THE MISSILES REACHED
DETECTION RANGE

without raising an alarm. At four kilometers a second, it took only eleven seconds to reach the Federation ship once they were within range. Heavy-compound fragments and blast shook the ship and punctured her armored hull.

Suddenly the lights and most of the ship's displays died. "Emergency oxygen, now!" the pilot shouted. "I'm sealing the ventilation. Going on autopilot for maximum climb—mark! All hands to escape stations!"

And then the hatch was off and those of them who were still alive were bailing out—into the heart of the frozen mountain range where their unknown enemy might well be waiting to pick them off one by one by one. . . .

☆ ⭐ ☆

STARCRUISER SHENANDOAH #2

Division of the Spoils

by
Roland J. Green

A ROC BOOK

ROC
Published by the Penguin Group
Penguin Books USA Inc., 375 Hudson Street,
New York, New York 10014, U.S.A.
Penguin Books Ltd, 27 Wrights Lane,
London W8 5TZ, England
Penguin Books Australia Ltd, Ringwood,
Victoria, Australia
Penguin Books Canada Ltd, 2801 John Street,
Markham, Ontario, Canada L3R 1B4
Penguin Books (N.Z.) Ltd, 182–190 Wairau Road,
Auckland 10, New Zealand

Penguin Books Ltd, Registered Offices:
Harmondsworth, Middlesex, England

First published by Roc, an imprint of New American Library, a
division of Penguin Books USA Inc.

First Printing, August, 1990
10 9 8 7 6 5 4 3 2 1

Map illustration by Pat Tobin

ROC ROC is a trademark of Penguin Books USA Inc.

PRINTED IN THE UNITED STATES OF AMERICA

To the memory of two men
who made ships fascinating for me:

C. S. Forester, master storyteller

Samuel Eliot Morison, sailor and historian

Principal Characters

A. Human

Major Nathan ABELSOHN: Federation Army commander, Armistice Zone.

Josephine ATWOOD: Reporter, Trans-Rift Media.

Captain Sophia BERGERON, A.B.R.: Company commander, Third Battalion.

Captain Pavel BOGDANOV, U.F.N.: Executive officer, *Shenandoah*.

Father Elijah BROTHERTONGUE: Member, House of Delegates and Military Council, Dominion of Victoria.

Colonel Indira CHATTERJE: Chief medical officer, Victoria Command.

Lucco DiVRIES: Former officer, U.F.N., now attached to Medical Corps, A.B.R.

Raimondo DiVRIES: Victorian organics farmer and Bushranger activist, brother of Lucco DiVries.

Sergeant Juan ESTEVA: Scout Company H.Q. and operative for Federation Intelligence.

Brigadier Domenic FEGELI: C.O., Alliance ground forces on Victoria.

Prime Minister Ronald FITZPATRICK: Prime Minister, Dominion of Victoria.

Commander Louisa GESELL, U.F.N.: C.O., 879th Attacker Squadron.

Governor-General Jeremiah GIST: Governor-General, Dominion of Victoria.

Governor Martin HOLLINGS: Governor, Freeworld States Alliance Territory of Seven Rivers, on Victoria.

Senator Philip KARRAS: Senator, Dominion of Victoria, and Chairman of the Military Council.

Major General Mikhail KORNILOV: Commanding general, Victoria Command.

Acting Vice Admiral Sho KUWAHARA, U.F.N.: Commander, Victoria Squadron, and senior naval officer, Victoria Command.

Brigadier General Marcus LANGSTON: Commanding general, Victoria Brigade.

Captain Paul LERAY, F.S.N.: C.O., heavy cruiser *Audacious*.

Captain Rose LIDDELL, U.F.N.: C.O., battlecruiser *Shenandoah*.

Brigadier General Houang LIU: Former chief of staff, Victoria Command.

Second Lieutenant Charles LONGMAN, U.F.N.: Launcher Division, *Shenandoah*.

Admiral Marya LOPATINA, F.S.N.: SOPS, Alliance naval forces off Victoria.

First Lieutenant Brian MAHONEY, U.F.N.: Training Department and J.O.O.W. under instruction, *Shenandoah*.

Commander Joanna MARDER, F.S.N.: Executive officer, *Audacious*.

Captain Lucretia MORLEY: Military Police officer, attached to Provost Marshal's office, Victoria Command.

Major Liw NIEG: Intelligence, Victoria Command.

Doctor Somtow NOSAVAN: M.D., attached to Medical Corps, A.B.R.

Colonel Sun Ji PAK: C.O., Alliance 96th Independent Regiment.

Major General (Retired) Alys PARKINSON: Former C.O., Victorian militia, and member of the Military Council.

First Lieutenant Karl POCHER, U.F.N.R.: Former C.O., tender *Leon Brautigan*.

Captain Candice SHORES: C.O., Scout Company, Victoria Brigade.

Captain Wolfgang STECKLER, U.F.N.: C.O., Victoria Dockyard.

Second Lieutenant Brigitte TACHIN, U.F.N.: Weapons Department, *Shenandoah*.

Rear Admiral Mordecai UZEL, F.S.N.: Chief of staff to Admiral Lopatina.

Colonel Ludmilla VESEY: Chief of staff, Victoria Command.

First Lieutenant Elayne ZHENG, U.F.N.: EWO, 879th Attacker Squadron.

Sergeant Major Raoul ZIMMER: Company Sergeant Major, Scout Company, Victoria Brigade.

B. Baernoi

Eimo SU-ANKRAI: Fleet Commander, Khudrigate Fleet.

Brokeh SU-IRZIM: Ship Commander First Class, Khudrigate Fleet.

Rahbad SARLIN: Observer, Special Projects, Office of Inquiry.

F'Mita IHR SULAR: Captain, chartered merchant vessel *Perfumed Wind*.

F'Zoar SU-WEIGHO: Retired Fleet Commander, Khudrigate Fleet.

Behdan ZEG: Commander in the Office of Inquiry, half-brother to Rahbad Sarlin.

Glossary

A.B.R.: Army of the Bushranger Republic.

AC: Armistice Commission(er).

AD: Air Defense.

AEW: Airborne Early Warning.

AI: Artificial Intelligence; also Action for Independence.

Antahli: Leading minority nationality in the Khudrigate of Baer.

AO: Area of Operations.

Baernoi: Sapient humanoid race, highly militarized, whose remote ancestors resembled Terran pigs.

CA: Combat Assault.

CC/ACC: Combat Center/Auxiliary Combat Center (aboard a warship).

C.O.: Commanding Officer.

CP: Command Post.

EI: Electronic Intercept.

EMP: Electromagnetic Pulse.

ETA: Estimated Time of Arrival.

EWO: Electronic Warfare Officer.

F.I.O.: Field Intelligence Operations, the covert-operations specialists of the Freeworld States Alliance.

F.S.N.: Freeworld States' Navy.

ftl: Faster than light.

Guidance: Baernoi term for navigation.

Great Khudr: Military leader who united the planet Baer under Syrodhi leadership.

HQ: Headquarters.

IFF: Identification, Friend or Foe.

IR: Infra-red.

J.O.O.W.: Junior Officer of the Watch.

kheblass: Merishi obscenity, literally meaning "too clumsy to climb."

KIA/WIA: Killed in Action/Wounded in Action.

K'thressh: Sapient octopoidal sea-dwelling race, never leaving their home planet but defending it with powerful projective telepathy.

Kytano!: Merishi warcry, literally meaning, "Long live victory!"

Merishi: Humanoid sapient race, descended from climbing omnivorous reptiles, ruthless and far-flung traders.

MOS: Military Occupational Specialty.

NCO: Non-commissioned Officer.

Office of Inquiry: Baernoi term for Intelligence.

okugh: Root vegetable native to Merish and basis for a potent (130 proof) distilled liquor.

OP: Observation Post.

P.I.O.: Public Information Officer.

POW: Prisoner of War.

Ptercha'a: The "Catmen" or "Catpeople"—felinoid sapient race, formerly mercenaries for the Merishi.

QR: Quick Reaction.

RDF: Radio Direction Finding.

RHIP: Rank Hath Its Privileges.

RTU: Return to Unit

Scaleskins: Derogatory term used by both Baernoi and humans for the Merishi.

SFC: Supporting Fires Controller.

SFO: Supporting Fires Observer.

Smallteeth: Derogatory term for humans popular with the Baernoi.

SOP: Standard Operating Procedure.

Special Projects: Baernoi term for covert operations, under the Office of Inquiry.

SSW: Squad Support Weapon.

Syrodhi: Dominant nationality among the Baernoi, from its leadership in uniting the planet.

TAS: Tactical Air Support.

T.O. & E.: Table of Organization and Equipment.

TOAD: Temporary Out-of-Area Duty.

TUCE: Taken Up From Civilian Economy.

Tuskers: Derogatory human term for the Baernoi, who have visible and non-vestigial tusks.

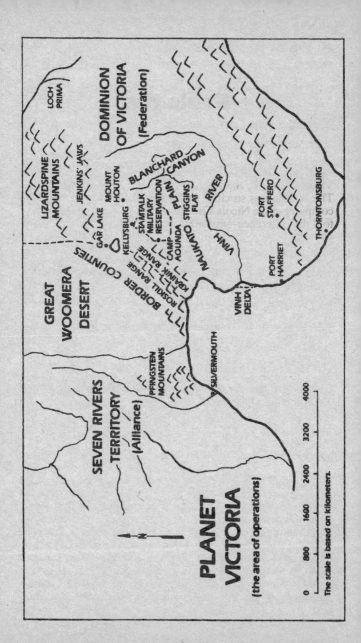

PLANET VICTORIA
(the area of operations)

The scale is based on kilometers.

0   800   1600   2400   3200   4000

SEVEN RIVERS TERRITORY
(Alliance)

GREAT WOOMERA DESERT

DOMINION OF VICTORIA
(Federation)

LOCH PRIMA

LIZARDSPINE MOUNTAINS

JENKINS' JAWS

GAR LAKE

MOUNT HOUTON

KELLYSBURG

BLANCHARD PLAIN

CANYON

STAMTALK MILITARY RESERVATION

CAMP AQUNDA

STIGGINS FLAT

NAUKATO RIVER

VINH RIVER

FORT STAFFERD

THORNTONSBURG

PORT HARRIET

VINH DELTA

ROSKILL RANGE

KRANIK RANGE

BORDER COUNTIES

PFFNGSTEN MOUNTAINS

SILVERMOUTH

Prologue

Four hundred million kilometers from the primary of the Victoria System, the asteroid tumbled gently through space. The tumble was so close to the original that even the main computer at the Nicola Chennault Observatory couldn't have told the difference—assuming that it had recorded the original tumble.

The Victoria System had a good quota of cosmic junk, but its famous observatory had its eyes turned and its resources committed to far larger and far more distant astronomical phenomena. If the asteroid's tumble after it was moved wasn't quite the same as the one from a glancing collision a few eons ago, nobody would be the wiser.

Moving the asteroid had changed its orbit a little more. Again, no alarm bells were likely to sound even if anyone noticed. The asteroid stayed on the opposite side of the system from the observatory and beyond the range of amateur astronomers on Victoria. It also lay close to the plain of the elliptic, in a patch of "junk space" that no ship would penetrate casually.

To guard against other kinds of penetration, the asteroid had an escort of rocks arrayed around it like raiders in formation with a heavy ship. Those rocks were in no sort of natural formation, but they were too small to be noticed even in a more heavily traveled system.

The simple existence of the escorts slowed any ship with working navigational sensors. Any ship without them wouldn't have penetrated this far into the asteroids in the first place. Slowed, a ship could be more easily tracked and attacked. Whether the attack would come from the escorts' lasers or from the cruiser *Fireflower* depended on a number of factors.

The most important was whether *Fireflower* was snugged down in the concealed dock, drifting among the rocks and trying to look like one of them, or off on her business elsewhere in the system. If she was generating "Mystery

Ship" sightings, the rock-mounted lasers had to do all the work, but also had a clear field of fire.

As she maneuvered *Perfumed Wind* past a rock three times its size, F'Mita ihr Sular was as alert as if the ship had no recognition equipment at all. The past three times, her cargo had been bulky enough to slow the ship and lethal only once it was delivered.

This cargo was light, a quarter of the usual weapons and equipment plus six containers that made even Fleet veterans like First Guidance Ehmad met-Lakaito perform rites of aversion when they thought their commander wasn't looking. Detonated by accident or treason, even one of those containers could destroy *Wind*. All of them together could destroy the asteroid as well.

The rock was falling astern when the alarm hammered ihr Sular's ears. The double-toned honking warned of a suspected intruder in the cargo spaces. She bared her tusks in disgust, shifted the alarm to "Battle Alert," and ordered the hold flooded with gas.

The gas was harmless to anything in the cargo except a few tightly sealed items, or to anything else that was supposed to be in the hold. It was violently irritating to the unprotected skin of any Lawbound of the Khudrigate of Baer.

If the intruder was wearing a protective suit, he could always seal it up. He would also seal a residue of the gas in the suit with him. A very rugged intruder might last a quarter-watch before the pain in his eyes and ears drove him to unseal.

A quarter-watch after that, the hold would be vented into space. This would permanently cure the intruder's pain, itching, and every other sensation—

"Commander, we have an inship call," met-Lakaito said.

Ihr Sular was already staring at the screen. Wisps of gas floated past the face there, without hiding its grin.

"I commend your security," the intruder said. "Anyone who hadn't been given immunity to K47 would really be in trouble."

"I didn't know there was an immunization."

"Did I say that there was?"

"Truthfully, you did not. But do you want to argue with me over the screen, or end this test and do it over a drink in my cabin?"

"What am I invited for?"

"You may be surprised." Ihr Sular looked at the displays and returned the grin. "Take those dummy charges you planted in the bombs with you, though. Otherwise it won't be a pleasant surprise."

Rahbad Sarlin lowered his ears and pulled his lips far down along his tusks. Ihr Sular couldn't miss the note of mockery in this gesture of submission.

She hadn't expected one of her passengers to be one of the Fleet's most distinguished Special Projects commanders. But anyone authorized to ride *Wind* to the Victoria System had to be someone out of the ordinary, so this was no great surprise.

She'd also succeeded in surprising Rahbad Sarlin. This was definitely beginning their association with all feet on the ground. Failing one of Sarlin's surprise tests had grounded commanders much senior to her.

Oh, she had Homeright in plenty on Petzas, and a husband who would never force her to rely on it. But being grounded would take away her Spaceright and leave her facing her husband's pity, which was almost worse.

She decided that she would go almost anywhere the invitation to Sarlin might lead. If they traveled far enough, she might even learn why someone was supplying sunbombs to the humans on Victoria.

One

Brian Mahoney waited until the last of the astronomers settled into their seats in the briefing room. He studied the four men and two women, trying to find some significance in the pattern of their seating, then stood up.

"Good morning. I'm Lieutenant Brian Mahoney, from *Shen—Shenandoah's* Training Department."

"Not the Public Information Office?" a thickset older man asked.

"Half my job's lecturing, so they thought I would do as well." *Probably better than any P.I.O. who's afraid for his next Evaluation if he doesn't hide what a muck the Army made of things.*

"I don't suppose this is in any way connected with interservice rivalry, is it?" the man asked.

"It's connected with my being available when you people needed a briefing," Mahoney said. *For any other connections, your guess is as good as mine.*

"Now could I ask a favor? No more interruptions until I've finished the briefing. It may actually answer a few of your questions, which will save us all some time."

Mahoney avoided eye contact with his audience while he set the display controls for keyboard activation, then punched a sequence he now knew almost as well as his serial number. A map of the settled continent of the planet Victoria appeared in the tank.

"I'm sure the media have covered Victoria's history up to the present crisis. So I won't go into detail on how it became a dual-sovereignty planet, with the Alliance's Seven Rivers Territory and the Dominion of Victoria under Southern Cross, a member of the British Union, an ally of the Federation.

"You wouldn't thank me if I did, either. The details don't reflect very well on anybody except the Victorians, who had to cope with the off-planet decision makers' mistakes. The

4

only excuse *or* explanation is that what became Seven Rivers started as an outlaw colony right after the Hive Wars, when everybody had their attention on more important planets."

Mahoney highlighted the Vinh River, trailing down across the dominion's northern half. "For nearly a century, the people beyond the Vinh led a pretty hardscrabble existence. They coped, but they didn't like it. Again, the details aren't pretty, and they don't make anybody except the Victorians look good."

He went on to explain how the early signs of unrest made the Federation high command decide to assign a naval squadron to Victoria. *Shenandoah* was commissioned as flagship of the squadron and rode her Stonemans out to the system just as the crisis turned hot.

"Didn't the Baernoi have something to do with the unrest?" another astronomer asked. Her name badge read "Academician Kovacs," and with that title she had to be a lot older than the thirty-five or so she looked.

Mahoney decided to field that question on the spot. "The Tuskers supplied some weapons and equipment, through Merishi intermediaries. Whether they were aiming the stuff at Victoria or just selling it to the Merishi traders to make *them* grateful, I don't know. Neither does anybody else in the Navy I've talked to.

"The only possible sign of a high-level Baernoi presence in the system is that mysterious ship I'm sure you've all heard about. That's why you're going out to the Chennault Observatory aboard light cruiser *Weilitsch*, not aboard *Leon Brautigan*. The supply ship can't run or fight if somebody does show up on her tail.

"*Weilitsch* won't be as comfortable as *Brautigan*. But she'll get you there, which is what the Navy wants."

Mahoney slowed the display to keep the maneuvers and incidents from getting ahead of his narrative and went on. The incident of the Blanchard Canyon, *Shen*'s ball-of-yarn flag-showing pass at low altitude, the accidental shootdown of Air Victoria's Flight 6 by the Third Battalion of the Victoria Brigade, the mutiny in the Fourth Battalion, open rebellion by the "bunch of bushrangers" north of the Vinh—

"With the forces we had available at the time, suppressing the—independence movement—was never feasible. We were more concerned with preventing a larger war. That did

5

threaten once, when the bushrangers shot at an Alliance Navy reconnaissance flight.

"The Alliance thought that the Federation was using the 'rebellion' as a cover for seizing territory along the frontier. Completely wrong, of course, but they had naval superiority by then. They thought they could move their ground troops into Federation territory to cut the 'infiltration' at its source.

"So we nearly got into war by mistake. Fortunately we managed to persuade them to stay out of Federation territory. I'm sure you've all read the media coverage of our tactics there, so I won't go into detail on that."

Not to mention that it would show on my face and in my voice, what it felt like to be aboard Shen *when Captain Liddell dared Baba Lopatina to start a war.*

If Mahoney lived two hundred years, he'd never forget sweating in his survival suit, watching the displays, knowing that six kloms below *Shen* was solid rock ready to tear her apart if either accident or hostile action made her drop that last little bit. . . .

He turned away to wipe sweat off his forehead. By the time he turned back, the display was showing the new Bushranger Republic in silver, between the red of Seven Rivers and the blue of the Dominion of Victoria.

"The Alliance promptly recognized the Bushranger Republic, and peace broke out soon after that. The Federation hasn't formally recognized the Bushranger Republic yet, but all parties are abiding by the Armistice."

"What's holding up a peace treaty?" It was the thickset man again. Mahoney's memory now put a name on him— Ludwig Brosky, an expert on quarks and also brother to an Agrarian Party senator. The lieutenant decided that he could stroke the man's political views without telling any detectable lies.

"I'm only a line lieutenant aboard the flagship of the Victoria Squadron, so this just a guess. But I think the problem is borders. Neither the Alliance nor the Federation wants to give up any more territory or people.

"But right now, the Bushranger Republic has about seven hundred thousand people and damned near no other resources except people. Nobody wants to be accused of sabotaging them, either."

Brosky looked mollified, if not totally convinced. Mahoney froze the display and looked at the astronomers. "Now— any questions?"

"What about dirtside security?" the other woman said. She was dark, jumpsuited, and handsome in a rather austere way.

"We recommend that you stay clear of the Republic's territory," Mahoney said. "Right now, it's a slack time for farm work, and a lot of people will be in town with nothing to do but drink more than they can handle. By the time you come down on regular leave, they'll all be back on the job and the bars will probably be delighted at extra customers.

"Federation territory is open. The Alliance is requiring all non-Alliance civilian visitors to register with the Ministry of the Interior and inform a prefect or the local military commander of their location once a day. We've had a couple of expulsions over violating that regulation, but one of those was rescinded when it turned out that somebody had just got on the wrong lifter."

Mahoney killed the display. "I can't emphasize too strongly that nobody official wants a war over Victoria. Some private citizens probably do, but our job is to knock them on the head as soon as they show up, before they can make trouble.

"I hope you'll be able to help us with that job when the time comes. Meanwhile, you can go about your work without looking over your shoulders. Thank you."

Nobody applauded, but Academician Kovacs rose and smiled. "Thank you, Lieutenant. We'll do our best."

She gathered up her colleagues with her eyes, silently challenging Brosky to say a word. The man kept quiet, although he was the last astronomer to leave and kept looking back at Mahoney until the lieutenant shut the briefing-room door.

Mahoney returned the terminal to the control of *Shenandoah*'s main computer and ordered the drink dispenser back to its station. As the robot rolled out the door Mahoney realized he should have drawn another cup of tea before letting it go.

He looked at his watch. If he jogged—not sprinted, not walked, but jogged—he might make it to the ward room before they pulled the dispensers to clean them for lunch.

If he wanted to sprint, he might even make it before the last breakfast brewing was too old to be drinkable.

Reckoning by the Standard Year, Captain Rose Liddell, C.O. of the battlecruiser *Shenandoah*, had been in the

Navy for twenty-seven years. Reckoning by the year of her native Dominion, it was twenty-three—hardly a difference that mattered, particularly since she'd spent a total of sixty-two days on Dominion since she was commissioned.

Since then, she'd eaten far more breakfasts with colleagues and superiors than she cared to remember. Right now it was 0947 (Ship Time) on the 183rd Standard Ship Day of *Shenandoah*'s commission. Acting Vice-Admiral Sho Kuwahara was Liddell's breakfast partner, and they had a full agenda to discuss before the admiral took the shuttle down to Fort Stafford.

Her steward, Petty Officer Jensen, set down a fresh pot of tea and vanished noiselessly. Liddell refilled the cups and ordered the terminal on. Figures scrolled across the screen, the order for the Victoria Squadron's resupply.

Liddell whistled as the number of missiles flashed on the screen.

"Storage problems, Captain?" Kuwahara asked.

"No. But is somebody planning on our fighting a war?"

"Planning on you being ready to fight a war, even if supply lines to Victoria are cut. I understand that Schatz is considering giving the Victoria Squadron an Open Allowance."

Federation S.O.P. was to give Navy and Army units a Standard Allowance of supplies, with resupply when they dropped below their quota. An Open Allowance would let the Victoria Squadron stockpile everything from missile-carrying buses to toilet paper, simply by asking for it.

Liddell now understood why Kuwahara had been given a temporary third star. Normally, only formations commanded by a vice-admiral or a lieutenant general were eligible for Open Allowances.

"I didn't ask for it, by the way," Kuwahara said. "I didn't want to look greedy when I didn't know if Schatz was facing Baernoi trouble elsewhere. He sent off the request on his own, on a denial-required basis."

"When?"

"Twelve days ago."

That meant that if Charlemagne didn't turn thumbs-down within eight more days, the Victoria Squadron could gorge itself full from Eleventh Zone's warehouses and depots.

Fine, if we can just deliver and protect all the goodies . . .

Liddell ran the list back to "Weapons."

"How are these coming out?"

"Aboard *Shankar*. She's got two new launchers and a full Combat Center."

"Good," Liddell said. "I'd hate to have that many weapons loaded aboard a ship that couldn't keep them out of hostile hands except by blowing herself up. I trust the transport crews, but I'm not sure I'd trust *myself* to pull that particular switch."

Kuwahara looked at the soundproofing overhead. "There speaks the captain who frightened off the Baba. Are you sure you wouldn't care to rephrase that?"

"No, sir," Liddell said unceremoniously, and changed the subject. "As far as your suggestion about exercises to remind people we're not back on a peacetime routine yet—let's hold off until we hear about the allowance. If it's approved, nobody's going to have time to sit around, and everybody knows what an Open Allowance means.

"Besides, I bounced the idea off my executive officer. He felt he couldn't recommend such exercises."

Kuwahara's eyebrows rose. Liddell wondered if he was as surprised as he seemed. Then she considered that Commander Bogdanov's mellowing might not be that well-known outside *Shenandoah*. His reputation as a martinet had been well deserved, even if it was a case of the devil finding work for idle hands to do.

Putting Bogdanov back to ship handling, his first love, had made life more pleasant both for him and for the rest of *Shenandoah*'s crew. He was still a great one for staying aboard ship and keeping quiet.

"You'd better be prepared to lose the Hermit," Kuwahara said. "I understand he's on the list for deep selection to captain."

"Fine, but there's no law against having a four-striper as exec on a capital ship."

"No law, but 'the needs of the service' have been known to do the same work."

"The needs of the service include the needs of *Shenandoah*," Liddell said. "Right now, one of those needs is *not* having to break in a new executive officer."

"I promise the orders transferring him won't come from me," Kuwahara said. "I also promise that I'll endorse any request you make for keeping him if *Valhalla* joins the squadron."

Liddell nodded, too relieved to say anything. It was long

9

odds against the big carrier going anywhere but Victoria when she recommissioned after her overhaul.

It was longer odds against anybody but the explosive, ambitious, and gifted Prange being the carrier's C.O. He'd virtually claimed squatters' rights on *Valhalla*, and the only way to get him off her bridge would be to give him a star. Liddell devoutly hoped that promotion would *not* be followed by sending him out to Victoria as second-in-command of the squadron.

Liddell sipped tea, then had an afterthought.

"What about Coletta?"

"What about him?"

"Do I keep Bogdanov if Coletta comes out to command the army?"

"If he does, he'll be junior to me. They may also put Victoria under I Corps, so Frieda Hentsch can pull the strings without leaving Shalimar."

"Shalimar is ninety-six light-years away. Those are long strings. They may also promote Coletta."

Kuwahara grimaced. "Captain, I think we should defer any further discussion of General Coletta until we have digested our breakfast."

"With pleasure," Liddell said.

Once a week, *Shenandoah*'s fifty-five officers dined formally, with Commander Bogdanov presiding at the head of one of two long tables and the senior department head at the other. Usually there were guests, sometimes even welcome ones.

Also once a week, Captain Liddell played host to a semirandom selection of her officers, usually either Bogdanov or a department head and anywhere from three to six others. Junior officers who'd begun by dreading these occasions soon found that Liddell was an excellent host, with a wide range of knowledge, a good wine cellar for those who drank, and an even better selection of tea and coffee for those who didn't. Not to mention that any good chess or *skat* player was automatically in Captain Liddell's good books unless they did something treasonous, destructive, or disgusting.

Apart from these bouts with formality, the junior officers ate cafeteria-style at four-seat tables; the senior ones had a screened alcove with two robots to save them steps. Second Lieutenant Brigitte Tachin had fallen into the habit of eating at table Red 9, and the rest of her roommates in D-4 joined her as often as duty permitted.

This morning two of the other three had been waiting for her. For once Charles Longman looked well rested, but Elayne Zheng was red-eyed and morose. Tachin remembered that Elayne had come in after 2300 and left before 0530, but it looked like something more than too much partying this time.

"—so Steckler has Commander Gesell on his lap, or so bloody close it makes no difference." Longman grinned. "Some people have all the luck."

"Who's the lucky one?" Tachin said.

"Ah, ah, Brigitte," Longman said, waving a callused forefinger below the tip of her nose. "Are you trying to delve into my secret passions?"

"Charlie, you haven't had a secret passion in your life," Zheng said, in something above a whisper but below a growl. "The only thing you haven't done is bounce on a live video circuit."

"Are you betting on that?"

"I—no, I don't think I will. But you'd better bet that Gesell's standards are well above yours—and you."

"Who said I had any such thoughts about a superior officer?" Longman said, looking around in mock indignation. "Who's the lying vine thief?"

"You've had them about both me and Brigitte," Zheng snapped. "I outrank you, and she's certainly superior in value to the service—"

Longman turned white and dropped his cup, which hit the edge of his plate and overturned. By the time Tachin had finished mopping up the spill, Longman was only red and Brian Mahoney was approaching with a loaded tray.

He set it down, swung his chair out, then stared at Zheng. "Elayne, normally I wouldn't roust you in public. But I heard that last crack. An explanation would be a friendly favor."

"Oh . . ." Zheng slapped both hands down on the table, then sucked a bruised little finger.

"I'm waiting, Elayne," Mahoney said.

"You can—" Zheng began. Tachin heard anger crackling in the other woman's voice and wondered if Mahoney wasn't working off a frustration or two of his own.

He'd certainly been jerked from job to job over the last three months, doing all of them well but not getting much closer to qualifying as J.O.O.W. He'd even had one narrow escape from becoming Captain Liddell's secretary—a necessary job that he could have done superlatively well, but more office time!

Tachin stood up. "Elayne, do you have your magnifier on you?" *Hope that's not too silly a question; she'd sooner forget her contra implant than her tool kit.*

"Sure, but—"

"Well, it's something a little private, if you don't mind."

"The heads?"

"That's closest. It may not be anything, but—"

"Let's celebrate when we're sure." Zheng rose before Mahoney could say a word, let alone move to stop her. Tachin had to hurry to catch up, but noticed that Longman was carefully looking everywhere but at his tablemates.

In the head, Tachin perched in lotus position on the bench opposite the washbasins and grinned at Zheng's expression. "Should I take my pants off to lend verisimilitude to an otherwise bald and unconvincing narrative?"

"It wasn't a narrative, just a one-liner, and I don't give a damn if it convinced Brian or not. Thanks for getting me out of there. I don't know what I would have said, but I know you wouldn't have liked to hear it."

"I'm quite sure I wouldn't have. What has you so ready to bite? Brian, or Lucco DiVries, or something more?"

"Lucco's a finished book." Tachin wasn't convinced and didn't think Zheng herself was, but said nothing. Even if the attachment hadn't gone deep, DiVries effectively joining the rebels must have hit Zheng in her very considerable pride.

"Brian—it's not his fault that somehow that great bumbling Irish bear has a dozen different talents, all of them somehow in demand. No, it's just that I'm in danger of being pulled out of the squadron and back here aboard *Shen*."

"I'm sorry."

"I rode attackers during the worst of the crisis. With the second squadron operating off the dockyard, *Mutti* Gesell doesn't need to keep her birds flying around the clock. I suppose if I come back, Captain Rosie will owe the 879th one. But I thought human sacrifice was against regulations!" Zheng sat down and looked ready for a first-class case of the grumps.

Tachin put a hand on her knee. "Elayne, I don't know

how much this is worth. But Brian mentioned that our training people are setting up a course for the reserve aircrew from the dominion. The Armistice Commission is trying to use local people as much as possible for the boundary mapping. Some of them need a little refresher training—"

"A little?" Zheng's laugh was a snee's hunting call. "They'll need a complete advanced course before they can find the Lizardspines without running into them!" She looked at Tachin. "You thinking they'll need some people for hands-on instruction?"

"I'm not an expert on training requirements—"

"No, but you're an expert at getting things out of Brian. I've known him five years, and this is the first I've heard of it!"

Tachin sighed. She had the feeling that trying to damp the crisis, she'd fed in more mass instead.

"How often have you been aboard when Brian wasn't up to his collarbone in work? And maybe he's being tactful in staying away from you until you get over—whatever else you've been wrestling with."

"You could be right," Zheng said slowly. "Oh, you *are* right. I was just looking—never mind what I was looking for. I'll start looking for a way to get on the instructional staff of this training course. If Brian can feed me a little advance intel—"

"I'll ask—"

"No, *I'll* ask," Zheng said. "I go off in a corner and sulk, and what happens? This fresh kid from nowhere finds out Brian's innermost secrets—"

Tachin knew she was blushing when Zheng broke off to guffaw. "You mean you *have* finally put all that privacy to the right—"

"It's hardly your business."

"No, but I've noticed that you strip off in front of Brian but not Charlie."

"Elayne, it hardly requires a giant intellect to tell Brian's ethics from Charlie's."

"No, I don't suppose it does. But if we sit here swapping pseudo-insights for much longer, Brian will start worrying that something's really wrong. I'd better go back and apologize to him, then try to enlist his help. Maybe I'll kiss his feet? On second thought I'll leave it to you."

Tachin was still blushing as she followed Zheng out of the head. Not for the first time, she wondered if there was any

13

point in staying out of Brian's bunk, when Elayne did everything short of locking them in it together.

Yes. Several points, actually. Sex with Brian wouldn't do her much good. It wouldn't close Elayne's mouth. It might open Charlie's—not to mention other parts of his anatomy.

Most important, sex with Brian for the wrong reasons might do *him* quite a bit of harm. She didn't know what the right reasons were, but she could wait to learn what they were—and wasn't that more thought than she'd been ready to give her last few partners?

Two

The man who called himself Eugene Van Gelder took one last look at the room where he'd lived for five years. He'd never let himself call it a home, but he hadn't lived so long in one place since he left the ship where he was born. In his profession that was a long stay.

Maybe too long. Being reclusive, securing your living quarters against both physical and electronic intruders, leaving few records and those conflicting, varying your routine randomly—none of these could keep a spy safe indefinitely if somebody wanted him dead.

Even now he might not be on Field Intelligence Operation's termination list. He would surely be on it before long, and then he might not escape by leaving Victoria. The Alliance's covert-operations experts had a long reach, but even they found it harder to hit a moving target.

He had savored the irony of having to move on just as the profits for a double agent on Victoria were increasing dramatically. But so were the risks, and under five different names on as many different planets, "Eugene Van Gelder" had been careful about taking risks.

It had been low-risk, acting as a channel for information that the officers of the Bonsai Force wanted to send to Fleet Headquarters without Intelligence knowing about it. Gratitude might not be in them, but they knew a profitable arrangement when they had it working for them. To keep that arrangement working, they could be relied on to lay false trails, enough to deceive Governor Hollings or even the local Field Intelligence Operations chief unless he had orders to call all hands to battle stations.

It had been almost as low-risk, feeding selected nuggets of that information to Brigadier General Liu, Victoria Command's chief of staff. The information upheld Liu's position both with his Federation Army superiors and with Victoria's various oppositions. As long as Victoria was at peace, telling the Federation what they would doubtless have learned themselves in due course was nothing to have anyone in Seven Rivers Territory sharpening their knives for him.

Now war had come to Victoria, not particularly bloody, but war nonetheless. Van Gelder refused to believe that peace was coming back after only one confrontation. Too many people hadn't been heard from.

Among them would be Federation Military Intelligence, which lacked its opposition's bloodthirsty streak—or at least was supposed to. Van Gelder and others who lived in the shadow world of the double agent knew otherwise. He would not live very long if he refused to provide more information about Alliance plans and operations.

Enough information to damage Alliance interests, perhaps kill Alliance soldiers and destroy Alliance ships. Then the Bonsai Force's officers would withdraw their protection, and F.I.O.'s ax would fall.

If it didn't, Colonel Pak might take direct personal action, and of course there were always the Merishi to be reckoned with. Van Gelder thought he had the measure of the local community, but he'd heard of younger, off-planet visitors with a combative streak,

Van Gelder decided that speculating about how he might die was a waste of time he didn't have. He knew enough, which was simply that he had to be off Victoria before the Federation's first damning request reached him, let alone before his refusal reached—who?

Probably that little major—Nieg, that was his name. He had an ex-Ranger's fondness for fighting the decisive battles himself, whether with data files or vestpocket fusers. A worthy opponent—but anyone who thought in those terms either didn't go into Van Gelder's line of work or didn't live very long if he did.

Van Gelder looked at his watch and keyed the shutters open. The view was an uninspiring stretch of the foothills of the Pfingsten Mountains, but it would look suspicious if the shutters stayed closed after dawn.

Out into the hall, lock the door, and down a half flight of stairs to the elevator atrium. The windbushes in their pots were beginning to bloom, and Van Gelder knew that was the scent that would always recall Victoria to him.

The elevator arrived; he looked inside, then behind, before stepping in. Normally he didn't take such obvious precautions; a man who behaved like the media's notions of a spy was more likely to be reported as one.

Today, he might add years to his life with a few extra minutes' precautions. Like standing in the middle of the transparent elevator cage as it sank twenty floors, then getting out on the eighth floor, still twelve levels above the garage. A walk across the eighth-floor bridge to the other tower, then down its elevator to the second floor, and down the emergency stairs to the garage in the basement that both towers shared.

Simple precautions, sufficient only if anyone on his trail was very sloppy or didn't expect him to be alert—which amounted to the same thing. But nine people out of ten *were* sloppy, and even the tenth had off days.

If spy catchers were as efficient as fiction showed them, Van Gelder knew that spies would long since have followed pimps into extinction.

He took a circuitous route to his car, stopping and looking in all directions every few meters. An ambush at the one point his enemies knew he would have to approach would save them the trouble of trailing him either in the building or after he left it.

Natural eyes and augmented ears tuned for the slightest unusual sound, he took ten minutes to cover fifty meters to his space in Bay 7. His little red Marcos shared the bay with a dozen other cheap groundwheelers.

Built into the bottom of Van Gelder's suitcase was a miniature fuse damper, short-ranged and short-lived but enough to keep opening the car door from setting off anything. Once he was inside, he could hook the suitcase's damper to the car's power pack, extending its life and range.

Everything worked according to plan. Van Gelder allowed himself a two-second sigh of relief, then started the motors and switched the controls to manual.

Building regulations said you were supposed to turn your car over to the garage computer on the way in or out. At this hour he'd be kloms down the road to the spaceport before anyone noticed that he'd left, let alone left under manual control.

If he turned his car over to the computer, on the other hand, it wouldn't matter if he went unnoticed by his fellow humans. An electronic hand couldn't be bribed, but it could be ordered to grip hard when you wanted it to let go.

At least he'd be beyond the reach of computers once he

17

left the building. That was one virtue of groundhuggers over liftcars. Aloft, you were plugged into a computer net every second, maybe harder to sabotage but certainly not impossible to tap for someone who really wanted to know who you were.

Then there were any number of ways to arrange an "accident," depending on how zealous the police were expected to be. If *they* had already been discreetly approached . . .

The ground—on foot if necessary—then space—that was Van Gelder's route to safety. More safety than he could expect on Victoria, anyway.

And how long would it be before he made his next stop too dangerous? He felt a chill that had nothing to do with danger or the early-morning cold as he realized he wouldn't have asked that question five years ago.

He powered up the wheels and backed the car out of the bay, on to the ramp toward the west entrance. It spiraled up past three more bays, holding progressively more and more expensive cars, up to a glossy green Petrovich that had to cost more than many lifters.

One more turn, and he was approaching the line of dump bins for the south tower. Only four apartment complexes in Silvermouth had their own sorter/recycler plants, and this wasn't one of them. Grinders fed organics to the sewers, and chutes fed the rest to the bins. Every morning the custodian gave the bins their orders, and they rolled off down Uspensky Boulevard to Plant Seven.

One of the bins was a little out of line. Van Gelder slowed to make sure he had room to pass, saw the heads-up display give him the clear signal, and fed power again.

As he did, he saw the bin move even farther out of line. One of the custodians must not have locked the wheels last night.

Not my problem anymore, unless I ding the car so that I have to walk—which might make me harder to trace, anyway—

Then the bin moved slowly but unmistakably into his path. He saw this in one moment; in the next he saw the thin wire running up the corner of the rolling bin.

Surging fear didn't slow Van Gelder's hands. He fed both the fuse damper and the wheels all the power he had. The car slammed into the bin, tipping it up on two wheels. It went over with a clang, still blocking Van Gelder's path. He backed off, rammed the bin again, heard his bumpers crumpling, heard the whine of the bin's racing wheels—

Until the explosion swept away all other sounds, turned the world to flame and a heartbeat's worth of pain, then blotted it out completely and forever.

Colonel Sun Ji Pak rose early and believed in personally conducting investigations that required discretion. So it didn't surprise the HQ duty officer to reach his C.O. over breakfast with Essteb Y'eel, owner of the Web of Hrar.

The colonel keyed in a scrambler code and looked at the owner. He rested his fingertips on his cheeks, one of the more formal Merishi gestures of assent, and left the table.

"Somebody blew a car bomb in the garage of the Ardis Towers," the duty officer said.

Pak remembered hearing a faint thump a few minutes ago. "Is Fegeli on base?"

"Negative. Want me to track him?"

If Brigadier Fegeli was anywhere near where Pak suspected he was, tracking him down would take too long and put him in a foul mood when he did appear. Pak had no intention of giving either Intelligence or the media that kind of free banquet.

Pak switched to his lifter's frequency.

"Power up and be ready to lift in two minutes. Load and lock sidearms."

"Yes, sir."

The Merishi reappeared to escort Pak out.

"May I summon a ground taxi? It would be nearly as fast."

"It would also make me a sitting target, in case this incident is the first of a campaign."

"As you wish. At least I pray that my hospitality was not deficient."

"It was excellent. As for what brought me here—tell Raukis and his brother to avoid anyone from the 96th for a month or so. I can hardly keep all my people from holding grudges. If they catch Raukis or his brother alone—our people don't think that the fight was provoked."

"Ah. Least said, soonest mended?" That wasn't a phrase in Commercial Merishi, and it came out distorted almost past recognition. Y'eel was still smiling at his own erudition.

"Something like that," Pak said. As he went out, he remembered to chamber a round in his own pistol.

The crew of the lifter had her powered up, their sidearms ready, and Pak's scattergun loaded and laid out on the rear

19

seat. The floor tilted even before he'd picked it up, and they were above the roof of the Web of Hrar before he'd strapped in.

Silvermouth was spread out, to allow plenty of room for natural drainage and ground cover. The lifter followed the main transit line three kilometers downhill, crossed the Public Gardens, and grounded on the landing pad of the Ardis Towers' commercial annex.

The military markings gave Pak a safe landing and his ID took him downstairs to the police CP. The captain in charge was an old acquaintance on the edge of being a friend. As a lieutenant, he'd been a watch commander in the district that included the "strip" outside the Silvermouth Military Reservation. Pak had called on him quite a few times, to quietly settle differences of opinion between soldiers of the 96th and the "strip's" business owners.

" 'Morning, Colonel. Any of your people involved in this?"

"Not that I know of. But I was in the area—"

"At the Tangled Web?"

"Is that what you call it?"

"When we want to be polite."

"We can compare notes on Citizen Y'eel later. As I said, I was in the area. I thought it would make any Army role in the investigation easier if I came over."

The captain frowned. "Two people from Field Intelligence are already on the way."

Pak was grateful for a naturally expressionless face. "I'll leave them alone, unless anyone from the 96th was a casualty."

"We haven't any identifiable bodies. The blast seems to have been a charge in a trash bin, and it wiped out all the other bins and a red Marcos passing by. We'll need the forensics people for an ID on the Marcos's driver. There wasn't much left."

A red Marcos . . .

"We're assuming it was either a resident or a resident's guest borrowing the Marcos. You have anybody missing?"

"I've asked for an all-hands check-in."

"We've got two residents not accounted for," the captain went on. "Sharon Farber—"

Pak laughed. "I'd wager a month's salary she's alive, healthy, and safe in bed. If you insist on knowing whose—"

"Not unless we suspect her."

"Good." Dragging Brigadier Fegeli back on duty would have been bad enough. Dragging his affair with the cantor of Temple Beth Israel on stage would be a declaration of war.

"The other missing character is a free-lance media agent named Eugene Van Gelder. He—did you know him, Colonel?"

"He did some work last year for our Public Information Office. Good writer, but kept rather to himself." *For better reasons than I hope you'll ever know, Captain.*

"Well, don't have your P.I.O. start writing up an obituary yet. The Forensics people will be here any minute, and you're on our need-to-know list."

"Thank you," Pak said, turning for the stairs. *And thank you for giving me this warning.*

If Pak had been on the scene when the Intelligence people arrived, only a miracle could have kept them from noticing him. As it was, they would have to rely on what they overheard to confirm his presence.

Police and Intelligence relations were no better on Victoria than they were elsewhere in the Alliance. Intelligence men asking questions about Pak would simply be sounding the alarm about their interest in him.

Pak waited until the lifter was halfway back to headquarters before he started recording a message for Paul Leray. Luck was with them; a courier was going up to *Audacious* that afternoon, too soon for Intelligence to react unless they already had enough evidence to court-martial both Pak and Leray.

Pak almost hoped that the rumor was true, about most of Admiral Lopatina's squadron being redeployed. It would weaken the Baba's influence. It would also make the ships and troops of the Bonsai Force indispensable to maintaining the military balance on Victoria.

The Bonsai Force, and its senior officers.

On Captain Leray's private screen, the image of the smoke-trailing Ardis Towers vanished and Colonel Pak's face returned.

"I have no intelligence on what other investigators besides the Silvermouth police are working at the Ardis Towers. Nor do we have any reliable sources at the Towers themselves to obtain this intelligence."

The colonel's hard face seemed to turn from stone to metal. It was impossible for his voice to be more expressionless.

" 'Reliable' now includes the ability to withstand a full-scale Field Intelligence interrogation, including the use of illegal methods. I am reluctant to accept a situation in which we may have to act without further intelligence, but under the circumstances I fail to see that we have any other choice."

The screen went blank. Paul Leray looked at Joanna Marder. The executive officer of the Alliance heavy cruiser *Audacious* looked down into her glass. It was nearly empty—had been empty, for a good ten minutes, in fact. Leray felt a glow at the sight, that his own two drinks couldn't account for. He also realized that for once he wouldn't have said a word if Jo had slugged down half the bottle.

He picked up the brandy and filled both their glasses, then raised his. Jo was doing the same when Leray saw the time. The scrambler that let them listen freely to Pak's message would cut out in ten minutes. Toasting "Eugene Van Gelder" would only waste some of those minutes.

Leave the man to God, who could reward or punish him as he deserved—and who knew his real name, anyway. Get on with the problems he'd left behind for the living.

Marder sipped her brandy. "I'm concerned about Pak's assumption this was an Intelligence hit. It would be more their style to snatch him, squeeze him dry, then put the pressure on *us*."

"That's a long-term solution," Leray said. "Field Intelligence doesn't always think in those terms."

"Then why did it get where it is today?"

"Because it started with people who did think in the long term. Unfortunately, it also started a century ago. Those people are dead or retired.

"The ones who set policy now are the field experts the founders sent out. Set policy, and pick the current generation of field chiefs. Know the master, know the servant."

"But what would Intelligence gain by simply wiping out Van Gelder, without learning more about him?" Marder asked.

"Don't assume they didn't already know. They might have even turned him—"

Marder choked on a swallow of brandy and closed her eyes. The tears on her cheeks weren't entirely from the choking fit.

"I see," she said hoarsely. "Turned him, used him, and then wiped him out to make us look over our shoulders."

"Make everybody else do the same, too. Nothing like a 'terrorist movement' to persuade a local government to give Field Intelligence a freer hand."

Marder cursed softly.

Leray gripped her hands. He didn't know if he was giving strength or taking it. The one seemed to be as badly needed as the other.

"Anyway," Leray said. "Pak is right. We have to be cautious for now. That's not as hopeless a situation as it might seem either.

"Intelligence will have to stage a few other incidents if they want a plausible 'terrorist conspiracy.' Then it won't be just them getting a free hand. The 96th's own intelligence people and the police Special Investigation Division will have to be allowed to move. Otherwise more people will be suspicious than even Intelligence can afford."

He leaned back in his chair and tipped his glass up until the last drops trickled down his throat. "Besides, we're lucky in one way. Van Gelder's whole job was making sure that senior officers back in the High Command learned what the Bonsai Force thought was happening on Victoria. Not Hollings, not Intelligence, but the field commanders.

"Now we've got a senior officer about four-tenths of a light-second away. One of her squadron commanders has access to her anytime he wants it. And she could probably give our late friend Van Gelder lessons about fuzzing Intelligence."

"Want to put that in our reply to Pak?" Marder asked.

"Any better ideas?"

"If you're going to record the reply, can you cut the visual?"

"Sorry. This has been a bad day—"

"And we're going to make it better before it gets any worse." Marder uncoiled from her chair and reached for the collar of her high-necked tunic.

Leray thought briefly of discretion or at least caution. He thought less briefly of human contact—starting with his lips on Jo's neck. He switched his terminal to "Voice Record" and spoke quickly.

"File Code Clio 96435. Concur in your recommendations, pending development of pattern of 'terrorist' action. Use couriers only in emergencies. Presence of cooperative senior

23

officer makes independent intelligence channel low-priority objective."

Pak's message vanished from his sliver; Leray's replaced it. In another thirty seconds, the package was keyed not only to Pak's code but his thumbprint.

Leray turned back, half expecting to see Jo already naked. Instead she'd only taken off her tunic and unfastened her shirt halfway down, leaving her neck and throat bare.

"You must have been reading my mind."

She threw her head back so that he could kiss her whole throat, from the point of her chin down to the cleft between her breasts. He spent a long time at that, with his hands gripping her buttocks, and hers twined in his hair.

"Split screen," Captain Liddell told the computer.

The picture on her terminal divided. The top showed Commander Bogdanov in his chair on the bridge.

When the executive officer was half-asleep, he looked like a coiled spring. When he was at full alert, as he was now, he looked as if it would be cruel to wake him.

The bottom half of the screen showed Baba Lopatina's chief of staff, Rear Admiral Mordecai Uzel. He wore full-dress uniform and the expression of a 'man with a full bladder who's just found the bathroom door locked.

"Good evening, sir," Bogdanov said, giving the sitting salute.

"Good evening, Commander," Uzel replied. "Do you have the duty?"

Liddell subvocalized the code for "Tell him yes." Bogdanov nodded.

Uzel's always been pretty casual about rank, which is what you'd expect from a Bar Kochban. Let's see if that bombing in Silvermouth jacked him up.

"Very well," Uzel said. "This is the verbal report of ship movements to the senior available Federation officer, required under Article 17, Clause B, of the Armistice Agreement. A permanent record of this report is being made aboard *Fei-huang*, and a document of the ship movement will be sent within eight hours, under Clause C of the same article."

"Acknowledged," Bogdanov said. Liddell saw him activate the recorder on his own screen. "We will also make a record. Proceed, sir."

"Battleships *Salamis* and *Erzburgerwald*, The Fourteenth

and Ninetieth Cruiser Squadrons, and the Fifteenth Transport Division will leave Victoria orbit between 2350 and 2430 tomorrow. They will proceed on a standard course" —Uzel swallowed—"to a position for transit out of the Victoria System."

"Acknowledged," Bogdanov said. "May I say that it has been a pleasure associating with Admiral Lopatina and her command. I hope that we may renew the association—"

"Admiral Lopatina is remaining in command of the Alliance naval forces in the Victoria System," Uzel said. No, *snapped*. If he'd been a Baernoi, he'd have bared his tusks.

"Then—"

"The transiting ships will be under the command of Admiral Eberle," Uzel said. Liddell wished she could reach across the forty thousand kilometers to *Fei-huang* and pour the man a stiff drink. He looked as if he needed one.

"Then I'm glad that our association with Admiral Lopatina and yourself at least will not be interrupted. Is there anything we can do to facilitate the departure of your ships?"

Uzel's face said, "Let me off this circuit before I scream." Bogdanov nodded graciously. Liddell had the notion that if he'd been standing, he'd have bowed.

"Please convey our best wishes for a safe voyage to Admiral Eberle. Acknowledging receipt of information concerning ship movement, under Article 17 of the Armistice Agreement."

Uzel's half of the screen went blank before Bogdanov could move on his. Liddell watched as the executive officer called up force tables and deleted the Alliance ships being sent out-system.

No, let's call it by its proper name. Being redeployed, to cut the Baba down to size while leaving her with enough firepower to have some control over the tactical situation—

"Losing those ships doesn't take the Alliance as far down as I'd thought," Bogdanov said. "They'll still have *Fei-huang*, *Brilliant* with her two attacker squadrons, *Audacious*, and four light cruisers."

"Also, Captain, with all due respect to you and Admiral Kuwahara—"

"Pavel, it's shaking my faith in your reputation, watching you charm Admiral Uzel. If you start trying to be polite to me, I won't know what to do with you."

"Yes, ma'am. Actually, I had very little choice. If I couldn't charm him, I would have laughed in his face. Since he and

25

the Baba are staying with us, that would not have helped matters. The Baba and her staff are worth at least another heavy ship."

"Agreed. I also think that order must not have much discretion in it, if the ships are still going out after the Silvermouth bombing."

"Not necessarily," Bogdanov pointed out. "All it could mean is that they are receiving no ground reinforcements. What remains could support the ninety-sixth, if it becomes involved, and still have firepower to spare for us."

Pleasant thought. An even less pleasant one was that they didn't know who was behind the bombing, who they were aiming at, and what they might do next.

Navies are so bloody useless at the down-and-dirty forms of killing. Unless they're ready to send their people down into the dirty, to kill or be killed. . . .

"Pavel. Grab some of your special brews and the first lieutenant. I don't care if Jackie's in the shower, bring her along."

"Captain, Commander Charbon is unlikely to respond positively to such an approach—"

"I want you, your tea, and her up here ten minutes ago."

"Aye-aye, ma'am." Bogdanov was both saluting and grinning as the screen blanked.

Liddell swiveled in her chair, to fish her ready-reference printout of *Shenandoah*'s crew roster from the credenza drawer. She wanted the ability to free-associate and play hunches that hard copy gave her, before facing Commander Charbon.

The first lieutenant liked to be generous with other departments' people and stingy with her own. If *Shen* might be sending a third of her five hundred people down to Victoria, Liddell wanted to be sure everybody shared the poverty.

Three

The eye-searing sky of Petzas's Inward Ocean was vanishing behind wind-driven clouds. Brokeh su-Irzim felt that wind against his skin, bare except for a loinguard, blowing hard enough to lift his ears. He pulled his cap out from under the wheel and flopped it roughly on to his head.

The wind gusted stronger, sending spray across *Dark Moon's* deck to sting su-Irzim's cheeks and eyes. The cap seemed to sprout wings and leap from his head, over the railing, and into the face of a foam-crowned wave.

"Eater of young," su-Irzim growled. He shifted in his seat to scan the other waves. They were also growing foam on their heads, sometimes even on their bellies, and they were all rising higher.

By now the sky was almost completely gray, one sign of a blow that would settle in for the rest of today and perhaps tomorrow as well. Su-Irzim decided to raise more sail and try to race the blow back to Kamo Harbor. The entrance might be tricky if the wind rose more, but it could rise only so much in the next watch. Even without the computer, he'd brought *Dark Moon* in past the Heads of Kamo in far worse weather than this.

To beat off shore would be more of a challenge, but he had barely enough sea room for that, and at best he would spend a night and a day and perhaps another night at sea. The Heads were no place for a prudent sailor to approach in the dark, computers, good boat, the favor of the Sailors' Judge, and everything else thrown into the balance.

Su-Irzim powered up all the winches, let the computer read the winds and currents, and watched the sails shift and spread. The surge of water under the hull became a steady thunder roll, the spray over the bow turned into a solid curtain, and the whine of strained rigging fought the whine of the wind.

He tightened his grip on the wheel until his nails gouged

through the padding into the metal. When he knew the wheel felt right, he eased the grip. Less than a watch was long enough to cramp hands, if you stone-gripped when you didn't need to.

But he'd not trust the steering to the computer. It was good enough for plain sailing and it did make it easier to charter the boat, for all that his cousin had said so. It was no substitute for hands on the wheel and feeling the life of the boat under you, as she fought the waves or yielded to them as might seem best, like a dancer or a team match in unarmed combat.

Behind *Dark Moon*, the wake began to bubble white as her speed mounted. Sometimes a wave overtaking and lifting her would spread the wake, but it always grew again. Su-Irzim savored the whiteness churned across the gray-green waves, until one wave lifted him high enough to show him the Head. No more than half a march away; visibility must have dropped as the wind rose.

He turned his mind from savoring the beauty of the rising storm to easing himself and his vessel safely into harbor.

On the screen, Fleet Commander F'zoar su-Weigho saw the steward at the master console. Lights flashed from yellow to blue as the shutters closed, sealing the house against the rising storm.

Steward Kumodz Dran kept his eyes on the displays until the last light turned. Su-Weigho swiveled his couch and saw that one of the study windows still showed gray sky and heaving gray-green sea.

"Kumodz," he called softly.

"Yes, Lord?"

"Window Three in the study didn't shutter. Check your instruments."

The steward hid tusks and ran the diagnostic program through the console. Several lights glowed yellow; the steward made rude remarks in several dialects.

"Forgive me, Lord. Shall I summon Maintenance?"

"After my cousin leaves will be soon enough. Have you heard from him?"

"The harbormaster acknowledged the message but said *Dark Moon* was not in sight from his post yet. If you wish, I can call the Sea Observers—"

"They will be up to their pouches in worse sailors with

28

worse boats, who may really *need* help in this blow," su-Weigho reminded him.

"No, and forgive me. With all due respect to your cousin, he would not thank us for it."

"My cousin's character is due a great deal of respect. I am not so sure about his manners."

"It is not my duty to have an opinion on that, Lord."

"No, but you perform all of your other duties so well that you are entitled to have one if you wish it."

The steward smiled. "Thank you, Lord. Will there be anything else?"

The fleet commander noticed that the offending shutter was closed. Just in time, too, judging from the thunder of the surf on the rocks below the compound.

No swimming, no matter who offers to join us, until the surf goes down and the staff has time to clean the live stingweed and dead fish off the beach.

The screen faded and su-Weigho swiveled his couch to contemplate his companion. Behdan Zeg lay on his back, looking dead or at least needing capsule care. Only the slow rise and fall of his massive chest and an occasional twitch of a muscle below the left ear said that life lingered.

Without rising or moving anything but his mouth, Zeg said, "Why not have your cousin sail directly here? Any message will be remembered."

Su-Weigho remembered that Zeg came from Amzgar. It had almost the opposite ratio of water to land from Petzas. Most of that water was shallow, stinking, and useful only to maintain a habitable ecology.

"Because in this storm, he and *Dark Moon* would end up on the rocks, drowned or battered to pieces. We might never even find the body."

"But a message is still—"

"My message to you is to have some respect for people whose cooperation the Coalition needs."

"It does not need you as badly as that."

"It undoubtedly needs me more than it needs you. Shall I ask them to choose: my support or another representative on Petzas?"

That drew more movement from Zeg than he had displayed since lying down. His face twisted in a way that suggested he would pull lips if asked, but that the one who asked would pay a high price later on for that humiliation.

For someone whose father kept a bathhouse, Behdan Zeg does a better imitation of a goldtusk than I do.

"Well?"

"There will be no need for you to send such a message. I still ask why you sent a message to the harbormaster, instead of having me go and bring your cousin myself."

Because my cousin would probably drop you into the harbor as an extra anchor for Dark Moon *even if the ensuing legal consequences outweighed the temporary emotional satisfaction.*

A more suitable answer took longer to phrase.

"Because you're a stranger, and the Bloodsand Coast is really a small town when it comes to remembering strangers. If my cousin argued, someone might even think he was being abducted and call the Guardians.

"As for the message—it's a code based on references to a party that took place twenty years ago, when I was my cousin's ship commander. Nobody who wasn't at that party—in fact, nobody who didn't take part in some of the practical jokes—will understand it.

"I was thinking of having lunch while we waited for my cousin. The harbor's only a tenth-watch away in good weather, but the storm will ground flyers and may flood part of the Coast Highway."

"As you wish. I am not hungry."

Nervous, lying, or afraid of being poisoned?

F'zoar su-Weigha reminded himself that he should not quarrel with the Coalition's leaders over the manners of their agent. He might well have been the only one available and had probably been rude to everyone else as well.

He still felt that enduring Zeg was a considerable price to pay for increasing the influence of the Antahali within the Khudrigate of Baer.

Brokeh su-Irzim wheeled his roadrider out of the harbor parking lot, threw a half wave, half salute at the harbormaster's window, and fed power to the wheels. They whined, spun, and sprayed gravel for a moment. Then the roadrider whipped around the curves of the entry road and onto the highway.

The rain seemed to be increasing—no, that was just spray from a roadhauler. With the uncertain weather of the Bloodsand Coast, a lot of cargo went by road. This meant a lot of great ponderous cargo vehicles making nuisances of themselves to honest roadrider pilots.

Su-Irzim had to pass a whole convoy of roadhaulers before he was clear of the spray cloud and facing an open road. More power, and the roadrider crept up to ten-march, about as fast as he wanted to try on a wet road.

Down the south slope of Wrymouth Hill, with the road winding in great curves, entry roads to estates and farms popping up at intervals, and the roadhaulers falling farther and farther behind. At the bottom of the hill, su-Irzim glimpsed in his rearview the whole convoy braking hard to avoid a tractor crossing the road from an inland field down to a marsh verge.

The thought of stew flavored with marshscent reminded him that he'd missed dawnfood and would probably be too late for haltmeal. It would not be the first time he had sat through a conference at his cousin's house on an empty stomach, then gone to the kitchen to find a charitable servant. That wasn't a hard search; those who remained had been there since he was a boy, and remembered the young commander home from his first Fleet assignment in his first, hardly worn wargarb.

Time to concentrate on his riding. From here almost to the Point, the road wavered not only back and forth but up and down, like the track of the crawler they'd fed ale at the party. Or like the movement of a woman's hips, as he and she rode each other to a state of bliss that could hardly have been purer . . .

Definitely too distracting a thought for piloting a wet road. Su-Irzim slowed until the clearviewing of his helmet could handle the rain, then oriented himself. The trees on either side of the road grew close to the shoulder and thicker than two bodies.

Virgin growth was easier to find on the Bloodsand Coast than on some other parts of Petzas. The Occali Flood had taught a harsh lesson about preserving ground cover only fifty years after the planet was settled.

Past the Stand, past three—no, four farms, since the Ikseh estate had been divided when Ahmd Ikseh lost his Houseright. A disgraceful affair, all around, but it was hard to blame Lyota. She had endured a great deal before she finally took a lover, and even then she took him because he would give her children a father's love as their blood father never had.

At least there had been no question of either side losing Houseright when his own marriage ended, nor any children

31

to suffer. He was not the first commander in the Fleet to find that his mate wanted more of him than duty allowed. He would not be the last. The pain was real, but there had been no disgrace to make it worse.

The road began to climb again. Su-Irzim slowed, knowing this was the last hill before the familiar gatehouse. A tenth-watch later, it loomed out of the rain, towering over the road in front of it and the walls on either side. A replica of the gate of a Warring States era castle, most of its volume was storerooms and dormitories for people on outdoor-staff duty.

Even distorted by electronics, the voice that hailed him as he pulled up before the gate was familiar.

"Hello, K'tama. You sound as if you've been expecting me."

"I'm too old to bother pretending not to know a secret when it jumps up and bites my tail off at the roots."

"You're twice as fine as any half your age, and you know—"

"I know that the longer I listen to your flattery, the longer you'll be out in the rain. Your card, please."

Su-Irzim shoved his Fleet badge under the scanner, which promptly played a quarter-passage of the "Glory of Union March." The gate slid back; he walked the roadrider through the gateway, to avoid triggering alarms by rapid movement. Past the scanned zone, he saluted the inner window where K'tama was probably watching her consoles, mounted up, and shot away up the road in a cloud of spray.

By the time he reached the main house it was hard to tell where the spray began and the rain ended. The wind was driving sheets of water almost horizontally across the road, and he'd seen a worker's shelter take wings and soar away on a blast.

At last the garage door opened before him, and he rode down into the warm smelly twilight. A light flashed on and off, then turned into a beam that guided him to his assigned place. As he unslung his baggage, he heard feet click behind him.

"Kumodz! This is an honor."

The steward was as immune to flattery as the gatewatcher. "You be the judge of that when the commander's done with you. Meanwhile, I'm to take your baggage straight to your room. They want you right away."

"They?"

Kumodz's face showed he realized he'd made a slip. "I mean—"

"The commander's not alone, is he?"

Silence gave the answer. Su-Irzim didn't press the issue. All four permanent servants of the commander's estate were nearly as old as the commander; none of them would find life easy if they had to leave.

The commander would do his best for them, but that might not be good enough if the Coalition decided it didn't need him. Even if he remained indispensable, the Syrohdi were not above petty cruelty to leading Antahlis' servants.

Su-Irzim pressed fingers with the steward and remembered advice from twenty years ago, from the man who would be his host in a few minutes.

"Don't waste time worrying about the easily avoidable mishaps. That wastes strength, too, and they become harder to avoid."

"Lead on, Kumodz. My fellow guests in this house have often surprised me, but seldom offended me."

Su-Weigho saw both surprise and anger on his cousin's face as su-Irzim as he entered the room and saw who occupied the third couch. Kumodz stood in the open door long enough for the cartload of refreshments to roll through, then pressed fingers together and closed the door—manually, so that he could make a check of all the security systems.

By the time the door was closed, su-Irzim had his formal face on. It had all the expressiveness of a Speaker's ceremonial headdress and didn't catch the eye nearly as much. The fleet commander hadn't lost his ability to read what particular form of turmoil the mask hid. His young cousin hadn't been this shocked since his mate asked for the dissolution.

"I suppose there is some reason for bringing me and this—one of the Instrument's stranger tools—"

Behdan Zeg exposed his tusks. Su-Weigho brought his nails down on the arm of his couch, hard enough to gouge the wood and raise echoes.

"Guestright is taken seriously in this house. It is not abused. Peace, both of you."

"I am here for a reason, which concerns you," Zeg said. He sounded about as conciliatory as a mining borer.

"Display File War Ax," su-Weigho said.

Lights faded, a display tank rolled over, nearly bumping the refreshments, and the couches swiveled. A gray-blue planet spun in the tank, oceans, deserts, and mountains nearly all the same dreary color.

"The planet Victoria," said su-Weigho's recorded voice. It occurred to him now that a Smalltooth—a human, as they called themselves—would have understood his pronunciation of the name easily. Just he had easily understood humans' pronunciation of Petzas, his own name, or even the twelve-part name of the First Khudr.

Perhaps that was part of the problem lying between "Smalltooth" and "Tusker." They not only wanted many of the same things, each could make the other understand that they wanted it—and what they might be ready to do if they did not receive it.

Between the stars, the Khudr's commanders no longer tried to govern the movements of each band and ship, as they had in some long-ago and still-shameful wars. In other ways, too much communication could still wreak the same havoc as too little.

The recorded voice told of the history of Victoria, from its first human settlement, through its coming under two sovereignties, to the emergence of political dissidents on both sides of the border. The history went on, describing efforts to supply the human dissidents with weapons and equipment through the usual Merishi agents. It concluded with a summary of the crisis on Victoria that ended in the armistice, half a year ago.

Su-Weigho nodded to his other guest as the tank faded into inchoate gray. "I have learned of a recent arms shipment," Zeg said. "Placed directly into human hands, this would let us influence our human allies without Merishi cooperation."

That was a long-standing goal of every faction within the Khudrigate. Working through the Merishi was slow, insecure, and expensive even when it was neither of the first two.

It also risked involvement with the strong-willed young Merishi, who so greatly resented being second to the humans that they were willing to run great risks to alter this circumstance. Among those risks was that of war between the humans and the People.

"It was considered, bringing in the Ptercha'a," Zeg added. "But they have few ships, and their one colony in the area is young and weak."

"Is there a single Ptercha'a colony that could really face

the anger of both the Smallteeth and the Scaleskins?" su-Irzim asked. "That seems to me a—time-wasting—quest."

"That is why I am in the Office of Inquiry and you are not," Zeg said smugly.

"The shipment would certainly give us a share in the victory of any humans who put it to good use," Zeg went on. He sounded almost smug. "It consists of twelve sunbombs."

"The fools!"

"Better fools than cowards!"

Su-Irzim sprang off his couch.

"Hold!" Su-Weigho's voice cut the shadows like a firebeam.

"I will hold," his cousin replied. "But if this—calls me such names again, he will be the first Office of Inquiry Commander in some time to fight a death duel."

"I think you hope in vain," Zeg replied.

"The others who were challenged had orders not to fight, that is true," su-Weigho said blandly. Then he bared his tusks. "But *you* would be ordered to accept the challenge. And may the Instrument find a place for you."

"You—" began Zeg. He sounded as if he'd looked in a mirror and seen a monster staring back at him.

Su-Irzim spread his fingers. "I think this decision is giving a quickgun to a child. But perhaps there is more to it than I see. Also, was it your idea?"

"You can hardly—" Zeg bristled.

"Answer your fellow guest," the fleet commander said. It was an order.

"I do not agree that it is foolish," Zeg said, more soberly than he had spoken so far. "But it was made at a far higher level than mine. My duty was to bring word of it to our host so that he could arrange for you to be sent to Victoria."

Su-Irzim looked as if Petzas's rotation had suddenly increased beneath his feet. He half sat, half fell onto his couch and gripped the back.

Su-Weigho smiled. "You are going back on Fleet Duty, aren't you?"

"At the beginning of the Planting Moons."

"If it can be sooner, you will be under Fleet Commander Eimo su-Ankrai."

"Maybe it can be. But what is a Syrohd doing, asking for a low-ranking Antahl like—" Su-Irzim stopped as he saw su-Weigho's smile return.

So the old cannibal can still have people with their own Fleets counting feathers for him.

"Very well. I will be happy to go back to the Fleet, at whatever time will let me watch events on Victoria. Fair?"

"You may be right to doubt what may come of the sunbombs. But how can we be sure, if we have no one we can trust with the ships at Victoria, watching and reporting? If the bombs cause more trouble than they are worth, then so be it.

"But if this is the way to make the Smallteeth work directly with us—if the Coalition can solve that ancient problem—"

Su-Irzim held up both hands to stop the other's oration. But the Inquirer was in full flight; nothing but death could have stopped him short of his conclusion.

At least that conclusion was a formal apology to su-Irzim. They pressed fingers before su-Weigho escorted the Inquirer to the door. By the time the fleet commander returned, his remaining guest had helped himself to a plate of rolls and half a dozen sidedishes of fried vegetables.

"Crude," he said when his mouth was no longer full.

"The cooking, the tactics, or—"

"The cook hasn't lost his art. Our fellow guest probably never had any."

"If you had fought, no one would have believed you were so easily drawn." Su-Weigho looked at his cousin's plate. "Or haven't you been eating properly? You should—"

"Consider walking out into the storm, if you are going to advise me to marry again." Su-Irzim's face twisted as he realized he'd gone too far.

"Forgive me. But will you answer—or at least, may I ask—one question?"

"You can ask any number."

"Only one. Were the sunbombs your idea?"

"No. Believe it or not, cousin, I am no longer an official Coalition representative anywhere. Not even on the Council for Strategic Review. I couldn't do justice to the job without spending half the year on Baer and half of the rest in space going or coming."

"I can see that."

Su-Weigho looked at the younger commander with wry compassion. "But can you see how much more I can do without being official? Holding office, everybody knows what I am, where I am, what I can do, and how to keep me from doing it. When for all our enemies know, I am sitting on my estates gossiping with my neighbors—"

"Don't underestimate the Syrohdi."

"I don't. But they may not learn soon enough. Sooner or later one of our crises with the humans will give the Coalition and our Antahli the chance we've sought for two generations. Victoria may not be that crisis, but it certainly looks promising."

"You can trust me, Commander."

"Good. And you can trust me to keep you entertained until it's time for you to leave. At least one party, I think—"

"Will Zeg be invited?"

"Yes, but so will enough others that he won't be noticed. Believe as you will, he is a good actor. He's half-brother to Rahbad Sarlin, and the talent runs in the family."

Su-Irzim frowned. Perhaps he realized what a narrow escape he'd had, considering what the Inquirers' near-legendary Observer might have said and done about a half-brother's death.

"It won't be like *the* Party, but I don't expect you'll lack for company," su-Weigho added.

"Can you provide one who likes to sail?"

"It's up to you to persuade them that you're worth sailing with!"

Four

Lucco DiVries stepped behind the rock outcropping and pushed up his mask. It was too high and too cold for mites, but in the open the wind was still loaded with dust to get in your eyes, teeth, and ears. The outcropping did cut off the view across the desert to Mount Houton, but DiVries didn't care. As scenery, both the town and the landscape around it were down to the standard of most of the rest of the Bushranger Republic.

After a moment Captain Sophie Bergeron unmasked, too. DiVries decided that the sand-gray mask looked more pleasant than Bergeron's face.

"What the Hades were you going on about when you climbed all over Sergeant Linzer?" she began. "You're not even a Republic officer, let alone in the chain of command."

"You know enough about ammunition handling to see what Linzer and his crew were doing wrong. You wouldn't have put in those revised procedures otherwise. Good ones, too."

"I'm so flattered, I could vomit all over your boots."

"Don't. They're my only desert-fit pair. Look, Sophie—"

"*Captain Bergeron.*"

"Yes, ma'am." *So she's going to be official. Wish there was some way I could be official right back.*

There was, and Lucco DiVries had known it ever since the Armistice. Renounce his oath to the Federation, swear one to the Bushranger Republic, and take any of the jobs they'd offered him if he did. Then he'd be as official as anybody could be in this pickup Defense Force of a pickup country.

DiVries decided it was his move next. "Captain, I'm not questioning anybody's basic competence, least of all yours. It's just that I used to be in Weapons, then I did three years aboard an ammunition transport, then I've taken the course in Baernoi weapons. So I know the Hades of a lot more

38

about how that stuff your people were tossing around can bite if you're not careful!"

Bergeron licked dust off cracked lips. She'd traded in her old sweater with captain's bars for something that looked as if its maker had heard of uniforms without ever seeing one. From twenty meters away she still looked like any bush farmer.

"I'm surprised you're so concerned. If half our ammunition reserve did blow up—"

"Slopping around with ammunition can kill more than the sloppy. Has it occured to you that *I* might go up along with the demos and grenades? That's a good-sized bang you've got there."

Bergeron forced a smile. "You mean you wouldn't gladly die to take the enemies of the Federation with—"

"Captain Bergeron, you can take—" DiVries took a deep breath. "You can let me finish."

"Go ahead."

"I'm not good martyr material. My brother got the family supply of that vice. I'm not even sure the Bushrangers are my enemies. Certainly they're not people I want to see blown halfway to Petzas by accident."

"They won't thank you for that attitude when you go home."

"Who's going to know about it, unless you or Sergeant Linzer grab a Fed Commissioner and babble in their ear? Are you planning to do that?"

"Lieutenant—Lucco. It's my turn to ask you not to insult my intelligence. What concerns me is how close you are to the limit for amnesty. You've had one extension because of your family obligations. If you don't get a second, you have to either go or stay within eleven days."

"I can make my own decisions, thank you."

"If the Federation lets you. But—Lucco, this isn't just something I was told to mention. It's something I would have mentioned—"

"So mention it, without the preliminaries, if you don't mind."

Bergeron slapped the rock, open-palmed, then shook stinging fingers. DiVries wanted to reach out and hold the sore hand until it stopped being sore, or else turned into a fist and knocked out a few of his teeth.

"You've been wandering around freely ever since you rode north with C Company. We owe you a lot, but that

39

means you've also seen a lot. Suppose Fed Intelligence puts it up to you after you go back—a loyalty downcheck, unless you spill everything you've seen and heard. That's a lot, Lucco. Enough to hurt us."

"I doubt if Fed Intelligence is so hard up for agents that they'll need to pump me. What their own people couldn't learn, I'm sure they've picked up from the Armistice Commissioners. I've heard your people whining and pissing about the AC's being 'legal spies.' "

Bergeron smiled. "The fanatics would have said that whether they believed it or not. The rest were worried."

"So let them go on being worried about real threats, not about my spilling to Fed Intelligence. In your position, I'd be a lot more worried about a snatch by the Alliance Field teams. The Alliance can bury somebody who's died under an illegal interrogation a lot easier than the Feds."

Bergeron turned away and started to pace back and forth. Her strides grew longer and finally took her out into the open, straight into a faceful of dust. She staggered back, coughing and gasping, eyes streaming.

DiVries pounded her on the back with one hand and opened his canteen with the other.

"Here, Sophie."

She took a hefty swig and gasped again. "What the—"

"Reesa's private stock, mixed with synjuice. Lemon, I think."

"Remind me never to try outdrinking your brother's wife. Are you sure this isn't a form of chemical warfare?"

"Nonlethal, certainly."

"I'm not so sure about that." Bergeron took a cautious sip, then a second, spit out a mouthful of dust, and handed the canteen back.

"Lucco, it's orders, to do something about you wandering around. But I do have some discretion. What about agreeing to be a prisoner-at-large, in custody of my company? You can't leave the company area, and you'll have an escort from the company everywhere you go inside it."

"Sure that won't leave you short of bodies?"

"We're up to strength, or as up to strength as we need to be unless serious shooting starts again."

"All right. You want an oath?"

"Yes."

"How about after dinner?"

"Better be after lunch. My company turns into the battalion's Alert Force at 1600."

"Will you let me buy the lunch?"

"If there's anything to buy, yes."

"Deal." They shook hands, and Bergeron started pulling her mask back on.

DiVries leaned back against the rock and stared out at a featureless patch of desert. Five lifters crept low along the horizon, looking as small as mites, their formation visibly ragged.

It could be worse. The orders could be to lock me up, and that would be painting a big bull's-eye on my ass for all the crazies.

So far the Victoria crisis had been controlled by the sane people on all sides. Not always the competent, but at least the ones who didn't *like* the sight of blood spattering or farms burning. The others had to be out there, and sooner or later they would find an opportunity, or at least imagine that they'd found one. That would be about the same thing as far as the victims were concerned. . . .

Attacker *Mahmoud Sa'id* cruised in circles at eight thousand meters, forty kilometers off the coast of the Bushranger Republic. The radar screen in front of Elayne Zheng painted a picture of the Krainik Range petering out before it reached the Gulf on the Republic's side of the border.

At the very fringe of the radar's reach, the Roskill Range flickered on and off the screen. The Roskills didn't peter out; in fact, the cluster of peaks on the coast rose high enough to be snowcapped more than half the year.

In the valley between the Roskills and the Krainiks, the Republic had an outpost. Officially it had a rifle company, a civil-action/rescue detachment, and a radar station for monitoring traffic over the Gulf. No one doubted the official T.O.&E; *Sa'id* had been tracked by the radar so many times than Zheng could have jammed it in her sleep.

The unofficial radar—or in Zheng's opinion, radars; she'd registered at least two distinctive signatures—was another matter. It was a Baernoi weapons-guidance radar, its signature laundered so that even Zheng was doing no more than playing a hunch when she labeled it.

"Coffee or tea?" came a voice behind Zheng.

"No caffeine." she said without taking her eyes off the

screen. The Roskills were fading now as *Sa'id* headed down the SE leg of her pattern.

"Milk or hot chocolate?"

"Chocolate." If they hadn't been airborne, she'd have asked for a slug of rum in the chocolate. She didn't need anything to increase her alertness; all her nerves were already out on her skin.

What she needed was something to let her monitor that damned mystery radar until it wasn't a mystery anymore. It would also help to be able to forget that weapons-guidance radars usually meant weapons to guide not too far away.

Good weapons, too, if they were Baernoi. Beamed energy weapons would be strictly line-of-sight and not too useful here; missiles were another matter. The Baernoi had some extremely effective ground-hugging pop-ups in that category.

Zheng had memorized all the available data on those missiles. So had Commander Gesell, C.O. of the 879th Attacker Squadron. That was the real reason she had *Sa'id* on post over the Gulf.

Sa'id's official duty was to provide "distant cover" for the teams surveying the border between the Dominion of Victoria and the Bushranger Republic. Nobody had said just how distant the cover could be. Commander Gesell was an expert at exploiting this kind of oversight.

She was just as expert at defining assignments to her own advantage. Sometimes for her own benefit; always for her squadron's. Zheng was still detached from *Shenandoah* because she was officially "critical support personnel for the border survey," which had Priority Ones and One-Reds slapped all over it.

She'd expected to end up riding a lifter in the Krainiks. It beat riding a seat aboard *Shen*, even a Combat Center console seat. Staying aboard *Mahmoud Sa'id* in the bargain—

Pwinnnngggg!

The alarm on the microwave sounded. Zheng reached behind her to take the hot chocolate, nearly dropped the cup, and nodded her thanks. As she popped the cover, the contact alarm sounded.

"Surface contact, bearing 242, twenty-eight thousand meters."

"Speed?" the pilot asked.

"No reading. Either something's glitched or—" She set down the chocolate and tapped a sequence into her console.

The visual scan went to high magnification, and an image flickered on to the screen, then steadied.

"Coastal freighter out of Silvermouth, heading—I'd guess—for the new Alliance base at Barnard's Crossing." She stepped up the magnification until she saw the foam curling over the curved deck of the ship, washing against the squat deckhouse aft.

"Low in the water, too. That and a plastic hull—explains why we didn't pick her up."

"Doesn't the Alliance have enough lift not to need surface ships?" the navigator asked.

"I think the freighter's going into service from Barnard's Crossing up the Mauger River, combined military-civil run," the pilot said. "Since she had to go out on her own bottom, they probably figured why not load her up? She could haul a year's rations for the garrison."

"Want to see if they've got any new films?" the copilot asked.

"Negative," the pilot said. "Just give them the situation interrogative, Lainie. If they don't need any help, we'll be on our way."

Before the ship replied to Zheng's query about their safety, the attacker was close enough for her to see the Alliance naval insignia on the deckhouse. But their radio operator and two men on the bridge both signaled the same thing—"all's well."

"Coming up on course change," said the pilot. "Three, two, one—mark! Course 270, same speed, same altitude."

Mahmoud Sa'id turned to the southwest, stern toward the coast of the Republic, as Zheng sipped her chocolate and scanned her displays.

The attacker's latest course change registered on Camp Chapman's radar, just like the previous seventeen changes. The duty officer wondered if the Fed crew was trying a new tactic—boring the Republic into coming back into the fold.

Nothing will do that. If they even try seriously, Action for Independence will show that Leon Brautigan *wasn't a real measure of our abilities.*

The duty officer's chair creaked as he swiveled to watch the screen and the shelter door simultaneously. Not that the view out the door was much more exciting than the Feds' pattern. Three more shelters, two lifters, a ground cycle with a one-man launcher slung across its handlebars, a lot of scuffed ground littered with scraps of plastic and bits of garbage.

One thing I'll say for Sophie Bergeron. She keeps things policed up. I guess that stays with you, if you were a sergeant.

Thoughts like that came more frequently than they had three months ago, when Bergeron put up a captain's bars while the duty officer only put up a lieutenant's. That was bad enough, an insult to Action for Independence as well as to Hermann Rourke.

Even worse was what she'd said when Rourke hinted how she might make him forget the insult and tell his superiors to do the same. Well, he now knew why she'd given him that answer. She'd already picked out that damned Feddie prisoner to service her, and Rourke's eight years in AI didn't count there either!

At least being down here at the arse end of the Republic had one advantage. He couldn't see Bergeron and DiVries together, and maybe it would be "out of sight, out of mind" before long.

Back to business.

"Check IFF on the attacker?"

"I just did it five minutes ago."

No "sir," not even a polite tone. Rourke decided not to ask about the routine diagnostic check on the programs. He'd enter another nominal report in the log and settle accounts with that surly radar-mechanic-turned-sergeant later.

Elayne Zheng dropped her cup as the distress-call alarm screamed. The copilot was already reading off the message.

"It's that Alliance freighter. They say—they've taken a *missile* hit."

"A what?" It wasn't a chorus because the pilot out-shouted the rest of the crew.

"That's what they're saying. Frag warhead, medium damage topside, two casualties."

"Dead?"

"They don't say."

"Elayne," the pilot said. "Any traces on your radar?"

"Playback?"

"Just be sure you've got the record. Maximum scan for any air contacts."

Zheng went to maximum scan and got minimum results. Nothing showed except the freighter, now sixty kilometers astern and dead in the water, and far to the south what looked like bad weather.

"Zero. Nul. *Nada*. Although I think that weather front's going to be up with us in another hour."

"Tell me something I don't know," muttered the pilot. "They were shutting up and shutting down at Port Harriet the last time we called in. Recommendations?"

Zheng swallowed. This moment came to any good E.W.O., when her attacker was just a platform for the sensors she commanded, and what that platform should do depended on what was best for those sensors.

It was a proud moment—*and pride plus a half-stellar gets you a cup of coffee.*

Displays showed that the pilot had already increased speed, begun evasive maneuvers, and armed the chaff and decoy dispensers. Zheng activated Level Three jamming—enough to confuse simple-minded radars, not enough to wipe out her own sensors.

"Put us on the deck right now," she said. "Call for ship and satellite surveillance of the area and a scramble of the rest of the flight. This isn't a one-ship job anymore."

"Amen," the pilot said. The deck tilted and the altimeter unwound rapidly. Zheng thought of playing back her recording of the time frame of the missile hit, then decided she needed her attention on what was happening, not what had happened.

Twenty meters above the sea, *Mahmoud Sa'id*'s plunge ended. At this altitude tall waves could hit them with spray, and the damaged freighter was beyond their radar horizon.

They were also below the radar horizon of any weapons launcher that wasn't practically underneath them, unless it had a satellite relay. Even then, orbital radars could lose an attacker in sea effect, and the lag time would give *Mahmoud* time to maneuver if somebody actually did lock on.

The idea of a missile launcher practically underneath them gave Zheng a brief chill, then an idea.

"Douse the lights."

"Everything?" the navigator asked.

"Everything. It's just possible our missile-happy friends fired on visual."

All the internal lights went off as well, proof that the pilot wasn't as calm as he seemed. When they came back on again, the copilot asked: "What if the missile really was friendly?"

"Then it was an accident, and it's not our baby. If it wasn't an accident, whoever fired it wants to start a war. They're not *my* friends, Jimbo."

The copilot grunted agreement. An air pocket bounced the attacker up ten meters and down fifteen. Zheng twiddled the adjustment knob on her harness until she had at least the illusion of a better fit.

"Damn," the navigator said.

"I suppose another twenty meters won't—" Zheng began.

"No, they just told me there's a ten-minute delay in giving us an orbital link. The rest of the flight's going off in five minutes, ETA twenty-five minutes."

Zheng didn't say anything, but her thoughts were sulfurous. *Mahmoud Sa'id* was alone and, at low altitude, nearly blind in the face of an unknown threat.

The missile-carrying drone passed too far from the camp for a visual, but Rourke watched it pass on the radar. He had to look over the operator's shoulder, and the company C.O. had to look over his, but they all saw the drone slide past at fifty meters and head out to sea.

As sea effect began to blur the image, the missile launcher came on the radio, to announce that they'd put a drone on station as a precaution. The three soldiers in the shelter looked at each other. Then the C.O. looked at the door. The half-dozen gapers there promptly found business elsewhere. This gave Rourke a clear view of the camp.

At the door of the nearest shelter, an argument was going on. Two men carrying a portable rocket launcher were waving their free hands in the face of a woman locking the shelter door. Rourke heard something about "issuing ammunition without a requisition" from the woman, and a couple of sexual epithets from the weapons crew.

"Would they mind telling us something we don't know?" the C.O. asked the world in general. "Such as why they launched for an attack on an Alliance ship? Will it do anything, except maybe lose us a drone and missiles because the Alliance thinks it's another attack?"

"Anyone who launched this attack is guilty of a provocation," Rourke said. "Provocateurs are universal enemies."

The radar operator looked at him, with an expression Rourke didn't have time to interpret before a major blip leaped on to the radar.

"In the critical area," the C.O. said. "Could be that Feddie spy ship, but—check the IFF."

The operator's mouth opened as if he wanted to say something, but his fingers danced as fast as ever. "No readings on the IFF."

"Diagnostic check on the computer."

"It's been made," Rourke said hastily. He wondered if the penalty for lying was worse than the penalty for neglect of duty.

"Put us through to the launcher and have them check," the C.O. said. His voice was steady, but sweat beaded his cheeks and throat. "Damn it, we don't want to screw up the way the Feddies did over Flight 6!"

"No time, sir," the operator said. "Whatever that is, it's in firing position for more than the Alliance ship. It could pop off at us—"

The C.O. gripped the back of Rourke's seat, careless that he was also gripping some of Rourke's hair. It wasn't that pain that made Rourke bite his lip.

"Recommend missile release," the C.O. said. The words were almost a sigh.

The launcher crew must have had their fingers hovering over the release switches. The fuzzy blip that was the drone suddenly became fuzzier, then split into three, two distinctly smaller than the first.

Mahmoud Sa'id's fate was sealed by a margin of no more than fourteen seconds.

Nobody aboard was happy about climbing to an altitude where they'd be on the Republic's suspicious radars. They were even less happy about staying on the deck, blind both offensively and defensively, only marginally useful against somebody who had, after all, used a weapon and caused casualties.

So *Mahmoud Sa'id* began a cautious climb back to five thousand meters. Elayne Zheng was fully occupied monitoring the area where the missile launcher almost had to be, if they'd launched and hit undetected.

Everything outside that circle got only cursory attention. So the Republican missiles reached detection range for their onboard radars without raising an alarm.

Then alarms tore at ears, but the missiles were already accelerating. At four kilometers a second, they took only eleven seconds to close the distance to *Sa'id* and make a perfect bracket. Neither was a direct hit, but with a perfect bracket they didn't need to be.

Heavy-compound fragments and blast shook *Sa'id* and

punctured her armored hull in half a dozen places. One of the punctures was in the weapons bay, where the supposedly stable propellant of a short-range missile blazed up. Another ignited armed flares ready in the chute, three seconds short of being ejected.

The alarms died, along with the lights and most of the displays. Zheng thought: *Power failure or power cut?* Standard procedure for a low-altitude emergency in an attacker was cutting power for all nonessential systems. They didn't need radar or air-conditioning; they did need altitude.

"Emergency oxygen, now!" the pilot shouted. "I'm sealing the ventilation." Zheng felt the air currents stop, but not the throat-tearing smoke. She coughed, spat, slapped her mask over her face, and unstrapped. A final pat to her dead consoles, and she was out of her seat.

"Going on autopilot for maximum climb—mark!" the pilot shouted, voice muffled by his mask. The deck tilted and slammed Zheng and the copilot against a console. Zheng felt something twist painfully in her shoulder and saw blood flower on the copilot's temple.

"All hands to escape stations," the pilot added. Trying to help the navigator with the copilot, Zheng learned that she had a dislocated shoulder. *So far, not too bad, but those escape capsules are hard enough to handle with two hands.*

The pilot heaved on the hatch to the escape chamber. A blast of heat and smoke leaped from the opening. The navigator hadn't pulled on his mask; he clawed at his eyes, dropping the copilot.

"Damn," the pilot said. He heaved himself back into his chair. "Hang on, people. I'm going back on manual, try to get us over land for a bare-ass bail-out. Lainie, can you rout out the emergency chutes?"

Zheng discovered that she could. She could even use both hands if she didn't mind screaming occasionally from the pain in her shoulder.

The copilot was out of it, and the navigator was nearly so, with a major toxic-inhalation dose. He managed to breathe between coughs, but Zheng was wary about masking him. If he vomited into the mask, he'd been finished.

At some point in their flight through Hades, it occurred to Zheng to wonder about further missile attacks. After all, the nearest land was Bushranger Republic territory. If they didn't show clearly as disabled, somebody might decide they were an attack.

48

At another point the pilot asked Zheng to take a vital-signs reading on the copilot, who turned out to be dead. Finally even a simple look out the one remaining clear port told Zheng that they were over land.

"Back on internal power," the pilot said. The main lighting system came on. Then *Sa'id* lifted like a surfboard on a crest as the pilot jettisoned the whole weapons-bay load.

"I'm going to blow the auxiliary hatch, then program the autopilot to roll her. Get on the ladder, grab the navigator, and fall out."

"Thanks." Zheng managed not to cry out as she grabbed the ladder to the overhead hatch.

"Hatch set—three, two, one—"

Whannnkkkk! Zheng saw a circle of gray sky overhead. She set the timer on the navigator's parachute release so it would deploy even if they were separate or he was unconscious. The deck tilted, and the circle turned to half sky, half snow-covered mountains. She felt the internal air pressure streaming past her as *Sa'id* rolled inverted.

She let go then, something tapped her on the leg, and the circle suddenly expanded to become her whole world. As she and the navigator fell away from the dying attacker, flames spewed from the hatch, a long tongue nearly licking her boots.

She cursed again. Electrical or maybe the evacuation-compartment fire, something had cut loose the minute fresh oxygen hit it. The pilot wasn't going to get out of this one.

Zheng's hand nearly froze short of the chute release. It seemed a lot simpler to plummet down through the sky and smash herself into permanent oblivion.

It would also be wasting the pilot's death, and maybe causing the navigator's. *They don't pay you attacker bonuses for simple solutions, Lieutenant Zheng.*

She made an eyeball altitude check and found that they had plenty. *Thank the Creator for small favors, since this seems to be Her off-day for big ones.*

A thumb punch, overriding the automatic timer, and the navigator's chute popped. Zheng flung herself backward as it did, then rolled into the dereve position to gain horizontal as well as vertical separation.

When they had enough of both, she popped her own chute. The opening shock made her scream again, with a new pain in her leg as well as the old one in her shoulder.

Swaying under the transparent canopy, she saw a cloud of

dust, snow, and smoke leap from a mountainside. *Mahmoud Sa'id* was now as dead as her namesake, and not nearly as honorably.

Another reason to stay alive. Dead E.W.O.'s can't take a piece of hide from the people who buggered the works and shot them down.

It was beginning to look as if getting out of the attacker was just the first step in that direction. The ground looked rugged, snow-covered in patches, totally uninhabited, and a long way from rescue posts if the Bushrangers had any to begin with.

Take things one step at a time. It saves worry, even if not always ass.

The first step was staying close to the navigator. He was floating down fifty meters above and a hundred away, drifting away slowly and apparently unconscious.

The second step was to make a safe landing. No, the second step was to check the survival radio. If she could get a signal out before they dropped behind the peaks, it couldn't do any harm.

Displays normal. Now, let's see if anybody's listening—

"Mayday, Mayday. This is Lieutenant Elayne Zheng and survivors of Federation attacker *Mahmoud Sa'id.* Mayday, Mayday."

A look at the ground told her that it was time for that safe landing. She set the radio for a continuous Mayday, checked its straps, and prayed that her leg was only sprained, not broken.

Five

Lucco DiVries couldn't sleep in the chilly, wind-shaken little shelter. He could daydream, but that didn't help the boredom of being neither quite prisoner nor quite free.

He knew he could also solve that problem by deciding on his allegiance. Since he had only five more days to make that decision anyway, the thought of that cure for his boredom was tempting.

But the cure might be worse than the disease. Since Bergeron's company moved to its new post five days ago, he'd asked three times to talk on a secure line to either a Federation representative or his sister-in-law Teresa. Three requests, three refusals.

He was beginning to think that taking prisoner-at-large status hadn't been the wisest choice. There'd been danger in confinement, vulnerable to any fanatic's potshot. There was danger here, different but not much less.

The main one was that he might only be allowed to talk if he agreed to provide military intelligence, or even act as a spy against the Federation. The Armistice terms prohibited this. So did quite a few agreements about prisoners and paroles. The prohibitions were about as effective as one might expect.

The Bushranger Republic undoubtedly had its share of people who'd trained in one or another intelligence agency. It would also have its share of those who achieved dubious ethics by pure natural ability.

Going into the field with Bergeron's company, DiVries was beginning to suspect, had put him where either kind could grab him by the short hairs with a minimum of sweat.

The thought of sweat reminded him to check the setting on his sleeping bag. It had crept down ten degrees since the last time he looked; no wonder he was too chilly to sleep. No wonder, either, considering the age of most of the equipment begged, borrowed, or stolen for the Defense Forces of the Republic. (Army of the Republic, actually; anything else existed in file.)

The power in the bag was all right; DiVries felt warmth beginning to creep back into it and around him. Before long his head sagged, and the daydreams turned imperceptibly into real dreams.

Elayne Zheng gripped a rock, and gripped edges sharp enough to feel through her gloves. If she'd been bare-handed, she would have been bleeding.

The standard Navy rig-out for a shirtsleeves environment wasn't the real survival gear that had burned or fried along with *Mahmoud Sa'id*. It still helped keep sharp objects out and body heat in, cushioned bangs, bumps, and jars, and generally improved the wearer's life expectancy.

Why, I might last a whole day, instead of just a few hours. That could be important. Her radio was pumping out a Mayday and should let her home in rescuers, when they showed up. It was "when" and not "if," in spite of what mountains, weather, and Victoria did to radio reception.

All Zheng had to do was be alive when they showed up. *Scratch that. Be alive, and keep the navigator alive, too, toward which the first step is finding the son of a Ptercha'a.*

Zheng pulled herself fully upright and looked out from behind the boulder. The pain in her leg shot down into her foot and up into her chest; there it collided with the pain coming down from her shoulder. It seemed a waste of time to scream when there was nobody to hear her, so she just bit her lip.

The leg felt more like a bone bruise than a sprain, definitely not a fracture. Another small favor was that her belt survival kit was still with her. Like her clothes, it was no substitute for the gear in the escape capsule, but it did include painkillers.

She choked them down dry, then sat with her back to the boulder until they started working. When she could stand without even thinking of screaming, she wondered if she had a concussion. The mountaintops looked blurred and wavering.

On a second look, she recognized fast-moving clouds. The winds up near the peaks, above three thousand meters, must be even fiercer than down here. Which also explained why there was no sign of *Mahmoud Sa'id*'s crash site. Any smoke would be blown away, and who knew how far she'd been carried from the site.

A mixed piece of luck—her quick-release gear had worked. She remembered seeing her parachute whip away on the wind, any shelter or clothing it might have provided vanishing into the murk.

Zheng only hoped that the navigator's stress-activated autorelease had also done its job, *and* in the right place as well. Chute autoreleases had saved many unconscious people from being dragged by their parachutes. They'd also dumped the people into water where they drowned, over cliffs where they broke every bone in their bodies, and in the paths of fires that roasted them alive.

She reminded herself that for downed crew to brood on the numerous and inevitable inequities of the universe was contrasurvival, and started scanning the scenery. No sign of the navigator or any chutes, but she thought she recognized the triple peaks of Mount Denholm.

That would put her on the northern side of the Hammerhead, the circular mass of peaks where the Roskills came down to the sea. Forty kloms inland, seventy from the nearest reported Bushranger base. Two hundred from the Alliance border, but how far from infiltrators that even the Bonsai Force probably didn't know about?

Priorities, Zheng, priorities. Remember the navigator.

She switched off the Mayday and listened on the rescue frequency for a moment. The moment turned into a minute, without the silence breaking. Zheng swore in three of her five ancestral languages and switched frequencies again.

The navigator's signal squealed and shrieked in her ears.

Another moment in Radio Direction Finding mode gave her directions—downhill, to the right, and from the signal strength, probably in the open. She tried to raise the navigator on voice, but got only more silence.

Zheng hoped the navigator was alive. Almost as much, she hoped he was in shape to pop her shoulder back into place before she ran out of painkillers.

Hooking her radio back on her belt and wishing for a staff, Zheng began her downhill trek.

In Lucco DiVries's dream, he was undressing Sophie Bergeron. Since he'd never seen her except fully clothed, her body somehow looked rather like Elayne Zheng's. This was absurd, Lucco knew, because Sophie was at least ten centimeters taller than Lainie and with that faded auburn hair had to be a lot lighter-skinned—

"Lucco. Lucco, wake up. Hey, I'm talking to you. I need you *awake*. We have a problem."

What somebody—it sounded like Sophie—wanted and what DiVries wanted were two different things. He rolled over without opening his eyes.

Suddenly the cot tilted under him and he rolled off it, to land on the floor with a thump. He woke up enough to recognize Bergeron standing beside the cot, wearing field gear and a grim look.

He lurched to his feet and sat down on the cot. Bergeron handed him a steaming mug. It held hot, strong tea laced with local "rum," a synthetic tipple that had nothing but potency to recommend it.

With the cup inside him, DiVries looked up. "Okay, you said a problem. Serious enough to wake me up for?"

"Yes, and what the Hades were you doing asleep at this time of day?"

"Not much else to do here, and anyway I'm not one of your corporals. I—"

The fans of two lifters climbing out almost directly overhead drowned him out. He saw Bergeron cock her head, listening.

"That's the last of the Quick Reaction platoon heading out." She swallowed. "Lucco. There's been another accidental shootdown."

The warmth from the tea evaporated. DiVries stood. "Who hit what?"

"One of our—the Republic's—our missile batteries covering the valley between the Roskills and the Krainiks. It shot down a Federal attacker by mistake. There'd been an attack on an Alliance coaster, and we thought—"

"ID on the attacker?"

"I've heard it's the one named after that Navy reservist killed aboard—"

DiVries knew afterward that he must have still been half-asleep. Otherwise he'd never have tried to attack Bergeron over something that couldn't possibly have been her fault.

At the time, all he could think was: *The goddamned Bushrangers just murdered Lainie!*

He swung on Bergeron, let the knee she aimed at his groin ride up his thigh, twisted to block a counterstrike with forearms, tripped over the cot, and fell backward onto the floor. He rolled again, got his feet tangled in the cot, and managed to end up with his groin protected but otherwise completely helpless.

Before he could worry about that, he understood what a spectacle he'd made of himself. He laughed.

"What's so bloody entertaining?" Bergeron began.

"Nothing, except maybe me. Can I get up?"

"Be my guest." She didn't help him, but stood back while he sorted himself out.

"*Mahmoud Sa'id*, is that the one?"

"So I've heard," she said.

"Okay. Any word on where, and how many survivors?"

"We don't have much orbital data. but it looks like they made feet dry, somewhere in the Roskills. We also have signals from one, maybe two survival radios."

Which can go on Maydaying up a storm long after their owners are dead as the Great Khudr.

"So far, not too bad. What's all this got to do with me, except that you mite-bouncers may have killed a friend of mine?"

"If we have—I'm sorry. Believe it or not, I am. But a lot of other people are alive, and you can help keep them that way. Come with me, when I take Second and Fourth Platoons out in twenty minutes. I want a witness, a reliable Federation witness, that the Republic's ground forces made a thorough search, didn't interfere with anyone else's search, things like that."

"What makes you think anybody down south'll believe me?"

"If you go back when we've settled this—"

"What makes you think I want to go back?"

Bergeron gaped. "You've decided—"

"I haven't decided a thing!" *No, that wasn't quite right.* "I'll go along with you, and do what you say. But if Elayne Zheng's dead—"

"I thought she'd be dumping you over your staying with us this long."

DiVries decided that jealousy wasn't the problem here. Even if it was, mentioning it might have him wrestling the cot again.

"Elayne and I weren't affiliated even before this. No, I just don't forget people who kill my friends."

Bergeron nodded, then stepped outside the shelter. Over the rising wind, DiVries could hear her doing a walkaround.

When she came back, a cold gust nearly blew her into his lap. It did blow a small black cylinder out of her hand, onto the cot. She picked it up, twisted the end, and set it down again.

"There. They'll think the bug's gone sand happy for a couple minutes. Happens all the time."

"The one disguised as a section of the cot's frame?"

Bergeron grinned. "That, and any others. Let's make this quick. I've already heard rumors of sabotage being involved. I don't have any opinions on that. But even if the people who want a war aren't responsible for this, that doesn't mean they won't take advantage of it.

"The Feds are going to be crawling walls over this as it is. If a paroled prisoner-at-large is shot while in Republican custody—and security in this camp's going to be shaky with most of the riflemen out on search . . ."

"I get the picture. Okay, but I'll need field gear and—"

"I'll have gear sent over, and you can take this. It's the only nontraceable weapon I could get my hands on."

It was a presentation pulse pistol, with a conventional folding stock and highly unconventional furniture of polished wood. DiVries recognized expert craftsmanship, and wasn't surprised to see a silver plate in the butt.

"To Sergeant Sophia Bergeron, from Company E, Third Battalion, 134 Brigade, in friendship and farewell."

"Long way from Pied Noir, aren't you?"

"It's a long story." She turned off the bug jammer, pocketed it, and stepped to the door. "The field gear's coming up in five minutes. See you at the pad in ten."

It took most of Elayne Zheng's concentration to keep putting one foot in front of another. The rest went to shutting out the pain from her arm and leg that the pills couldn't handle, not to mention the suspicion that she had a mild concussion and the beginnings of hypothermia.

So it was a good five minutes before she realized that the navigator was off the air. She stopped, listened for another minute, then gave a minute to each frequency the radios could handle. She heard a lot of static, but nothing intelligible, from either the navigator or anybody else.

She wanted to cry, except that dehydration would bring the hypothermia on quicker. She reminded herself that the navigator might still be alive. If he was, she was about his only remaining hope.

Zheng went back to the one-foot-in-front-of-another routine. At least it would keep her from freezing, in any sense of the word.

How long this went on, before the pulse pistol opened fire from downslope, she never knew. She heard the slugs *wheeeett* past her, except for one that *spnnnggged* off the rocks. She hit the ground, hard enough to cut her lip and start a miniature avalanche.

As the gravel and lumps of ice rattled away down the slope, she saw a figure break from cover. It wore what looked like Navy coveralls and a helmet, carried something in its left hand, and stumbled as it tried to run.

The navigator was left-handed.

Zheng leaped to her feet, waved her good arm, and screamed.

"Hey, Jock! Jock, it's me, Lainie! Don't shoot!"

The figure stopped and half dove, half fell behind a boulder. A faint shout came up the hill.

"Elayne? Is that really you? Are you alone?"

"It's really me. Who else should it be?"

"Come on down, keep your hands up, and let me make sure."

Zheng wondered about a head injury on top of the facial burns and smoke inhalation. Then she remembered the radio silence, and suddenly the wind was even colder.

He's picked up somebody else out here. He thought—thinks—I might be them.

She stood up, held her hands out in front of her since she couldn't raise both of them, and started down the slope.

Captain Candice Shores swung herself up on to the table at the front of the briefing room. Too late, she remembered that she'd forgotten to switch on the main display, and it wasn't voice-commanded.

She resisted the temptation to stretch out one long leg and activate the display with a foot. That would save a whole four seconds. It would also tell the platoon leaders and platoon sergeants of Victoria Brigade's Scout Company that their C.O. was nervous.

"Top, switch on the display."

"On the way," Raoul Zimmer said.

The flatscreen display showed the Gulf coast of the Bushranger Republic. A red square showed the area of the search for *Mahmoud Sa'id*'s survivors.

"All right. I'll give you everything they've given me. If I get any more, I'll give it out before we lift. We're supposed to get a lot more on the way, but don't bet anything you can't afford to lose on that."

The laughter was faint but real. "We're taking 1st, 2nd, and 4th platoons, with an extra weapons squad apiece and doubled cooking equipment. Twelve lifters, with all the high-wind gear we can scrounge up in the next thirty minutes.

"We'll be riding loaded and docked with three attackers from the 879th. That's partly to cut transit time and partly to let us orbit offshore if necessary. The diplomats are supposed to be making talk-talk with the Bushrangers over letting us in. Maybe they'll succeed fast. Maybe they'll take a while."

"And if they fail completely?" somebody asked. The silence seemed louder than the laughter before.

"Why do you think we're ready to go in shooting?" Shores replied. "Make sure everybody stays loaded, locked, heads up, and buttoned down for emergency undocking."

She saw nods and went on, hoping nobody thought that meant she wanted to go in shooting. What she really wanted was to hide the fact that nobody all the way up to Victoria Command seemed to know what to do if the Bushrangers stonewalled.

"Our primary job is to provide security for the crash site. If we find any survivors, of course we bring them in. But the Bushrangers have more people and more local knowledge, and we expect to have some teams from the border survey on hand as well. They've got every kind of sensor and weather gear on their lifters that I'd ever heard of and a few I hadn't."

"Any word on who popped off at that Alliance coaster?" the platoon sergeant of 4th Platoon asked.

"Who the Hades cares?" somebody else snapped. "It's the Bushrangers who hit—"

"You'd damned well better care," Zimmer growled, carefully not looking at the speaker in case they were an officer. "That somebody is just as crazy as the Bushrangers, and *all* crazies are dangerous. If they haven't killed any of our people yet, it's just their bad luck or our good luck. Right, ma'am?"

"Good point, Top. We're not interested in vengeance until we know exactly who did what, and maybe not even then. We are interested in preventing any more incidents that the crazies can exploit even if they don't cause them. Anybody who goes north with anything else in mind is going to be incredibly unhappy, or maybe a civilian, when I find out.

"Any questions?"

The silence was a relief. Shores resolutely kept her eyes on the map until the last footfall died.

"Captain?"

She turned to face Sergeant Esteva and Corporal Sklarinsky, a third of Scout company HQ and two-thirds of her bodyguards. Both were fully armed and suited up, except for sealing their thermal vests. Between them they had her field gear and personal weapons, plus a shoulder bag that thumped when they set it down.

Shores prodded it with a toe. "Liquid or solid?"

"Liquid," Esteva said. "The last of what you—the Company—got from—in Fort Stafford last summer. We can turn it over to the medics if you want, but I thought you might need a little for making talk-talk yourself. Never seen a Bushranger yet who could turn down a drink."

Some of the Bushrangers belonged to Temperance sects. Shores decided that encountering one of those would exceed her daily quota of bad luck.

"Sling it in with the HQ gear," she said. She sat down and started pulling off her boots. "And lift out, both of you. I don't need help, and some of those people they sent out after the Armistice may need watching."

"Yes, ma'am."

Elayne Zheng walked the last ten meters to the navigator almost as blind as he was. The wind was rising, slicing clouds of snow and grit off the slopes and flinging them into her eyes.

She finally knelt down in front of the navigator, raised his free hand to her face, and let him feel his way over her features, from ear to ear and forehead to chin. Even through the glove and on half-numb skin, the hand felt cold.

"Thank God," he said finally. "It is you."

"Who did you expect? The people who made you go silent on me?"

"Maybe. I don't know who they are. What I heard—it was short, not in clear, but not in any code I could recognize. It had to be close, though. Reception in these mountains is—well, it mostly isn't. The weather—Lainie, what are you doing?"

The navigator grabbed for his radio as Zheng switched it back on and turned the Mayday up all the way. She fended him off with both arms until he suddenly doubled up in a coughing fit, then did the same with her own radio.

"Jock, I don't know who else is out there. But some of our friends must be. We've got to let them know where we are. Besides, now that I'm here, somebody who can see will be holding the pistol if the bad guys do show up. Or was that your usual standard of marksmanship?"

Cracked lips twisted in a smile. "I can tell light from shadow, most of the time. I fired at the sound. Thought I'd got lucky, too, when I heard that little avalanche."

"Damned good thing you—"

Zheng held up a hand for silence, twisting her head, praying to every ancestral god and spirit that the wind would drop for ten whole seconds. Then she grabbed her radio and popped open the rear panel.

"What—"

"Do you have any flares?"

"No, but—"

"One radio's all we need. Remember about converting a power cell into a flare?"

"I never could get the trick of that."

"Bloody theorist!" Zheng's fingers completed their work. The radio's power cell was now ready to discharge its stored energy in one spectacular flash, if it hit something hard.

Zheng wound up and threw. The power cell soared downhill and vanished into the twilight and the driving snow. She prayed again, that she'd really heard a lifter, that the cell would flare, that the lifter was friendly and would see—

Light blazed downhill. Zheng had just time for her eyes to adjust to the glare and make out the light reflected from the belly of a lifter less than five hundred meters up. Then she clutched at the radio, in a way that would have crushed any bed partner's ribs.

"Mayday, Mayday," she screamed. "Survivors of *Mahmoud Sa'id.* We are about one hundred meters directly uphill from the flare site. Repeat, one hundred meters directly uphill—"

Zheng didn't need any reflected light to see the lifter as it broke out of the overcast and wobbled down toward them. No secret intelligence operation would use a piece of junk like that, barely able to navigate in this kind of weather.

She turned her face into the wind, until it dried the tears on her cheeks, then switched her radio to receive and sagged into the navigator's arms.

"—too windy to lift off now, so we're setting out ground anchors. Even if we get snowed in, your people'll be warmer'n they'd be out on that bloody slope."

"Thanks, Mr. McGuire," came Elayne Zheng's voice. "He forgot to mention that he and his daughter set my shoulder, salved Jock's eyes, and treated us both for frostbite and exposure. We owe him more than I know how to pay.

"This is First Lieutenant Elayne Zheng, concluding her report"—a yawn—"her interim report, on the *Mahmoud Sa'id* incident."

The recorded broadcast ended and routine announcements replaced it on *Shenandoah*'s intercom. Brian Mahoney let out a long sigh of relief and gripped Brigitte Tachin's hand.

Cahrles Longman lounged back on his bunk. "Pity Lainie's so tired. Otherwise she'd know how to pay off the farmer, though maybe not in front of his daughter unless the girl goes for—"

"I am going to go for you with something sharp if you don't shut up," Tachin said briskly. Before Longman could bristle, the private-signal chime sounded.

"D-4, Lieutenant Mahoney speaking."

It was the first lieutenant, Commander Charbon. "Lieutenant Mahoney, the captain presents her compliments and would like you for a ground assignment connected with this incident. She says your experience with the Armistice Commission—"

There was more, but Mahoney heard just enough of it to keep from having to ask stupid questions. He heard mostly his own anger.

Damn it! Another dirtside slot! Do they really think I'm good at all these odd jobs? Or are they just afraid to tell me that I'll never qualify for Junior Officer of the Watch?

He must have said the last aloud, because Charbon was looking startled and Tachin alarmed when the screen went blank.

"Brian," Tachin said. "A thought. I have nearly as much time with the Armistice Commission as you do. If Commander Zhubova can spare me, why shouldn't I volunteer, too? I'm sure they'll want a weapons—"

Mahoney was hugging Tachin so hard she squeaked before he realized that she might have more to say. He held her out at arm's length, glared at Longman until the other man stopped grinning, then hugged Tachin again.

"Well, privacy at last," Longman drawled. "I at least will know what to do—"

Mahoney's eyes met Tachin's. They turned together, grabbed the privacy curtain on Longman's bunk, yanked it down, and latched it in place. While Mahoney held it down against Longman's profane efforts to get out, Tachin pulled out her bunk's storage net, dismantled it, and tied the components across the curtain.

As a final touch, Mahoney borrowed a laser welder from the emergency locker in the passageway outside and welded the curtain's latches and all the fastenings of the harness in place.

"Charlie," he said from the door. "Brigitte and I are going down to volunteer. When we come back, if you are very polite and apologize about Elayne, we may let you out. Then you can hold an orgy if you want to.

"Otherwise—" he turned to Tachin and offered his arm with a courtly bow. "*Mademoiselle* Lieutenant?"

"*Enchantée.*"

Six

Admiral Kuwahara was only one man, and not a particularly large one. Rose Liddell decided that his presence in Combat Center for this practice alert was so tangible because it reminded everyone that the next alert was likely to be real.

Liddell's attention returned to the main display. It showed a simulated defense of the Vinh Knuckle by two companies of the Second/215, groundbound and facing an opponent with air superiority.

Not that this was a particularly plausible scenario. The Second Battalion, 215 Brigade, had adapted quite well to Victoria since its arrival a month after the Armistice, apart from being a good regular outfit to begin with. It would take a lot to knock out their organic lift transport, never mind their aerial fire support.

Still, coping with the implausible was a good test of the Combat Center people, and one that so far they were passing. The fire-support board had just called in a strike at coordinates Liddell didn't catch, when her intercom signal squeaked in her ear.

"Combat Center, Captain Liddell."

"Captain, I have the analysis of the strike on the Alliance coaster. *Eriksen Gamma*." It was Commander Bogdanov, in the Auxiliary Combat Center. Since the exercise was primarily for the main CC people, half of the ACC capacity was on standby. Bogdanov had been using it to try unraveling at least the first of the several mysteries that made up the present crisis.

"Good." Liddell hand-signaled to Admiral Kuwahara, then switched the connection to a secure three-way. "Go ahead, Pavel."

"We have no traces of any airborne launching platform and no sure signature for the missile itself, which is hardly surprising. It would have been a small weapon, probably with a low metallic signature, skimming the waves. Even an interceptor-configured attacker with lookdown radar might have had trouble detecting it."

"But not the launch vehicle?"

"No. We may learn otherwise when we study *Mahmoud Sa'id*'s sensor records and interview survivors."

"I don't know about the survivors," Liddell put in, "but from the pictures of the crash site, I doubt there will be any usable records."

"Very well," Bogdanov said. "Then I will—go out on a limb? Yes. I think the missile was launched from a submarine, submerged or awash."

Kuwahara muttered something Liddell didn't understand, but with a note of "Why didn't *I* think of that?" Liddell decided to administer a ten-cc dose of tact.

"That's an interesting hypothesis, but doesn't it depend too much on coincidence? There aren't that many submarines on Victoria."

"There are not," Bogdanov said cheerfully. "But we still don't need coincidence. I also had the radio log scanned. The departure time and route of *Eriksen Gamma* have been public knowledge for more than a week. We have been flying the patrol on which *Sa'id* was shot down for five days. All three—political administrations—on Victoria have ports within two days' submerged travel of the ship's route."

"I see," Kuwahara said. "At least I think I do. Somebody took advantage of a security leak—or rather, of our thinking that there was no need for security."

"Us, the Alliance, and for all I know the Republic as well," Liddell added. "I suspect there's enough blame to go around."

"I hope so," Kuwahara said. "Because I intend to call in everything both the Army and the Alliance owe me to get to the bottom of this. Get to the bottom of it, and fish up whatever I find there to the light of day, even a Victoria day."

"May I pray for your success?" Bogdanov asked. "As well as helping in the line of duty?"

"By all means," Kuwahara said. "Start by praying for some cooperation from the Alliance. They own at least half the submarines on Victoria."

"That might be praying for a miracle," Bogdanov said. "But I will do my best."

"Your best is usually very good indeed," Kuwahara replied. "In fact, it's been good enough to have you selected for promotion. Congratulations, Captain Bogdanov."

Liddell didn't hear all of Bogdanov's graceful reply. She was torn between indignation at Kuwahara's not telling her and distaste—to put it mildly—at the thought of losing her invaluable executive officer.

"I'll add my congratulations to the admiral's," she said finally. "It's nice to know that the Promotion Board occasionally gets something right. Is there anything else?"

"No, except for permission to scan and sort all the data on Victorian submarines. That may narrow the range of our search a little."

"Go ahead," Liddell said. As Bogdanov cut off, she noticed that the exercise was over. No, not quite over. With their seniors' eyes off them, the CC people had turned the scenario into a wargame, with a couple of ringers thrown in, Baernoi Death Commandos on the "enemy" side and the crack 101 Light Brigade coming to the rescue of Second/215.

Liddell watched the exercise slog forward to a predictably bloody but decisive Federation victory. *I hope I never have to really watch a fight between two units equally determined to lose their lives rather than their reputation.* The thought took away some of her pleasure at Bogdanov's promotion.

Liddell rose, waited for the CC people's attention, then grinned. "Well done, if not quite what I'd planned. I apologize for woolgathering, but something came up in connection with our pet crisis. We have a line of inquiry, which is more than we had ten minutes ago. That's not only all I can say, it's all I know."

She turned to Kuwahara. "Admiral, if I might offer you the hospitality of my quarters?"

As Kuwahara unstrapped, the intercom announced the launch of the shuttle carrying *Shenandoah*'s investigation team down to the crash site.

Paul Leray wished the screen circuit was private. Even more, he wished Joanna Marder was not on a shuttle two hundred kilometers from *Audacious* and ready to break out of orbit.

Anyone else looking at her would have said she was grinning from ear to ear at the thought of seeing action. Leray knew the set of that wide mouth and mobile lips too well. She was bottling rage and humiliation, to keep herself from exploding like uncontained antimatter.

"Wait until we hear how long this ground duty will be," she said. "If this fuss blows over in a day or two, Pak will gladly loan me a short-term kit. I don't want to come back to *Audacious* and learn that my gear's on the way to the prefect's office in Barnard's Crossing."

"No problem, Jo."

"Oh, and if you do need to pack up and ship off, ask Leading Hand Cantacazune. He can help prioritize if there's a limit."

Meaning he knows where your liquor is, and how to smuggle it down. Leray considered arranging for something non-fatal but awkward to happen to Leading Hand Cantacazune.

"Paul?"

"Sorry, I was making a mental list. And no, I won't tell you of what. Not over an open circuit. God keep you, Jo."

"You too, Paul, *and* our ship. I've got almost as good a territorial claim to *Audi* as you do!"

"I won't forget."

As the screen blanked, Leray's hyperalert ears detected footsteps outside the door. He punched it open, to face a startled Admiral Uzel. The admiral took a step backward and glared.

"I haven't added spying to running errands for the admiral," Uzel snapped. "If you will close the door, sit down, and stop making me want to draw the sidearm I'm not carrying—"

"Aye'aye, sir."

Uzel remained standing for a moment after Leray sank into the chair in front of the screen and swiveled it to face the other man. Then he unfolded the emergency seat by the door and sat down.

"I think you'd better tell me what's bothering you about Commander Marder's detachment," Uzel said. "It's more than losing your exec temporarily. Or have you exaggerated how well trained *Audacious* is?"

The possibility of lying to Uzel passed through Leray's mind and departed quickly. Uzel had served with Lopatina for a good third of his naval career. He was the man she called on when she wanted a knotty problem untied unofficially. Lying to Uzel would be an invitation to official action.

Apart from what that might mean for him and Jo, it would weaken the Alliance squadron at the worst possible moment. Until the redeployed ships were recalled or replaced, the Bonsai Squadron was a third of Alliance strength, and the one most familiar with Victoria.

Which meant that the Baba probably wouldn't do anything official now. But she would remember that Leray and Marder had *deserved* official action, and the Baba's long memory was a Navy legend.

"*Audacious* can do without Commander Marder for as long as she's needed on the ground," Leray said. "The navigator and I can divide the exec duties. My administrative load as commodore of the Low Squadron is minimal, for now."

"Good. If that changes, and we can't get your exec back, I'll send over a couple of lively specimens from my people. In fact, I think I'll do that anyway."

"Thank you, Admiral, but . . ."

"Is keeping Commander Marder busy that important?"

It was too late to go back on his decision to tell the truth. Leray nodded.

"I thought so. It didn't escape the Baba, that you refused to give Marder *Audacious* when you became commodore. You don't seem to be as blind to her problem as some people think. However, you still need to convince those people."

"Any suggestions?"

"Seeing if she could function in a highly demanding position without you. That's one reason for her detachment. Another reason is that she's the best for the job. We needed a senior naval officer from the Bonsai Squadron dirtside *fast*, and it was a choice between you, her, and Commander Lithgow. You're needed as commodore and Lithgow doesn't have a first-class exec."

Uzel fumbled in his shoulder bag. "May I smoke?"

"Go ahead," Leray said, turning up the ventilation and activating the filters.

Uzel made an elaborate business of lighting up a thick aromatic, then puffed in silence until it was noticeably shorter. When he spoke again, he was avuncular, almost paternal, although he couldn't be more than a couple of years older than Leray.

"Paul, has it occurred to you how good you are? I'm here because the Baba thought we needed you aboard *Audacious* more than me aboard *Fei-huang*. Also because some of what you needed to hear was private, but a message disk could have done that as well.

"If you weren't spaceborn, I'd tell you to bet anything you own on ending with two stars. As it is, if we pull this one out of the fire, and I'll tell you to at least not bet against them.

"You're damned good, but you may have a serious weakness. Can we trust you to take care of that weakness before we have to take care of her for you?"

Leray set his face into his most diplomatic mask, hardened his voice, and said, "If Commander Marder is that kind of weakness, certainly it's my duty to deal with it. But I think the question is still open. Otherwise, you would hardly have assigned her to her new post."

"Point to you," Uzel said, looking around for the waste slot. Leray pointed it out, watched the half-smoked aromatic vanish, and held out his hand.

A little hypocrisy goes a long way. And maybe I just thought I heard blackmail—dump Jo if you want stars.

Leray also knew that her new assignment would keep her on duty nineteen hours out of the twenty-six. Not to mention under Pak's eye, or the eye of someone close enough to the colonel to be effective and discreet.

Effective, discreet, and without Leray's personal involvement warping their judgment. Leray turned back to the screen and punched it up.

Has it reached the point where my involvement is hurting Jo rather than helping her?

"Another sherry?" Captain Liddell asked.

Kuwahara was contemplating his empty glass when the intercom signaled.

"The exec's compliments," said the first lieutenant, Commander Charbon. "He has a prioritized list of Victorian submarines ready for transmission."

"Prepare to receive file," Liddell told her computer, then picked up the sherry decanter. Kuwahara shook his head.

"Your sherry is as fine as ever, but I just realized that I hadn't had lunch."

"Jensen can do something about that."

The "something" turned out to be chicken salad, a selection of hot breads, and a half bottle of wine. As she munched, Liddell studied a printout of the submarine file.

Nothing obviously suspicious, but Bogdanov's done his usual good job. Hate to lose him.

"What are you planning to do with Com—Captain Bogdanov, if you don't mind my asking?"

"I didn't put him in for a special promotion, if that's what

68

you mean," Kuwahara replied. "I knew he was being considered for deep selection and would probably make it. I just asked that if he did make it, that I be told Priority Red and Command Secret. We need another good four-striper off Victoria."

"But not necessarily aboard *Shenandoah*?"

"Spines down, Captain."

That was Schatz's phrase, and hearing it from Kuwahara didn't soothe Liddell.

"Doctrine doesn't prohibit two four-stripers aboard a battlecruiser," she said, more politely than she felt. "It's too bad this isn't a carrier. Then you'd have three four-stripers to play with—"

"And if this was a carrier, she would probably be *Valhalla*, and you would be Captain Prange, which is a thought calculated to ruin my digestion of a very excellent lunch," Kuwahara interrupted.

In the face of Kuwahara's smile, Liddell's indignation faded. "All right, Admiral. What were you planning on doing with Pavel?"

"Two suggestions. One is to make him commodore of the Up the Sleeve Squadron, when we call them back on Victoria station."

"Two of the captains are senior to Pavel."

"Yes, but they're both ex-attacker types. With Bogdanov's reputation, they won't quibble about seniority. Particularly if the squadron gets the down-and-dirty work."

Liddell contemplated the idea. The Up the Sleeve Squadron was officially the Eighth Light Cruiser squadron. It was part of the half of the Victoria Squadron officially redeployed, in accordance with standing orders, when the Alliance reduced their strength.

However, Admiral Schatz's orders for that redeployment left out one key phrase—"out of the Victoria System." Instead they read "off Victoria Station."

This small difference in phrasing made a practical difference measurable in light-years. Under their senior captain, the four light cruisers were now drifting in the Victoria System's Oort Cloud. It wasn't much of an Oort Cloud, but enough to hide them from anybody who wasn't actually looking for them.

Well supplied, undoubtedly well bored by now, they were still reinforcements for the Victoria Squadron, eight days away instead of twenty-one to twenty-four. If this little flare-up of the Victoria crisis brought Alliance reinforcements hot-jumping back . . .

"And the other job?" Liddell asked.

Before Kuwahara could reply, the intercom called again. It was Bogdanov.

"Our crash crew and the Scout Company security force are on station, but the diplomatic formalities aren't completed. They've been asked to orbit."

"How long?" Kuwahara and Liddell asked together.

"At least two hours. This means the Republican forces will reach the crash site first. We have radio intercepts and orbital sensor readings that put their point flight within half an hour of the site."

'Very well," Kuwahara said. "I want a continuous all-sensors surveillance of the crash site. Deploy satellites, drones, manned craft, and anything the Army can spare."

He stood and flexed tension out of his shoulders. "Most of the Republican military are ex-Federation. Between that and the crash damage, I don't think they'll learn anything compromising from the wreckage. I also trust them to do a thorough job searching for other survivors.

"I still want hard data on everything they do so we look alert and they look honest. There's going to be too much suspicion running around as it is. The people who want to make a war out of this incident will feed on it."

"Aye-aye, sir," Bogdanov said.

Kuwahara sat down again and silently held out his glass. As silently, Liddell refilled it.

When she'd joined the Navy, she'd been appalled at the number of times senior commanders seemed to eat, drink, and make merry on the eve of battle. She'd had Sam Briggs's words drummed into her, but only now that she commanded a capital ship did she really understand them.

"The best thing to do when you see a crisis coming," Briggs had said, "is catch up on your sleep, meals, bathing, and anything else you need to catch up on. That way you'll be ready to go without, when the crisis actually arrives."

"Anything else" now didn't include another sherry, but it did include the matter of Pavel Bogdanov.

"So Pavel might go to the Up the Sleeves? Where else?"

"Would you consider his taking over *Shenandoah* and you becoming my chief of staff with the rank of acting commodore?"

Liddell was glad she hadn't taken another drink, because she would have dropped it. It was more solid praise than almost any medal. Not to mention a more practical solution than the alternative.

Pavel could certainly do the job. He could also handle Charbon, who would certainly be the new acting exec. Fujita had too little line experience and Zhubova was indispensable at Weapons.

"I admit I haven't given up all hope of being allowed a few extra people for key staff positions," Kuwahara said. "But when one considers how heavily the Army was reinforced for dropping the ball, and how little we've been given for scoring the first goal . . ."

He shrugged. "A compromise. If I leave you as C.O. of *Shenandoah*, will you find yourself a secretary? That might ease the load just enough so that you can handle both jobs."

"Secretary coming up," Liddell said, "on one condition. I won't have Lieutenant Mahoney."

"He's the best qualified, and he's worked with you before."

"He's also well qualified for other jobs, including J.O.O.W. If we keep taking him off line assignments for odd jobs and staff posts, he's going to start doubting himself again."

"Do we have time for therapy on even the most promising lieutenants?"

"I do, when it's not a life-or-death situation."

Eyes met over the nearly empty sherry decanter. Liddell knew that the difference between her and Kuwahara had just come nakedly into the open.

Both of us can see people, ships, and ourselves as expendable when it's life-or-death. He can do so at other times as well. I can't.

Kuwahara was the first to lower his eyes. He shrugged again. "I won't make Mahoney a direct order. I won't even make a secretary an order.

"I will request staff reinforcements again. I will also request you to start thinking about how we can come up with a staff out of our own resources. And I will pray that I get more cooperation from you than I expect from Eleventh Fleet!"

"I'll drink to that," Liddell said.

The decanter held just enough to cover the bottoms of their glasses.

Seven

"Scran Gold, this is Scran Green. We have a visual on the crash site. Permission to deploy and land?"

"Scran Gold here. Permission granted."

"Acknowledging. Should we light up?"

Captain Bergeron's look was one Lucco DiVries knew well—an officer with a subordinate who's just asked a silly question.

"Scran Green, of course you light up for landing and searching the wreckage. We don't want any more crashes or to miss any bodies. But put your security perimeter outside the lights and give them all the sensor gear you have."

"That's not much, Scran Gold, but we'll do our damnedest."

"That's all anybody can do. Safe landing and good luck."

The relief on Bergeron's face was clear, even in the dimly lit cockpit of the command lifter. DiVries looked past Bergeron, trying to catch a glimpse of the platoon deploying for the crash site.

"As soon as we've set up security for the survivors, I'll have you lifted over to the crash site," Bergeron said. "The QR platoon's reported some unidentified radio signals, but no sign of hostile action."

"Thanks, but I'd rather see *Sa'id*'s people first."

"We need a witness at the crash site—"

"You also need one with the survivors. Not that I don't trust McGuire or your medics, but a Mark I Eyeball inspection—"

Bergeron glared. DiVries had the feeling that only the need to keep her dignity was damping down her temper. What did she suspect? A reconciliation with Elayne? Ridiculous. Mixed loyalties? Not so ridiculous, but not the key factor here.

"Look, the whole idea of my being here is to settle much of this unofficially."

72

"Two of your people are dead. Two more and two Alliance people are hurt. That may take a lot of settling."

"It will. But I've been in bars where that was a normal casualty list for a weekend's brawls. I don't think anybody's going to be hitting the panic button. What they'll be doing is asking a lot of questions. The more answers we can get unofficially, the better for everybody."

"You think Zheng and the navigator will talk to you more willingly than to me?"

That hadn't been the direction DiVries intended the talk to go, but since it had gone there—

"It's worth a shot, isn't it?"

"Anybody could begin to wonder what side you're on, Lucco."

"You're not anybody, Sophie—Captain."

"No, but neither are your Intelligence people. Entrapment is a court-martial offense, and when you do it for people who are technically rebels against the Federation—"

The deck tilted and the note of the fans changed. DiVries saw a snow-plumed ridge slide underneath and beyond it a valley slope with a ring of silvery yellow lights twinkling halfway down it. He checked his straps, then grinned at Bergeron.

"Let's do it my way, and don't forget Lainie's temper. She may not tell me anything. In fact, by the time she's through with me, there may not be enough left to court-martial!"

Outside the McGuires' lifter, the wind was strong enough to dimple the shield of Elayne Zheng's stretcher. The Bushranger bearers had their eyes screwed tight against the blast, and slid and stumbled on the rough ground. Zheng still didn't like being helpless in Bushranger hands, but knew that she'd have been a damned fool to try walking.

The open door of a field shelter glowed invitingly. The stretcher bearers lurched through and set the stretcher down at the feet of a woman in civilian clothes with a medic's armband.

She bent over, folded the shield back, and started pulling off Zheng's clothes. This went fast; Zheng wore Kathy McGuire's spare bush suit, at least three sizes too large all around.

"That didn't hurt as much as I'd expected it would," the medic said. She pulled a scratched and dented bioscanner out of an even more battered carryall and applied it to Zheng's shoulder.

73

"Kathy popped it back in."

"She knew what she was doing. Now let's have a look at the leg."

The alloy-tube splint had to be removed for the scan, and that did hurt. The medic had just bent over the scanner when the door opened again. Cold air stormed in, followed by the stretcher bearers with the navigator, and another man.

"Lucco!"

"Hold still, or—"

Zheng couldn't have held still to save her leg, maybe even her life. For the first time in more years than she could remember, she wanted to cover herself in front of a man. The fact that the man was a former lover made the impulse even more outrageous.

Embarrassment turned to anger, anger to rage, and rage back into something she could at least put words to.

"Lucco, what the Hades are you doing here?"

"Lieutenant Zheng—" the medic began.

Zheng ignored both leg and shoulder to swivel on her buttocks and kick the scanner out of the medic's hands. It *whamped* against the far wall. The two stretcher bearers nearly dropped the navigator in their haste to get clear before the medic ordered them to restrain Zheng.

"Medic—" DiVries began.

"Sergeant Pike, you damned Feddie—"

"Let's not argue theology, and I'm not quite a Feddie. I'm a prisoner-at-large, who helped negotiate the safe passage of Sophie Bergeron's troops out of Port Harriet during the—war of independence."

"You're Lucco DiVries?" Pike now sounded ready to be at least polite.

"I don't have a clone that I know of. What I do have is some things to say to Lieutenant Zheng. You have another patient to help. What about our not trying to do each other's jobs?"

"All right. But—Lieutenant Zheng, if you broke my scanner . . ." She couldn't stalk away indignantly in a room three meters wide, but her back was stiff as she turned it on the two officers.

"Lainie, these people don't have a lot of equipment. If you broke the scanner—"

"If you come down on me again, I'll break a lot more than the scanner. I—what's so bloody funny?"

DiVries's smile turned into a chuckle. "I wish Sophie could see us now. I think she was worried you might try to talk me back into Fed service."

"Sophie?"

"Captain Bergeron."

"You've been—no, sorry. It's been a rotten day and I'm not sure you're going to make it any better."

Zheng lay back on the stretcher. She didn't have any claims on Lucco even if he was bouncing Bergeron, and he'd never seemed like the sort of man to let that influence his loyalty.

"Lainie, if you're not up to talking, fine. Just listen to me for a minute and I'll leave you in peace."

It took him more than a minute to explain why he was with Bergeron's company and why he was here in the medshelter instead of at the crash site. By the time he'd finished, Zheng's arm and leg were hurting worse than ever.

Medic's busy with the navigator, though, and he's worse off than I am. Besides, I need a clear head for talking with Lucco.

"Sounds like you've decided to stay north."

"I haven't."

"How much more time do you have?"

"Lainie, I can read a calendar. Four more days."

"Why the Hades—"

"Have I waited so long? Lainie, there's been a hell of a lot I could do by staying north that helped the Bushrangers and didn't hurt the Federation. Like tonight—coming with Sophie's people to help them stay on their good behavior. They don't know if I'm going back south to describe every time one of them picked her nose or didn't shine his shoes!"

"Well, damn it, you ought to know. Or you aren't the man I thought you were."

DiVries looked half-puzzled, half-amused. "Are you really saying that I owe you a decision?"

"Sounds that way, doesn't it?"

"You've got a pretty high opinion of your bouncing skills, you know that."

Zheng grinned. "I'm not the only one. But—Lucco, make your decision, and I'll brief you on the shootdown. Go on phoomphering around, and I'll be quiet as a dead sand-scrabbler."

"Too bad we can't switch positions. You'd make a better spy than I would."

"Maybe, maybe not. I lie a lot. You don't lie to anybody but yourself, and not much then."

She pulled the blankets back over herself with her good hand and turned on one side. "Well?"

"One condition. I can make the decision either way."

"Either—" It wasn't pain that cut her off, but a suddenly dry throat.

Definitely a better spy than me. I walked right into that one. Can I get out of it?

If she briefed him after he said he was staying with the Bushrangers, she'd be morally and maybe legally abetting a change of allegiance. Not something to have witnesses to, at the very least.

But if she backed down, she'd be leaving just about the only attacker type the Bushrangers had in the dark. Just about the most useful man they'd have for getting to the bottom of the shootdown.

Some jobs are important enough that you don't worry about loyalties when somebody volunteers to do them. Sounds like Sophie Bergeron knows that. Do I want Lucco's last memory of me to be that I was dumber than Bergeron?

"Okay, Lucco."

"Green Three undocking—mark!" hit Candice Shores's eardrums. She winced but kept her eyes on the screen. A shadowy shape dropped away from attacker *Louis Ferraro*. It fell free long enough to make Shores frown, then slowed and stabilized as lift-field and gravity balanced each other. A moment later it began climbing up to the altitude of the rest of the Scout team.

"Diadem Force Leader to Shield Leader, we have formation," Shores said. "Setting course 325, speed 180, altitude two thousand meters."

"Everything nominal that we can see," came the voice of the senior scout pilot. "They've got both the camp and the crash sites lit up like an airgypsy outing. Recommend you stay high, though. We got a couple of unidentified EIs from the area, didn't sound like anybody we had on file. The Bushrangers may be the only ones out here tonight, but don't bet on it."

"Gambling's for attacker types," Shores said. "Don't worry." She switched from the air-ground to the all-hands circuit.

"Diadem Force, we're going in as planned. Second Platoon proceeds to the crash site and cooperates with the Republican force there. The rest head for the main camp. Hover for five minutes. If we don't have any instructions from the Republican C.O. by then, we'll ground in standard defensive formation on a beacon.

"No radio silence, but blackdown until we're challenged. Then light up *everything*. There may be some unfriendlies out here, but they won't be nearly as dangerous as another mistake."

The chorus of "Rogers" was varied with a couple of "Amens," and followed by an unfamiliar voice.

"Diadem Force, this is Scran Gold, the Republican C.O. We have you on our radar. Can you light up now? Also, you can land in any appropriate formation at least a hundred meters west of our perimeter. We don't want to be hitting each other if somebody infiltrates."

"Sounds okay to me—ah—"

"Captain Sophia Bergeron, Company B. First Battalion. Is this Captain Candice Shores?"

"Yes, but—"

"Are you the senior Federation officer present? And are you still an authorized Armistice Commission Observer?"

Shores glared at the radio. "What the hell business is it of yours, Captain Bergeron?"

"It wouldn't be, except that we have a change of allegiance to process. I thought that if you were qualified to act as the Federation observer—"

"Lucco DiVries!"

The words were out before Shores could stop them. The impulse made her angry; the sound of Captain Bergeron trying not to laugh made her angrier still.

After a couple of deep breaths, she could speak.

"Diadem Force, light up."

Outside the stars faded and the black rocky slopes striped with snow took shape below as twelve assault lifters turned on all their lights.

"Formation Eight-Six," Shores added. The patterns of lights swayed, swung, and began to disperse. It would take longer to land the formation, but they'd be a harder target on the way in.

"It is Lieutenant DiVries, isn't it?" she added.

"I'm afraid so," Bergeron replied. She still sounded unreasonably cheerful.

Shores thought of asking for a talk with DiVries, but

decided that the situation was already embarrassing enough. Besides, Lucco wasn't the kind to change allegiance on a whim—or change back on anything Candice Nikolayevna Shores could say to him.

"Get your people ready, then," she said. "Diadem Leader out."

Captain Bergeron slipped her arm through Lucco DiVries's as they watched Captain Shores and her party climb the hill toward them. Bergeron told herself that she wanted human contact only against the cold wind, not against the tall officer with the grim face striding toward her.

Bergeron had known many leaders described as having "command presence" who didn't live up to the description in person. Candice Shores was not one of them. Her height, her wide dark eyes, her stride like a big predator's—she gave the impression that if she ordered the rocks in her path to move aside, they would obey.

She stopped in front of the Republican party and motioned her companions forward. One was a sergeant with a grenade launcher, the other a corporal with a camcorder rig on his helmet.

"Captain Shores, Sergeant Esteva, Corporal Sklarinsky," she said. "Sklarinsky, start recording."

Bergeron had been through allegiance-changing ceremonies a dozen times in the last four months, beginning with her own. She had the phrases memorized, and if it had been anybody but DiVries, she'd have gone along with Shores's obvious desire to get the business over with as fast as possible.

They went through identity, rank and branch of service, intention, reasons (where DiVries exercised his right to remain silent), renunciation of claims on the Federation government—

"Do you renounce any right to bring legal action against citizens of the United Federation of Starworlds, for refusing to permit transfer or inheritance of private property currently held in the territory of the Federation."

"I do not."

"DiVries—" Shore began in a voice that cut like the wind.

"It's irrelevant. There isn't any such property. Besides, I think that provision could be challenged."

"DiVries, do you want to be a bedroll lawyer or a Bushranger?"

"Citizen of the Bushranger Republic, if you please," Bergeron said.

Shores wasn't pleased, but she let it pass. Her anger seemed entirely for DiVries. "Make up your mind. If you want to risk an invalid change of allegiance, it's your tail in the crack if we catch you."

"All right, all right. My response to Clause Fourteen is yes, I do renounce any and all such rights."

The ceremony rolled on, to where DiVries swore "not to serve in the armed forces of the Bushranger Republic for five Standard Years from the date of this oath."

"Which means that I want you in civvies and preferably out of here before *we* lift out," Shores added.

Bergeron decided that ignoring Shores's temper had gone on long enough.

"Captain Shores, that sounds like a threat. If you or anyone under your command attempts to remove Mr. DiVries from Republican territory, you are likely to start the war I thought we were all trying to prevent."

"She's right, Candy," DiVries said. "Besides, I won't go. Elayne Zheng kept her promises. How about you being an officer and a lady and doing the same?"

For a moment Shores looked ready to pull out large handfuls of somebody's hair—her own, if that was the only hair she could reach. Then she jerked her head.

"I'll withdraw that request. Only be careful—I don't think we're alone out here. I can vouch for my own people, but—"

"What makes you think that?" DiVries asked. "Have you been picking up some odd radio signals, too?"

"What do you mean, 'too'?" Now Shores reminded Bergeron of a predator who's scented prey.

"Elayne's navigator overheard some, and we heard one signal on the way in. We couldn't record or get a position, though."

Shores grinned. "No, you couldn't. But *Ferraro* has a recording of what might be the same signals. What about I have them tight-beam it down to us, and you and the navigator can listen?"

"Captain Bergeron and I will be glad to listen," DeVries said. "As for navigator—if you wake him up, Elayne will knock you down and Sergeant Pike will jump on you."

"Okay," Shores said. She looked at Sklarinsky. "You've been recording all this?"

"Sorry, Captain."

"Oh well, in for a shilling, in for a stellar." Shores stood to attention. "By the authority vested in me as senior officer present of the Federation Armed Forces and as an Observer of the Victoria Armistice, I declare that former First Lieutenant Lucco M. DiVries, Federation Navy, has freely, completely, and irrevocably renounced all allegiance to the United Federation of Starworlds.

"Okay, Sklarinksy. Cut, and let's get back and call up *Ferraro*." Before her NCOs had turned around she was on her way back downhill.

The boulders, Bergeron saw, didn't make a path for her. They didn't need to. She seemed to dance around them or leap over them as if her feet had their own sensor array.

She turned as she felt DiVries's arm around her waist. "I wish it hadn't been Candy," he said. "She's pretty high up on my list of people I don't like to disappoint.

"But I guess my brother and Reesa and their kids—yeah, and maybe you, by now—they're higher. Oh well, I'm not the first soldier in this bind and I won't be the last. Crying over it just risks dehydration."

"Being around here doing military duty risks more," Bergeron reminded him. "Or will Shores turn a blind eye?"

"She might, but I don't know about all her people. I'm damned sure Intelligence has planted a few people with the Scouts, too."

"Hmmm. Do you have any medic training?"

"Just first-aid."

"That should be enough. Sergeant Pike now has a civilian assistant. From what I've read, that five-year rule is usually enforced only for the combat arms anyway."

"Know any rituals for averting bad luck?"

"No, but I know one for averting freezing to death. A cup of hot tea. Several cups, in fact."

"Lead on, Captain."

Eight

Hermann Rourke, acting C.O. of Camp Chapman, stepped inside the shelter and wrestled the door shut. The wind didn't clutch a sliding door the way it did a swinging one, but ice was forming in the tracks.

As the door *chunked* shut, the radio operator dashed around her partition, her face half-red, half-pale, in a blotchy pattern. She nearly collided with Rourke, and she did collide with a technician carrying a cup of tea.

Rourke mopped tea splotches off his sweater, nearly kicked the technician, and glared at the radio operator.

"Well?"

"Emergency signal from the missile battery. They're under attack!"

"Attack! What's happening?"

"Sir, all I know is what the message said. They've been hit by at least twelve rockets. They've lost two launchers. The rockets are Federation Mark 82, they think. Three outposts have reported small-arms fire, and one is off the air."

Before Rourke could close his mouth to reply, somebody on the other side of the partition muttered an obscenity.

"What is it?"

"The whole bloody missile battery just went off the air. Somebody screaming about another incoming salvo, then silence. Maybe the static's jamming, but it sure as hell isn't our people."

Rourke nearly knocked the partition down in grabbing the radio.

"All hands alert! Repeat, all hands alert! Our comrades in Battery 12 are under attack by Federation forces. We can expect to be next. All personnel draw full ammunition, protection, and medkits, then report to your defensive positions. Repeat, all hands arm and take defensive positions. Good luck. That is all."

Rourke looked around to see how the rest of the sensor operators were reacting to his display of alertness. None of them seemed to be reacting to anything except their screens or displays.

Alarms shrieked. "Incoming!" several operators shouted at once.

Rourke didn't wait to find out what was incoming. He knew that if he stayed inside, he might try to crawl under a console. Better get outside and see what was coming, even if it might be his last sight.

He half stumbled, half fell through the door, two of the technicians following him. As the camp's troops boiled out of their shelters and scurried past, Rourke looked northeast.

A raw, flaring yellow light seemed to cover half the horizon. His first thought was that the missile battery's ammunition was exploding. His second thought was that the battery was fifty kilometers away.

The high-pitched shriek of incoming rockets slammed him back against the shelter wall, as if the sound was a physical blow. He was already falling through the door when the first rocket hit.

He saw sparks blaze where it hit and knew that it was a hypervelocity slughead. Then three rockets with explosive warheads instead of slugs ambled in overhead and tore the roof off the shelter.

The blast sent Rourke flying feet-first out the door, but all the fragments missed him except one that skewered his left thigh. The two technicians weren't so lucky, and neither were several soldiers passing by.

Rourke wasn't sure if it was his people screaming or more rockets. Just before he lost consciousness, he decided it was both.

Lucco DiVries not only should have been somewhere else, he badly *wanted* to be somewhere else, like back in the dining hall of the refugee camp at Gar Lake, telling his niece and nephew about his adventures in the Great Fourth Company Mutiny—

No, what he really wanted was to be in bed with Sophie Bergeron. Maybe he hadn't really crossed the border into desiring her. Maybe it was just the old urge to grab a last bit of life before you died, which seemed a distinct, even imminent possibility.

Meanwhile, Bergeron and Shores were glaring at each

other in a way that made DiVries want to either step between them or step well clear.

"I'm not saying that it's impossible the Federation has retaliated—"

"Considering that you've sent in Rangers, I'd say it's damned near certain," Bergeron snapped.

"The Rangers are a *rumor*, blast it!" Shores almost screamed. "Rumors don't rocket-spray military installations!"

"Do we have anything besides your word on that?"

"I suppose that's not good enough?"

"What do you think, if you're capable of—"

"Captain Bergeron, I don't think insults will get us anywhere," DiVries said.

The interruption turned both women's glares to DiVries, but that might at least delay their drawing sidearms on each other.

"We need to send somebody to at least one attack site to be sure it's really Federation work," Shores said. "Anybody can pick up a load of Mark 82s. I'd bet Alliance Intelligence could outfit a whole firing battery of them!"

"That's right, blame the Alliance for your own—"

"Federation troops are going to one of the attack sites," Shores said. "They are going with or without your permission. They will—"

"They'll be shot out of the sky if they come in without authorization," Bergeron shouted.

"With what?" Shores said. She almost controlled a sneer. "Do I have to remind you that firing on a Federation unit will be an act of war? If that happens, our attacker support won't need authorization to enter Bushranger airspace. Don't bet on who shoots whom out of the sky then."

DiVries poised himself to grab either woman if they started to draw. What he would do if they both drew simultaneously, other than step in front of the one he'd grabbed, was a problem he'd worry about when it came up.

Several daylong seconds passed. Then Bergeron crossed her arms on her chest. "All right. But tell me—what happens if you're interfering with a genuine retaliatory raid?"

"Then I suppose they'll hang me by my toes from the flagpole on the Fort Stafford parade ground as a warning to other Scouts to mind their own business. I'd rather risk that than what might happen if I don't investigate."

"Just so you know—"

"Assume I'm sapient, Captain Bergeron, and let's get moving. I'll take the reserve platoon—"

"Two squads."

"Three, and my two bodyguards. I don't want some hot-head tempted to shoot at us because we look weak. Besides, we may need extra hands for first-aid."

"It won't be just hotheads ready to shoot anybody in a Federation uniform. Can your people change clothes?"

"Into what? Cold-weather gear makes everybody look like an Inuit, and *they* aren't suspected, I hope!"

Bergeron managed a crack-lipped smile. "Not yet. Okay. Three squads and your CP, but hurry."

"That's what Scouts are for." Shores turned and shouted downhill, loud enough to make DiVries wince even over the whining wind.

"Esteva! Three squads from 4th Platoon. Load now, lift in five minutes. Sklarinsky! The CP rig and extra ammo!"

Faint shouts acknowledged. Shores turned and scrambled past the two Bushrangers, up to McGuire's lifter. She drew her sidearm and banged the butt on the cockpit door.

The door opened, framing McGuire's face and the muzzle of a snub carbine. DiVries's mouth gaped wider than the door, then Shores's arm shot up, The carbine barrel slammed against the top of the door with a loud *tannnkkkk*!

McGuire was neither small, elderly, nor out of condition. He still couldn't move his weapon. Maybe he didn't want to, DiVries realized. He was staring straight into Candice Shores's eyes from a distance of no more than forty centimeters. That could paralyze a Baernoi strike commando, let alone a Victorian bush farmer.

After a moment the grip relaxed and the muzzle vanished. The farmer's face remained, stubbled and sour.

"Bloody hell. Bad enough a working man's got to try to doss down in the middle of a bunch of soldiers. Then great galumphing Amazons come and bang on his ear. What do you want?"

"Sorry, Citizen, but none of us are going to be sleeping for a bit."

Shores described the situation. The man's face grew sourer, but his daughter joined him and neither drew a weapon.

"I may not be coming back," Shores concluded. "In case I don't, I've recommended you for a Civil Assistance Award or whatever equivalent the Republic lets you accept. But I wanted to say thank you, personally. You saved a friend of mine and you may have helped prevent a war."

"Well, all right, if you put it that way . . ." the farmer grumbled, then stuck his hand through the door. Shores gripped it, then turned and stalked downhill.

"Doesn't she ever walk like a normal human being?" Bergeron muttered to the wind.

"I think her stories about her father being a Bogatyr artist are crap. She's really the first human–Ptercha'a cross."

"I can believe it," Bergeron said. "But I'm really beginning to be glad she's around."

DiVries nodded. "We'll need somebody like her when we fly into the—"

"What do you mean 'we,' Lucco?"

"I mean that I'm coming. There are casualties. I'm a medical assistant. How much credibility will that position have if I don't come?"

"How many places will you go that you don't have to?"

"Ask me tomorrow, and meanwhile, just remember that I hate overprotective women." He slapped her on the shoulder, then headed across the snow-whipped slope toward the medical shelter.

It was beginning to look as if he'd made the right decision in changing allegiance. Whether the peacemakers were blessed or not, Victoria was certainly going to need a lot of them.

It wasn't certain that he could be a better one as a Bushranger citizen than as a Federation Navy officer. But this was a situation without certainties, and the only thing on his conscience was not realizing that weeks ago!

The combined troops flew to the radar station in two Federation lifters and three Republican ones. Both sides kept loose formation, free to maneuver and to fire—even on each other.

If it came to that, Shores knew her people would be the ones who flew away. The Bushrangers had one air-to-air-capable weapon among them, and two of their lifters had no armor.

Forty kilometers from Camp Chapman, Bergeron's command lifter blinked a warning, then slid out of its own formation to fly wing on Shores's. From the cockpit an elderly signal laser started blinking on tight beam.

"COMPANY A, THIRD BATTALION, HAS SECURED MISSILE BATTERY AND SURROUNDING AREA. COMPANY C.O. WARNS THAT ANY FEDERATION FORCES APPROACHING WITHIN FIVE KILOMETERS WILL BE CONSIDERED HOSTILE."

"What the hell's the bastard going to do about 'em?" Corporal Sklarinsky asked.

The blinking went on.

"THIS ORDER APPARENTLY ISSUED BY COMPANY C.O. ON OWN INITIATIVE. OFFICER IS STRONGLY ANTIFEDERATION. RECOMMEND COMMUNICATIONS BLACKDOWN TO PREVENT RECEIPT OF SIMILAR ORDER FROM HIGHER LEVELS BEFORE ARRIVAL AT RADAR SITE."

Shores laughed.

"Signal 'concur,' " she told the copilot.

The Bushrangers must have had a nervous moment when the copilot swung the turret to use the aiming laser for signaling. They must have also recovered quickly, because Bergeron's reply came almost at once.

"THANKS. ALSO RECOMMEND PROCEEDING AT LOW ALTITUDE THROUGH WILLARD PASS. I WILL TAKE POINT."

"MY TURN TO SAY THANKS," Shores replied.

The lifters bobbed and weaved into their new formation. Shores watched the Republicans with the eye of a professional soldier and an amateur pilot. They were slower than Feds would have been, but not sloppy, considering that they had less maneuvering power and less experience in formation flying.

With a little time and experience, they'll do well enough. I hope they get the time, because it looks like they're going to get the experience whether they need it or not.

In single file now, the lifters slowed to one hundred kph and slipped into the Willard Pass. Shores had the feeling that she'd been here before, maybe on a training exercise. Even the patterns of shadow on the slopes looked familiar. Snow plumes whipped from hummocks almost close enough to touch. And was that smoke from the chimney of a crumbling shelter? No, just more snow. Still, so much about this night flight seemed familiar.

Shores grimaced as she realized why she had the sense of being here before. On a night like this, in terrain like this, Sam Briggs had executed one of his most famous tactical maneuvers, taking five brigades through the Black Ram Pass on Rurik to break the independence forces past recovery. She must have seen all the films and most of the dramatizations before she made first lieutenant.

But Sam Briggs had been dead for centuries, she had five

lifters instead of five brigades, and at the end of the pass lay a mystery caused by human stupidity instead of an honorable opponent to defeat in a desperate, history-making battle.

Stupidity isn't an honorable opponent, Candice. It's much more common, and much more dangerous.

Shores was used to hearing her conscience address her in her mother's best diagnostic tone. This was the first time in many years that the voice had warmth in it as well as good sense.

"Mother?"

Nobody answered. Nobody heard, either, except the copilot, and she kept her eyes fixed on the displays. Shores adjusted a strap that was gouging her left breast and listened to low-voiced conversation behind her.

"How much longer, Sarge?"

"Ask the Old Lady, if you want to walk home," Esteva replied.

"Isn't there something in the rules about keeping the troops informed?"

"Could be, could be. I'd have to check."

"But—"

"Why don't you seal it?" the squad leader said. "Besides, I heard that a little adrenaline stimulation is good for you."

"This isn't a *little* stimulation, Corp. It's—"

"It's time you sealed it, like the lady said," Esteva put in. His tone was the one he used when the next step would be a discreet appointment with the offender for some unofficial but effective discipline.

It worked. The lifter was silent as it droned down the pass, except for the whine of the fans and an occasional crackle of static in Shores's headphones.

The orbit-bound shuttle went supersonic just above the hilltops. The boom rattled everything in Colonel Schapiro's office, including the boots Joanna Marder was pulling on.

"Have to watch that," Schapiro said, switching the shutters closed. "This area's more seismic than you skyjockeys seem to realize. Every spring we get quakes up in the Roskills, when the glaciers shrink and shift.

"And speaking of ice . . ." He gestured at Marder's glass.

She pulled on the other boot and shook her head. Maybe it wasn't a test and certainly she couldn't afford to get paranoid with the C.O. of the battalion she'd be working with. She still wasn't going to take chances.

"All right, Commander," Schapiro said. "You were wished on me on even less notice than you had. I've fired off a polite request to Pak for an explanation. Can you maybe save me a little time in getting one?"

"Is that an order?"

"It's a request, but maybe not a polite one. Commander, I'm senior, I'm on my own ground, and I'm mad. Enough explanation?"

Marder fought a sudden urge for another drink. So what if she failed Schapiro's test? Was his opinion worth a counterfeit credit slug?

"You may not be as mad by the time you get through listening," Marder said. She sucked the last ice cube out of her glass and rolled it around on her tongue while she organized her thoughts.

"I'm down here because Bonsai Command and the Baba both want to set up a two-battalion task force here. The coastal end of the Bushranger Republic is looking like the main trouble spot. A task force that size will need its own naval liaison. I was tapped."

"Two battalions. Any idea what's the second, and when it's coming in?"

"No to both." *Although I hope by all that's holy Pak or someone senior to you comes with it.*

"Then what are you supposed to do now, other than insult my liquor?"

I think he is testing me. But for whom?

"I'm supposed to coordinate attacker support for *Eriksen Gamma* in case your air cover needs any—"

"It doesn't."

"I didn't say it did." The shuttle had overflown the coaster on the way to Barnard's Crossing. Schapiro's battalion had four lifters with full air-to-air loads continuously on station over it. They'd been so alert they nearly missiled the shuttle when it broke out of low clouds before they had a verbal confirmation of the IFF.

Let's hope the Fed patrols stay well inshore toward the Republic, or there might be another Fed attacker downed by mistake.

"I just noticed that the weather's getting up," she went on. "I don't think that storm's going to head quite so much to the northeast as we'd expected. In that kind of weather, attackers can stay on station better than Army lifters."

"You really know that much more about bad-weather flying?"

Marder decided there was a second argument against taking another drink in Schapiro's office. If she had a glass in her hand the next time he said something like that, she might throw it in his face. That would be "assaulting a senior officer" by law, even if it might be "abating a public nuisance" in fact.

"Not necessarily. But our extra power—"

"Isn't worth doodly if you're down in the surface gust pattern, with nothing but eyes and arse to guide you. Yeah, I've heard about what your sensors can do from up high, but I've never seen it and I don't want to risk anybody on it now."

For the first time, Marder noticed the command pilot's wings on Schapiro's faded battledress. *Maybe he should have stayed with tac air. Now he's my problem as well as Second Battalion's.*

"Do you have an ETA on *Gamma*?"

"0430 tomorrow. Weather permitting, of course. We'll scramble all the air and post the Narrows. . . ."

The boastful description of Second Battalion's plans went on for quite a while. Marder took mental notes and realized that if Schapiro had begun with the explanation, she might have ignored the insults. He and his battalion seemed to be reasonably ready for trouble, assuming it didn't come in wholesale lots stamped "Made in the Federation."

"Thank you," Marder said, when Schapiro started looking as if he expected to be praised. "It sounds as if we have more time to bring in attackers than I thought. I also begin to suspect they won't be needed."

"Glad to see we agree on something. Okay, Commander. I've got your card for billet and kit. Give HQ your room number for emergencies and get off your feet." He pushed the bottle across the desk toward Marder.

Her fingers cramped, resisting the urge to take it. But the test was so transparent, and even without the testing this was no place to seek that comforting glow. She had to be alert even when she slept, and not only alert but awake in—God, *five* hours?

Camp Chapman stayed off the air all the way down the pass, where Shores hadn't expected to hear anything anyway. She wasn't happy that the silence went on when the joint flight hit open air.

The two command lifters flew wing and blinkered a short exchange. Shores would rather have used telephone or face-to-face, but Bergeron's Fed-surplus command lifter had lost its line jacks and docking gear.

They went in treating the camp as a hot LZ. One lifter from each side dropped a squad at the mouth of the pass, then the Fed lifter took the high spot while the Republic's took the low. Bergeron would have been happier with it the other way around, but her lifter was the only Bushranger machine equipped for high watch.

The other three lifters went straight in and landed in a trefoil, rear hatches inside, bow guns and personal weapons covering a complete 360 degrees. They'd just landed when somebody finally came on the radio. It was a strained male voice, that a Bushranger identified as one of the camp medics.

"Hunh—took your"—something unintelligible but probably obscene—"time. Are those Feddies—"

"This is Captain Sophie Bergeron, B Company, First Battalion. We are here to provide security and medevac, in cooperation with Federal forces under Captain Candice Shores."

"*Kheblass* Feddies—" Pause for an unmistakable bout of vomiting. "Guess—guilty for what—they . . ."

By the time the medic came back on the air, each side had deployed two full squads. Shores's feet itched to be with them, but she sent Esteva instead and remained by the radio, with Sklarinsky and the medics.

"People who made it—out under cover, waiting for the Feddies to finish us off. Rest—in shelter. Blue one—blue one with a door."

Shores nearly popped the cockpit door off its tracks, hitting the ground. She was halfway to the shelter before Sklarinsky caught up with her.

"Captain, there's a fine line between leading from in front and sticking your ass out too far."

"What are you going to do if I cross it?"

"Nothing, except pull it back—if I can,"

The exchange let Bergeron catch up. "Captain Shores, I don't think those people in there want to see Federation uniforms right now."

"I keep telling you, we didn't do this!" Shores waved a

long arm over a scene that included half a dozen clearly visible corpses. Ugly ones, too. Blast could leave a soldier looking asleep, but fragments and hypervelocity slugs were more vicious.

"I'm beginning to believe you. But the people in there—they're hurting, they don't know what I do, and I didn't hear the medic say they'd all been disarmed. I'm going in first."

She was running toward the shelter door before Shores could move.

Hermann Rourke woke for what he knew must be the tenth time since the attack. Something was different, besides his hurting a little more. The painkiller that took hold as the shock wore off must be running down.

He'd expected that. He hadn't expected to hear someone knocking. *Knocking*, as if they were friendly. Maybe the Feds weren't following up with a ground assault?

Cold wind blew over Rourke as the door opened. He heard cries from some of the wounded, further inside. He recognized one cry. One of the technicians, with her wounds maybe already swollen with mites from dirt blown into them. Her eyes would be hypersensitive to light—

A silhouette in the doorway. More than a silhouette, a soldier in cold-weather battle gear. Rourke tried to focus on the soldier's face.

For a moment it came clear. Bergeron, and behind her—they looked too neat to be Republicans. They had to be Feddies the bloody traitor had brought in!

"Hello?"

Rourke rolled to his carbine, gasping with the pain, making someone else scream as he crushed a foot, wanting to vomit from his whirling head as he raised the carbine and groped for the trigger. . . .

Rourke's groping slowed him just enough for Sklarinsky to step in front of both Bergeron and Shores. It didn't keep him from putting four rounds through Sklarinsky's faceplate and the face behind it. Shores and Bergeron, already on the way to the ground, weren't hit by anything but pieces of Sklarinsky's head and helmet.

Shores landed with her own sidearm drawn. Knowledge that there'd be the devil to pay if she shot a wounded Bushranger reached her hand just in time. The other hand groped for something to throw, found it, balanced it, and threw.

Thrown left-handed and cross-bodied, the empty fire extinguisher still smashed into Rourke's jaw hard enough to knock him flat. His carbine rolled from limp fingers as the Republican medic staggered around the corner.

"You—Feddie bitch—"

"One of your wounded just blew away one of my people, you mite-brained turd!" Shores still had her sidearm drawn. Bergeron stepped between her and the medic.

Not trusting herself to speak, Shores waved the flight's three medics forward and stepped aside. Then she grabbed Bergeron's shoulder and spun her around.

"Call in the radar station security perimeter. Everybody on it, right now!"

"Captain Shores—"

"Now! Or I give the order myself and signal my high spotter to fire a warning shot. I don't want anybody from this radar station where I can't see them."

Bergeron tried to pluck Shores's hand off her shoulder. She might as well have tried to arm-wrestle a power-pile waldo. Shores's peripheral vision showed her Esteva drawing down on Bergeron, Lucco DiVries looking ready to try disarming everybody in sight, and the turrets in both command lifters pointing at each other.

Shores felt the tension go out of Bergeron's body and lifted her hand. The Republican captain gave a jerky nod; Shores hand-signaled Esteva to shift aim. By the time Bergeron reached her lifter, the two turrets were carefully pointing 180 degrees away from each other.

Esteva half led his C.O. back to the Fed command lifter. Shores slumped into the seat, trying to remember Sklarinsky's next of kin, holster her sidearm, and monitor her troops at the same time.

She'd just acknowledged a report of footprints when a sharp female voice came on the main ground-air frequency.

"Browser to Diadem. Scramble and report." Commander Gesell's voice promptly climbed two octaves and turned into gibberish.

Shores added setting the current scramble code to her list of jobs and found herself all thumbs. She was back on the air just as Gesell finished deploying what sounded like most of the rest of her squadron.

"Diadem Leader reporting," Shores said, and reported.

"You're way out on the edge of your orders about facilitating the investigation by cooperation with the Republicans," Gesell said.

Do you have airtime to tell me things I already know?

"I'm SOP for the time being," the commander went on. "I'll let you know when that changes. Meanwhile, you've done pretty damned well. Keep it up, and you can even transfer to the Navy when this is over."

"Thanks."

Shores cursed, less at Gesell than at the circumstances. The commander was good, she was willing to listen, she didn't like Bushrangers, and she was a Navy attacker jockey and not an Army groundpounder.

Gesell's four qualities just about balanced each other out. General Langston would have been a lot better. Where the Hades was he, if Gesell was SOP?

Shores came up with a couple of possible answers, then realized they were scaring her almost as much as Sklarinsky's firefight. When she tried to holster her sidearm, she realized that her hands were shaking.

Esteva brought her a cup of tea. She'd just finished drinking it when 2nd Platoon came on the circuit.

"The Bushrangers are refusing to let the crash investigation team from *Shenandoah* land. Repeat, the Bushrangers are—"

Static and screaming filled Shores's ears. Jamming or a glitch in the scrambling? "The Bushrangers are what?"

More interference, this time definitely jamming. A couple of phrases squeezed through: "Lieutenant Mahoney is trying—" and "possibly as hostages."

The signal went completely to noise.

"Captain, we don't have a lot of cups."

Shores realized she'd been pounding the teacup on her knee, handed it to Esteva, and stood up. She realized that to save her life she couldn't think of what to do next, but that an ancient phrase and a young NCO might just save her.

"Carry on, Sergeant Esteva."

Nine

Brian Mahoney was angry. Probably angrier than he should have been, since he was the senior Federation officer fit for duty in this "hostage" situation.

But if he hadn't been so angry, he'd have been shivering. Either the lifter that was the Bushrangers' combined CP and detention cell didn't have a heating system or it wasn't working. Being out of the wind was about the only difference between the CP and the bare mountainside.

Shivering wouldn't help. Those mite-brained Bushrangers would be sure to take it for fear, and try to tough the situation out.

Mahoney looked at Gordon Uhlig, lying on a pallet in the corner with Chief Petty Officer Lowenstein bending over him. Lieutenant Uhlig had been C.O. of the crash investigation party, until he resisted the Bushrangers and became the incident's only casualty. So far.

Lowenstein gave Mahoney the angled thumb that meant "Okay for now, as far as I can tell." It would be nice if they could borrow an Army medic, but the Scouts had left only one. The Scouts' X.O., Lieutenant Piccone, wasn't letting the medic anywhere the Bushrangers could grab him too.

"Okay," Mahoney said. He was looking at the Bushranger command group, but pitching his voice so everyone in the CP could hear him.

"You've stepped on it two ways. One is holding hostages. That's nonnegotiable, by Federation law. As soon as a hostage situation is officially declared, we're expendable.

"If we're expendable, there's nothing to stop the Scouts from cleaning out Republican forces here and at Camp Chapman. That will leave the whole coastal region of the Republic open to anything the Federation cares to do."

"Don't bet anything you can't—" began an NCO. A lieutenant (at least it looked like bars sewn on his sweater) stopped her.

"That's what you were setting up when you took out the radar and missile posts, wasn't it?" the lieutenant asked.

Mahoney ignored what must have been the twenty-fifth accusation against the Federation. These people had a jammed disk on that point, and maybe a brain lesion or two.

"If we were, why do you think I'm offering you a way to prevent it?"

"I haven't heard any offers yet. If I did, could I believe them?"

Mahoney wondered if the lieutenant knew as little about Federation doctrine on junior officers' initiative as he did about Federation law on hostage situations. Against hostility or honest error he could make a good fight. Against invincible stupidity he was in trouble, and the other six Navy people in the investigation party along with him.

"Wait until I make the offer, then use your judgment. There's another nonnegotiable Federation demand. Searching the wreckage for the flight-data recorder. We're reasonably satisfied it wasn't jettisoned, so we won't ask for a search permit. We aren't even sure it survived the crash, although it's designed to. But we can't go home without making the search."

He sat down without being invited. Sometimes standing gave psychological dominance. Right now it was more likely to make him look like a defendant before a panel of judges.

"Suppose we agree to investigate the crash without any Scouts around for security? We don't need much, except for a couple of people to keep equipment from blowing away or rolling downhill.

"The rest of Scout Company pulls out, to an agreed-on position outside the valley. Maybe even outside Republican territory, although I don't recommend that. I think they'd be more useful down at Camp Chapman—"

"As reinforcements for an attack on the missile battery?" the NCO said. The lieutenant looked sour but said nothing. Mahoney wondered if the NCO was some sort of political commissar.

Hadn't heard that the Bushrangers were putting them in officially, but there's always somebody who'll appoint himself if the local C.O. won't stop him.

"More hands and more lift for medevacking wounded, I would put it," Brigitte Tachin said. "Also reinforcements, yes, but against whoever attacked the posts in the first place."

Mahoney nodded. "That's what I'll recommend to Lieutenant Piccone and Captain Shores. Meanwhile, we can get on with our work at the crash. We'll be hostages de facto, because if our friends do something you don't like you can always reel us back in.

"But we won't be hostages de jure, which means our friends won't *have* to do anything you don't like. Give us six hours, and we'll be out of your hair and your territory both."

Assuming we don't lose anybody to hypothermia, falls, or radiation leaks, but let's look on the bright side since all the others are too damned depressing!

"If we go this route, and you pay compensation to Lieutenant Uhlig for your mistake, the whole thing will blow over before this storm does. We might even be friendly witnesses at any investigation into—whatever you want to call this initiative you took, as soon as Captain Bergeron was out of sight."

What I want to call it is "mutiny," but tact has its uses.

"We've done nothing that calls for an investigation," the NCO said. It sounded arrogant but not a bluff, and the lieutenant and the rest of the command group were nodding.

Mahoney felt colder than the wind could have made him. If these people had something in the works that would keep them from being punished for mutiny and risking a Republic–Federation confrontation . . .

"So forget that," Mahoney said. "But what about the rest?"

The lieutenant looked around the command group. "I'll have to ask you to step outside while I consult my superiors."

This was an invitation to do exactly what he'd planned to ask for. Mahoney managed not to grin.

Lowenstein shook her gray head. "I'd better stay with Lieutenant Uhlig. Something happens to him, it hits the fan no matter what." She was also hand-signaling Mahoney that she wanted to talk.

They stood in the rear as the others filed out into the windy night. "You think I'm negotiating illegally?" Mahoney asked.

"Damned if I know. I know attacker power plants and tapestries and how to be a doting grandmother. I also know common sense when I see it. I think I see it here."

Mahoney felt warmer. "Thanks."

"One piece of advice, though. Let everybody go on rec-

96

ord for or against. You're right on the edge of the law. They'll obey better if they think you know it."

"No problem. So what's your vote?"

"I'm for it, of course."

Mahoney felt so warmed by that, he nearly forgot to seal his parka as he stepped out of the lifter.

Darkness hid the gray waves and their white foam caps from Joanna Marder's command lifter two thousand meters up. It didn't hide the lights of *Eriksen Gamma,* plowing through those waves on the last twenty kilometers of her voyage. It didn't hide the lights of the five other lifters and three attackers flying escort on the coaster.

Marder stretched, wanting a drink badly but a massage desperately. The massage would be safer, too. She knew that once she'd drunk enough to feel the warmth glowing in her, she'd go on until the glow blotted out the rest of the world.

The lights ahead weaved and bobbed as the convoy rode the storm winds. In the display tank other lights sparked— the attackers patrolling five hundred kilometers east, off the Republican coast, and the command attacker on high station in the middle of the Gulf.

They'd be all lit up, too, because Fegeli's orders were to be highly visible. Anybody who wanted to shoot at them, the sooner they did it, the sooner they'd be squashed. Anybody else shouldn't have any excuse for "mistakes."

"Signal coming through on the Fed crash investigators," the radio operator said. She listened, then signaled Marder to put on her headphones.

"—fragments of flight-recorder capsule recovered have been loaded. We are lifting out at 0410 for rendezvous with friendly forces. Lieutenant Uhlig is conscious and coordinated. All members of team are suffering minor exposure and possible minor radiation dosages.

"After the initial misunderstanding, we have received full cooperation from the armed forces of the Bushranger Republic. No hostile action was intended.

"This is First Lieutenant Brian Mahoney, F.N.S. *Shenandoah,* signing off."

The voice would have been familiar even without the name. Mahoney seemed to be a jack of all trades, Armistice Commission, briefing visitors, and God knew what all aboard *Shen.*

"Trust a Killarney man to tell a good tale," the radio operator said. Then she straightened up.

"Message coming in, on COMMAND SECRET scramble." Marder slipped her card into the radio console and heard gibberish turn into Colonel Pak's voice.

"Commander Marder. I'm on my way to Barnard's Crossing with the Fourth Battalion. ETA 0700. We are picking up enough radio traffic and vehicle movements in the Republic to suggest some military action. No evidence of Federation involvement or combat yet.

"All coded intercepts are being sent undeciphered to Point Unicorn. I have assigned Signal Chief K'ung to secure their transmission."

Marder grinned. "The K'ung drill" was the Bonsai Force's current code for an order that wasn't being obeyed or shouldn't be obeyed. Governor Hollings—"Point Unicorn" —might want to keep the Bonsai Force in the dark about what was going on the Republic, but they wouldn't play that game. If anything going on in the Republic spilled across the border or out into the Gulf, it would hit the Bonsai Force long before it hit Governor Hollings.

"What are your current orders, Commander?" Pak asked.

"Complete the convoying operation, maintain surveillance of the Gulf, and keep all vehicles and crews in nominal condition." she recited irritably.

Why couldn't somebody have passed the word to Pak? The Baba certainly was keeping an eye on the situation, or she'd never have ordered the attacker squadron C.O. to take orders from Marder.

And if the Baba was too busy, what about Paul? The thought hit like a meteor hitting a ship's shield, didn't penetrate, but registered on every sensor just the same.

"No sign of hostile or Federation activity?"

"Blank all around."

"Good. I recommend you land and recharge as soon as *Gamma*'s inshore. I can push our recon flight out a little farther forward."

"Need any air guides for the last stage?"

"Negative. I have half a dozen pilots who grew up around here. Two of them can fly point."

"Thanks for the help. Marder over."

"Pak out."

The commander stretched again and rubbed eyes that seemed to have breeding mites behind their lids. So far the

Mahmoud Sa'id affair hadn't done more than cost her a night's sleep and a display of Colonel Schapiro's temper. Even the "hostage" situation at the crash site had defused itself while she droned over the Gulf.

Now something was going on in the Republic that threatened to change that. Time to warn her people.

"Set up for Gold Security transmission," Marder ordered the radio operator. As the operator's hands called up the right colors on her board, Marder pulled the com terminal toward her and started tapping in a message.

Chief Lowenstein stared out the cockpit window. "If somebody will give me a white horsehair and a black horsehair, I'll try to tell them apart. If I can, it's dawn."

Brian Mahoney murmured, nearly in Brigitte Tachin's ear, "I'd rather tell a Bushranger horse's ass from a Bushranger with sense."

Elayne Zheng must have overheard, in spite of the whine of the fans. "Is there a difference?" she snapped, then went back to changing the dressings over the navigator's eyes.

"Now just a bloody—" began Josh McGuire, from the pilot's seat.

"If there wasn't a difference, would Mr. McGuire and his daughter be flying us out?" Mahoney interrupted. "Elayne, I think that calls for an apology."

"Is that an order?"

"It's an order to either apologize or shut up. Take your pick."

Zheng shut up. Trying to find explanation if not excuse, Tachin decided the E.W.O. must have strained her shoulder changing the dressings.

No, we're all of us a bit edgy, more than injuries could account for. None of us would be complaining if we were in a Federation lifter.

Not that *Shelia* was the piece of junk she looked at first. Outback lifters on Victoria seldom competed for beauty prizes, but they needed long range, heavy payloads, and bad-weather maneuverability. High speed and fancy electronics were almost as much luxuries as beauty, and almost as hard to find.

They could have done worse. Instead of McGuire's volunteering to fly them across the border, they could be riding in a Republican lifter whose pilot had God only knew what orders or impulses. They could even be sitting on their *culs* on the frozen mountainside by *Mahmoud Sa'id*'s wreckage, waiting for the diplomatic talk-talk to permit the return of their shuttle.

Tachin shivered and hugged her coat closer with one hand, Brian with the other. The McGuires had cut the heating down to the minimum needed for the wounded, in order to stretch their range. It was going to be close even so, unless they could fit the power packs for the crash kit to recharge *Shelia*'s cells.

"Hang on, people," McGuire said. "Another pass coming up. But that's the last one before we hit the coastal plain at the south end of the Krainiks."

Lowenstein looked around for a piece of wood to touch and finally tapped her forehead. As she finished, Zheng stiffened.

"Don't look now, people, but we're being followed."

Tachin saw the fuzzy picture on the rearview screen—a dark-colored lifter, with oversized fans and a slimmer hull than anything she'd seen in the Republic, civilian or military.

With that configuration, she wasn't surprised to see it overtaking them as if they were standing still. She was surprised when the floor tilted wildly, throwing everybody into a heap at the forward end. The McGuires were taking *Shelia* down, and Tachin's stomach heaved from more than the maneuvers as she realized why.

The lower they were, the less distance to fall if their pursuer shot out their lift.

A moment later eye-searing light wiped out the picture on the screen. *Shelia* bucked, a fan screamed until one of the McGuires cut its power, and Elayne Zheng grabbed a cutting torch.

"What the bloody—" Kathy McGuire shouted.

"Let me set this for explosive discharge and toss it out. When I toss it, you get us on the ground. Maybe they'll think we took a lethal hit."

Tachin certainly thought *Shelia* was doomed, when the torch's power pack discharged in one dazzling flash. Both McGuires fought their lifter down onto the ground more by touch than by sight. They hit hard, bouncing their passengers off the overhead, bulkheads, deck, and each other. Tachin was sure for a moment that she'd join Lieutenant Uhlig with a concussion.

A cold wind blew the smell of sweat, fear, and ancient

cargoes away from Tachin. She looked up and saw that the landing had sprung the top hatch.

"Better close that—" she began.

Mahoney shook his head and stood up. "No. If they're watching for signs of life, closing it might give us away. Brigitte, if I give you a boost on my shoulders, can you peek out and see what our friends are doing?"

Tachin was dizzy and sick and her feet and hands did what she told them slowly and reluctantly, but the best cure for everything seemed to be action. She scrambled up Brian as if he was a tree, but holding on more tightly than she'd ever embraced the old pear tree in the backyard.

Perched on his shoulders, she had a good view over an arc of about two hundred degrees of the sides and rear. Off to the left, the attacker was climbing slowly and drifting right. Tachin saw a two-seat tandem cockpit, what looked like weapons pods under stub wings on either side, and what had to be a chin turret just below the cockpit.

"Some kind of gunship—" Tachin began.

One of the weapons pods spewed flame. Kathy McGuire screamed "Mayday, Mayday. Under attack by unidentified—" Something drew a trail of flame halfway to *Shelia,* then arced downward to churn up snow, smoke, and bits of rock. Tachin felt *Shelia* rock, slammed against the edge of the hatch, yelped as something sharp stung her cheek, then felt herself slipping and clutched the rim of the hatch.

As she did, the weapons pod flamed again. At the same moment, fire lanced down from the sky. An invisible fist punched the gunship, like a child punching a house of cards and with the same result.

The gunship disintegrated, first from the punch, then from its ammunition exploding. Tachin lost the trail of the second missile in the blast, then ducked inside, pulling the hatch closed.

The explosion of the second missile nearly flipped *Shelia* on her side and knocked Tachin off Mahoney's shoulders. This time she didn't worry about a concussion, but she thought a couple of teeth were going to need replacing.

The McGuires were bellowing into the radio, a duet in bass and alto. "Who's up there? Who? This is a Mayday from lifter VA 21465, property of—"

"Hey, hey. Calm down, people. This is Gold Four, Command Warrant Officer Hussein. Are you ready to ditch that clunker and ride out in comfort?"

The McGuires looked ready to have strokes in unison. Tachin sucked blood from where her teeth had been and heard Mahoney fill in the silence.

"Hey, we may still be airworthy. Mr. McGuire?"

The farmer's face stayed red but his eyes and hands moved surely to make a check. "We've got lift, three fans, and no major structural damage. We could use a little juice—"

"What's your maximum airspeed?" Hussein said.

"About 150 kmh with this load. But we only—"

"Negative. You'll have to ditch and ride out with us. We can't stooge around in Republican territory long enough to convoy you. There's been a putsch in the Republic, and there may be civil war any hour."

"What?"

"Lieutenant Mahoney, I'm an attacker pilot, not an ear doctor. I said somebody's trying to overthrow the Bush-ranger government. That gunship we blew may have been on the rebel side."

Mahoney's face took on the look of a man pushed too far and now ready to push back. Tachin grinned in spite of her aches and pains.

"Mr. Hussein, is ditching *Shelia* an order?"

"Well, sir, my orders were to avoid any unnecessary danger to my attacker—"

"The danger involved in saving *Shelia* is necessary. I will take full responsibility. Standing orders are to reward civilian cooperation to the maximum extent feasible. The McGuires haven't just cooperated, they may not have a home to go back to or any other property in the universe except *Shelia*.

"Mr. McGuire. Can you dock with a Navy—okay, can you take a tow from one?"

"I think we lost one hook for a Y-connection."

"Can you replace it?"

Kathy McGuire nodded. "That's my job. Give me some of your tools and a spare pair of hands"—Lowenstein held out hers and McGuire nodded—"and ten minutes, and I can rig for a Y-tow and a power umbilical as well."

"Got that, Mr. Hussein?" Mahoney said. "In fifteen minutes, I want you to be down here with a tow and an umbilical. How far is that gunship you blew out?"

A short muttering ended in, "About seven hundred meters away, bearing 065 true."

Mahoney whistled. "Did you jam his missiles?"

"No, sir."

"Then his maintenance or his guidance stinks. We should have been potted the first shot. Well, it's too far to send out a ground party to search the wreckage. Can you make a low flyby and take pictures, at least?"

"Is that an order?"

"Yes, Mr. Hussein. That is an order."

"Aye-aye, sir." Before the radio went dead, Tachin heard muttering in a language she didn't recognize. Elayne Zheng laughed.

"Tell us, Elayne, and maybe we'll all be entertained," Mahoney said. Tachin gripped his arm, feeling muscles hard as launcher pistons under the coveralls.

"That was the beginning of a prayer, that he not be cursed or endangered for obeying a madman," Zheng said.

The two women beat their planned time by enough to answer the attacker pilot's prayer. Fifteen minutes from the signoff, *Shelia* was under way, bobbing at the end of a towline, an umbilical feeding power to her lift generator, and an insulated container from Gold Four giving Mahoney's people their first hot meal in more than a day.

Ten

The meeting was small enough to get work done, even by Admiral Kuwahara's rigorous standards.

Major General Mikhail Kornilov, C.G. Victoria Command (although for how long, higher ranks only knew). Brigadier General Marcus Langston, C.G. Victoria Brigade. Colonel Ludmilla Vesey, Victoria Command's chief of staff. Major General (Retired) Alys Parkinson, representing the Military Council of the Dominion of Victoria. And himself, an acting vice-admiral commanding the Federation's Victoria Squadron. Five people, enough to get work done—or undo the work of everyone who had tried to make a home of inhospitable Victoria over the last two hundred years.

Kuwahara focused his attention on the map display, where Colonel Vesey was concluding her account of events at the Armistice Commission Extraterritorial Zone. It had started life less than half a Victoria year ago as the Federation's Camp Aounda. Now it housed the Armistice Commission, a growing population of highly placed tourists, and a security detachment drawn from all three armies on Victoria.

Correction, the Detachment *had* been drawn from all three armies. Colonel Vesey was explaining why there'd been some changes made in the six hours since the attempted coup in the Bushranger Republic became official.

"There were no civilian casualties in the efforts by the Republican rebels to provoke an Alliance–Federation incident. Federation casualties were one KIA and five WIA; Alliance casualties, no KIA and four WIA. Republican casualties are unknown, but may have exceeded ten KIA.

"All prisoners taken in the incident are under criminal detention. All Republican forces have been requested to withdraw to a distance of not less than ten kilometers from the zone. This withdrawal was completed as of 0945.

"General Kornilov has ordered the use of lethal force against any Republican troops violating the ten-kilometer limit. He hopes for cooperation from the Alliance, but will act unilaterally if necessary."

Kornilov's massive head jerked. "If anyone has an alternative to suggest, other than evacuating the whole zone . . . ?"

Kuwahara held his peace. He couldn't think of any improvement, and any other comments would be pointless. Worse—it would sound as if he was arguing with Kornilov simply for the record.

Vesey started to sit down. Parkinson impaled her with a look. "What about the situation in the Republic?"

"Well, we're short of hard data—" Vesey began. The Victorian's look sharpened. Kornilov cleared his throat.

"What we know about the situation in the Republic is based on radio intercepts, some orbital sightings, a few intelligence reports, and a lot of guessing. If you want what we've learned from that—"

"I do," Parkinson said. Her tone made Kornilov cough. Kuwahara nodded, drawing Kornilov's glare. The admiral put on his blandest face and waited for Kornilov to remember who was senior here.

Kuwahara hated to pull rank, particularly on someone in Kornilov's position. But he would hate even more what would happen to civil-military relations on Victoria if General Parkinson went back to the Military Council and reported that Victoria Command was withholding vital intelligence.

"Let's admit the limitations of our knowledge, but discuss the situation within those limitations," Kuwahara said. "Colonel Vesey?"

The chief of staff rose again. "The people behind the attempted coup seem to believe that the Republic is helpless against its enemies without more outside help than the present government is willing to seek. Who those enemies are, who's going to provide the help, and how much effort the rebels made to put their position across peacefully, we don't know."

"You don't think the Alliance is innocent, do you?" Langston asked.

"I'm sure they haven't helped, but they don't seem to be the main supplier of the weapons the rebels have used. We do think that supplier may have had something to do with the *Mahmoud Sa'id* and *Eriksen Gamma* incidents. The rebels went into action suspiciously soon after the shootdown."

The looks around the table told Kuwahara that everybody

else had already reached that conclusion, too, and liked it no better.

"Fighting seems to be confined to an area north of a line from Gar Lake to Mount Houton. We have sightings of firefights all the way up into the Lizardspines, and one report from our outpost at Loch Prima.

"The only place where both sides seem to be getting ready for a stand-up fight is Mount Houton itself. This may be prestige, it may be arms dumps, it may be industrial resources—most of the lifter-maintenance facilities are there.

"However, neither side is trained or equipped for a house-to-house fight. At the moment they're both lifting in all the troops they can spare elsewhere and doing a bit of sniping."

Parkinson looked satisfied. "How is our intelligence network coping?"

Vesey frowned. "We've had few reports from our local sources. It's not impossible that some of them have been terminated. It's likely that many of them are either lying low or happen to be where nothing's happening."

Parkinson now looked not merely satisfied but smug. "General Kornilov, Admiral Kuwahara," she said formally. "With your permission, may I invite another member of the Military Council of the Dominion of Victoria to brief this meeting?"

"I'd prefer to wait until after we've made a few decisions," Kornilov said.

"I think this briefing will help the decisions," Parkinson said. She waited just long enough not to be usurping Kornilov's authority, then opened her com circuit.

"Father Brothertongue, can you come in now?"

The fact that Father Brothertongue had been chaplain to the Victorian militia before his election to the House of Delegates didn't make him a more plausible member of the dominion's Military Council. Kuwahara agreed with those who said it was his old friendship with Prime Minister Fitzpatrick.

The priest entered, wearing a clean but rumpled bush suit and a sober look. Parkinson held a chair for him, and he sank into it with an unmistakable sigh.

"Good morning. I apologize for my clothing, but I had to come directly here without going home. I've just returned from the Bushranger Republic."

Kornilov frowned. "Members of the dominion government aren't authorized—"

"Ah, but ordained or recognized religious ministers are," Brothertongue said, so deferentially that he defused Kornilov's wrath at being interrupted. "There was a legitimate matter of an ordination being questioned that had me in the north these past few days. But I could hardly avoid hearing and seeing some of the—ah, secular activity around me."

"Get to the point," Kornilov said. Kuwahara wished the same thing silently, if only so he wouldn't have to mediate between Kornilov and Parkinson when Mikhail unloaded all his frustrations on this interloper. If he was one.

Father Brothertongue's impressions of the politics of the rebellion were very much the same as Colonel Vesey's. So were his views on the strategic situation—stated so clearly that Kuwahara suspected the man had once been something besides a chaplain in somebody's armed forces.

"What may be decisive is the rebels' access to outside sources of arms, possibly even off-planet sources. What I hope we can arrange here is some way of restoring the balance.

"If we do that in the next few days, the government forces should be able to clear Mount Houton. That will break the rebels' morale and reduce them to the status of a guerrilla force."

"That will be more the Navy's affair than the Army's," Kornilov said. "Admiral, can we seal off Victoria from any unauthorized landings?"

"Not without either reinforcements or the cooperation of the Alliance," Kuwahara said. *Cursed if I'll discuss the Up the Sleeve Squadron until Brothertongue reveals what he has up his!*

"We've already requested reinforcements. We can also ask for the cooperation of the Alliance authorities. I want to be cautious, of course, in phrasing the request. If they reject it openly, we'll simply have made matters worse."

"I don't see how they can get worse," Brothertongue said. "Whatever we may think of the Republic, only the innocent will suffer if it falls into chaos."

"We won't save them by crossing the border in force," Kornilov said. "We have two combat-ready battalions available, which might not even be enough to meet the rebels. It certainly wouldn't be enough if the rebels called in the

Alliance. Even if the 96th didn't cross the border, the Alliance would certainly step up its own supplies to the rebels."

"I don't think the problem is numbers," Parkinson said. She leaned back in her chair and appeared to be contemplating the map. "Suppose that Victorian volunteers were to run supplies across the border to the government?"

"Where would the volunteers come from?" Kornilov asked.

"The dominion's militia brigade, of course. Since they weren't mobilized, they're fresh and up to allowance on supplies."

Kuwahara frowned. Parkinson was in for a nasty surprise when she inventoried the brigade's rations. The militia themselves hadn't been mobilized, but a good part of their food was now aboard the Up the Sleeve Squadron. All the records would turn out to be in order when anybody asked, but that wouldn't feed hungry Victorians.

It also wouldn't soothe Parkinson. An unsoothed Parkinson added to an abandoned Bushranger Republic could mean a great deal of new anti-Federation sentiment on Victoria, ready for exploitation.

No time to let Mikhail come around gradually, even if he will.

Kuwahara tapped his display controls. The map turned holographic, vividly displaying contours. He focused on the rugged Blanchard Canyon area, running northwest from the upper Vinh River, across the border, almost to Mount Houton.

"General Parkinson. Could your volunteers handle bringing the supplies up through the canyon?"

Either Parkinson had been expecting cooperation or she was a fine actress. "If we pick for bush-ready lift and bush pilots, yes."

"Very good. This is rugged terrain. If your supply runs stay low, only somebody directly above them with a look-down radar or IR sensors could detect them. The Navy will be flying attacker patrols all along the border. Every time supplies are coming up the canyon, we can concentrate our patrols in the area. That should keep anyone from getting directly above your people."

"You won't be able to cross the border, though," Brother-tongue pointed out.

"They won't need to," Parkinson said, rising to join Kuwahara at the map. "Five-sixths of the route was still in

Federation territory, the last time the Border Committee met.

"Once our people reach the border, the government forces may be able to make pickup there. If not—volunteers are a venerable institution. In fact, it might even work out for the best if the rebels detect our presence. They'll have to split their Mount Houton force, and that could put the government on top without a fight."

Except for whatever the rebels do to your volunteers, Kuwahara thought.

Still, the plan made both political and military sense. It would be Victorians helping Victorians. It would also be exploiting local resources to the maximum extent. This was such a fundamental point of Federation military doctrine that it probably explained why Kornilov hadn't been relieved for not calling up reinforcements.

Meanwhile, Kornilov was nodding ponderously. "I assume Governor-General Gist has been informed of this proposal?"

Unmistakably, Parkinson was surprised. Brothertongue, just as unmistakably, was not. He smiled. "Of course, he'll be informed. He has to consent to our enlisting citizens of any other Union planet.

"Which reminds me, General Kornilov. Has General Parkinson mentioned how many volunteers we wanted?"

Parkinson's acting was back up to standard. She slapped her forehead. "Sorry, Mikhail. Here I am, asking you to buy a horse without even knowing that it's not a grumbler."

The discussion turned irresistibly to drawing up a table of organization for the volunteers.

Kuwahara's copilot/aide vanished down the passageway, his mission arranging in-flight meals for the shuttle's trip out to Task Force Borha. As the aide vanished, Kuwahara heard a familiar heavy footfall closing from behind. He waited until General Kornilov pulled up beside him.

"Would you like to join me for a drink?" Kuwahara asked.

Kornilov looked unpacified. "Did you have to jump to Parkinson's support so fast and so completely?"

"In the sense that I was under no coercion to do so, I did not *have*—"

"Admiral, I think this is too serious for word games."

Kuwahara decided that even the slightest wit was out of place, with Kornilov in his present frame of mind.

"I thought it was a good idea, and I still think so." The admiral went on to explain the supply situation.

"Why didn't they notice long before this?" Kornilov asked.

"We'd stowed a good part of our rations and amenities with a private contractor," the admiral said. "We didn't have storage space in orbit or any dirtside facilities at all.

"The private contractor appropriated part of that—or at least let somebody else appropriate it. We are inclined to think the latter, although the contractor wasn't the poorer for it.

"We offered to refrain from formal charges if the contractor would replace the supplies on a one-for-one basis. He couldn't offer fast enough."

"You expect me to believe that you didn't know he was offering militia reserves?"

"Yes. The repackaging and renumbering was a professional job."

"It sounds as if he had expert advice," Kornilov said.

He probably did, and I think we both know whose.

Kornilov had replaced Brigadier General Liu as his chief of staff on the eve of *Shenandoah*'s arrival. He had gone on to relieve Liu as commander of a battalion-sized task force as soon as the Armistice was signed. Now Liu was sitting in a gilded cage as an advisor to the Armistice Commission, looking for an opportunity to retire with either honor or profit, preferably both.

"You don't suspect any political aspect to it?" Kornilov pressed.

"This is one of those situations where you can't tell where greed ends and politics begins," Kuwahara said. "Do you suspect General Parkinson?"

Kornilov looked up and down the passageway, then pulled the admiral into an alcove. The double-paned window showed a drift of virgin snow banked half against the building, half against the windbreak stretching north from it. The beervine that held the windbreak in place was brown in winter dormancy; the storm had carried off the last of its blackened leaves.

"Frankly, I don't trust anybody on the Military Council with regard to Federation property," Kornilov said. "What concerns me more is the capabilities of the militia. Only one battalion has more than six hundred people on the roster, and the whole brigade barely tops two thousand. All their vehicles are local, their electronics commercial models, and half their weapons personal property. They have exactly 123 veterans of regular service in any military force, and the brigade commander isn't one of them!"

Kuwahara nodded. Like General Liu's desire to retire rich, the limitations of Victoria's militia brigade was something they both knew. It was one reason the brigade hadn't been counted as an asset, let alone mobilized, during the previous crisis.

The admiral also suspected that the Federation wasn't entirely innocent in this matter. To keep the Victoria Brigade up to strength as cheaply as possible, Eleventh Zone command had systematically stripped the militia of their best people for the two territorial battalions carried on the T.O. of the Victoria Brigade. The four left under the dominion's Ministry of Defense had to fight for the dregs, with barely a decent cadre of veterans to whip them into shape.

"So what we have is Parkinson volunteering people who aren't much above the level of cannon fodder?"

Kornilov nodded. "And neither of us is such a barbarian that we believe in winning by attrition. But that might be the only way to win if the rebels come out from Mount Houton and seriously hit the volunteers."

"Not if the volunteers have advisers."

"Did I hear quotation marks around the last word?"

"No—well, maybe not. But consider what a hundred people could do for maintenance and communications. I can't imagine Parkinson putting more than five hundred people in the field, so that could give us—them—advisers down to platoon level.

"Also consider what happens if the rebels do move. We'll have to pull our people out, of course. But they'll certainly be armed and ordered to return fire in self-defense. We might even have to lay on a few tactical attacker sorties to complete the extraction safely."

Kornilov grabbed Kuwahara in a bear hug, then held him at arm's length. "You crafty bastard! A man after my own heart."

"I suppose that's better than being a woman after your own job?"

"Aghhh." Kornilov pretended to scrape dung off his shoe. "If Frieda Hentsch wants my job, I'm sure she will do it well. Only let them take away either me or the Hentschmen.

We're matter and antimatter, and the containment field is weak."

"I'll join that wish."

Admiral Schatz and General Berkson were slipping into a cardinal error. They were neither showing their confidence in Kornilov nor removing him in favor of someone they trusted. They might have explanations for this, but where was the excuse?

"Will you join me for lunch?" Kornilov asked. "My quarters, and perhaps a sauna afterward?"

Kuwahara's sense of duty drew all its weapons to do battle against temptation. Then he realized the battle was quite pointless. With the rebellion flaring up and a counterattack to plan, his idea of flying to Task Force Borha needed revising.

The Navy people there deserved praise, both the landing party and *Mahmoud Sa'id*'s survivors. But he could hand that out just as well at Fort Stafford. All he needed to send north was his shuttle. While it made the round-trip, he could sit down with Kornilov.

"Lunch, certainly. The sauna depends on how fast my shuttle returns from Task Force Borha. I'm sending it up to bring the Navy people back south."

"Fine, although if you can wait half an hour, I have a few high-priority loads it can carry."

"Give me a list, and I'll ring up my pilot. Also give me a list of what advisers you want the Navy to provide." *No need to tell him that Rose Liddell's had a landing-party roster drawn up these past five days, or he'll simply ask for everybody on it.*

"Done." Kornilov handed Kuwahara a mess card. "Go on ahead and claim a private dining room with a secure terminal. I want to check on those loads."

A knock on the door of the bunkroom interrupted Brian Mahoney's changing the heatpak on Brigitte Tachin's left hand.

Elayne Zheng lifted her head and stared at the door. "If this was *Shen,* I'd swear that was—"

"Hey, anybody home?"

"It *is* Charlie," Tachin said. She stood up, pulled up her one-piece underwear, and pulled on a sweater.

"Welcome to Frigid Prospects," Zheng said as the blond

112

lieutenant sauntered in. "Or is that what you've got now? And how did you—ah—"

"Break out of where these—this lady and gentleman—put me? Oh, I was taken from that county jail by a set of curious Chances. Three lovely red-haired sisters, Lori, Martina, and Susan Chance."

"Right," Mahoney said. "And they were so curious they just now let you go?"

"No, they thought my presence on Victoria was indispensable to peace."

"How do you spell that last word?" Zheng asked.

"That depends on whose—" Longman began, then actually cut himself off before anyone else could even glare.

"I found an access plate, and put a glitch in some wiring that brought the maintenance people around," he said. "Then the Hermit—he's put up a fourth stripe by the way—he suggested a short dirtside assignment to the Armistice Commission."

"I thought the commission was supposed to promote peace," Tachin said.

"So it will, if I'm with it," Longman said. "At least peace in D-4. Meanwhile, you people are supposed to be packing for a trip back to Fort Stafford and *Shen*."

"I thought we were supposed to be dressing for Kuwahara's inspection."

"Plans change. The shogun sent out his shuttle, with me and a few other high-priority people. It lifts off in half an hour, with or without you on board." He kicked a small traveling case under the one vacant cot and sat down.

"So it goes," Mahoney said. "Brigitte, can you pack my stuff while I say good-bye to Candy—"

"Shores? Last I saw of her, she was crying on the shoulder of a major—Abelsohn, I think."

"Her old C.O.," Mahoney said, hand on the door. "Good for him."

"Making major, or helping Shores?" Longman said. "If I was as sure of a medal as she was, I wouldn't be crying on—"

Mahoney swung around so fast that everyone except Zheng flinched. "Charlie, do you want to reach the Armistice Commission in pieces?"

"All I said was—"

"Enough to prove you've never lost somebody under you in a stupid fight."

"Well, when all's said and done, when the hell did that happen to you, Saint Brian Mahoney?"

"Shut up," Zheng said. "Charlie, you've put your foot in it again. Brian, Charlie's right. I'm the one here with the right to talk about losing and hurting. This is my third time in seventeen years.

"But don't worry. You'll all probably have the chance to catch up, as long as the crazies don't run out of ammunition." She lay down again, her back turned. Mahoney relieved his feelings by slamming the door on the way out. The only problem, he realized, was that he wasn't sure what feelings he'd relieved.

Eleven

"*Fireflower* has outreached our passive sensors," Ehmad met-Lakaito said.

F'mita ihr Sular gave a slack-lipped sigh. It was not entirely one of relief.

Putting twelve sunbombs into the hands of humans of unknown reliability and judgment could do as much harm to the Khudrigate as to the humans. She very much wished that she had an Inquiry Authority to ask where the bombs were going once they reached Victoria.

But that was knowledge which Rahbad Sarlin had made it bared-tusk plain that he would kill to keep from her. Also, the bombs' intended destination might no longer matter.

With the rebellion in the new Republic, any of the human factions who could not draw on the great powers' arsenals might quickly become desperate. Then the bombs stood a good chance of being used, not necessarily by the people to whom they had been sent.

"Commence active sensor scan," said a perfect imitation of met-Lakaito's voice from behind her. She whirled, hands in slice-stroke posture, to see Sarlin smiling at her.

From met-Lakaito came a strangled noise that might have been born as either a laugh or a curse. Ihr Sular glared at both of them.

"I have decided that the sunbomb is not the deadliest weapon in the Khudrigate's arsenal," she said. "The deadliest is a Special Projects officer with a curious notion of humor."

"Certainly better than a Special Projects officer with no notion of humor," Sarlin said. "Have you ever met my half-brother?"

Sarlin now wore the standard shipboard shorts and sleeveless vest, with the toed half boots that most of the older crew favored. From his odor, ihr Sular could tell that he'd been exercising hard before sponging himself down.

"Be that as it may," she said politely, "was that an order?"

"I should give orders aboard *Perfumed Wind,* in the presence of its commander? What do you take me for?"

"Not the fool you took me for," met-Lakaito said shortly, and turned back to the displays.

Ihr Sular gripped Sarlin's left wrist, hard enough to dimple his wristband, and led him out of the pilot chamber. When the hatch shut behind them, she bared her tusks.

"*Never* jest with discipline aboard a ship! For once, I wish we were of the Fleet. Then it might be a while before even Special Projects was able to wedge you aboard a ship!"

Sarlin's posture of submission was so exaggerated that his rump hit the grab rail on the bulkhead. Ihr Sular's hands straightened into slice-stroke posture of their own will.

"Forgive me," Sarlin said finally. Unlike his posture, his voice held no mockery. "You understand that I anticipated being on board that ship along with the bombs. When I had to endure humans bringing me proof that the orders had been changed, and I was to remain here . . ."

"Ship starvation set in?"

"If it had not already done so. I say nothing against your ship or your crew, but the first keeps the second busy. My work is on Victoria. Or it was supposed to be. I wonder who Special Projects had underground, with the right to give me orders?"

It occurred to ihr Sular that the answer might be "nobody." Special Projects authentication codes were supposed to be impossible to break or reproduce. Ihr Sular's experience led her to believe this was unreasonably optimistic. But that would occur to Sarlin in his own time, given his natural suspicion. More urgently—

"Were you serious about the active scan?"

"It might have detected any observers who have hidden behind asteroids, waiting for this rendezvous. If our friends ended up with someone on their trail, we should know and they should be warned."

"They wouldn't be the only ones warned if we went to active mode. Our sensors aren't Fleet models. We don't need to run at high speeds in asteroid belts. Just creep up on particular asteroids slowly and quietly."

"Will you let me take a listening watch on passive scan?"

"Are you qualified?"

116

"Another pair of eyes, ears, and hands. Is that enough qualification?"

First Guidance met-Lakaito watched over his navigational gear with the intentness of a new mother over her first child. He still needed to eat, sleep, and purge himself.

So much for the conceit that Special Projects officers are above nature. Ship starvation can flay them like common folk.

"Yes. But I'll have your hide for gloves if you switch to active without my permission or that of the First Guidance."

"If I commit such a folly, I'll peel my hide off myself. Honor bound!"

They gripped thumbs to seal the gesture, then returned to the pilot chamber.

With a vicious whine, the night wind flung itself at the hastily assembled field building. Rattles and creaks assaulted Candice Shores's ears from all directions. She tried to shut them out and go on with the job at hand.

"—loyalty to superior officers and an outstanding degree of initiative. This is demonstrated by—"

The words on the screen might have been in Merishi for all the logic she could find in them. So had all the previous words she'd tried out for the letter of commendation for Lieutenant Piccone, Scout Company's X.O.

Here we go. Maybe.

Erase two lines and start with:

"After Lieutenant Mahoney announced the result of his negotiations with the Republican forces, Piccone displayed an exceptional degree of initiative and leadership of a high quality in disengaging the remaining personnel of Scout Company. To this initiative and leadership is largely due the fact that—"

Someone knocked on the door of the cubicle grandly named the C.O.'s office.

"Yes?"

"It's Sergeant Major Zimmer, ma'am."

The walls of the building being about the thickness of toilet paper, Shores didn't swear. She didn't even think any curses. She stored the text, hoped she could store the inspiration, kicked the heating pad under her feet out of sight, wedged her feet into chilly boots, and said, "Come in, Top."

She instantly realized she needn't have worried about the heating pad. Zimmer was wearing a pair of hopelessly non-regulation heated boots, a lined sleeveless vest over his battledress, and a purple scarf at his throat.

"Top, I thought you'd be used to this place by now."

Zimmer smiled. "Ma'am, my part of Pied Noir is mostly sunshine and vineyards. My bones remember that, at least in the winter."

"Pour some tea and sit down, then. What do you need?"

"Well, I'd like to know if you're going to be at the chess club tonight."

"Short a referee?" Zimmer was the usual referee at Company chess matches, because nobody else in the Company could play at his level.

"Well, not exactly."

"Then I'll have to beg off. I'm trying to put together a letter of commendation for Piccone. It's one of those binds where you know what to say but not how to say it."

"Okay, but Sergeant Strauch was hoping you'd be there."

"He's way out of my class."

"I'm not sure it's a match he wants."

"If it's 4th Platoon business, he ought to start with Lieutenant Khabi."

Zimmer's face took on that remote look he used to remind young officers that he'd been in the Army longer than they'd been alive.

"All right. What haven't I heard that I was supposed to?"

"The platoon's pretty unhappy about none of them being allowed to volunteer for the Mount Houton run. I know, you were afraid they couldn't be trusted around the Bushrangers. But they weren't badly treated as POWs."

"They still lost friends. Besides, I need the veterans to keep the newlies up to standard."

"There's only a quarter of the platoon brand-new now that all the lightly wounded are back on duty. They could have spared three or four, I'm sure."

"I wasn't. Some of those wounded more or less deserted from the hospital. I'm not sure they're up to watching newlies in combat."

"You were sure that Sergeant Esteva could be trusted, though. He and Sklarinsky were *copains* from years back. I think it's Esteva's going off that's got the platoon unhappy, more'n anything else."

Shores wondered what answer would satisfy Zimmer without exposing Esteva's work for Intelligence. Major Nieg hadn't exactly ordered her to let Esteva volunteer, but he'd said that both he and Scout Company would benefit from having Esteva observing the rebels firsthand.

"What about Esteva's being captured by somebody who suspects what he's up to?" she remembered saying.

"He knows what to do, to make sure they don't find out," Nieg had replied. His face was as wintry as the hills outside Task Force Borha's camp.

She brought her attention back to Zimmer's long dark face and decided that satisfying Zimmer had an overriding priority. Otherwise she might not find out what else was wrong, when it could be something serious enough to get her people killed.

"Esteva's working for Intelligence. Not internal security, at least not anymore. Strictly who's who in the opposition. It was suggested that he could do a better job if he went with the volunteers."

"I had a feeling it might be something like that. If you'll forgive me for saying so, you aren't the kind of officer to let somebody go off for personal vengeance when it's going to hurt the Company."

"I'll forgive a lot of compliments like that. If I'd had a completely free hand, Esteva's about the last person I'd have sent. I can't afford to break in *two* new bodyguards at once!"

Zimmer smiled. "Want me to look around for a couple of people who can work with Esteva when he gets back?"

"Be my guest."

Now, what should I offer in return? Not for the first time, Shores decided that there ought to be a class in company-level small-group politics at OTC. The leadership class barely scratched the surface.

"I guess the letter of commendation can wait. I'll be over for chess. I also have a nasty feeling that the Mount Houton mess is going to need a few more volunteer advisers before long. Sit down with Strauch and pick a few reliable names from 4th Platoon to throw into the hat.

"Oh, and how close is Strauch to being command-qualified? I know he's good, but does he look good on the record?"

"With things the way they are, he'll need a couple of waivers."

"Maybe I can arrange that. No promises, and don't let Strauch get his hopes up. But I'll see what I can do."

"Thanks, Captain."

"See you about 1930."

Shores wondered where would be the best place to start to get Strauch formally qualified to command the platoon. If she could swing that, then she could go on to swing Lieutenant Khabi by his—no, that would be little harsh.

The fact remained that he'd ignored a problem with his platoon until it put his platoon sergeant and the company Top in the embarrassing position of having to bypass him. They were good people, with something like fifty years of service between them. Zimmer wouldn't have been here unless he saw a crisis looming.

And if it turns out that Khabi promised to talk to me and then didn't keep that promise . . .

Composing what she would say to the lieutenant in that event was more than emotionally satisfying. It seemed to release a plug on her creativity somewhere. Piccone's letter of commendation seemed to roll off her fingers.

The altitude display showed seventy kilometers. To the east, the horizon showed a distinct curve. Joanna Marder realized that this was the first time she'd climbed so high since the Bushranger rebellion began.

In the seat beside her, the civilian who called himself Lorne was sweating as if the attacker cabin had been a sauna. Cosmophobia? If he was Intelligence—and he certainly smelled of it—Marder was sorry that they weren't going high enough to bring on a full-scale attack.

On the ground, the sunset line now lay well to the west of Mount Houton and was creeping toward Kellysburg. Marder's hands itched to step up the magnification and see if the fighting in Mount Houton was visible. Light infantry weapons wouldn't be, but if any of the rumors were true about heavier stuff coming in—

"Radar lock-on," the pilot said. "At least three different scans."

"Any IDs?" Marder asked. She modulated her voice carefully. SOP filled no vacuum here, not when she wasn't rated attacker crew.

"One Federation, one of those Bushranger sets—I think— and something I can't even guess at. Only reason I can make the Fed set clearly is the power. Everybody's interfering with everybody else."

"Let's hope it doesn't blank out our IFF."

Lorne rewarded Marder by sweating even harder. The pilot set the IFF to max power to make sure that it would punch through all the radar interference and tell the world that this was Alliance attacker BK 721 on an authorized flight to the Armistice Commission Zone.

They'd topped out their trajectory at eighty kilometers and were on the way down before any acknowledgment came. They were clear as far as the Bushranger government troops and the Federation were concerned.

If the rebels heard, they didn't reply. The pilot looked at Marder. She decided to hand the credit he wanted to pass right back to him.

"Our orders are to avoid any incidents or provocations. Can you bring us right down the hole on top of Commission HQ?"

"That won't protect us against heavy AD weapons," Lorne said.

"The only people who have any are the Feds," Marder said. "Unless you suspect that the rebels have acquired some, or the Bushrangers have redeployed some from the Mount Houton area."

Lorne's look confirmed Marder's suspicion that he was Intelligence. It also made her suspect that she'd exceeded the amount of probing what Intelligence allowed to line officers.

She decided to be more careful. If Lorne ended up wanting her court-martialed for "noncooperation," she wanted to be innocent.

The altimeter began unwinding. Seventy-five kilometers, seventy-two, seventy—

"If you can bring us down the hole, do it," Marder said. The pilot nodded.

"If you can't, bring us in over Republican government forces. They may be a little less trigger-happy."

"Shouldn't we make an all-modes sensor scan and recording if we do that?" Lorne asked.

They dropped to sixty-four kilometers before Marder decided she wanted an explanation for that question.

"If they've got any sort of receivers, they'll pick up the scan. What if they regard it as a hostile act?"

"I didn't think about that. Sorry."

Right. Sorry as Genghis Khan about sacking a city.

121

"Think about it. Your ass is riding in this bucket along with ours."

"All right, all right." The glare didn't come back, but the petulance was a blatant act. "I just thought the recording might be a nice present for the Federation. A goodwill gesture, to get reopening the Commission off on the right foot."

"Maybe, but I'd say it's not worth the risks."

Lorne now looked sulky but said nothing. If he went along with her on this in front of witnesses, he'd have a job getting her for noncooperation. What charge would he try then?

Probably depends on what his superiors will threaten to do to him if he comes back without the recording.

Marder decided that Lorne would need watching the whole time they were grounded in the Commission Zone. The trouble was that might be as much as two days, and she couldn't stay awake that long, trust anybody else to watch Lorne, or signal for help.

Oh well, at least it's another incentive to stay sober.

Actually that was turning out to be easier than she'd expected. For a week she'd been surrounded by people who either didn't know about her problem or didn't think anything they said would affect it. If she stayed sober, fine; if she got drunk, fine, as long as she was fit for duty at the right time. The prospect of her drinking didn't twist a knife in anybody's guts the way it did to Paul.

"Fifty-five kilometers, people," the pilot said. "Strap in. Arm all decoys and warm up the jammers."

"Coming up, skipper," chorused weapons officer and E.W.O. Like Marder, the copilot looked silently at the screen as Mount Houton dropped out of sight below the steadily advancing horizon.

"That's the last trach set," Lucco DiVries said, handing Dr. Nosavan the wrapped package.

The doctor didn't even raise an eyebrow until he had the set fixed to the latest throat-wound case. Then he said something in his ancestral Thai that DiVries decided wouldn't bear translating.

Nosavan started to wipe his forehead with his left hand, then remembered the blood on his gloves. "Get me a sweatband, Lucco. Check the oxygen bottles on the other trach sets on your way, too. Can you change a bottle?"

"Well—"

"Yes or no?"

"Sorry. I could change them if we had any fresh bottles. Every charged bottle we've got is in use."

"That may be about to change," came Sophie Bergeron's voice. DiVries turned, to see the captain weaving through the cots, with BoJo Johnson leading her. BoJo, DiVries decided, was mellowing a bit. The hospital's twelve-year-old self-appointed security guard and reception committee now kept his pistol holstered inside the hospital, even if he kept the flap unsnapped.

"For the better or for the worse?" Nosavan snapped.

"Doctor, that's defeatist—"

" 'Defeatism' is a disease of little commissars' imaginations—"

"The bullets in their guns aren't imaginary, Dr. Nosavan," DiVries put in. "One way things could get much worse very fast is for you to find that out the hard way."

Nosavan raised his eyes to the patched and scabby ceiling of the storeroom-turned-hospital-ward. "I prayed as hard as I could that all the commissars would join the rebels. It seems I am not worthy to have such a prayer answered."

"Don't waste time prayin'," shouted somebody from a nearby cot. "Just get me up and around. The pols who don't join the rebels'll wish they had!"

DiVries led Nosavan, Bergeron, and BoJo toward the foreman's alcove that now housed Nosavan's desk and heavy equipment. That was far enough from the eighty-odd wounded to mute all but the loudest cries and screams. There weren't as many of those as DiVries had expected at first, but when he learned why, he'd rather have had the noise.

Medevac was sporadic, so a lot of the badly wounded didn't make it to the hospital. Then the triage left more of them stuck quietly in corners, loaded with painkillers and prayers for their quick death.

People who weren't badly wounded, Nosavan and his assistants patched up as quickly as possible and sent back to their units. If they got as far as the hospital in the first place, that is. On his three medevac runs, DiVries had seen at least twenty legitimate wound stripes walking around, weapons in hand.

"So, what's going to change things?" Nosavan asked when they reached the alcove. He turned to warm up the kettle, discovered that it was still hot by upsetting it on his leg, and hopped around on one foot while DiVries sloshed cold water on the scalded leg and Bergeron tried not to laugh.

BoJo didn't try. He curled up in a chair, holding his sides and laughing until the chair rocked. It finally fell over; he leaped up and gave it a sharp kick.

"Enough," DiVries said as he rolled up Dr. Nosavan's pants to apply burn ointment to the scalds.

The boy glowered but sat down again. DiVries smeared on the ointment and wondered again why the orphan boy seemed to obey him even when nobody else could so much as get him to acknowledge their existence.

Maybe BoJo was picking up on DiVries's thoughts about him: *There but for the grace of God and Raimondo go I.* Without his older brother growing up overnight and taking charge, Lucco DiVries might have been like BoJo, a child thrust out into the streets from a disintegrating home, living by his wits until no one would foster him, dragged into an orphanage that was one step better than prison or the grave but no more. . . .

Not to mention the whole orphanage being chased up here to what they thought would be safety when the Republic seceded, then finding that the war had caught up with them.

"I'm on my way back from a battalion briefing," Bergeron said. "The first group of volunteers is bringing in their convoy tomorrow. They didn't give us an ETA."

"They don't trust the company commanders?" Nosavan sputtered.

"They probably don't know themselves," DiVries said, although privately he wondered if the doctor might not be right. Security in this civil war was somewhere between negligible and zero. The only reason this hadn't done much harm so far was the mutual lack of resources to take advantage of it.

This might be about to change. If the rebels could prevent the convoy reaching the government troops, or even better, capture it intact . . .

"The convoy's bringing in ammunition, medical supplies, some food. We're going on Alert One at midnight tonight because we think the rebels may try to attack us before we're resupplied. Or they might pull troops out to attack the convoy, and we can hit them here while they're weak."

She hesitated. "This isn't an order, just a suggestion. It might not be a bad idea for all the hospital people to have a gun handy."

124

"The rebels—they—how?" Nosavan was so outraged he could barely speak for a moment. "We have a good many of their wounded with us, not to mention prisoners. Do they want to start an atrocity competition?"

Bergeron nodded. "Some of them do. Or at least that's the rumor, but you know that rumor in war always makes the enemy out to be a monster. . . ."

Sometimes it isn't just rumor, DiVries thought. *And what's worse, as often as not all the monsters aren't on the other side. What some of our would-be commissars could do with a "massacre" at this hospital . . .*

DiVries decided that regulations, oaths, Armistice terms, direct orders, or God Almighty notwithstanding, he was going to find himself a gun as soon as he could!

Through the open door, Brian Mahoney heard the sound of the wind, pallets rattling across a spraycrete floor, and Brigitte Tachin's voice raised in polite indignation.

"I know those fuse testers are combat-rated," she was telling some unseen Victorian militia volunteer. "But I spent half a Standard Year on Alcuin learning how many ways combat-rated electronics can go out. Believe me, if you treat them like bricks, some of them will be as useless. People can be killed by undetected fuse faults."

"All right, all right. Don't get all that nice hair up your arse," came a grumbling male voice. At least the man sounded sober. "I'll get Wally over for loading them. He used to be a cargomaster for Jervis Haulers."

"I'm sure Wally knows his business. Just remember that the loading is still your responsibility, for better or worse."

The man's reply was inaudible, but the tone didn't sound any more insubordinate than Mahoney had come to expect from the Victorian militia. They seemed to feel that the Federation was in their debt simply because they'd volunteered. Anything else, such as obeying Federation officer "advisers," was an unreasonable imposition.

Tachin stepped through the door and slid it shut behind her. She looked so drawn and pale that Mahoney vacated the one chair in the cubicle for her. She slumped into it, then put her hands between her thighs. After warming them there for a moment, she started rubbing them together.

"Frostbite kicking up again?" Mahoney asked.

"A little bit. But I can't wear gloves in the warehouse. Not when some of those volunteers aren't even wearing shirts! You know what they'd say about fancy-dancy Feddie offisahs."

"Too bloody roight," Mahoney said. His imitation of a Victorian accent made her smile.

"That's better. Tea, coffee, or chocolate?"

"Coffee."

"Anything in it? It'll have to be local whiskey—"

Tachin pretended to spit decorously. "Straight coffee, thank you. The company commander said he expects a movement order in the next hour or so. We'll be lifting out before midnight."

The cold of a Victorian winter night seemed to rip through the warehouse walls, the office walls, and Mahoney's skin, to chill his vital organs. He forced himself to his feet, and by the time he'd drawn two cups of coffee he could trust his voice and his hands.

"Just remember that you and I have done our share of being heroes," he said. "Keep your head down and give somebody else a chance."

"Oh, I will be careful. If I can, without losing authority over these *sacré* volunteers. Even sober, they can't always tell care from cowardice."

"Blast the volunteers!"

"If we don't reach Mount Houton in time, the rebels may do just that."

Pouring himself another cup of coffee was the best answer Mahoney could think of. The steady attrition of the fighting in Mount Houton had changed the original plan of having the Federation advisers stay south of the Republic's border. Now half of them were riding the supply convoys all the way north to Mount Houton, armed for "self-defense," but not equipped with their own heavy weapons or provided with air cover. Mahoney liked to think that he would have called this a half-assed solution, even if Brigitte hadn't been one of the advisers going north.

Tachin set her empty cup down on a pile of folders. "Be sure to take your own advice, too. Your frostbite was worse than mine and this base could draw a rebel attack. What happens if they rocket you out of this nice cozy office and you have to run around playing soldier again?"

"Then maybe I can put in for that J.O.O.W. qualification instead of another commendation. Dr. Mori's recommended taking me off waiver for full shipboard duty. Says my lungs are completely cleaned out."

"Wonderful."

She stood and leaned her head against Mahoney's chest, pretending to listen to his lungs. His arms went around her, holding her gently. The embrace he wanted to give might break her; it would certainly break the moment.

"Now," she said. "Can I use your office for changing into my field gear?"

"Be my guest."

Mahoney heaved the dark blue bag on to the table as Tachin began wrestling her sweater over her head.

Twelve

The drone of small-arms fire and the thump of grenades slowly faded. In five minutes it faded enough that Lucco DiVries and Dr. Nosavan could talk without shouting. From the looks on the faces of the wounded, it hadn't faded enough.

"That sounds like the last of it," the doctor said, picking up a bottle of wound sealer and plugging it into a battered sprayer.

"Or it could be just another lull. That was the fifth mad minute in the last two hours."

"Are the people on the line just nervous and shooting at shadows? Or do you think something's happening?"

"The two aren't mutually exclusive," DiVries said. "If the shooting at shadows goes on long enough, one side or the other's going to start thinking the opposition's up to something. Then they'll react to what they think is happening."

"At least neither side has the troops for a full-scale offensive," Nosavan said. He looked at the small Buddha on the corner of his worktable.

DiVries hoped that was still true—or that both local commanders believed it was true, which amounted to the same thing. Not for the first time, it struck him that any career soldier could teach any psychiatrist a great deal about the effects of delusions on behavior.

Two of the teenage orphans who'd volunteered as orderlies picked up a stretcher case and started toward the diagnostic center. Until two hours ago, it had been easier to move the diagnostic scanner to the patients. Then the aisles between stretchers got too narrow for the scanner.

If this goes on for another two hours, we won't even have aisles wide enough for the stretcher bearers. It also occurred to DiVries that they hadn't seen anyone from Bergeron's company since before the first mad minute, not even casualties.

As the orderlies set the stretcher down, DiVries saw BoJo snap around and aim his pulser at the back door. It was three sizes too big for him and made him look like a boy playing soldier, until you got close enough to see his eyes.

"Who's there?"

"Friend."

"Immortal," Bojo said, giving the sign.

"Memory," came the countersign, in a high-pitched voice distorted by the heavy door. At a nod from the doctor, DiVries unlatched the door.

Amy Tucker almost fell through the door. The oldest of the orphans when the Bushranger Republic seceded, she'd come of age a month later and promptly joined the Army. DiVries remembered her as a round-faced, rather slow-moving girl. Now her face was no longer round, her movements were slow from exhaustion, and if there was anything of the girl left, she was hidden deep inside the dirty, red-eyed woman in bush suit and helmet who half walked, half stumbled into the room.

"They sent me with a patrol since they couldn't get you on the radio."

"Somebody winged the antenna for the main set, and the handhelds don't have scramblers," DiVries said.

Tucker glared at him. "Who appointed a Feddie the com off—"

"He's no Feddie, you stupid—" BoJo began.

"Enough," Nosavan said wearily. "What's the message?"

"The hospital's going to be evacuated. The patrol will provide security for anybody who can walk, and weapons for anybody who can use one. For the rest, they're going to lay on a medevac flight. How many will you need?"

Nosavan punched up figures on the computer lying next to the Buddha.

"About ten flights."

"Good-oh. What's signal strength from inside here?"

"What are you carrying?" DiVries asked.

"A 10-6B."

"Better step outside. I'll cover you."

"Hey, Lucco," BoJo almost whined. "You're med and under oath. Let me go."

"I'll let you go sometime when it's dangerous. You can't prove anything on a milk run like this."

Tucker opened the door and led DiVries into the back alley before BoJo could reply. They crouched, waited in silence for two minutes that felt like half an hour, then started working their way down the alley toward the open street.

They'd reached a trash bin when DiVries, who was leading, detected movement halfway along the next stretch of alley. Armed soldiers—definitely more than one—were apparently climbing out of the solid street.

"Tucker," DiVries whispered. "Report unidentified troops in squad-plus strength, climbing out of an access hole in the alley between the seven-hundred blocks of Ness and Fitzgerald streets."

"Will do."

DiVries lay down and started counting while Tucker slipped back behind the trash bin. "Apricot, Apricot," he heard her whisper. "Apricot to College One—"

Pulsers droned from the distant alley, and solid slugs ripped into the trash bin. A burst chewed up filth-caked plascrete, driving grit into DiVries's left eye. The right one still showed him the flashes, then the incoming concussion grenades.

The grenades fell a little short. If they'd landed farther back in the alley, the blast trapped between the buildings would have laid out both DiVries and Tucker the way the enemy intended.

Instead the grenades spent most of their energy flipping the trash bin up on end. DiVries's ears rang and his eyes watered as garbage rained down on him. Through the ringing he heard a scream.

Blinking his good eye clear, he saw that the upended bin had caught Tucker across the thighs. She was writhing desperately to get out from under the crushing weight. DiVries started crawling toward her.

"No, damn you!" she screamed. "The radio. Here—I'm Apricot Two, calling College—oh, God!"

"I heard you," DiVries said, snatching the radio. *I only hope God or somebody else does, too.*

"Apricot Two calling College One," DiVries said. "Apricot Two calling College One. Come in, College One. Hostile report from Apricot Two to College One . . ."

He prayed to hear a voice instead of static, and tried to shut his ears against the faint animal whimpers from behind him.

*   *   *

A thousand kilometers to go, to Mount Houton.

Brigitte Tachin stared through the frosted side window of her lifter at the darkness rushing past outside. It was the kind of darkness that an unimaginative poet would have called "velvet."

Tachin knew better: a Victorian winter night rasped like a file on your skin. She didn't want to feel that rasp again. She wanted to feel something like velvet, or better yet, the touch of warm human skin. Best of all, the touch of a particular warm human, Brian Mahoney.

Danger doing things to one's hormones was no longer a theoretical concept for Tachin. But doing anything about those hormones was. *Discipline, Tachin. Without it both you and Brian aren't going to survive long enough to compare notes on your hormones.*

At seven hundred kilometers, Tachin's seat tilted as the lifter swung onto a new course. In the darkness for twenty kloms on either side, sixty-odd lifters were supposed to be doing the same.

Tachin was prepared to bet they'd do it—probably as well as a similar contingent of Federation Army cargo haulers could have managed, at night, at low altitude, without lights or major navaids, and maintaining radio silence. Victorian bush pilots, she decided, could get more performance out of less capable equipment than any other pilots she'd known.

At 450 kilometers, Tachin's superior night sight picked out a new lifter joining the formation, in their eight-o'clock position.

"Should we ask for an ID?"

The pilot shook his head. "Naah. Probably some local civvie bus. Besides, there's bound to be somebody locked and loaded in *his* six o'clock, and the C.O.'s keeping a listening watch. This bloke does or says anything he shouldn't, he'll get it up the arse so fast it'll come out his ears."

Tachin had the feeling that she'd been told as much as she was going to hear without being told everything she needed to know. From the expression on the face of Sergeant Esteva, the senior Army adviser aboard, he had the same feeling.

At three hundred kilometers, the Victorian C.O., Colonel Borrie, came on the radio.

"All hands. We have to make a slight change of plans. Reports from Mount Houton indicate a major rebel attack

131

is under way. Our positions in the city have been hit both frontally and by infiltration through the sewers.

"Also, rebels in company-plus strength have been airlanded to the south of the city. Their reported positions are within four kilometers of where we are supposed to land. We have no additional information at this time on rebel weapons or air support."

Esteva and Tachin looked at each other and missed the next few words—

"—hot LZ. At the very best, we can expect to have to assist the support troops coming out from the city in providing security for the ground vehicles. So we're going to make a preliminary landing in Formation R, then regroup by companies."

Tachin tuned out reminders about battledress, camouflaging skin, and drawing full ammunition loads. She wondered if the landing wasn't sacrificing too much time, then decided that Borrie knew what he was doing.

The enemy almost had to know they were coming by now, even if the radio message had to be relayed by a series of rebel stations. So the best thing to do was organize to fight their way into Mount Houton, and the best way to do that was land. In a remote area, visual signals or even messengers could handle communications, and the lifters wouldn't be eating into their power reserves while they regrouped.

All lifters were flying with less than half their maximum payload, to make the whole hop from the border to Mount Houton nonstop. They still had at most a two-hundred-klom margin for error. A little too much circling time plus an unexpected headwind could land them all too far from Mount Houton to play any role in the battle except that of helpless target for rebel missile-sniper teams.

Colonel Luvic, senior Federation adviser, added her bit when Borrie went off.

"There's no question of bad faith by the Republicans. Anybody's intelligence can slip. Our job is to get those supplies into Mount Houton and into the hands of the Republican forces. If we have to shoot off some of the ammunition in order to deliver the rest—well, we all knew we weren't joining the Civil Action Corps!

"Good luck."

The copilot started glaring around the cabin when Luvic

mentioned "bad faith." She went on glaring until Esteva glared back, and the pilot put a hand on her shoulder.

Tachin thanked God she hadn't been the one to decide what to say. Mention bad faith, and offend the Republicans? Or ignore what every Fed would be thinking, and make your own people suspect you were keeping them in the dark?

And speaking of darkness—there were now three shadows at the eight-o'clock position, holding formation not only on Tachin's lifter but on one another. Tachin fought down an impulse to pull on her night-vision goggles; that would strain her eyes and reveal her suspicion.

She probed the darkness until the position indicator showed two hundred kilometers to go and eyestrain was ready to set in naturally. When she gave up, she still had no more than a suspicion, but it wasn't a pleasant one.

The three shadows reminded her of the gunship that had so nearly killed her and Brian and everybody else aboard *Shelia* only a few days ago.

The display tank filled the whole left half of the admiral's conference room, and the holographic display filled the whole tank. Red and blue lines crawled over the area around Mount Houton, the Blanchard Canyon area north of the supply depot, and the Armistice Commission Zone.

In one corner, General Kornilov's heavy face and broad shoulders obscured a section of the Gulf. Rose Liddell noticed that Kornilov was wearing battledress, an affectation if he was recording this briefing in his headquarters.

Be fair, Rosie. He may have recorded it just before lifting out to Task Force Borha or someplace else closer to the shooting. When Kornilov led at all, he did it from in front.

"If such a diffuse operation can be said to have a *schwerpunkt*, the rebels are clearly making Mount Houton theirs," Kornilov said. "They have attacked along the existing lines, infiltrated platoon-strength parties through the sewers, and airlanded the better part of a battalion to the south of the city."

The attacks in the city were apparently keeping the Bushrangers too busy to provide progress reports. The airlanding battalion was being engaged by government troops pulled out of the city, as well as the supply convoy's volunteers and their Federation advisers.

133

"Reports on that engagement are fragmentary but optimistic. The rebel troops appear to be either very reluctant to use their weapons or very short of ammunition—"

Or both, Liddell thought. In fact, both made more sense than either one alone. Given rebel strength according to the last intelligence reports, they must be making a desperate final push, scraping the bottom of the barrel for both troops and supplies.

"Substantial air and ground movements in the Blanchard Canyon area suggest that an assault on Border Base One is being planned. This might involve a border crossing, in which case I intend to invoke the right of hot pursuit and interpret it generously.

"The TAS company of our TacAir battalion is on pad alert for supporting the base. I would request that the Navy have one flight of attackers on station as well."

"We'll have two," Commander Gesell said. The C.O. of the 879th was in flight gear, except for her helmet. She'd piloted the attacker that brought Kornilov's recorded briefing up to *Shen*.

Kuwahara gave Gesell a double thumbs-up and turned back to the display as the Armistice Zone expanded to fill the tank. Red and blue squiggles—they hardly formed continuous lines—surrounded it.

"The government forces here amount to nearly a light battalion, with organic heavy weapons, transport, some AD, and communications. Their intervention in either Mount Houton or the Blanchard Canyon area could be decisive.

"Unfortunately, a political decision has apparently been made to retain them in position until the rebels withdraw their forces. The Republican government apparently wishes to avoid the appearance of abandoning the zone to the mercy of the rebels, even though this may cost them the war."

It occurred to Liddell that the Bushrangers might also want to avoid a situation where the rebels might come into direct conflict with regular Federation or Alliance forces. This was assuming the Alliance forces wouldn't take the rebel side and escalate the whole confrontation into something where the arming cards might be slotted into the warhead controls.

At what point do *good intentions start paving the road to hell, instead of reducing collateral damage?*

"I want to simulate an attack by Bushranger reinforcements on the rebel units in the zone area. This will force them to either redeploy or withdraw. In the latter case, the government can move its battalion to one of the active theaters. I am informed that arrangements for high-speed air transport have been made on a contingency basis."

Liddell wondered if that was the hand of Intelligence at work. Almost certainly it was the same people who'd apparently come up with three gunships for the supply convoy, if the electronic signatures picked up in the last couple of hours meant anything.

"The Zone Army commander, Major Abelsohn, has been briefed on his role. His first task is to neutralize Alliance forces presently in the zone as a source of intelligence to the rebels. His second will be to simulate the ground elements of the government attack."

An overlay of green squiggles writhed back and forth across the zone, looking more like worms having an orgy than infantry on the attack to Liddell. Kornilov's face and the red rebels vanished together, but the voice remained.

"If the Navy concurs with this initiative, I would be grateful for their support plan before 0345. If the Navy does not concur with this initiative, I must request Admiral Kuwahara, as the senior Federation officer in the Victoria System, to relieve me of my command.

"Thank you."

The cube blanked. An admiral, four captains, and a commander stared at one another. It was the commander who broke the silence.

"Subtle, isn't he?" Gesell said. "But—I'm sorry if I'm out of line—"

"You have the floor," Kuwahara said.

"Don't need it for long," Gesell said. "Just long enough to say—let's do it. I want to get those damned rebels reacting to *us* for a change. Maybe we can help the Bushrangers clean them out. At least we'll be learn just how deep the rebels are in the Alliance's pocket."

That's going to be expensive knowledge, if the price is shooting it out with Baba Lopatina, even if the Up the Sleeve Squadron's coming in.

It was also knowledge the Federation desperately needed. Liddell's head told her that, at the same time her guts were telling her that Gesell was right.

"I concur," Liddell said.

Kuwahara looked at Bogdanov and the two senior cruiser captains. Three sets of shoulders with four-striped boards shrugged. Three heads nodded.

"Good. I'll order Commodore Steckler to button up the dockyard and then we can get down to serious planning." He looked at the clock on the control panel of the display tank. "We have exactly an hour and ten minutes before Commander Gesell has to be on her way down to Kornilov with our plan."

Thirteen

"Sixty kilometers to go. ETA twenty minutes. The ground convoy's left the perimeter." The pilot's voice sounded as if his mouth was as dry as Tachin's. She was glad she didn't have to talk now.

"Any updates on hostiles?" The voice sounded like Sergeant Esteva's.

"The closest is about ten kloms up toward Shanklin Ridge from the LZ."

"Wish we had some gunships," Esteva said. "Even one pass might help."

"SOOL, chum," the pilot said. Tachin caught the hesitation in his voice, though. Did Esteva smell something, too? Or was he trying to draw the pilot?

Meaningless questions, when there was no privacy and Esteva would answer only when he wanted to.

Tachin shifted to unsnap her carbine from its hull bracket and laid it across her knees to check the magazine. Helmet and mask, battledress, medkit, rations and a canteen, and a Sobelev H65-II ordance computer were most of her load; infantry combat wasn't her MOS even tonight. But just in case, she was carrying an M-9 carbine, one magazine in and three belted, and four hand grenades.

She hoped somebody else would get the job of throwing the grenades—an irony that somebody might appreciate, considering how much time Tachin had spent working around multikiloton warheads. She'd done enough pest hunting on the farm to know her way around a pulser; the magazine came out smoothly, then slipped back in—

"Excuse me, ma'am. Can I look at that?" It was Esteva, reaching for her pulser.

She reversed the weapon and handed it to him butt first. He read the telltales on the magazine, then popped it out and pulled off the rear plate.

"Hoy! What are you—"

"Thought so. Somebody loaded it up to the full thirty-five rounds." Esteva pulled a multitool out of his vest pocket and extracted two of the 7mm slugs. "That cuts down the strain on the coil. Otherwise it can pop in the middle of a firefight and ruin your whole day."

"Thank you. Now, can you tell me if there are any surprises we should expect?"

Esteva's neatly trimmed beard twitched as he grinned. "I'd bet on a whole bunch, but not on any particular one. Don't sweat it, though. Infantry's not your job tonight, I hope."

Tachin bristled. Her hoping that was one thing. Esteva saying it out loud, as if he'd read her thoughts—doubting her courage, male protectiveness, or something worse?

"Sorry, ma'am. There are some things I can't tell you, but you don't have to worry about me being Big Papa. Captain Shores said I might run into you, and that you were a friend of her friend Brian Mahoney, and that if I missed a chance to help you, at least around the edges—well, she'd fry parts of me for breakfast that I might miss."

"Doesn't Captain Shores have enough on her mind?"

"It's a pretty big mind, Lieutenant."

Tachin unhooked her chest harness, pulled out her own multitool, and began removing the extra rounds from the three reserve magazines. Numb and unsteady fingers made for slow work. By the time she'd finished, the ETA was down to four minutes and everybody else had strapped in.

Her fingers were still numb, but they seemed to have the shakes out of them. She was grateful to the harness for cooperating, and to Esteva for not offering to help.

As the last link tightened around her diaphragm, fire scarred the darkness ahead.

"—electronics only, or decoys, too?" *Weilitsch*'s captain asked.

The space around Kuwahara's display was cramped for six senior officers at the best of times. When they all had computers on their laps and trays beside their seats, the matter density was completely out of hand.

Rose Liddell shifted in her seat, kicked over somebody's fortunately empty cup, and hoped Kuwahara would vote for decoys. If he didn't, she'd have to speak up, and take her chances on sounding afraid—

"About fifty-fifty," Kuwahara said. "The sensor people

want you to believe their megastellar toys can confuse God, but that's only to justify their budget slice. Besides, the only ship with a big enough sensor suite is *Shen*, and we need her in a better tactical position."

Thank you, Lord, who has granted Admiral Kuwahara common sense in spite of his being an admiral.

"No argument there," Bogdanov said. "But can the 879th deliver all the decoys?"

"We can, but they'll have to ride outside. That'll slow us down. Besides, if the Alliance gets a good visual on us—"

"Then we'll have the intelligence we want when they pass it on to the rebels," Kuwahara said,

"Admiral, I'm not worried about anything the rebs can do," Gesell snapped. "Not the Baba either, unless she's come down with the stupids all of a sudden. But taking three, four attackers for decoy dropping—that's so many we can't use for close support."

"I think I can solve both problems at once," the light-cruiser captain said. "The whole squadron's got its full load of decoys. We can send one down with the attackers, and use a pop-up launch for her load. Then she can stay low and be in position to help the attackers if they need it.

"Meanwhile, we can put *Novy Pskov* on call for close support, if the Blanchard Canyon folks jump the border. I had the squadron rendezvous just before we hit junk space and consolidated our whole air-to-ground load aboard her. She's no good in a space fight, but she's worth a whole attacker squadron down low."

What most impressed Liddell was that Commander Gesell let the slur on attackers pass. Kuwahara nodded.

"Well done, Captain. Captain Liddell, can you start your Weapons Department breaking out all your spare decoys an hour ago? Commander, how fast can you have four attackers up here and loaded with all the decoys *Shen* can spare?"

Gesell bent over her computer, fingers flying. Liddell shifted again, kicked another cup, and this time felt luke-warm liquid running over her foot.

Time to ring for Jensen to clean up, even if nobody wants seconds!

Sophie Bergeron's first warning of the ambush was a ring of fire around a distant hilltop as the rebels salvoed rockets. Then the radio erupted in screams, shouts, and static as mines and snipers ripped into the middle of the road convoy.

She slapped the shoulder of a pilot who needed no warning. The command lifter was already plunging toward the ground. Bergeron switched the radio to the all-hands frequency and ordered the rest of the air escort to do the same.

A hundred meters up, the rockets aimed at the escort caught up with the diving lifters. One lifter blew apart in midair and reached the ground as smoking debris. A warhead chewed up two fans on Bergeron's command machine and punched fragments through the rear hull and two riflemen sitting there. The HQ medic scrambled aft as the pilot swung the remaining fans to full descent.

They got down safely, by a margin of seconds. Another rocket screamed overhead and chewed a trough in the crest of the next hill. Bergeron and her com operator sprinted for the nearest cover, a ring of boulders; the pilot and the company clerk with the HQ computer followed.

This left four riflemen, two of them wounded, and the medic. Before they could get out, a rocket burst overhead, spraying bomblets. One went off directly behind the open rear door of the lifter. No one came out after that, only a few moans and smoke from frying electronics.

"Better get the SSW out of there," the Top said, and sprinted for the lifter. Bergeron gripped a boulder with both hands and wished that whatever was shaking, her or the ground, would stop.

Her mouth was dry and her sphincter tight; this was the normal reaction to danger. But why had her body shut down the blood supply to her brain and fingers?

It hadn't. Somewhere in her brain was embedded the notion that she was still a sergeant, who could command the troops around her and leave the rest to the company commander. *That* was shutting her down.

She told the notion to shut up instead. After long enough for the Top to return with the long-barreled SSW and its ammunition it did. She greeted him almost normally.

"Anybody alive in there?"

"No, and the night sight's out, too."

The clerk pulled her head out from under the display's night hood. "Getting lots of message fragments, Captain. Looks like the rebs are hitting hard, but strictly from the north."

Bergeron stuck her head under the hood and stared at the screen. The clerk was right. The next stage in ambushing a surface convoy after taking out the air escort was a pincer's movement against the immobilized vehicles. So far the rebels were only engaging with fire, most of it heavy weapons, and from the hills to the north of Highway 11.

Bergeron realized her brain still wasn't working right when she couldn't remember the number of the platoon riding in the trucks. Never mind, they'd know who they were, and everything else was falling into place—

"Sourball Leader, all-hands call to Sourballs. Sourballs Three and Four, take position on the military crest of"—what was the damned ridge?—"Sleeping Grumbler Ridge. Sourball Two, hold across Killick Road, south of Holmes Farm.

"Abandon all road-bound vehicles. All-terrain vehicles, pick up road-bound crews and proceed south on Killick Road to Sourball Two position. Sourball One, home in on my position."

She set the radio for repeat and scramble and prayed that all her platoons still had leaders and all the leaders still had working, scrambled radios. At least radio conditions were above average tonight, in spite of the cold—which cut both ways, because it also made command-guided rockets more dangerous.

Bergeron drank from her canteen until the inside of her mouth no longer felt ready to flake off. Then she handed it to the sergeant.

"Thanks, Captain. Think they're after just pinning us down while they go for the supplies?"

"Maybe. But if we go haring off toward the LZ without regrouping, they could push a couple of ground columns in among us. Then we'd lose the whole company."

"Not arguing, Captain. Just—bleeding Christ, what was *that*?"

The northern horizon turned into a miniature sunrise, so bright that for a moment Bergeron's brain stalled at one gruesome thought.

Nuclear explosion.

She was looking around for high ground for better observation when the night seemed to snow lifters. Bergeron had her carbine up and aimed before she recognized the markings of her own company.

Dust whipped past as a command lifter grounded less than twenty meters away. Sourball One, the leader of 1st Platoon, ran up.

"Sorry we broke contact, Captain. But right about the

time you went down, three gunships joined us from the supply convoy."

"Gunships?"

"Configured that way, sure as hell. Don't know just where the militia dug them up, but I'm glad they're on our side. One of them ran a pass to draw fire from the AD battery, then the other missiled the battery. The third one passed us hard data on the rebel positions."

The sergeant held out a data card. Between nerves and cold it took Bergeron three tries to slip it into the computer, but the results justified the effort.

She'd been right: the rebels were strictly to the north. What was more, their position could be turned into a death-trap with a little bit of luck.

A lot of luck, actually. We'll need it, to get those volunteers to move out shooting, if the Feddie advisers won't help. It didn't surprise her anymore, to think of her old comrades as "Feddies," although she avoided some of the ruder terms for Federation people.

A whole lot of luck. Either I have to push my company north against heavy weapons, or the people in the city have to push from the east.

"Sergeant. Did those gunships give you a call sign and a frequency?"

"Salamander Flight, and the standard TacAir frequency."

"Good. You get on the horn to them and get an update, including what just blew up north." If that explosion had been the rebel ammunition supply, maybe B Company wouldn't be butting heads against heavy weapons after all.

"Top, you and your oppo in the 1st deploy the platoon for dispersal and all-around defense."

"They aren't one hundred percent compatible, Captain."

"Oh, shove compatibility. Sorry, don't overdo the dispersal. I think we may want to move out of here damned fast on short notice, if I'm guessing right."

If she was guessing wrong, of course, she was risking her company and maybe the Republic. But at least she was at the point where she could risk it on her own wrong guess, not wait for somebody else's.

Keep this up, Sophie, and you may be a real officer swine before you know it!

The intercom signaled three times before Charles Longman realized that the call was coming in on the secure line. He punched in the codes and saw Major Abelsohn's face on the screen.

"Mr. Longman. How's the laser coming?"

"Pretty good. We're waiting—"

"For what?"

"For Chief Dalmas to get back with the new integrator board. He's going to test it before he leaves the storeroom so we won't have a dud."

"Applause, I think," Abelsohn said. "How fast is that likely to be?"

Hamilton looked at the overhead, three centimeters above his sweaty, tangled hair, and uttered a mental prayer to Murphy, God of Engineers.

"Twenty minutes after Dalmas gets back."

"Good. I'll tell him that it's an emergency and provide an escort for him."

"Escort—" Longman began, but the screen was blank. For a moment, so was his mind. Then he added the scrambled line and the "escort" together and came up with the sum of *Trouble*.

If the Armistice Zone was about to see another round of fighting, that meant another D-4 bunker with his tail on the line. The best-shaped tail, Brigitte Tachin's, was already on the line with the supply convoy. Brian Mahoney might have to go north, and even if he stayed at Border Base One, he might be standing on a target.

The only D-4 who was safe tonight was Elayne Zheng, probably going slowly crazy in *Shen*'s sickbay. Correction: she was safe tonight unless *Shen* got caught in the shooting. Then she would be the only D-4 who could neither run nor fight back.

Longman realized that he'd be perfectly happy to do either, but fighting would do more to cure the boredom of Armistice Zone duty. Abelsohn had given him a chance at a fresh start, making him assistant maintenance officer, but there just wasn't that much work in the job.

Part of it was the maintenance officer, an ex-warrant who liked hands-on work even more than Longman and didn't have a family of admirals to inhibit the impulse. Part of it was the low profile the whole zone was keeping. The civilians were gone, likewise all Bushranger troops on either side. Just outside the zone, half a battalion of government troops was keeping the rebels from making trouble for anyone.

Inside the zone now was a weak rifle company from each major power, plus a small mixed technical staff. With everything this bobtailed garrison didn't need stowed and locked, maintenance requirements were minimal.

Longman had disconsolately pushed data until tonight, when the auxiliary communications laser went down. Abelsohn had called a department heads' meeting, so Longman was left to entertain himself by helping Chief Dalmas run the diagnostic tests, then dig into the hardware itself, sleeves rolled up, sweaty, dirty, and happy as—as a man doing what he really enjoyed doing.

"Lieutenant, you in there? I've been knocking for five minutes."

It was Chief Dalmas. Longman cringed at the thought of what Abelsohn would say about his woolgathering, but managed to punch the door release.

Dalmas scurried in, the integrator over his shoulder, and two more Navy chiefs behind him. Hamilton rose, recognized one, and almost had to sit down again.

Master Chief Gunner Lo ignored the officer's surprise, as he usually ignored almost everything officers did short of direct orders or indecent propositions. He sat down at the console, tested the major programs, then ran one final test.

A satisfied grunt, and he leaned back in the seat. Hamilton risked a look over Lo's shoulder. As he'd suspected, the laser was now ready to be tight-focused at full power. Tight-focused at full power, it could still be a communications device, but it was also a ship-killing weapon.

The noise of the wounded in the hospital seemed to double every five minutes. Lucco DiVries knew that was only his imagination, compounded by the crack on the head that he'd taken in the alley.

The noise was increasing, though, in direct proportion to the decrease in Dr. Nosavan's supply of painkillers. He was now doing minor work like cleaning the grit from DiVries's eye without any painkillers. What he had left was reserved for major casualties, like Amy Tucker with her broken thighs, crushed kneecaps, and probable internal injuries.

Head, eye, and all, DiVries still considered himself fit for any work that didn't involve standing or walking. He'd just finished an inventory of wound-dressing supplies and handed about half of the depressingly small amount to a nurse when he realized someone was actually *knocking* on the front door.

A moment later the back door echoed the knocking, and a moment after that someone let off a pulser burst outside. The burst's echo was an uproar of shouting, including threats to dismember the fool who'd wasted ammunition and endangered his comrades with ricochets. DiVries would have enjoyed the uproar more if it hadn't included several rebel political slogans.

Well, I've really been expecting this since the rebel push, and nobody can say I'm anyplace illegal.

Correction: nobody could say it and be right, but somebody who was concerned about creating an incident instead of being right—

The nurse put down the dressings and walked to the door. "This is a hospital, serving civilian and military casualties of both sides," he called. "Have you come to evacuate any rebel—"

"Action for Independence!" a voice outside snarled. DiVries had the feeling he'd heard that snarl before.

"Casualties?" the nurse concluded.

"We have to come in, secure any weapons, and post a guard for everybody's protection," a deeper voice said. "Now, can you open the door or do we have to torch it?"

"Blow it!" came the snarl again. The deeper voice's reply was unintelligible and probably unprintable. Before the dialogue could continue, Dr. Nosavan nodded to the nurse. The door slid open, and six rebels walked in.

Actually, five walked and one, who'd been leaning against the door, fell. He quickly got up and started glaring around the room, as if trying to find the one who'd been responsible for his loss of dignity. DiVries's years as a recruit training petty officer made him smell drugs.

The rebel leader was a thickset dark man, with graying hair revealed by his thrown-back hood and a lieutenant's bars inked on the shoulders of his jacket. But DiVries's eyes promptly shifted to the man standing behind him.

Now he remembered where he'd heard that snarling voice before. It was the fanatical lance corporal from Company C of the Victoria Brigade's Fourth Battalion, who'd favored killing the fleeing officers when the company mutinied. Now the man wore a sergeant's stripes, but the same hungry look and eyes that sought something to destroy or at least hurt. DiVries felt sick at the thought of those eyes finding him.

He couldn't stifle a groan. All the rebels looked at him, but the lieutenant was the first to speak.

"What's the trouble with him?"

"Concussion," Nosavan said briskly. "He got it pulling in wounded. If you'd like a breakdown of our casualties, I'd be happy to give you . . ."

DiVries didn't listen to Nosavan's relentless recital of medical statistics. He was too busy thanking higher powers for the doctor's quick wits. He was also trying to remember the rest of the symptoms of concussion. Pretending to be more seriously hurt than he was might not help, but it certainly couldn't do any harm.

Fourteen

Brian Mahoney scrambled down the last meters of rubble-strewn slope, nearly pitched onto his hands, but caught himself in time. His precariously regained balance promptly vanished in fanwash as the last six lifters of the second convoy took off.

This time he landed sitting. He stayed down until the last lifter had rounded the spur of Cheek Hill. By then the chill of the ground was nibbling through even his insulated battledress, but he'd counted five K/G-96s out of the six lifters.

That made a total of eighteen K/G-96s out of the twenty-five lifters in the last convoy. A fact that might be random coincidence, unless one correlated it with another fact.

The Kobayashi/Gusewitz-96 was license-built (or assembled) on more than fifty planets. One reason for this popularity was that its basic design included onboard power supply, circuitry, and socketing for a variety of military conversions.

Mahoney stood up, brushing grit from his clothes. Now that he thought of it, the cargo manifests he'd wrestled with these past two days had been remarkably reticent about the contents of a good many crates. Weight and dimensions were there in all the necessary detail, because no pilot would lift out otherwise. But contents were frequently such fuzzy categories as "lifter spares" or "ammunition: handle with care."

A big lifter with four contrarotating drive props floated in, caught the ground-anchoring gear, and pulled itself down on to the pad. As the props whined into silence, a familiar square figure on a trail bike emerged from the dust and started climbing the hill toward Mahoney.

"Hi, Karl. One of these days that bug's going to scramble the air controllers' sensors and Major Wausau's going to scramble you."

Karl Pocher seemed to have been issued a new face since his battle against the hijackers aboard *Leon Brautigan,* one incapable of smiling. He managed a jerky nod as he dismounted, then shifted the sling on his magazine scattergun.

"Brian. I've just heard they want me as the Fed adviser aboard our big friend." He pointed at the lifter, its rear ramp now dropping to the ground.

"Where the hell are they taking her, that the crew needs advice? That bird must have come off a Category One passenger route."

"She's a quick-changer, so it might be cargo, but yeah, I see what you mean. Hell of a big target to take up north."

"What makes you think she's going north?"

Pocher's bleak look told Mahoney that he'd put his foot in it. There was nothing behind the thought except Pocher's desire to get a shot at the people who'd killed his crew.

"If she's not going north, I'm not going with her."

Pocher had a certain amount of license, for winning *Leon Brautigan* back. The waiver for active duty, the trail bike, and the scattergun proved that. Mahoney doubted that the license extended to disobeying direct orders.

The argument was ended before it could start, by the sudden wail of the alarm siren. Pitched to cut through even the heaviest ear protection anywhere on the base, at a range of fifty meters it made Mahoney want to scream. He clapped his hands over his ears, while Pocher switched on his helmet radio.

The siren died; Pocher listened for another half minute, then turned back to Mahoney. "They've spotted unidentified movement in the southwest quadrant, inside the kill zone. Can you keep an eye on the bike? I've got to run."

"Sure."

Mahoney gripped a handlebar of the bike. As he did, six Federation advisers burst out of the air-control shelter just downhill. They wore full combat gear—"advisers" suddenly transformed into an augmented rifle team, complete with SSW.

Mahoney had swung one leg over the seat of the bike when the sky blazed with patches of artificial daylight as high-powered flares burst over the base. A laser on the edge of the landing pad started picking them off, its beam lost in the glare.

Two 150mm launchers started slamming rounds into the sky. They were firing either shells or inert rockets; no trails told Mahoney where the friendlies were aiming.

The enemy didn't leave him so ignorant. Rocket trails scarred the sky as the last of the flares died. The laser shifted targets and the launchers started firing AD frag clusters. Four rockets still got through, leaving eye-searing blue-white flames spreading where they hit.

Pocher swore. The big lifter's props were turning again and her ramp was going up. The ground crew scattered as the props went into reverse. The lifter careened across the pad, heading backward away from the nearest of the flames.

Mahoney tried to plot the four marker-rocket hits and draw his sidearm at the same time. He succeeded in dropping the pistol without plotting any of the hits except the one by the pad.

"Here." Pocher handed him the pistol muzzle-first, sights activated and all telltales reading clear.

"Thanks." One blaze on the pad, one over by the launchers but not on them, thank the saints for small mercies, one on the crest of Cheek Hill, and one—

"Blast!"

One blue-white flame danced on the hillside right above the ravine where shelters for half the remaining supplies were dug into the rock, and a cave entrance led to the rest. A blue-white flame, sending out a thermal impulse that would register on the most simple-minded heat-seeking guidance system. A guidance system like the rebel rockets that would certainly be coming in soon, with infantry probably not far behind them—

"Karl! Hop on." Mahoney straddled the bike, holstered his pistol, then switched on the power.

"What?"

"I don't know if we have any decoy flares ready. If we don't, maybe we can improvise something from the reserve supplies."

Pocher nodded. The bike churned dust and gravel, then started climbing the hill. The motor's whine set Mahoney's teeth on edge and every bump threatened to knock them loose, but he didn't dare slow down.

Thirty seconds. That was the time it would take incoming rockets to lock on to the thermal targets. How long it would take them to reach the lock-on point, and how long after that before they hit, Mahoney didn't know but wished he did. The answer might be how long he had to live.

The last squad of volunteers had drawn their grenades and marched off into the darkness. Brigitte Tachin saw that a half-empty case remained. She also noticed that most of its contents were illuminating grenades.

Shielding her four frag grenades with her body from the crew, she slipped them one by one into the crate. When she stood up again, she had four illuminating grenades in their place on her harness.

"Defectives, ma'am?" a voice said behind her.

She nearly had her carbine in firing position when she recognized Sergeant Esteva.

"Oh, hello, Sergeant. No, or at least the grenades aren't defective. My knowledge of how to throw a frag safely may be. So I thought I could light things up without hurting anybody."

"Maybe, maybe not. Thing is, Lieutenant, you've got to throw them just in the right place if you don't want to light up your friends. Also, they can burn a hole right through your body armor and your body if they light on you."

"I'll remember that."

"Heard anything on the fighting?" the sergeant asked.

"The ammunition parties have all come from their companies' reserves. Nobody's come back from the firing line to tell me anything."

"I think Borrie and Luvic want to keep up the pressure. Thing is, looks like we may have lucked out. *Something* took out most of the rebs' heavy-weapons ammo—"

"Those—things that look like gunships?"

"Maybe. Maybe somebody pissed on a live fuse and shorted it into action. I don't know. But the rebs seem to have gone to ground in front of us. They're trying to push south, but they aren't having much luck there either."

"I thought there wasn't anything but the convoy from the city to the south."

"Yeah, but they seem to be putting up a hell of a fight. I hear it was Sophie Bergeron's company flying escort on the convoy. Don't know about the rumor that she grabbed off the lion's share of the ex-regulars for her cadre, but she's got a good head."

"No arguing there."

"No. We'll probably need some help from the city once they've sorted things out there. I hope they don't wait until the second convoy arrives."

"It's on the way?"

"ETA about 0900."

"Then I can let my people get some sleep."

"Make sure they get something hot first, and have a couple awake at all times for security. The rebs can't be completely ready to pack it in, or they wouldn't have hit Camp Sklarinsky."

Tachin frowned.

"Sorry, ma'am. That's what the troops have nicknamed Border Base One. I forgot it's not official. We don't even use the name around the Vickies. They probably want to name it after the first trooper they lose. Oh well, if the rebs are pushing at it, they'll get their chance."

Tachin nodded and sat down. "Thank you, Sergeant. Let me know as soon as you learn anything more about the attack. I'll be taking the first watch myself, after we eat, so there's no rush."

"Sure, Lieutenant."

Esteva was a fleeting silhouette against the flickering glow on the hilltops, then he vanished. Tachin sat on the crate until she had her legs and voice under control.

Tracer streamed overhead and played along the line of trucks. Four streams at first, then three; Sophie Bergeron thought she heard cursing from where the fourth SSW had jammed.

"Sourball Leader to Sourballs Two and Four," she radioed. "Commencing supporting fires. Move on my visual signal. Counting down, ten, nine, eight—"

At "zero" the shadows around her broke apart into fixed and moving shadows. The moving ones scurried or scrambled or sometimes staggered down the slope toward the road. Even with night-vision goggles, it took a little imagination to see them as two platoons of Republican soldiers, counterattacking toward Killick Road and the abandoned convoy.

Bergeron waited until most of the moving shadows had pulled well ahead, then signaled to her com operator. They picked their way down a steep slope, then broke into a trot as they reached level ground.

The SSWs ceased fire; Bergeron heard the platoon leaders calling them forward. She hoped the gunners would hurry. In her old regular brigade, an attack like this would be supported by at least one SSW per squad, just like the T.O. said. Three SSWs for two platoons was spreading it thin, even against an enemy with a good deal of the fight knocked out of them.

The rebel attack across the road had slowed when they lost heavy-weapons support; wherever the gunships came from, they'd earned their pay. Booby-trapped trucks and mines handed out a bloody nose. Then in open country south of the road, untrained and shaken troops faced SSWs, snipers, grenades, more mines, and even a couple of hearty troopers who liked to go hand-to-hand with knives.

The rebels never got to the main position of Bergeron's company and the convoy crews. The two platoons going forward now had the job of finding out where they'd stopped, and pushing them back if that was too close.

One of the SSWs opened up again. Grenade launchers flared in the truck line: rebels still holding and fighting. The first SSW ceased fire but another and a rifle squad opened up, then grenades were going both ways and trucks started burning—

A power pack blew in an eye-stabbing flare as Bergeron broke into a run. Being with a two-platoon assault at all wasn't normally part of a company commander's job, but the casualties hadn't all been on the rebel side. Bergeron's company was short an X.O., 3rd Platoon its leader, and about twenty other recovered casualties were crammed into a grounded lifter serving as aid station and warming hut.

Bergeron caught up with the rear of 3rd Platoon as the other two SSWs opened up again. Over the last stretch of broken ground moving and fixed shadows mingled again, and she didn't dare shoot. Nobody shot at her, either, and she reached the road with a hand free to help the com operator climb the embankment.

Through the gaps between the trucks Bergeron scanned the ground north of the road. A few immobile heat pulses showed enemy wounded or maybe would-be surrenders. She'd have to put a squad out there soon to police up. Otherwise the surrenders might get their nerve back, and the cold would kill the wounded as dead as the rebels lying by the trucks, shredded or gutted by the booby traps.

Someone scrambled up on top of a truck cab to get more range, and promptly fell off. Bergeron heard a woman cursing ice, too loudly to be seriously hurt.

"Sourball Leader to Camperdown. We are on the objective, and it is secured. Light resistance and light casualties on both sides."

Camperdown—Brigade HQ—didn't reply for ten minutes. That was long enough for Bergeron to update her casualty figures, send the squad north, and hear that the Top was coming forward with an ammo resupply.

She was actually on the radio when the resupply arrived. The first thing she knew about it was when the Top shoved a steaming cup under her nose.

"Yech!"

"Sourball Leader, repeat that last message."

"Sorry, Camperdown. Just got a surprise package from my first sergeant." She wrapped one hand around the cup, letting the heat seep through her glove while she went on talking.

"I've got two platoons on the position, but both are short a leader now. Yeah, the 2nd's got a slug in the knee. Probably going to be short a leg for a while." *Maybe quite awhile, considering that the only good regen facilities are in the Dominion now.*

She turned to the com op. "Map Six."

Rebel positions flashed onto the screen. Bergeron shifted the cup to warm the other hand, and she and the Top bent over the map.

"How fast can we put somebody out on Wogus Ridge? Depends on how many somebodies—oh, okay. If we're going to have thirty minutes, I can make it two platoons. But we'll need air assets, fire and lift, that far out."

Brigade couldn't promise too much fast enough. Bergeron looked at the Top, they both shrugged, and she said, "Okay. That's an affirmative on Wogus Ridge, starting at 0445."

The sergeant was looking at the map. "Think they're planning on pushing something out from the city? 'Cause if they do that in the north and we've got Wogus Ridge in the south, the rebs are going to be surrounded."

"Give the man a stuffed pink snee. That's why I wanted enough time to regroup and resupply. Also put in a new leader for the 2nd."

"Are you looking at him?"

"Are the Lizardspines rugged? Akers is doing all right with the 3rd, but the 2nd's going to be a bit soggy."

"I'll head down there right now. Oh, they're sending around hot food in the medevac lifter. If things stay quiet out front, they'll bring the lift straight on to the road."

"Can't hurt."

If Brigade was thinking of pulling troops for a northern thrust out of Mount Houton, that had to mean the rebels were fading all over the place. So a lot of things couldn't hurt now, like dreaming of climbing into a hot tub with Lucco DiVries—if there was a hot tub functioning within a hundred kilometers.

Major Abelsohn waited until Joanna Marder had picked a glass from the serving robot before starting the briefing. He waited, she noticed, with one eye on Councillor Lorne and one eye on what she chose.

She'd lost her faith in personal secrets about the same time as her virginity, and both losses were fairly disappointing. At least sex had improved. Gossip hadn't.

She sipped her Kaloris eggnog. If it had any spiking, it was very light. *Serve everybody right if I pretended to get drunk and did something outrageous, like dancing on the table or sitting on that good-looking blond Lieutenant Longman's lap.*

Except that Marder knew she couldn't pretend, not tonight. Not with all the possible outcomes of tonight's events weighing on her mind.

She put her eggnog down, waited until everybody else had served themselves, and cleared her throat.

"Major Abelsohn, on behalf of the Alliance personnel here I'd like to thank you for your hospitality. But I'd also appreciate it if you explained as quickly as possible why we're all here."

"With pleasure—well, not quite that. We've got a bit of trouble coming up. Information received from sources I can't discuss suggests that the Republican forces in the zone are planning an attack on their rebel counterparts.

"I've already alerted all Federation units. I'd appreciate it if the Alliance forces could also go on Alert One until further notice.

"We've already evacuated the tourists, civilians, and major items of equipment for the Armistice Commission. To further avoid accidental casualties, we're going to declare the airspace over the zone a free-fire area. Anything that penetrates the airspace after 0500 will be treated as hostile."

Marder looked at the clock. Somewhat less than an hour to either get the attacker out of here or be prepared to button up and ride out the shooting on the ground, a sitting target if it got too wild—

She realized she should have looked at Lorne. Red-faced and sweating, he was glaring at Abelsohn.

"Yes, Councillor?"

"You can't give us that choice without endangering the ship! That's a violation of the Armistice Agreement. We can't possibly take off in less than two hours."

"Then you'll have to accept the danger and stay on the ground. Believe me," Abelsohn added. "It will be a lot less dangerous on the ground, under the zone AD umbrella. Unless you suspect Alliance AD is less adequate than Federation?"

Most of the Federation people fought back smiles. Even the Alliance ground C.O. looked away. Lorne's face got redder.

Marder decided to set off a countercharge before the councillor exploded. She slammed her glass down hard on the table. Silence fell as everyone stared at the spreading pool of eggnog.

Now we find out if Lorne is just an Intelligence informant or an actual agent.

"Councillor Lorne has been misinformed. Naval SOP for a vessel in this kind of situation is to be ready for space at thirty minutes' notice." She ignored choking sounds from Lorne and stared laser-eyed at Abelsohn.

"Major, I appreciate whatever concern you feel for our safety. Your real concern is whether the Alliance is behind the rebellion. Every Fed troop has been pissing their drawers over this prospect since the rebellion started. If we are backing the rebels, you're afraid we might overfly the rebel positions and warn them, or overfly the Republic's positions and give the rebels intelligence for a counterattack.

"If we wanted to do that, you couldn't stop us. There's crew and equipment aboard our ship right now. If we don't give them an all-clear signal in ten minutes, they'll take off and act as the safety of the ship and the right of self-defense dictates."

Abelsohn didn't laser-eye back; he just frowned. "An unauthorized takeoff would be a violation of the Armistice Agreement, too. It even might be construed as a hostile act, giving us the right of self-defense."

" 'Us,' Major?" the ground C.O. snapped. "If you think I'm going to let you fire on an Alliance naval vessel—"

Three bluffs on the table, Marder thought. *Now let's see if anyone wants to call them.*

"We're not going to fire at anybody who isn't firing at us," Abelsohn said. "Commander Marder, your threats were unnecessary."

"What about yours?" Marder said. This time it was mostly the Alliance people who fought down smiles, except for Lieutenant Longman, who was biting his lip to keep from laughing.

"I think if you want us out of the line of fire in thirty minutes, you can have it. In return, I'd like that load of fresh water you've been promising for the last day and a half."

"Will you agree to climb vertically within the zone air-space until you reach two hundred kilometers?"

That would wipe out any opportunities for intelligence gathering except by EIs, but Marder's orders had read only "take available opportunities for gathering intelligence on potentially hostile forces." She was prepared to argue that an opportunity that risked a shootout with the Federation wasn't "available."

"Yes."

"Fine. Mr. Longman, if you can take charge of the watering party . . . ?"

"Aye-aye, sir."

The young man rose with a grace that made Marder's eye want to linger on him, but she decided Lorne deserved a little attention now. She turned his way, to find his seat empty.

Did he dematerialize? Or head for a radio? Oh well, the best I can hope for is to find out when we hit orbit.

Marder swigged the last bit of eggnog and rose to follow Longman.

Fifteen

"Flare ignited at 878—no, 879651," Karl Pocher said.

The same figures came up on the map display between Pocher and Mahoney. Then the tearing-cloth sound of an incoming rocket made both men hit the ground for the twentieth time. They also shielded the electronics with their bodies and wished somebody would improve frag protection for field sensors.

The rocket burst fifty meters up and two hundred meters away. Light, sound, and shock wave blasted past the improvised OP, but no fragments.

"Low-yield detonation," Pocher said to no one in particular.

The explosion at least yielded a sudden burst of speed by the volunteer working party coming out of the ravine with the last crate of flares. They sprinted out of the ravine, then swerved toward the crest of Cheek Hill. Mahoney shouted coordinates after them, but doubted they heard.

"Damn those egg-sucking cowards!" he raved. "If we'd been able to get the flares down across the field to the launchers—"

Pocher waved a hand at the landing pad and the buildings around it. The air-control shack was smoking wreckage from a direct hit. Three overturned lifters and pieces of a fourth were strewn over the pad. Even in the intermittent light of the rocket bursts, Mahoney could count a dozen sprawled bodies.

"Ask the volunteers to cross that?"

"You did more."

"I was angrier. I was fighting back. And I was winning."

Mahoney shut up and turned back to the radio. *Maybe the rebels have finally knocked out enough of those yammering volunteers to clear the air . . . .*

He wished the flares had gone downhill, to be fired to their positions by the heroically served launchers. By refusing to cross the rocket-swept open ground to the battery position, the volunteers had in the long run increased their own casualties, but if they wouldn't listen even to Karl Pocher—

Another rocket came in. This one was picked out of the sky by a suddenly resurrected AD laser. Mahoney tried to call the battery but got only something that could have been either static or a message in a code he couldn't unscramble.

Mahoney cursed low-capacity scramblers, gun-shy volunteers, Victoria's poor radio conditions, and the fog of battle in general. In the twenty minutes since he and Pocher rode up to the ravine, the battle around the base had reached a mathematically perfect state of chaos. Or at least all the signals Mahoney picked up did nothing to make him doubt the evidence of his eyes.

From half a dozen points around the camp, the rebels were lobbing rockets into it. The 150s were doing good counterbattery work, but two of them, then one, could do only so much. The AD lasers had gone from three to two to one to none and were now temporarily back to one after repairs or recharges.

Meanwhile, even a few message fragments told Mahoney that a major infantry assault was building up to the northeast. The expected direction, of course, and the volunteers and advisers had been deployed to meet it. If they hadn't taken too many casualties—a small miracle—and the 150s still had enough antipersonnel rounds—a larger miracle—

No, not all the saints in the calendar together could work enough miracles to save the base.

Flares blazed uphill. A moment later, shells burst—a rapid-fire sequence of five, searching along a line just beyond the crest of the hill. Shells, not rockets. Mahoney raised his own binoculars, adjusted the magnification, and saw the remaining 150 rocking as it pumped out shells with flashless cold-gas charges.

"Karl. We've got to warn the people who ran into the cave. They thought they'd be safe, getting out the rear entrance. They're going to run right into rebel infantry."

"Damn! I should have reminded them about that movement in the southwest quadrant. Of course the people who sighted in the rockets would have somebody with them. A security detail, if nothing else."

Mahoney took a brief, shameful satisfaction that even Pocher couldn't think of everything. Then he scrambled down into the ravine, looking for the telephone line. If the volunteers were still working their way through the narrow passages that led to the far side of the hill, maybe he could warn them—

Laser-detonated shells burst a thousand meters up. Mahoney stopped caring about the electronics. He wanted something more than battledress between him and rebel weapons, now that they'd brought up a laser. The next stage beyond blocking the counterbattery fire was pushing home an infantry assault, with or without launcher support of its own.

The ideal amount of armor, Mahoney decided, would be about sixty centimeters of Grade Eleven composite—the thickness of one of *Shenandoah*'s main spheres. Joining the infantry, he decided, had not been the wisest career move he could have made.

Then four flares blazed at the four points of the compass, dwarf white suns that swung in tight circles as they slowly fell. Mahoney gaped—those were Navy flares—then stood up, his gaping turning to a grin.

A Federation light cruiser rode down across the sky over Cheek Hill, the flares lighting up her 150 meters of hull from bow to stern. From the gun turret under the bow, past the open hatches for the rotary launchers and the second, dorsal turret, to the flare and decoy dispensers at the tips of the fins—

The cruiser was so low that Mahoney saw the bow turret swinging north, the dorsal turret swinging south. Lasers darted in both directions, illuminating targets for the turret sights.

Both 150mm guns let fly at once. Twenty rounds a minute from each barely made the cruiser rock as her helmsman balanced lift, drive, gravity, atmospheric resistance, and the recoil of the guns.

"Somebody sharp at the controls," Pocher said, almost reverently.

"Yeah. They must have popped the last shells from the 150 with their laser, because they were already coming down into firing position."

"They could have signaled," Pocher said.

"Tonight, with the radios . . ." Mahoney couldn't go on analyzing. *My apologies, ladies and gentlemen*, he told the saints. *You* could *manage a big enough miracle*.

Then he and Karl Pocher were dancing, hugging each other, kicking up discarded packing material, snow, dust and rock fragments, and screaming, "Go it, you beauty! Go it, Navy!"

Elayne Zheng felt someone standing by the head of her bed just as the intercom screen lit up. She put her book down, sketched a brief salute to Commander Gesell, and waved her to a chair.

Instead, Gesell assumed the perfect position on the rug as Captain Liddell's face appeared on the screen. To Zheng, the captain looked like someone who'd spent the night doing something demanding, even exhausting, but rewarding.

"Good morning," Liddell said. "Since we are going to Alert One in twenty minutes, I thought you would appreciate a brief update on what's been happening on Victoria."

A map replaced Liddell's face. Her voice remained, to take *Shenandoah*'s crew on a two-minute tour of the Bushranger rebellion's desperate and now increasingly unsuccessful push for victory.

"The rebels have been held both in and outside Mount Houton. Thanks to their border violation, both the light cruiser *Novy Pskov* and the 879th have gone into action supporting the volunteers' base camp.

"The Republic hasn't put us on the need-to-know list for their next move. But we suspect they are planning on a major advance in Mount Houton. There are also signs of an attack on the rebels in the Armistice Zone."

Gesell laughed, and went on chuckling, a muted background to the rest of Liddell's briefing. Zheng wanted to throw something at the intercom to shut it up. She didn't care what attackers would be escorting *Shen*, where the support ships would be, or what the Alliance might do. She was going to sit out all of it—rather, lie it out, in this damned sickbay, and her C.O.'s laughter wasn't helping!

When Liddell finally signed off, Gesell noticed Zheng's clenched fists under the blanket. "Sorry, Lieutenant. I was just laughing about the Armistice Zone fight. I'm taking a flight down there to help simulate one, to goose the rebs without actually shooting at them. I'd be on the way now, except that the crew loading the decoys seems to have been hatched yesterday. They—Lainie, what's wrong?"

The use of her first name made Zheng realize that her eyes had overflowed. Gesell unfolded gracefully and kissed her lightly on the forehead.

"Come on, you wild and crazy electron pusher!" the commander said. "You can't even sit at a board for a full watch yet, let alone take Gs. I'll bet a bottle of anything you can find on Victoria that's fit to drink this won't be our last combat mission."

"Commander, you've got low tastes in liquor if you think that bet's worth making."

"So think of something else by the time I get back. I'm not going to miss pinning on your Distinguished Service Medal myself. Maybe then I won't have to remind you that you did a damned good job in *Mahmoud Sa'id*."

"I'd better get moving," Gesell added, looking at her watch. "After that Alert One goes, I'll have to kick someone into opening every hatch between here and the launcher. Too much wear and tear on the boots, if I want to save them for real bad guys." Gesell dashed for the door, nearly bowling over an attendant shepherding two carts of lunch.

The whine of the water cart's pump drowned out Charles Longman's footsteps until he was almost on top of Commander Marder. When she whirled to face him, they were close enough to embrace.

Which, under other circumstances, might be a damned nice proposition.

"Mr. Longman." The roughness in her voice might be the icy air, the face mask, or the drinking problem rumor said she had. It was an attractive sort of roughness. "Any problems?"

"Not with the water. Two more minutes, and we can disconnect. But I thought I'd better warn you. We had your power level monitored right through from when you grounded. We all knew Lorne was lying. Thanks for saving us the trouble of calling him down on it."

"You think I don't know that?"

"No, ma'am. I'm sure that's why you called down Lorne yourself. But if he's going to make a habit of telling bloody stupid lies to military professionals—couldn't somebody save us all a lot of trouble by telling him it's a bad habit?"

Marder nodded. "Somebody, but not me, and I don't know who." She smiled, and it was a nice smile, too, one that said: *I know you're probing to find out who Lorne really is. I'm not going to tell you, but I don't resent the question.*

"Thank you, ma'am."

"Thanks can go both ways."

"Really?"

"Mr. Longman, do you always mentally undress superior officers of the interesting sex?"

"Only when they're superior in quality, not just rank."

"Flattery won't get you more than another thank-you, but—"

Someone shouted from inside the attacker. Longman couldn't hear all the words, but he heard the name "Pak" mentioned twice.

"Stow it, you idiot!" Marder yelled up the hatch. When she turned back to Longman, all the warmth seemed to have crept deep inside her.

"Sorry, Mr. Longman. We've just had news of an emergency in Silvermouth. It doesn't concern this base, but if you can disconnect now . . ."

She was lying, Longman knew, but he was already at the limits of junior officers' initiative. One did not call a commander in any Navy a liar to her face.

"Aye-aye, ma'am."

She vanished into the hatch as Longman cut off the pump. The pipe unhooked and telescoped back into the cart, and he jumped on the cart as it rolled away toward the equipment shed.

Chief Dalmas was waiting for him at the shed door. "Both lifters loaded up, sir. Here's the weight and crew tables."

Longman took the printouts of the tables for the two lifters that would be leaving as soon as the attacker was clear of the zone. Both carried heavy loads of noisemakers, flash-bangs, flares, and dust projectors. Both also carried Bushranger IFF to make sure any Alliance sensors wouldn't recognize them as Federation.

Judiciously distributed at low altitude, the various devices would make a fine uproar starting in about an hour. A fine uproar—simulating for nervous, untrained rebel troops and overly curious Alliance sentries a series of infantry firefights. The kind of series that might be set off by a Bushranger attack on the rebel positions—

"What the hell? My name's not on the crew roster, for either one. Is there a third?"

"Sorry, sir. The flight leader didn't put you on."

"You let a bloody Army pill do that?"

"I had to let him give a direct order, sir."

"Did he say why?"

"Well, sir . . ."

"You're getting another direct order. Tell me what he said."

"He said, 'We don't need a Navy discipline case who wants to buy his way back aboard *Shenandoah*. Christ knows I wouldn't mind seeing the back of him, but tonight his weight in flares will be more useful.' "

Whatever Longman would have said in reply was lost in a sonic boom as the attacker accelerated into her climb. The lights dwindled, then were lost in the stars.

"Sounds like the pilot is working off his temper with a bit of a heavy hand on the power," Dalmas said judiciously.

"I think they had some sort of bad news, too," Longman said.

Lucco DiVries was laboring under a number of handicaps, only two of which were his watering eye and his headache.

He wasn't an infantryman. He didn't know ground combat or Mount Houton. He couldn't talk with any of the Republican wounded who were infantry, not without being overheard by the rebels. He couldn't talk with anybody at all, in fact, without breaking his act of being disabled by a concussion. So he had to sit or lie, groan occasionally, and itch with the ignorance of what the sounds from outside the hospital might mean.

The noise of infantry fighting was definitely getting louder. It seemed to be coming from the west. This might mean the rebels were trying to advance again, or that the government troops were doing the same. It might even mean that the government advance had driven the rebels into a retreat that would take them past the hospital, defeated, desperate, and generally bloody-minded.

The rebel guards seemed to have no communication with their own troops. DiVries tried to guess what guesses they were making, but didn't want to spend too much time looking at them.

That would blow his act, at the wrong time and with the wrong people. The lieutenant seemed rock-solid, but the sergeant commissar was sweating and the drug-case corporal's pupils were dilated. Not to mention that the lieutenant was relaying all orders to the corporal through the commissar— and if the lieutenant's authority was eroding, it didn't matter how solid he was—

"Dr. Nosavan," the lieutenant said. "I assume the phones are out?"

"You assume correctly."

"Then I'm going to ask for a volunteer to go out and find out how the battle's going. Either side will do. I'll write out a safe conduct for a government—"

"There's no way you can trust any of the government types—sir," the sergeant growled. The "sir" was enough of an afterthought that even Dr. Nosavan noticed it.

The lieutenant ignored the interruption and turned his back on the sergeant to survey the room. "Any takers?"

DiVries and Nosavan were the only ones who noticed the corporal grabbing the sergeant's arm and whispering something into his ear. No, BoJo noticed it, too, because he crawled under one of the operating tables.

Too street-wise to want to get caught in a fight among the bigger kids

"Any takers?" the lieutenant called again.

"Bugger off," someone said. That was the only verbal reply. A few gave traditional but nonregulation salutes.

The lieutenant's shoulders sagged. "All right. Josk, you know the town best. Dr. Nosavan, if I can use your computer to write out a message . . . ?"

"Certainly." DiVries thought that Nosavan seemed reluctant to leave his desk, and when he left it he didn't turn his back on the rebels.

Glory be, maybe our good doctor isn't as hopelessly civilian as I'd thought.

The lieutenant sat down, shifted files, and started on the message. In two minutes it was done. He ripped it off the printer and handed it to Josk—Private Josk, if the single black smear on either shoulder of her filthy sweater meant anything.

Josk saluted and picked up her rifle and coat. As the rear door closed behind her, DiVries saw the corporal shift almost imperceptibly to the left. At the same time the commissar shifted right, until he stood between the main room and the closet where the weapons were stored.

As he did, he turned his back on DiVries. DiVries's groan was more convincing than usual. Now he couldn't read the man's expression. He'd have to wait for him to act, and he looked like a man who could act very damned fast once he'd made up whatever he used for a mind.

Which means I have to guess faster than he can act. "Thank

164

you, Dr. Nosavan," the lieutenant said. He started to rise. As he did, a long burst of firing outside ended in a scream.

"I hope that wasn't your messenger Josk," Nosavan said. He seemed fidgety about getting back to his desk, which was understandable except that it was also drawing the corporal's attention.

"You sound concerned."

"Lieutenant, I'm concerned about any unnecessary casualties at this stage of the war. It will take a miracle for you to win, and even if you take over the Bushranger Republic—"

"Damp it, you—" the corporal snarled, raising his pulser.

"Corporal!" the lieutenant began. As he spoke, he turned away from the sergeant.

The sergeant gripped his carbine by the barrel, tossed it to the other hand, and raised it for one-handed fire as his free hand darted for his pistol.

He hadn't squeezed either trigger when Lucco DiVries slammed into him from behind. Adrenaline and desperation drove DiVries's ninety kilos to a respectable velocity. The sergeant went sprawling, with DiVries on top of him.

The lieutenant jumped out from behind the desk as Nosavan dove for it. The two men collided, falling onto the top of the desk and sweeping the computer off it. As they and DiVries tried to untangle themselves, the corporal set his back against a wall and raised his pulser.

For DiVries, the world shrank down to the knowledge that the corporal was as doomed as anyone else in this room, but that a lot of people would die before he did. DiVries scrabbled around blindly, feeling for one of the sergeant's weapons, not caring if the movement made him the first victim—

Fvvvmmppp!

A pulser carbine went off. A point-blank burst slammed the corporal against the wall. It also shredded his chest. His body armor, if any, wasn't proof against point-blank small-arms fire. He slumped to the floor, dropped his pulser, and died looking surprised.

DiVries cautiously raised his head to see an apparently self-levitating pulser sticking out from under a table. Then the pulser acquired a pair of disembodied hands, and the hands acquired BoJo Johnson's body.

"Lieutenant, hands up," he said cheerfully. "The rest of you rebel bastards, drop your weapons or I blow the lieutenant, then this turd—" He jerked his head at the sergeant.

"Blow that pisspot politico away, for all I care," shouted one of the rebel wounded. "If it wasn't for his kind, we'd none of us be here."

"Quiet!" the lieutenant shouted.

"No more orders, please," Dr. Nosavan said. He had finally opened his desk drawer and now pulled out a heavy-barreled thump pistol. DiVries recognized a five-round Police Model Steurmann 76. Its drug-loaded frangible rounds weren't lethal, but they would put a man to sleep for long enough to decide the battle for Mount Houton.

DiVries had the sudden, agreeable feeling that he wasn't the only one in the hospital who'd been putting on an act. *I should have remembered what Candy said about Dr. Nosavan. "He has his head screwed on with the eyes facing the way he's going," or something like that. High praise for a civilian, coming from her.*

DiVries borrowed clothing from one of the dead to bind and gag the sergeant. He was tempted simply to hit the man over the head, but was afraid he might hit too hard.

By the time the sergeant had run out of obscenities and threats, Nosavan and the lieutenant, whose name was Jonah Waterhope, had negotiated an agreement.

"All government walking wounded, please retrieve your weapons," Nosavan announced. "All rebel walking wounded, please keep your hands in sight if you don't want to be restrained."

"You'll have to restrain me from stamping that bloody mitebouncer into the floor!" shouted someone.

"I'm afraid we will," Nosavan said. "I think he's a valuable source of intelligence. Wouldn't you say so, Mr. DiVries?"

At that point DiVries would have agreed to the theory of spontaneous generation to preserve the feeling of relief and to give himself more time to recover. He nodded.

"Very good. Now, if the battle goes as I suspect it will, all rebels will be POWs, subject to the decision of the government of the Bushranger Republic. However, you can expect correct treatment at the very least.

"If by some chance the battle goes the other way, we will of course surrender the hospital to the appropriate authorities of the Freedom Party. We trust we can expect correct treatment."

Lieutenant Waterhope lifted his face from his hands long

enough to say, "I suppose so. Only what you hoped to gain by this—"

"We've already saved a good many lives, including yours, I suspect," DiVries put in. "Lieutenant, do you really think this turd would have left you alive after massacring the patients?"

"I suppose not."

"And H-bombs produce superficial burns! Lieutenant, even if the rebels win, I have a few contacts on the Fed side. Maybe I can wangle you political asylum—"

Waterhope glared. "Mr. DiVries, I know you're a brave man. So why are you so ready to suspect me of being a coward?"

"Sorry."

"You damned well ought to be. If the Freedom Party does win, it's all the more important to fight people like him." He pointed at the sergeant.

"Amen, Lieutenant!" shouted quite a few voices. The ragged chorus sounded to DiVries rather like the end of a prayer meeting. Outside, the firing swelled again, and now DiVries could hear the whine of low-flying lifters.

Sixteen

The continuous roar of the light cruiser's guns and exploding shells had died to a rumble in the north. The captain must think the threat from the southwest was gone. Certainly Cheek Hill hadn't taken a rocket in almost five minutes.

The volunteers popped out of the cave almost at Brian Mahoney's feet. He started and nearly fell into the ravine on top of them.

"Who's there?" Karl Pocher shouted.

"We're 4th Platoon, A Company, First Volunteers," a thin, middle-aged man said.

"Where were you?"

"We thought the enemy might be attacking from the rear. We planned to take defensive positions just outside the rear entrance. But the Navy was hitting them so hard that it didn't look like we were going to be needed. So we came back here."

Pocher and Mahoney exchanged looks. They suspected that the volunteers would have run, if they hadn't had to run through the cruiser's barrage.

Let's pretend to believe them and see if they've got their nerve back.

"Did you leave anyone on guard?" Mahoney asked.

"Ah—"

"Send a squad back. You got somebody who knows booby traps, maybe tangler mines?"

"Schick," someone said.

"Okay," Mahoney said. "Send Schick back with the squad. Leave another squad—"

Two attackers swept out of the north, silent until the sonic booms of their passage jolted the base. They pulled up in near-vertical spiral climbs over Cheek Hill. Mahoney saw large dark objects drop from both of them. Curiously soft explosions sounded from beyond the crest as the sonic booms died away.

"The Navy's just laid some minelet cannisters on the far side of the hill," Mahoney said. "That should make the squad's job easier. Now, leave another squad here, for security on this side. Karl, have you reached any of the flare parties?"

"Two of them are coming down, or so they say," Pocher said. He shrugged. "Want me to stay until they do?"

In a pig's arse I do. "Negative. I want some backup when we move out." *To protect me from the volunteers more than from the rebels.*

"Move out?" the volunteer leader said. "Where?"

"The rest of your platoon is coming with us. We're going to clear the pad, try to make contact with the artillery, and recover any friendly wounded."

"Oh." The man sounded dubious, but not more so that Mahoney would have if he hadn't been temporarily SOP. *Very temporarily, please God, if I haven't used up all my favors tonight.*

"We'll be ready to move out in five minutes, sir."

One of Brigitte Tachin's classmates had brought a bottle of wine disguised as a thermos jug of fruit juice. Now that Mother Yvonne was stretched out on her blanket in the sun, shoes off and a handkerchief over her face, it was time to break out the wine.

It was good strong wine. With the sun and the scent of the flowers it was so strong that Tachin's head began to swim. She pulled her own shoes off and wiggled her bare toes in the grass, still delicately damp from yesterday's rain.

A little stream curled around the bottom of the slope, forming a pool under a gigantic swordnut in full bloom. Tachin stared at the pool, saw bubbles rise from the dark cold water, then saw the bubbles turn into foam.

A man rose out of the pool, tall and dark, his hair hanging lank almost to his shoulders. He was naked as a baby and neither handsome nor ugly, but so made that his presence reassured more than it aroused.

Tachin pointed, then shouted, then grabbed her friends by the shoulders. She was afraid of waking Mother Yvonne, who would certainly send the man on his way, but she was afraid even more that her friends wouldn't see the man and be reassured the way she was by his presence. . . .

But her friends seemed to be blind and deaf, and when she touched them it was like touching wooden statues. They

169

didn't move, they didn't speak, they didn't even seem to breathe as the man stepped to the edge of the pool, up on to the grass, and toward Tachin.

She could move, so she stood up. She thought of taking off her own clothes, but decided that would be jumping to conclusions. This man had come for his own reasons, and if they involved her undressing, too, she would know it at the right time.

The right time.

Time.

"Time to wake up, Lieutenant," a man's voice sounded in her ear. "Hey, Lieutenant, we're alerted for a mission."

The cold and the darkness around her told Tachin that her dream was over. The mission the man was talking about had nothing to do with the work of the Aquinan Order back on Charlemagne.

She pulled down her sleeping bag and crawled out. She'd slept fully clothed except for her boots, so she was outside with Sergeant Esteva in two minutes.

"Sorry to bother you, Lieutenant, but they need some more bodies in the city. Specifically, somebody qualified as a SFO."

"Me? All I had was the basic course—"

"That's more than anybody else they can spare. Or find," Esteva added. "I kind of leaned on the colonel, though. I'm taking four of our people and handpicking a few more volunteers. We're also supposed to get a squad from the city's reserve."

"Thank you, Sergeant." Tachin would have been more grateful if his roster of the OP security detail hadn't implied doubts about her courage. "How are things going?"

"Could be a little better, could be a lot worse. Not all the rebs are ready to cut and run, but out here it's mostly mopping up. They started off pretty short of ammo, then didn't get a resupply they'd counted on. Some of them are a little pissed over that."

"I don't blame them." They must feel toward their backers rather as she felt toward Frieda Hentsch. If the general did have forty-odd Hentschmen to spare for Victoria, couldn't she have come up with a few more qualified SFOs among them?

Calling down supporting fires, ground, air, or space, was a skilled job at the best of times. Calling them down in a built-up area was an art as well. She prayed she could acquire both the skill and the art tonight.

Grit and snow stung her cheek, and she heard the whine of fans. "That's ours?"

Esteva pulled down his goggles. "Yeah." He watched for a moment, hand-signaled something, then nodded to Tachin.

"We're ready when you are, ma'am. One of the Bush-rangers even wangled some hot tea."

"Bless him," Tachin said to Esteva's rapidly retreating back. Then she abandoned dignity and ran, to keep up with the hurrying sergeant.

Mahoney's sweep of the pad cost only sweat, not blood.

His party reached the far side carrying three friendly casualties. They'd counted close to thirty dead, from both sides, extending the search line as far as Mahoney dared with a scratch outfit like this. It chilled Mahoney more than the night to know that the comparatively bloodless phase of the Victoria crisis was over.

A line of smashed revetments and wrecked lifters marked the far side of the pad. Beyond these lay more bodies, so shredded by antipersonnel rounds from the 150s that Mahoney only assumed they were rebels. He was kneeling, looking for insignia or equipment, when someone shouted from up the hill.

"Who's there?"

"Lieutenant Mahoney and the 4th Platoon, Company—"

"Company B."

"First Volunteers."

"Advance and be recognized."

Mahoney stepped into the open, arms spread wide.

"All right, Lieutenant. Pass."

The party scrambled up the hill and into the battery's perimeter as if it was the last lifeboat from a ship with an unstable drive. Mahoney found himself facing Sergeant Major Miguel Kimura, the senior enlisted adviser in the camp.

Kimura saluted. "Good to see you, sir." He gave a list of officer casualties that went on until Mahoney wasn't surprised at the concluding words—

"So I guess you're in command of the base for now. Any orders?"

Yes. Get on the horn to Scout Company and tell them to please come over, just Candy if they can't spare anybody else. More than anything else, Mahoney wanted to see

171

Candice Shores or somebody like her striding down the hill, tall, tough, and above all knowing what to do in an infantry fight. Until that happy event, however, the base would have to make do with Katherine Hanrahan Mahoney's last and favorite son, Brian.

"Sergeant Major, I suppose you could use some more hands here?"

"What we really need is more ammo, but some warm bodies won't hurt."

"All right."

Mahoney nodded at the platoon leader. "The sergeant major's acting battery C.O. You're under his orders. Put your people where he tells you. Karl, signal the people on Cheek Hill to assume a defensive position until further notice."

Pocher raised the signal laser while Kimura and the Victorian bent over a scrawled map of the battery position. It took two minutes for Kimura to give his orders, and when the volunteers moved out, it looked to Mahoney as if they had their nerve and wits back.

First-combat jitters had made a lot of good soldiers look like bad ones until they passed off. The problem was that they also turned a lot of soldiers into corpses before they could learn enough to stay alive.

"Lieutenant," Kimura whispered when the last volunteer was out of earshot. "How did they stand up?"

"Most of them started off a little skittish, but I think they've got over that. I don't know what would have happened if the air support hadn't showed up."

"It'll do them good to be around my people, then. Most of them stuck in there real good. With two more tubes, we might not have even needed the Navy!"

The conviction of artillerymen that tactical air support was a decadent way of winning battles was as unalterable as the rotation of the galaxy. "Fine. Now, have you people had any luck reaching the Navy, or *anybody* outside the camp?"

"Sending, no. But we've picked up a lot of fragments, and—sir, I haven't mentioned this to anybody, even my own people—"

"Give."

"Some of the fragments—they sounded like Merishi. High Merishi, not the commercial lingo."

Mahoney looked at Kimura, certain that he was hallucinating.

Kimura looked back. "Sir, I'm not dusting you. I'm telling you what I heard."

"Any recordings?"

"The recorder was about the first thing the rebs blew away."

Mahoney turned away, to face Karl Pocher.

"Brian, I think I'd better head back over to Cheek Hill. The people there sound a little nervous."

Mahoney didn't ask for details. He only gripped the reservist by both shoulders. "Go ahead. But remember, if you get yourself killed, I'll have you court-martialed for disobeying a direct order."

"What's that?"

"To stay alive until morning."

Pocher's salute was traditional, military, but totally non-regulation. Then he grinned. "I'll do my best."

The lights of General Kornilov's lifter winked out as the big M-476A passed over the camp perimeter. Candice Shores looked from General Langston to the soldiers drawn up around the pad, then back to Langston.

The brigade commander nodded.

"Dismiss special security detail," Shores told Raoul Zimmer. She listened to the order passing down the chain of command, watched the squads and individuals disperse, then turned back to Langston.

"Special security detail dismissed, sir."

"Well done, Captain, and thanks for getting out of bed at this un-Christian hour. May I offer you breakfast?"

Shores shivered. *And why, I'd like to know. With a father from Bogatyr, I ought to have more genes for resistance to cold!* Her stomach rumbled, but it was the rumble of resistance to food, not hunger.

"Thank you, sir. But could you make it lunch? I'd like to get back to my office, clean out the paperwork, then stretch out for a couple of hours."

"1300, then?"

"Fine."

A false dawn was creeping into the sky when Shores reached the migrant laborers' barracks that now housed most of Scout Company's quarters and offices. RHIP, so her own space was the former registration office, which was almost large enough to turn around in.

She sat down and watched Scout Company's contingent of

173

the security detail for Kornilov's visit trail down the hall to their bunks. Behind them came one of the security-cleared civilians who'd stayed on to help maintain the place. He was a small, wiry man, with an ageless Asian cast to his face.

Shores ran off a list of the security detail and posted it, with a note that they were exempt from reveille today. She'd have liked to let the whole company sleep in after the way they'd worked moving in yesterday. She'd expected to have to unpack and set up her own office, but when she came in, it was all ready for her, with a bouquet of flowers in a stoneware vase on the worktable.

Well, the work was done, and in this barracks you didn't need heating pads for your feet! She pulled her IN basket and started to work.

It no longer surprised her that official correspondence seemed to multiply both sexually and asexually, although the first seemed faster. Leave two letters unanswered overnight, and there'd be ten the next morning. Leave one, and it might have fissioned into three or four at most.

Charges of insubordination against Lance Corporal Awal, 2nd Platoon. Investigate.

Recommendation for promotion to sergeant for Corporal Hoberman, 1st Platoon. Endorse.

List of supplies and equipment over normal platoon allowance that the 3rd Platoon had drawn from the company reserves when it was assigned to the Quick Reaction Force. Note. *(Also, pray for the success of 3rd Platoon and stop worrying about not being with them.)*

Analysis of possible toxic content of paint in first-floor latrine. Forward to laboratory on Priority One, along with samples from other latrines in case somebody had used the same suspect paint in all of them. . . .

On the screen, false dawn had given way to true dawn by the time the last letter vanished. Shores's remaining energy was threatening to do the same. She pushed back her chair, raised her eyes, and found herself staring at the civilian. He was stood in her doorway, in one hand the controls for the floorkeeper, in the other a bottle of whiskey.

"Citizen, that's military-issue liquor. If you return it immediately, I won't say anything—"

"I have a perfectly good claim to military-issue liquor," the man said in a familiar voice.

Shores gaped. "Major Nieg!"

The Intelligence major bowed deeply, at the same time

raising one foot high enough to punch the door control. It slid shut behind him as Shores came out from behind her desk and gripped the little major by both hands. He pulled up a chair, put the bottle on Shores's desk, and sat down. "Want to drink to our—nondefeat?" he asked.

Shores nodded. A clear head didn't matter much now—or at all, until after she'd got some sleep.

Nieg unsealed the bottle while Shores fished two cups from her desk. He poured with one hand while adjusting his robot controller with the other.

"There," he said. "Just in case somebody's bugged your office."

"What else can that controller do?"

"Play music, project flatscreen films, emit sleep gas—do you want the complete fable, or do you want the facts?"

Shores sipped, then swigged. It was good whiskey, and at the moment she'd have drunk home-brewed beervine pressings. "I guess the facts, if I can concentrate."

Nieg poured her another cupful, "Don't let me help you concentrate if you don't want to."

"I'd better, 'cause somehow you've got your priorities in order, for a professional spook."

"Thank you. To our—to having won this time."

They clicked glasses. "What about next time?" Shores asked.

"It's remotely possible there won't be a next time," Nieg said. "There was a chain for supplies to the rebels—Baernoi to humans *and* some Merishi, humans and Merishi to half a dozen political factions among the rebels, political factions to the rebels' field forces.

"We broke that chain. That's one of the reasons I needed to send Esteva. I needed a reliable observer on the battlefield to see how badly the rebels were coming up short."

"From what I've heard, breaking the chain hurt them pretty badly. The volunteers and the Bushrangers putting up a good fight did the rest."

"That's about it. The problem is that we did our job almost too well. The rebels didn't get a lot of things they were expecting. Reinforcements, ammunition, fire support, medical supplies, and medevac, you name it, they came up short.

"They'll be looking for someone to blame, and when they find that someone, they'll be ready to fight again if the Bushrangers will let them. If they won't, the Republic will have an embittered, vengeful minority among their citizens, looking for someone to help them."

"Alliance Intelligence may be able to deal with some of the factions. The rest—I think one of them has started already."

"Somebody really did try to take out Pak?" She'd heard the rumor as she was suiting up for Kornilov's visit, with other things on her mind.

"Yes, and try to make it look as if the Merishi or their criminal allies had done it. That could be one of the Field Intelligence–backed factions. Losing Pak could give F.I. a chance to put some of their people in key places during the command shuffle."

"Think they did it, then?"

"Low probability. If the truth leaked out, Hollings would have to sacrifice any contacts he has in Intelligence to Baba Lopatina and the Bonsai Force. If he didn't, they'd come after him as well. Even low forms of life like Hollings have some instinct for self-preservation."

Shores decided she needed the rest of her drink and part of a fresh one. As she drank, Nieg continued.

"So far, nobody seems ready to blame the Baernoi. So if they show up all shiny and loaded with gifts—"

"May their tusks be filed down to the roots without anaesthetic." Shores saw that her glass had been refilled. "Now I see why you brought the whiskey. You didn't want me to have nightmares."

"I did not want to have them myself," Nieg said. "Has it ever occurred to you that Intelligence people like to do their work properly?

"At least I do. I left the Rangers for that reason. I was becoming very tired of killing people because another's blunders had allowed them to do the things for which they had to be killed. I wanted to see if I could avoid the blunders in the first place."

Shores noted that fatigue, depression, or whiskey seemed to be hitting the major. His English was growing steadily more formal.

"Oh, I almost forgot the most important fact I learned. We are receiving the new brigade Kornilov requested. Twenty-two to twenty-eight days."

"Which one?"

"As one would expect: 215, with all its organic units plus

176

another tactical air battalion. Probably other augmentations as well."

"A Scout battalion?"

"No. I think I would have heard about that."

Shores slipped off her boots and leaned back with her feet on her desk and her cup on her stomach. A full battalion of light infantry assigned to scouting for Victoria Command would give her people a badly needed rest. They hadn't been shot at during the Armistice, but they'd had more than their share of being hustled around to deal with emergencies that never arose.

The regular Scout Company that went with a brigade, on the other hand, would be more headache than help. It wouldn't take the load off her people until it learned it's way around Victoria. But its C.O. would almost certainly be senior to her, and if the C.O. wasn't willing to listen to her unless she went over his head . . .

She emptied her glass and set it back on the desk. "Thanks, Major. Really. How soon can I break it to my people?"

"Two or three days."

"Fine. Now, I'm going to totter down the hall and take a shower. Then I'm going to sleep until either the mess opens for lunch or the Baernoi attack."

"May I join you?"

Shores raised her eyebrows. "You didn't get a good enough look the last time?"

"A wise man can always find a new aspect of the beautiful."

"I've been told that so often I'm beginning to think maybe it's true. Besides, I know that people your height can't help where your eyes end up looking."

"Captain, my eyes are at least at the level of your shoulder blades. Not that they are your best feature, you understand, but I do rise to greater heights than some of my fellows."

"Are you suggesting we prove it?"

Nieg actually looked taken off guard. "The idea does appeal to me, I admit. *You* appeal to me. But the appeal may not be mutual. Also—forgive me for being blunt—but I think dealing with Intelligence professionally strains your loyalty enough."

It wasn't very often that Candice Shores like to hear someone rejecting the idea of sex with her. This time, Nieg might have read her mind. She concluded that he was not only with Intelligence but had it.

Which is a bloody sight rarer than simple bedroom talent, and not to be traded for it by anyone with the wits of a sandscrabbler.

Shores stood up. "Let's start in my room, Major. I do have a spare bathrobe, or you can borrow my heavy nightgown—"

"A little respect for superior rank and inferior stature, Captain, if you please."

"Okay, the bathrobe it is. But you'd better belt it up, or you'll be tripping over it every time you turn a corner."

Nieg made a rude gesture and recapped the bottle.

Brigitte Tachin watched the target data come up on her screen. The green light flashed on; she raised both hands in a thumbs-up to indicate to the observer that her computer had the data. Then she pressed the button to transmit the data to the Brigade SFC.

A minute later, another green light flashed on, and the screen displayed the words "TARGET DATA RECEIVED AS FOLLOWS." She checked to make sure that nothing had been garbled in transmission over Mount Houton's battered, bruised, and lame telephone system.

Nothing had. She signaled "DATA RECEIVED CORRECTLY," yawned, and punched in a "WEAPONS CHOICE" request. Brigade might tell her as soon as they'd decided between tubes and gunships. They might also wait until two minutes before the shooting started. If they told her soon, she might just have time for a cup of tea, if that volunteer Esteva had assigned to the kitchen on the fifth floor had managed to bring it back to life—

Being an SFO was turning out to be an easier job than she'd thought. This was only her third call, all of them in daylight and two of them over the telephone system. The security detail had no security to worry about, because the rebels hadn't even detected the OP, let alone shot at it.

The only drawbacks were the icy dawn wind and the dismal spectacle of Mount Houton. Against the wind, everything she had on seemed as much use as a bathing suit, and eight days of fighting had done nothing to improve the city's looks.

Neither side had unlimbered too many heavy weapons (since they didn't have them). Most of the damage wasn't visible unless you looked closely, but Tachin had been doing that for two hours now.

Not to forget that low flight to the OP, creeping down streets below rooftop height, bumping the fan guards on balconies, and staring through broken windows into gutted apartments—

A flight of gunships rose into sight. At the same time, the first salvo of shells burst.

"Two hundred over and a hundred right," the observer shouted.

Tachin punched in data, cursed Brigade for not warning her, watched the second salvo burst and the gunships closing—

The alarm on her computer clawed at her ears. The volunteer climbing out of the stairwell started, lost her footing on a patch of ice, and went sprawling with a tray of food and hot drinks.

When she'd caught her breath, Tachin realized that the third salvo hadn't come in, the gunships were climbing away to the west, and her screen was flashing a PRIORITY ONE message.

"URGENT REPEAT URGENT. TARGET REPORTED BY REPUBLICAN FIELD HOSPITAL FOUR IS REBEL COMPANY COMING IN TO SURRENDER. CEASE FIRE REPEAT CEASE FIRE."

"They could have told us themselves," Tachin muttered.

"They probably tried, but couldn't get anybody but Brigade," Esteva's voice said from behind her. "It's going to be weeks before you can get a call through in this town without trying three times."

The bloody hue of a Victoria sunrise faded from the eastern sky. Three of the gunships vanished into the still-shadowy west. Tachin thought she saw one of the salvo rockets before she lost sight of it.

The fourth descended to just above the rooftops and circled Hospital Four. Borrowing the observer's glasses, Tachin saw that it was a standard K/G-96 with podded weapons hung all over it.

"Name?" asked the volunteer clerk.

"Juana Lorenz," the stocky rebel woman said.

"Rank?"

"Rifleman first class."

"ID?"

Lorenz pulled a plastic disk out of the breast pocket of her sand-colored sweater and threw it on the clerk's desk. It bounced, rolled off onto the floor, and rolled under the desk.

The clerk bent to pick it up.

"Let her do it herself," Lieutenant Darlington snapped.

"Go bounce—" Lorenz began.

Darlington motioned the two guards forward. Brian Mahoney raised his arms to block them.

"Hey, people. The orders were correct treatment. Let's not break that over trifles." Before anyone could stop him, he reached down, retrieved the disk, and handed it to the clerk.

"ID number 10978," the clerk said, recording it.

"Okay," Mahoney said. "Any medical problems?"

"No. But has my sister showed up? Conchita Lorenz, lance corporal, ID—"

"We've got better things to do than keep track of everybody's relatives," Darlington snapped. "Outside and to your right. Group Blue. Don't cross the orange wire or you'll be restrained."

Lorenz threw Darlington a mocking salute and marched out. "Any more?" Darlington shouted.

There were thirty-eight more, making a total of ninety-two prisoners in this third batch since dawn. By the time the last rebel had been recorded, Mahoney was glad that he'd taken the "good guy" role while Darlington played "bad guy."

He couldn't have kept up the growling, swearing, and glaring required for Darlington's role without falling over on his face. Brian Mahoney couldn't remember having been so exhausted since recruit training.

It wasn't "the burden of command," at least. His tenure as C.O. of what everyone now called Battered Base One lasted only about twenty minutes. Then two of the five missing senior officers turned up, and a third regained consciousness. Mahoney rejoined Pocher on Cheek Hill and had a fine view of the Navy chasing rebels without having to do much himself.

As naval fire lifted, the QR force arrived—a platoon of Candy's Scouts and a company of Second/215, both aboard attackers that must have pushed their low-altitude Mach limits all the way. They cleared the perimeter, then headed north aboard all the lifters that could be put into the air. A flight of attackers followed them.

Mahoney got his boots off, put his head down, and slept for half an hour. He'd planned to sleep for two or three, but both friends and enemies had other plans.

Before the infantry hit their LZs, the attackers had hit a major rebel supply dump in the Blanchard Canyon. Before it stopped exploding, the rebels started surrendering, in person if they could find somebody, over the radio if they couldn't. A few diehards held on, sometimes doing more damage to their ex-comrades than to the Federation troops, but the last of these was gone before daylight.

The rest just wanted any way out of the war that would give them food, water, medical care, and someplace to warm up. The Federation, the Bushranger Republic, and the volunteers settled down to give the prisoners what they wanted, as fast as they could be processed.

The Battered Base had processed more than three hundred survivors of the force attacking it when the big lifter returned. Its crew looked smug, but were closemouthed about where they'd been all night.

They were promptly commandeered to fly out the first two batches of POWs, who now considerably outnumbered the able-bodied survivors of Battered Base. Then the third batch came in, and Brian Mahoney found himself commandeered—or volunteering, if one wanted to be delicate about it—for the job of prisoner interrogation officer.

The lifters with the third batch had just taken off, and Mahoney was dreaming of breakfast and more sleep (in whatever order they were available), when he heard an incoming lifter. It had at least one fan badly out of sync and a barely modulated lift generator.

He ran outside to see two lifters float down to the pad. It had been cleared of bodies but not of wrecked lifters, and the first lifter bumbled its way into a collision with one of the wrecks. The wreck's forward window dissolved and a fan on the other lifter ran wild with a scream and a cloud of smoke.

Somehow the damaged lifter managed to land safely. Mahoney hardly noticed the second lifter touching down until Darlington nudged him and pointed to his holster.

"Lock and load. I think they've brought in a few of the diehards."

Mahoney now saw that the second lifter was one of the K/W-96 conversions, and its bow gun was pointing at the first lifter. It was also disgorging a squad of fully armed Scouts.

Mahoney and Darlington reached the first lifter as the Scouts surrounded it. The squad leader motioned them back, then signaled to the cockpit. The side door opened, and two figures carrying a stretcher stumbled out.

Mahoney swallowed. The first stretcher bearer was human, but the second was unmistakably Merishi. So was the figure on the stretcher. Behind them in the lifter, Mahoney could make out three more Merishi.

Darlington found his voice first.

"What the hell—"

"Some of the Scaleskins flew into our perimeter," the squad leader said. "They had a deader and a couple wounded aboard, and some human friends." The squad leader spat. "They said they were claiming political asylum."

Mahoney closed his eyes. It helped stop the landscape from whirling around him, Merishi and all. Maybe when he opened them, the Merishi would be gone.

A soft voice spoke in what Mahoney recognized as Merishi, but not the commercial lingua franca. It went on until he opened his eyes.

The Merishi were still there. In fact, a medic was bending over the one on the stretcher, and a second stretcher was coming out of the lifter. The Merishi on this one had the blanket pulled over his face and the ceremonial death sign painted on both clawed feet.

That settled the question of hallucinations. *Now what about the other ninety-six questions raised by the Merishi being here?*

"Greg, can you take this? I'm going to get off my feet."

"Sure, Brian."

Seventeen

It was another high-level secret briefing in the same room where the one the first day of the rebellion had been held. But both the atmosphere and the company were different.

Kornilov was taking the briefing himself. He faced not only Alys Parkinson and Father Brothertongue, but Senator Karras, chairman of the Military Council, and Prime Minister Fitzpatrick. Instead of a developing crisis with everything including the outcome unknown, he could report a sweeping victory.

Kornilov flexed his shoulders and stepped up to the display controls. He wore full-dress uniform complete with sidearm. After eight days spent mostly in battledress, he felt cramped and confined. The feeling of new vigor and youth the battledress gave was gone.

He hoped it would come back before Indira Chatterje finished organizing a medical task force for the Bushrangers and had two spare hours. She wasn't going north herself, and he hadn't even had to make that an order. But shoring up the tottering health-care system of the Republic without stripping Victoria Command bare of medical personnel was a delicate and time-consuming juggling act.

Kornilov stood at attention and saluted. "Ladies and gentlemen, I wish to report a victory."

"Why you instead of Colonel Vesey?" Senator Karras asked.

"Colonel Vesey has worked herself to exhaustion. I ordered her to get some sleep."

"At Fort Stafford?"

"Senator Karras, have you ever tried to make a new contingency plan every six to ten hours, for eight days in succession?"

"Oh, is that what it was? I thought she was just holding the fort while you pranced around Victoria."

Kornilov punched codes into the display as if each button

had been a nerve point on Senator Karras. By the time the screen lit up, he had his answer ready.

"Senator, I'm not going to discuss my movements during the rebellion. But I have something else to tell you.

"Brigadier General Liu, the former chief of staff of Victoria Command, has been arrested. The charges are gross financial irregularities, including misappropriation of both federal and dominion funds, and possible breaches of security."

Kornilov locked stares with Karras. The senator didn't look away, but the general saw him beginning to sweat.

"Can I visit him?" Father Brothertongue asked.

"Certainly, although I didn't know he was a Christian."

"I have to try to help anyone in Liu's situation," the priest replied.

"Help him as much as you can, but just remember two things. One is that except for confession your talk with him will be monitored. The other is that he's probably not going to be tried on Victoria."

The prime minister's bushy red eyebrows rose. "Are you that sure about Federal jurisdiction?"

"I am, but Liu would be entitled to a change of venue even if we weren't. It may turn out that some of what he's done has caused the deaths of people of Victoria Command, his former comrades. Under these circumstances, would you trust us to give him a fair trial?"

Everyone seemed to accept that. Kornilov punched in troop positions and movements, split the display to cover Mount Houton and the Border Base/Blanchard Canyon areas, and let the display and his recorded voice go to work.

By the time the last rebel unit fled to the northeast, off the Mount Houton segment, the faces at the long table were a good deal friendlier. Kornilov ran a finger around the inside of his collar. Maybe he'd been doing Karras an injustice; this room seemed to be noticeably overheated.

"Thank you, General Kornilov," the prime minister said. "But you mentioned four victories, and have only shown us the two battles around Mount Houton and the fighting along the border. What's the fourth one?"

"I was coming to that. I can only give you a verbal description because no Federation forces were involved in the ground fighting." He tapped a control and the Armistice Zone replaced the eastern ADs on the screen.

"We carried out a deception operation, intended to simulate a Republican attack on the rebel forces to the west of the zone. It worked so well that the local Republican commander decided to move on his own.

"Either he thought the Federation was openly on his side, or that whatever we were doing would cover his movements. The second estimate was entirely correct. His battalion caught the rebels with their pants not just down but *off*! The rebel forces in the area were almost completely annihilated."

"Another point to Intelligence, eh?" Karras asked. He sounded almost jovial, but Kornilov wasn't deceived.

"The deception operation was carried out by regular Federation forces, Navy from the 879th Squadron and Army from the zone garrison. Intelligence operations were limited to penetrating the rebels' logistics support—"

"In plain English, the Merishi who were peddling them arms?" Karras asked.

Kornilov frowned. If he hadn't already mentioned Liu's arrest, this would have been the time for it. He hadn't intended for the Merishi to be mentioned except in the even more secret briefing 'Milla Vesey was about to give Governor-General Gist. However, the cat being out of the bag—

"Some of the Merishi in Seven Rivers seem to have been up to their usual tricks. We suspect that the attempt on Colonel Pak's life may have actually been aimed at the Merishi he was visiting at the time. The Merishi made a lot of promises, didn't keep many of them, and probably made enemies among the rebels still at large."

"I will pray that they are few," Father Brothertongue said.

"I think that prayer has already been answered," Kornilov said. "The highest estimate we had of rebel strength was under six thousand. Over forty-six hundred have already been killed, wounded, or taken prisoner."

"What about guerrillas?" General Parkinson asked.

"In the Republic, during the winter, they'll find it hard to keep the field. However, there are two things the dominion government can do to counter that threat.

"One is to recognize the Bushranger Republic. As a self-governing dominion, you can do that. I know you value good relations with the governor-general, Southern Cross, and Outback. But none of them have a five-thousand-klom border with the Bushranger Republic.

"You do. You may not help the Republic by recognizing

them, but you should stop them from suspecting you're trying to hurt them."

"We can certainly consider that," the prime minister said. "What's the other thing?"

"If you can afford it, keep the militia brigade fully mobilized. Use the volunteers with combat experience as cadre, if that won't mean breaking up too many units. I understand that most of the volunteers did well for green troops, some of them very well.

"My request for an additional brigade has been granted. It will be augmented by at least one tactical transport battalion. That should give your militia some combat-worthy lift without stripping the civilian economy even barer!"

"It will certainly help restoring transport to outlying communities," Brothertongue said. "That's been my chief concern for some time now."

"We'll run bus and cargo services if you need them," Kornilov said. "But our main concern is high mobility for our troops. With two regular brigades and the militia, we should have ten thousand troops plus the Republic's own forces to throw against any guerrillas. The warm-body problem will be solved, and we won't have to rely so heavily on Intelligence operations."

Karras' smile seemed almost friendly. "Sounds like a better show every minute. You won't hear me complaining if it works out that way." From the looks on the other faces, they felt the same way.

The prime minister rose. "General Kornilov, on behalf of the government of the Dominion of Victoria, I would like to thank you and your troops. 'Well done' is something I've wanted to say to a general ever since I was a corporal in 103rd Light Brigade. Also, it's the truth."

Kornilov saluted, shut down the display, and left the room. He was about four meters down the hall when his aide materialized, holding out a message:

Corson Hospital, 1120

Mikhail,
What about dinner in my quarters tonight, starting with drinks around 1730? The task force will be on its way north by 1500, or I will personally man a laser and singe their tails until they take off!

Indira

186

Kornilov didn't dance a *gopak* on the way down the hall, because neither his build nor his uniform allowed it. He sang "Snowstorm" all the way to his lifter, however, ignoring the quizzical looks from his aide and everybody else he passed.

The Shepherd's Inn served not only the Mount Houton airport but all the transients on the west side of the town. So it had plenty of room for a brigade headquarters and anything else compatible with the security of the HQ.

It helped that what the Bushranger Republic considered a properly staffed brigade HQ would have been just enough for a light battalion in the Federation regulars. However, Lucco DiVries couldn't help noticing that everyone assigned to the HQ was armed up, down, and sideways. Given time, the Republic's armed forces would undoubtedly develop a rear-echelon leisure class, but so far so good.

One of the facilities sharing the hotel was the brigade medical company, where DiVries came to deliver the records of Hospital Four's experience. He wasn't surprised to see that the rest of the wing of the hotel had been turned into a hospital.

He was surprised to see Captain Bergeron standing under the Red Cross that marked off the hospital area. Her fatigues would have been thrown out by any charitable agency, and her eyes were the same color as the cross.

"Captain . . . ?"

"Lucco!" She didn't raise her voice, but exhaustion didn't hide her pleasure. She couldn't have been more flattering if she'd kissed him. "What are you doing here?"

"They made me errand boy for the records on Hospital Four."

"I've been visiting my company's wounded." She licked cracked lips. "Did they say when you had to be back?"

"No. The beervine says the Feds are sending a load of medics to let us get off our feet."

"Want some company?"

Then she did kiss him, and the rest of the world spiraled away to a vast distance. When it returned, a thought came with it.

Was it really time to match the real Sophie Bergeron's body with the real Sophie Bergeron's face, instead of dreaming of a composite of Sophie's face and Elayne Zheng's body?

"The Shearers' Lounge is open," he said, testing the water.

"I don't suppose room service is still working?"

"I don't know if there are any rooms to serve."

"Let's find out."

They were lucky, after a short side trip through the Shearers' Lounge. A contingent of HQ types had settled in, looking all ready for barstool-to-barstool combat once they'd drunk the place dry. Fortunately some of the drinkers recognized Bergeron and a few recognized DiVries. Since both of them were unofficially heroes, this persuaded the bartender to part with not only a bottle but lunch.

The elevators weren't running, which left the fourth and fifth floors to the sound of wind and limb. The first couple of doors DiVries tried were unlocked because the rooms inside had no water or the windows blown out. The third door opened on a room that looked as if it had been used for exactly the same as DiVries and Bergeron intended.

Neither of them wanted to stand on ceremony about turning intentions into reality. In fact, neither of them wanted to stand at all. Bergeron was stripped and darting for the bed by the time DeVries had stowed the lunch. He liked what he saw, so much that he stopped worrying about fatigue and began to worry more about the consequences of months of celibacy.

Bergeron noticed his reaction. She settled her head on his chest and twined some of the hair around her fingers. "Is this a case of any woman will do?"

"You're not any woman." *What the Hades, she knows about Lainie.* "I've been dreaming of you for quite a while."

By the time DiVries finished describing his composite dream woman, Bergeron was burying her head in the blankets to keep from laughing. "How does reality compare with your dream?"

"I wish I could do it justice."

She ran rough-skinned hands delicately down his chest and stomach. "I think you can."

A moment later he knew she was right.

She threw off the blankets and straddled him. He gripped her by the waist and they sought and found a rhythm that drew them both along. She bent forward until her hair brushed his face and he could kiss her breasts.

For a little while at least they could forget that there was such a thing as war.

Since the day *Mahmoud Sa'id* was shot down, three storms had spread snow over the Pfingsten Mountains and Barnard's Crossing. The peaks blazed in the sunlight, and the ice that stretched five kloms out into the Gulf was knee-deep in sparkling white.

The only cloud Joanna Marder saw was the mist spiraling up from her mouth and Colonel Pak's. Here on the terrace of the hospital, they were out of the wind, and more important out of easy reach of detection.

"You look better than I'd been led to expect," she said.

The colonel's hard face twisted in what might have been a laugh on someone else's. "I feel better. All I had was temporary deafness and a couple of fragments in one leg. If I had less faith in human stupidity, I would almost say that the bomb couldn't have been intended for me."

"Maybe it wasn't."

"I know. That's the maddening thing about this entire affair. We don't know how many of the rebel factions think they were betrayed or who they think betrayed them. We don't know which of the factions have people in place here or anywhere else, or which of the people are potential assassins and which just have large mouths and small scruples. We don't, in fact, know that *every* senior Alliance officer isn't on somebody's termination list."

Marder had been living with that thought for days now. "Intelligence undoubtedly knows," she said.

"One of the stupidest things I've ever heard, in proportion to the intelligence of the person who said it," Pak growled. "They almost certainly know. But they will tell us three days before the heat death of the universe, unless— Commander, are you planning on getting drunk before you go back topside?"

"Have you joined the Jo Marder Protective Association?"

"If I have, I hardly need your permission. But if I promise not to, will you answer the question?"

The idea of somebody actually trusting her that much warmed Marder. "I was thinking about settling down and getting down to the real black," she said. "But if there's a reason—"

"I'll tell you what I'm planning and you can judge for yourself. I'm staying in the hospital for an extra day or two, because I suspect some people in the 96th are working for Intelligence. Ours, theirs, possibly both.

"If I'm not around, they may be careless, in plain sight of a few people working for *me*. If anything they do is off limits, I'll finally have a hold over Intelligence."

"Not much of a one." It annoyed Marder, to realize that Pak, instead of Paul and her, had come up with this elegantly simple plan.

"With the help of Admiral Lopatina, who still has her rank and will have some more ships within ten days, it may be enough. If not, they still don't have spare C.O.'s for the 96th growing on bushes."

"I see. So you'd like me to keep sober until this is settled one way or another."

"You need to know. I can't afford to have anybody else know. Make a professional judgment." Pak pulled up his hood and started to turn away, then stopped.

"Oh, by the way, Commander. If you absolutely insist on your binge, one of my reliable people has an in-town apartment. She maintains it quite legally, out of her own income. It's been used for discreet—almost anything you could name."

Temptation, get thee behind me, Marder quoted silently at the colonel's retreating back. Then she gripped the railing until the edges pressed hard into her hands even through her gloves.

She could almost taste the warm liquor and feel the warmth creeping down her throat and out into her body. It was almost a pain to know that the warmth wasn't real.

It could be real. Pak had offered. Intelligence could hardly do anything to her over a private binge that they couldn't already do to her over the Armistice Zone business.

She wanted the reality. She didn't want the morning after, which seemed to be getting worse each year. She didn't want to offend Pak or anyone on his side (and therefore hers) against Intelligence. She also didn't want to listen to Paul, but she realized that without the other two points Paul wouldn't have carried much weight.

"Colonel?"

On the windless terrace, Pak was just within hearing. He turned and stepped closer.

"I'll pass on the offer. Any messages for the squadron?"

"You have the only one I want to send." He looked at his watch. "Now let's go in and watch the news. Captain Liddell is doing a live press conference in another ten minutes. I have a taste for low comedy."

* * *

"The naval reinforcements on the way will certainly include at least one capital ship, probably more. I can't give you any details now because I don't have them myself," Captain Liddell added.

"Why not?" the reporter from Anzac Media asked.

Liddell wanted to laugh. "You have heard of communications lag, I hope? At the time the reinforcements were promised, Admiral Schatz couldn't be sure what ships would be available.

"He's certainly going to try to send the best and most cohesive force available. The Victoria Squadron is willing to live with that."

Liddell gripped the podium with both hands. "We hope the reinforcements won't be needed for anything except balancing Admiral Lopatina's incoming ships. With only its present strength, the Victoria Squadron helped local friendly forces to a decisive victory over the Bushranger rebels.

"They were the only people so far who have seemed determined on war to the death. We hope they've lost some of that determination, along with most of their strength.

"Everybody else on and around Victoria is as much in favor of peace as ever. We're increasing the squadron's strength for the same reason the Republic is asking for medical volunteers from off-planet: more resources to work for peace."

This oratorical flourish drew cheers, applause, and one loud "Amen!" in a voice that sounded maddeningly familiar. But somebody else popped up with a hand raised and a question ready before Liddell could scan the room.

"Chubin, *Novaya Pravda*. Is it true that Navy personnel on medical waivers were sent down on to the surface of Victoria and became involved in combat?"

The familiar voice said something impolite, but Liddell had other concerns. Somebody had blown the word on Mahoney. Knowing the lieutenant, Liddell was sure it wasn't any kind of personal enemy. It might be some Navy type with a general grudge or wanting the media on their side after they pulled the plug.

Walk delicately, Rosie. This one's mined.

"First Lieutenant Brian Mahoney is the person involved, I believe?"

"Yes."

That much honesty plus a half stellar gets you tea in the ward room.

"Lieutenant Mahoney's waiver prohbited only EVA in vacuum. Otherwise he had no restrictions. He was both qualified and available for his first ground assignment, the investigation of the wreckage of *Mahmoud Sa'id*.

"After his return from that incident, Lieutenant Mahoney received a complete physical examination as part of his treatment for mild exposure. He was found fully qualified to perform all duties, and was not on any sort of waiver when he volunteered as an adviser with the militia volunteers.

"In both assignments, Lieutenant Mahoney displayed outstanding qualities of initiative, leadership, courage, and diplomacy. I would say that he lived up to the highest standards of the naval service, except that frankly we aren't usually that good. He is being recommended for the Distinguished Service Medal."

More applause, then the familiar voice spoke. "Josephine Atwood, Trans-Rift Media Association. Does that mean that Federation 'advisers' will be eligible for combat awards?"

Liddell mock-glared at the nuggety dark woman near the back of the room. "Josie, take the quotations off 'advisers' or you may get a surprise in your drink."

"Yas'm, Captain. But will you answer the question?"

"With pleasure. Yes. Any more questions?"

The silence lasted long enough for the senior correspondent to rise and bow. "*Frau Kapitän*, it has been more pleasure than work to have you for this conference. May we have the pleasure again soon."

"Don't bet anything you can't afford to lose, people," Liddell said. "And if you're praying, pray for peace. Thank you."

Liddell managed to get out into the hall and halfway to the transit stop before Josie Atwood caught up with her. The two women embraced. Classmates and roommates at Thatcher College of Dominion University, they'd never completely seen eye to eye after Liddell joined the Navy but never dropped completely out of touch either.

"Well," Atwood said. "Is there anyplace around here for a civilized drink?"

"I was on my way to the Officers' Club right now," Liddell said. "Is that enough?"

Atwood's gray-shot eyebrows wavered. "Officers' Club. My, my. What's the price for taking me to the inner sanctum?"

"Telling me what you're doing on Victoria. I assume it's not to set up the Josie and Rosie Show again?"

"Hardly." Atwood fell into step beside Liddell. "What about leaving the drinks out of it? I'll tell you what I'm doing here, and you answer one question of my choice."

"Off the record?"

"Absolutely. It's for background only."

Liddell remembered that Atwood's definition of "background" was as elastic as any good reporter's. She decided to finish the questions before they started the drinks.

"Done. So what are you doing here?"

"Goosey thinks Victoria is about to get hot again. Even if the shooting's over, there will be a bunch of newsworthy visitors showing up along with your reinforcements."

Liddell fell short of swearing but not of showing what she thought of that development.

"Sorry, Rosie," Atwood said. "I didn't send them, and you can't shoot them down on the way. It will help that you got the ones in the Armistice Zone out nice and easy. They're feeling kindly toward the armed farces for the time being."

"My delight still falls short of being overwhelming. Is Goosey still a good poker player?"

"The last time we played, I was bare in every sense of the word inside of an hour."

"Okay, so he's playing another of his hunches. I suppose he thinks that if you help him take the pot, it will be worth a—what's next up from where he is now?"

"Senior editorship," Atwood replied. "The thing is, if he's a senior within two years, that gives him a reasonably good shot at editor in chief within five more."

"Never let it be said that I stood out of the way of a reporter's ambition. Particularly when he's right. The shooting may be over, but the shouting's going to be loud for quite a while."

"My impression exactly. My turn?"

"Hold it a minute."

They stood in silence for more like ten minutes, letting three minitrains slide past. The fourth one had two empty cars. Liddell glowered at a collection of junior officers until they left the front one empty for her and Atwood.

"Your turn," she said as the train glided out of the HQ stop.

"How badly did Kornilov step in it?"

"You're thinking of the mutiny?"

"Ah, you've had your turn."

"That was a background question, Josie."

"I should have remembered that you could divide up a bar tab remarkably fast for somebody with low math scores. Okay, I won't argue. It's the mutiny."

Liddell crossed both hands on a raised knee. "Kornilov made a mistake. It was a serious mistake, and it got people killed.

"But he made it for the right reasons. He made it because he overestimated the loyalty of troops under his command."

"Tell that to the survivors."

"I will, once I've rehearsed it on you."

"Oh, God."

"I don't have Her private number, and anything else gets you put on hold. Meanwhile, I promised you an answer. Do you want it or not?"

"I'm not sure I *should* want it, but I suspect I'll get it whether I do or not."

"Right. So here it is.

"Kornilov made a mistake that any senior officer has to be ready to make, as long as the only ft1 communication is by ship. If we get the round-trip time for a high-capacity interstellar link down to hours instead of weeks, it will be a different matter. But I'm not on the Benford Institute's mailing list.

"As we stand now, senior officers in isolated commands have to trust the people under them. One alternative is an independent surveillance force. That's been tried under Stalinist/Hitlerian regimes. It usually ends in either civil war or paralyzed armed forces.

"The other alternative is training senior officers to be paranoid about everyone under their command. Then you have to authorize them to be investigator, judge, jury, and if necessary executioner. You wind up giving an ambitious local commander more power, rather than less, and life under someone like that—"

"Becomes like General Colettta—'dull, nasty, brutish, and short'?" Atwood finished.

"Close enough."

Two stops went by in silence. By the third, it had started to snow again. A sonic boom rumbled briefly as some attacker or shuttle pilot crowded the Mach limit too soon and too low. Atwood finally stirred as they slid out of the Main Barracks stop.

"Rosie, if you ever want to run for public office after you get out—"

"And if you ever want to join the Sulei Monarchists—"

"Seriously, Rose. If you do, I'd like a job as your campaign manager."

The two women shook hands as the loudspeaker chimed, then proclaimed, "Next stop, Club Complex. Next stop, Club Complex. Please have your IDs or vouchers ready."

Eighteen

The frail metal skeleton under Brokeh su-Irzim reminded him of his roadrider. But the road beneath him was the surface of Petzas, with the Hook and Hammer just coming into view to the north. On either side of the road rose black banks growing stars.

One of the stars ahead winked brighter, then acquired a visible shape. Two, then three more did the same. The metal under him vibrated. So did his ears as his helmet radio brought the voice of the cargo lighter's pilot.

"Better come back into the pod and strap down, Commander. We're coming into visual range of the squadron."

Su-Irzim and the pilot didn't care about violating the rules against passengers riding on the cargo racks, but too many aboard the squadron were the rule-bound sort who did. There was small point in offending them at his first appearance.

He scrambled back into the control pod and closed the hatch behind him as the lighter passed the outer ring of raiders. He was strapped in by the time *Night Warrior* loomed against the stars ahead.

Night Warrior was a third larger than a human ship of comparable power, which would probably be a *Asok*-class battlecruiser. Little of that extra space was wasted. Su-Irzim had read articles in human military journals complaining that the People's ships had more vacuum storage space and used it better than their own warships.

Almost straight ahead, a cargo hatch gaped, docking arms extended and safety net already deployed just inside the hatch. The net probably wouldn't be needed; su-Irzim had seen the pilot's deft assurance at the lighter's controls. But no ship carrying Fleet Commander Eimo su-Ankrai would be slack with even minor safety precautions.

The stars vanished behind *Night Warrior*'s immensity; the lighter braked to a stop. Jointed docking arms unfolded, rattled into sockets fore and aft, then drew the lighter into the loading bay.

The loading crew waited until the ship's internal gravity had the lighter firmly pinned to the deck, then disengaged the docking arms and switched them to crane mode. The first of the lighter's cargo containers was already sailing overhead on the hook of one arm as the pilot shut down the lighter's systems.

When all displays were dark, he leaned over until his helmet touched su-Irzim's. "Any baggage, Commander?"

"Most of it went on the passenger shuttle. All I have is this."

He pulled the vacuum-proof canister out from under his seat and clipped it to his shoulder harness. It held the few items he refused to let out of his sight.

"Thank you for a fine ride. I'd wager you see more of the stars than I do."

"I don't bet with officers, Commander. Particularly when I know I'm going to win. Resent it, they do." The pilot unstrapped his harness without breaking helmet contact.

"Takes some thinking, it does, to remember there isn't enough out here for all of us."

"Does that include the Smallteeth?"

Su-Irzim heard a hiss of indrawn breath. *Probably thinks I'm trying to trap him into admitting defeatism or whatever this year's favorite term is.*

"It does for me," su-Irzim added. "The only problem is the humans who don't think the way I do. Until they're powerless, all the People have to work together to make sure we get our share."

"So be it," the pilot intoned, so reverently that no one could have ignored the note of mockery.

They hooked thumbs and su-Irzim stood up. His suit bore no rank badges, and he had to flash his ID three times at self-appointed security guards and once at real ones before he was allowed off the bay deck.

In the first dressing room he came to, he stripped off his suit and examined himself in the mirror. Even if working dress was allowed for meeting fleet commanders, what he had on was past salvage. He bundled up his suit, tagged it for delivery, then realized he didn't even know his own cabin number.

His ID in the internal data system and a query produced a surprising answer.

"Ship Commander First Class Brokeh Su-Irzim, Red Seven. Requests?"

He tapped in, "Request correction of error in rank and quarters assignment."

Night Warrior was designed to serve as a Fleet flagship; her Red Deck was generously designed to accommodate not only her own senior commanders but a good part of the Fleet staff. It would still be overcrowded quickly, if mere ship commanders second class were allowed on it.

The IDS seemed to be taking its time. Su-Irzim was thinking of unpacking his teeth cleansers when a robust voice came from the system's loudspeaker.

"There is no mistake, su-Irzim. While you are on my staff, you hold the special duty rank of ship commander first class."

"Yes, Lord. I mean, sir."

The fleet commander's ancestors held land when the Great Khudr's own forefathers were salt merchants, so the old honorific was a natural error. It was also one that su-Irzim had heard enraged the old hero.

Instead, he heard what sounded suspiciously like soft laughter, then: " 'Sir' will be enough. I am no more Lord here than you. Now, I imagine that you need rest and a bath after your rather irregular mode of travel to *Night Warrior*?"

So—the rumor had better be taken seriously: Eimo su-Ankrai had eyes in his tail and ears in his thumbs. Su-Irzim swallowed and said, "Yes, sir. But if you want me—"

"I would enjoy your company, but it would be putting the ale and meat before the porridge and water. Report to my quarters at the half of the first night watch, ready to work."

"Yes, sir."

Prime Minister Fitzpatrick's desk would have been large enough for the four people General Kornilov had briefed eight days before. Adding the deputy minister of justice, the deputy minister of defense, Alys Parkinson's chief of staff, and the prime minister's own confidential secretary crowded it to the point of elbows in ribs and chair feet pinching toes.

But they needed security. That meant all of them, in the one place Fitzpatrick could guarantee was bug-free. *To get this far and then muck it up because somebody didn't get the word would be adding stupidity to treason.*

"All right," he said, rapping the desk with the bowl of his empty pipe. "I've spoken with the president. She agrees in

198

principle, and will present our case to the governor-general. She will also order the police not to take action against any peaceful measures for union, in case Justice lines up with Defense. Sorry, Charlie, but you don't have the police in hand the way Alys has the troops."

The Justice deputy shrugged. "So what else is new? I'm too good a lawyer to be very popular with policemen."

"With the president on our side, we can move whenever we think wise. That's why I've risked this meeting. I want everyone's opinion."

"What I want," Karras said, "is a time machine. We ought to have moved the day after Liu was arrested."

"Liu's arrest by itself wouldn't have been a real problem," Brothertongue put in.

"Cold feet all of a sudden, Elijah?" Karras grumbled.

Fitzpatrick wasn't going to let this, of all meetings, degenerate into sniping. He rapped the table again.

And he rapped the table again.

"Elijah, could you explain yourself? Briefly. please."

The priest frowned. "I only wished to suggest that if General Liu revealed any of our dealings with the Bushrangers, what could happen to us without the extra brigade? How could General Kornilov rule the dominion with the forces he has, after putting the government out of action? With the brigade, he may be tempted to try."

"Kornilov might have tried anyway," Parkinson pointed out. "He's at the point where he feels he's been pushed around too long. He wants to push back. I'm not sure he's too particular about whom he pushes."

"Very well," Brothertongue said. "That the peacemakers are blessed does not, I think, mean that one cannot fight for peace. Certainly General Kornilov does not seem to favor it."

"I think we need to move on," Fitzpatrick said. "Anybody else with a strong preference?"

"Not a preference, just a notion," the Justice deputy said. "Wait until the brigade's in-system but not on-planet. We may catch Kornilov off guard."

Karras made what sounded like a remark about Kornilov's sexual habits. Parkinson snorted.

"Kornilov's had his lesson there," she said. "He's not going to be easy to catch off guard. Besides, we want to move while our militia and the Bushranger army are still fully mobilized, and before they start pardoning the rebels. That will give us a three-to-two troop edge, and the Navy won't be that big a factor."

Brothertongue grinned. "I hope that does not turn out to be an underestimate of the Victoria Squadron comparable to Admiral Lopatina's."

"What do you—"

"He means exactly what he says," the prime minister said, strangling a sigh instead of his militia commander. "We know we'll need several pieces of good luck. That's one of them. Go on, General."

"If we wait, we won't have so many troops in the field. Then Kornilov may think he can hold out until the brigade lands, and take the offensive. He may be right, if our weakness makes a lot of people sit on their hands or even choose the Feds. I think we all agree that a prolonged civil war is exactly the sort of thing we're trying to avoid."

Everybody agreed with that, or had the wits to keep quiet if they didn't.

Parkinson concluded. "Finally, if Liu's a factor, we want to move while he's still on-planet. Any day now they might ship him up to *Shenandoah* or the dockyard. We don't have many sympathizers aboard the dockyard, and aboard *Shen* he might as well be on Aphrodite."

"If Liu's a factor, we need to be careful what we do with him or for him," the Justice deputy put in.

Karras didn't say "cold feet" again but Fitzpatrick saw his lips twisting. "We're a committee making a decision, not a bunch of bloody oracles!" the prime minister snapped. "The next person I have to ask to explain themselves is going to spend the crisis weeding the duckpond!"

"All right," the deputy said. "Do you want the explanation in legal language or plain—sorry," he said as seven glares hit him together.

"It's simple. We're not technically seceding from the Federation. We're simply passing an act of union with the Bushranger Republic. Since the Republic *has* seceded, this means we automatically enter into a new relationship with the United Federation of Starworlds.

"They can let us determine the relationship de facto. They can formally negotiate to determine it de jure. They can even try to find some pretext for suppressing the new Victorian Union with armed forces they won't have when it goes into effect.

"But since we're not legally an independent country, we can't offer Liu political asylum. We'd technically be harboring an escaped criminal, one charged with some very serious offenses. Not turning him over would be obstructing justice, and get us off on the wrong foot with the Feds. Particularly the armed forces. They don't like Liu."

The prime minister himself didn't much like Brigadier General Liu. He'd been only a moderate success as an officer and his becoming a general was something of a surprise. His ending up in polite exile on Victoria wasn't, nor was his decision to do something to ensure a comfortable retirement without much caring what it was.

"I suppose you've got a point," Karras said. "But can any of us really afford to have Liu tell everything in return for a lighter sentence? If the Feddies have the wits of mite-rooters, that's what they'll do."

"Are we willing to be suspected of revolting simply to hide our tracks?" Brothertongue exclaimed.

This time the prime minister was sure that Karras' accusation was much stronger than "cold feet," but it was in Hellenic, so nobody understood it. Parkinson was the first to raise her voice above the senator's.

"I once read somewhere about 'He who wills the end, wills the means.' " She set her belt comp on the desk and flipped it open, knocking two of the prime minister's pipes onto the rug in the process.

Since the prime minister spoke only Anglic, he said nothing about the general, at least not out loud. He merely glared while she checked some figures, then snapped the cover down.

"I think our friend from Justice has just given us an option. Remember those Merishi who came in asking diplomatic asylum after the shot at Pak? Well, if we're not seceding, we're still part of the Federation. That means that we can grant them asylum and offer them protection just as legally as the Federal Army."

"What do the Scaleskins have to do with—" Karras began. Then his mouth hung open, his eyes widened, and he slapped both knees.

The general merely smiled benignly. "Exactly. They're a priceless intelligence source. The Federation will do a good deal to get them back. This might include dropping charges against General Liu."

"And I thought I was a good lawyer," the Justice deputy muttered.

"You are," Parkinson said. "But good laws need to be backed up with good soldiers."

"Enough trading compliments," Fitzpatrick said. "Can we arrange this without risking a confrontation with Federal forces? Because the minute they decide to shoot to defend the Merishi, our legal position becomes irrelevant."

"No," said Father Brothertongue. "It becomes hopeless."

Each stage of su-Irzim's journey to the fleet commander's cabin impressed him more with *Night Warrior*'s size. She was large even by the standards of the People, although elderly for a ship still in full commission, even in a "training squadron."

Indeed, she was large *because* she was elderly. A hundred and fifty years ago, the People occupied a much smaller volume of space. At the farther reaches of that volume, a ship or even a whole fleet might be expected to "fight, feed, and fix" for a year without supplies or reinforcements. Much of *Night Warrior*'s internal volume came from huge storage compartments and generous magazines.

Now that the People had fully equipped bases a single passage from human space, a fleet hardly needed to be its own base. Ships like *Night Warrior* were too large and needed too many in their crews, not to mention needing many spare parts that were no longer readily available.

So they were mostly out of first-line service. Overhauled, as *Night Warrior* had been, however, they were still formidable. With a crew that included only enough "in training" to give the right flavor, *Night Warrior* should be a match for any two human ships off Victoria.

That thought stayed with su-Irzim through one airlock after another, down passageways that constantly threatened to create interdimensional singularities, past bunkrooms and messes where the gabble and smell reminded him that he was overdue for lunch, and finally onto the Gold Deck. There the blue-clad guards examined his ID as if it might carry toxic contamination before passing him on down the final stage of his journey to Eimo su-Ankrai's cabin.

The private dining room was small, but it was another mark of the ship's size that it existed at all. It was not too small to hold four couches. Not full-sized couches; su-Irzim's former wife would have fitted comfortably onto any of them.

But couches, instead of chairs that sprouted from the deck like snoutweed from a marsh or even worse, hung down from the bulkheads like the kind of vine that produced nothing but berries you put in a bloodfeud opponent's ale.

Su-Irzim realized that he had been ground-bound long enough to forget the challenge of adjusting to the austere quarters of ships. Or perhaps he was just getting too old to see it as a challenge?

He bowed to the fleet commander and saluted the other guest, the squadron's chief Inquirer.

"Let my house be yours," su-Ankrai said, waving su-Irzim to the only vacant couch. A half-empty tray of appetizers filled the last couch, and saliva filled su-Irzim's mouth as he caught a whole new set of appetizing smells. Felkis in three different kinds of leaves, uhrims marinated in spices and then boiled in ale—good ale, too—a watering mouth was no longer an adequate response. His stomach rumbled.

"Did you hear me?" su-Ankrai asked.

Su-Irzim realized that he'd been about to give a mortal insult by appearing to refuse the fleet commander's hospitality. He filled a plate, drew ale into an antique mug, and settled down to quiet his stomach.

"It is a pleasure having you aboard," su-Ankrai said.

"It is a great honor," su-Irzim replied around a mouthful of uhrims. "But it is one that I—"

"Do not insult my old friend by implying that his judgment is failing," su-Ankrai said. "How is he, by the way?"

Profoundly disturbed at what the Victoria crisis may produce, if it escapes intelligent control, would have been truthful but untimely. Su-Irzim considered oblique ways of learning his commander's views without revealing his own, and finally settled on one.

"I should say he does magnificently. How else could he endure Behdan Zeg?"

Both senior commanders wrinkled their snouts. "I always said we should have switched Zeg and Sarlin!" the Inquirer muttered.

"Even had we been allowed to grip the decision, that might not have been wise," su-Ankrai replied. "Zeg lives down to the worst ideas the Smallteeth have of us. Sarlin can charm any sapient being so subtly they will reveal all their ancestors' vices to him before they know it. Besides, would our comrade here care to work with Zeg?"

Su-Irzim's shudder was not an act.

Conversation turned to shared memories of grand parties while the steward cleared away the appetizers, brought in dinner, and turned on both the screen and the music synthesizer. As the door slid shut behind the steward, the Hook and Horn crept on to the upper left-hand corner of the screen.

"I have you here because your work will be complex and the time you have to learn it less than we had hoped," the fleet commander said.

"How much less?"

"We leave in four days."

That was a considerable change from nine. "Is my work the same?"

"Yes."

"Then I swear there is no danger of my failing in my duty."

Su-Irzim did not expect to be forsworn, because F'zoar su-Weigho had provided him with information about his duties in advance. They were indeed complex, needing three titles to cover them all—chief of the intentions of the enemy group, assistant to the chief Inquirer, and liaison with Victoria System Inquiry Operations. The only fact he had been unable to learn was whether "Inquiry Operations" included only friendly ones, or whether he was supposed to keep a thumb on the humans as well.

Much study and a judicious mixture of meditation and exercise had let him build on previous experience in this kind of work, which had occupied ten of his twenty-two years in Fleet service. Four days less to learn what had to be learned aboard *Night Warrior* would not cripple him. It was barely even cause for annoyance.

"Before you become as complacent as you look," said the Inquirer, "I should say that there are some new developments in the Victoria crisis. If you are complacent on the basis of plans made from previous intelligence—"

"Come, come," su-Ankrai chided. "Let us not name our new comrade a fool. If he wishes to be thought one, let him offer evidence."

The Inquirer sounded even less pleased than before at having a lower-ranking Antahli interpreting the humans for him. This was no surprise to su-Irzim.

The Syrohdi are not always easy to bear, but bear them one must more often than not, or the People will be an easy

204

prey to any foe—and the humans are not the most dangerous we might face.

"You can think anything of me that you please, sir, if you'll fill my cup concerning Victoria. I assume the data is either recent or highly secret?"

"Both," the Inquirer said brusquely. "We meant no offense by withholding it until you were aboard. A reliable messenger is on his way to Fleet Commander su-Weigho at this moment."

This hardly guaranteed that there would be a secure way of discussing the new data with his cousin. It did promise well for the Inquirer's being willing to help su-Irzim do his work.

"The rebellion against the Bushranger Republic has failed," the Inquirer said. "There were a number of reasons for this, including secret Federation assistance to the Republican government and sabotage of the rebels' supply lines and air support. The military defeat of the rebels is complete, although some of their prisoners may be assigned to new Republican labor or service units."

"The immediate problem this gives us is the fate of *Fireflower*."

"Has she made another unauthorized mission?"

"That is the problem. We can't be sure."

Su-Irzim no longer felt anything remotely resembling complacency. The Merishi-designed, Baernoi-purchased converted medium cruiser *Fireflower* had been the link between the Baernoi depots in the asteroids and the regular commercial ships that brought in the concealed military shipments.

Loaded aboard those ships at their planets of origin, the cargoes would have been vulnerable to Federation Intelligence. Transshipped in space, the Federation could find them only by examining ships' logs. The Federation was not presently or prospectively able to examine the logs of Alliance or Merishi ships.

The combined Merishi–human crew aboard *Fireflower*, however, hadn't been content with running freight. They had used their ship's speed to spy on the Victoria Squadron, among other human activities. It seemed that *Fireflower* was as fast and sensor-loaded as many human warships, although she carried only a light self-defense armament.

"It appears that some of the Merishi aboard her are former Fleet personnel, instead of merchants, as we had been led to believe. It also appears that the humans aboard her belonged to a faction that feels seriously betrayed by the Alliance. They do not seem to know the role that Federation Intelligence played in cutting off their supplies, and blame the Alliance."

Su-Irzim frowned. It was not at the various qualifications—they were the common coin of intelligence work.

Nor was it at the presence of Merishi Fleet personnel aboard *Fireflower*. The Scaleskins as a whole were not warriors, and su-Irzim would swear by the Great Khudr's potency that their primary objective was to fling the People and the Smallteeth at each other's throats and profit from the resulting chaos.

The Merishi Fleet, however, was most honorably warlike. Its crews were skilled, determined, and well able to do their own fighting. Not all of them were opposed to the presently superior position of the humans, but those who were could make their opposition more effective than their merchant or banker counterparts. Much more effective, if they had access to sunbombs.

The cold of space seemed to enter the cabin at that last thought, piercing su-Irzim to the bones. He recited several Aids to Meditation and found no comfort in any of them.

He did find his voice, however.

"Where are the sunbombs?" *And if they are not meant to be discussed here, then perhaps it is not expected that I shall really do useful work.*

"They *were* in the hands of the Victoria branch of the People's Independence Front," the Inquirer said.

"Where are they now?"

"We do not know," su-Ankrai said.

Su-Irzim wanted to purge himself in the ale vat of whoever had lost the trail of the sunbombs, but they probably did not know who that fool was either!

He took a deep breath. "It seems to me that the disposition of the bombs depends primarily on two factors. Are the Merishi aboard *Fireflower* either in control or at least able to prevent unauthorized use of the bombs? And if there are no controls aboard the ship, or the bombs are not aboard it any longer, is anyone likely to warn the humans?"

"We don't know," the Inquirer said. Before su-Irzim could even think of gouging out his throat, he added, "There are devices built into all the bombs that make them comparatively easy to disable. There are several agents in place to whom orders can be sent, to activate the disablers. Those orders have been sent."

But have they been received, will they be obeyed, and could the disablers themselves be disabled if Smallteeth and Scaleskins allied their wits?

"I can see now why it's urgent for us to reach Victoria," su-Irzim said. "Shall I start preparing a list of alternative ways of pressing the bomb holders to refrain?"

"Yes. You are excused from the staff reception tonight. The first full staff conference will be tomorrow at 1030."

Thumbs rose and the fleet commander came as close to baring his throat as a Syrohd of his rank would ever do to a Antahl of su-Irzim's. Su-Irzim bowed himself out.

In the passageway, he mused his way back to his cabin, past sentries who looked hard at him to be sure he did not need assistance. He excused them for their good intentions.

Nineteen

The Mount Houton branch of Hennessey's had become an unofficial annex to the Brigade Officers' Club. In fact, since the official Officers' Club had two rooms in the Shepherd's Inn, little furniture, and even less liquor, Hennessey's did more business than its official counterpart.

It had one disadvantage, as Lucco DiVries realized when he saw his brother Raimondo approaching his table. Civilians could get in, whether they had an invitation (as he did from Sophie Bergeron) or not.

"Hullo, Luke."

"Hi, Ray."

The brothers' greeting was so tepid that Bergeron frowned. She hooked a stray chair with a foot and pushed it toward the elder DiVries.

"Sit down and have a drink."

"Kay still working her miracles?"

"She could make liquor out of mite eggs, I think."

Ray took the offered drink, gulped, and gagged. After an exaggerated fit of coughing, he put the glass down.

"I think she did exactly that, and now they're hatching."

"Go to Hospital Two," Lucco said. "That's where MedForce unloaded all the mite-treatment supplies." He didn't try to keep "Three's a crowd, brother mine" out of his voice.

Ray tried a bit harder to lighten the atmosphere. "No, I think it's only the shells dissolving. Ah, that's better." He finished the drink in two more gulps.

Respect for the brother who'd raised him wasn't going to keep Lucco's foot out of the seat of Ray's bush pants much longer. Fear of involving either of them, let alone Sophie, in a public brawl might keep his foot on the floor.

He pressed her foot under the table and she smiled back. "So what brings you in from Gar Lake, Citizen DiVries?" she asked.

"Actually, Gar Lake's down to a caretaker party and a few remaining locals. Most of the people who haven't—gone home—are putting up in the workers' barracks north of town along with the other refugees. I came over to make sure that the black-marketeers hadn't hijacked our clothing shipment."

Sophie and Lucco raised eyebrows at each other. Ray hadn't mentioned a third category of Gar Lakers, the ones who'd joined the rebellion and were now either dead, POWs, hospital patients, or fugitives in the wilderness. Ray himself was suspected of having turned a blind eye to the rebels' planning much longer than he should have.

Nothing would come of that suspicion, if he didn't step on his equipment again. There were a lot of people like Ray, walking around free because the Republic could either assembly-line try them or use due process and get nothing else done for the next year. Since the first was a political and the second an economic impossibility, Ray and his cohorts were free as the dust—for the moment.

"There's a lot of that around," Lucco said. "The Fed advisers who stayed on have been riding shotgun on some of the shipments. Maybe you should scare up a couple of them for the next load?"

"The Feds still around?"

"For oh, three, four more days. They're pretty busy teaching their counterparts in the volunteers—"

"Three or four more days? You're sure of that?" Ray asked.

Lucco thought he detected excitement in his brother's voice. He was damned near sure he detected suspicion on Sophie's face.

"Pretty sure, and what's the big deal? I haven't heard that it was a secret. Either that, or the Republic's got a weird notion of 'need to know.' "

"No big deal. It's just that it might take longer than that to haul everything for my people."

"So hire a kid I know. BoJo Johnson. He's an orphan, about twelve, thirteen Standard, but any black-marketeer tangles with him, he's going to wind up being sold for meat to his old customers."

Ray blanched. "They haven't really—"

"No, nobody's turned cannibal," Sophie said. "Nobody's getting fat either, but the dominion's doing its share and the Feds aren't stopping them."

"Good," Ray said. Something seemed to pass between him and Sophie; he poured himself another drink. "You know, I hope you two make something out of it. It'll be a change for me, being uncle to Baby Brother's kids instead of his being uncle to—"

Sophie's glass shattered in her hand. Lucco was untying his neckcloth while she was still staring at the dripping blood. He thought briefly of using the neckcloth to strangle his brother, but the look in his eyes was enough. Brother Ray had vanished toward the bar by the time the bleeding stopped.

"All right, Sophie. What is it?"

"Lucco, remember what you said about being overprotective?"

"I do. I also note that Brother Ray just put his foot in it. What's to keep me from doing the same, if you don't tell me?"

"How much does having children mean to you, Luke?"

"It has occurred to me that I might want them if I married a woman who also wanted them. Farther than that, deponent hath not got."

She gripped both his hands with her good one, a feat only her long fingers made possible. "Lucco, I might be the wrong person for you, whatever you wanted. But children— that's worse."

"You're sterile?"

"No. I left the Army after ten years, to get married. Two years later, we had a little girl. I had a bad time and mite trouble. Hysterectomy."

"Hey, they've had the regen techniques for that down for centuries."

"Not up here. The only full facility in the Dominion is down in Thorntonsburg. It didn't matter at the time, because I thought one was enough.

"She was crawling around one day, at the caregiver's. She crawled into a doorway, and the wind blew the door shut on her. It caught her skull. Brain-dead before they got her to the hospital."

Her words echoed in the silence Lucco was maintaining inside his head, so he wouldn't miss anything. He even stamped on his anger at Ray.

"That can do for a good marriage, and ours wasn't so good by then. My husband tried to beat me up one night. He forgot my combat training, and got as good as he gave.

"The jury did the right thing. Self-defense for me, and five years in prison for him. But he had friends in the Defense Ministry. I don't know what strings they pulled, but I wound up being transferred down from the Second Battalion to the Fourth."

Reservists had full medical coverage, including regens for non-service-connected disabilities. Territorials and militia didn't. Private plans varied; on Victoria, Lucco knew that most of them ran toward the low end of the scale of benefits.

Victoria wasn't Monticello or Charlemagne or Akhito. It never would be. But damn it, it could be better than it was, which was why Lucco DiVries had decided to stay and help it along. Whether or not he was with Sophie, and speaking of her—

"Sophie, you might end up getting the regen. You might end up not wanting children. You might end up not wanting me—although I hope you don't. But just in case we want to make babies—what about going back to quarters and staying in practice?"

Sophie knocked over two glasses and looked ready to throw one of them at him, then started to laugh and cry at the same time.

"With pleasure, Citizen DiVries."

"God, I hope it's not out of a sense of duty!"

Brigitte Tachin sat at a corner table in Hennessey's with a slice of mutated pizza and a glass of alleged brandy in front of her. She was reading a pocket print on career planning for junior officers.

This was a new—call it a subject for contemplation. Until the last few days she'd expected that the family situation would be resolved long before she reached the rank of lieutenant commander.

Now her TOAD, her volunteering, and her forthcoming commendation would all take years off her time to making rank. She might find herself with two and a half stripes before she was thirty, with the family situation still hanging fire, and some hard decisions to make.

This meant some thinking in advance. She knew she didn't want to accidentally condemn herself to staying a lieutenant commander for the rest of her service. Now what did she need to do to avoid that?

Half the pizza, thirty pages of the book, and most of the drink vanished before she noticed it. She'd just emptied the glass and thought of a second drink when Sergeant Esteva materialized at the table beside hers.

He was wearing civilian clothes and gave her an under-the-table hand signal to act. She tried to disguise a frown as an appraising look, then pushed her extra chair toward Esteva.

"I don't like to drink alone, if you want to know the truth."

Esteva feigned making up his mind, then nodded and shifted to the offered chair.

The waitress——about fourteen, probably one of Kate Hennessey's stray war orphans—brought another round of drinks. They clinked glasses.

"Is there anything else you don't like to do alone?" Esteva asked.

Tachin rolled her eyes to the ceiling in mock indignation at this brusque approach. Inside, a small voice was whispering that Esteva wouldn't be hurrying matters if he didn't think they needed it.

"Take walks."

Esteva rose and offered his arm. Tachin took it and they drifted across the outer dining room, through the weatherlock, and into the icy darkness of a Victorian winter night.

Twenty meters from the door they rounded a corner; five meters farther they found a niche suitable for one couple and fortunately unoccupied. They slipped into an embrace that would have deceived anyone more than a meter away and waited, to see if anyone had followed them.

Esteva's embrace was entirely professional—well, *almost* entirely. Tachin had a little trouble keeping hers the same way. Fraternization didn't appeal, and frankly neither did Esteva, but she hadn't been held at all in so damned long!

Now that the combat-induced hormonal high was long past, she wasn't sure how far she and Brian would let matters go. She did know that she was going to hug him harder than anyone had in years, and let him do the same to her.

"Okay, I think we're clear," Esteva said.

"Good. As long as this isn't real, I'm going to freeze solid in ten minutes."

"No problem. I just had another kind of proposition, from Ray DiVries."

"Lucco's brother? I thought he wasn't—"

"Not that kind of proposition. He wanted to know when the advisers were going home. He was real concerned about getting the date. Said he wanted to ask some of us to ride shotgun on supplies he's picking up for refugees from Gar Lake."

"Gar Lake. That was a rebel stronghold."

"About half and half. DiVries brought in the half who weren't rebels. At least he says they weren't rebels, but—I wouldn't take his word."

"He wouldn't be asking Feds to guard what he was planning to send to the rebels." She licked chapped lips. "Unless he was planning an ambush?"

"Haven't heard he's that sort, and doesn't seem like it," Esteva said. "But I'm going to put it around among the troops that we should go out in threes or fours when we go out. That way anybody wanting a cheap incident will have to pay full price. Can you do the same among the officers?"

"I can, but I know what the colonel will say. 'We can't show that we suspect our allies. Such suspicion is more likely to cause incidents than prevent them.'"

"Which colonel?"

"Borrie, but Colonel Luvic will probably go along with him."

"That doesn't mean you have to."

"Sergeant, I'm the second most junior officer among the advisers—"

"And afraid for your commendation?"

Tachin stiffened. Esteva decided to respond as if this had been passion and tried to kiss her neck. He got a mouthful of her synfur collar.

"Ptahh!" he said, spitting out hairs. "Serves me right. Sorry, ma'am."

"I shouldn't have snapped at you. But I don't see what—no, wait a minute.

"Suppose I suggest that officers log in and log out at their destinations. 'More efficient use of available transportation,' or some catchword like that. It'll cut the time that an incident can go undetected, at least."

"It can do more," Esteva said. His hug was now like a proud older brother's. "I can put a couple of reliable people on monitoring the log. Then we can be sure that there's a QR force ready to move. Besides any official one," he added.

"Unorthodox, but it should work," Tachin said.

"Orthodoxy plus two hundred stellars gets you a nice memorial," Esteva said. "Now, since we're not going to make this for real, *I'm* going to start freezing if we don't go inside." Hand in hand, they turned out of the niche and back down the street toward Hennessey's.

A kilometer below the surface of Riftwell, Rear Admiral Naomi Xera, Eleventh Fleet's chief of staff, sat at her desk. Her desk display glowed in front of her, locked to her private computer.

Three thousand kilometers overhead, the reinforcements for Victoria swung in orbit. In the last two days, the work of getting them ready to depart had slackened enough to notice. Xera had swum, played a round of handball with the chief of neurosurgery at Riftwell Base Hospital, considered playing something else with him, and composed a letter to Sho Kuwahara.

Now she even had enough time to write it.

Dear Sho,

By now you will have all the vital sadistics on what's coming to (or at) Victoria, so I won't bore you with them. I will say that Prange is no nicer than before, but he has done his usual fine job of whipping *Valhalla* back into operational condition. He also gets along all right with Ostrovsky of *Baikhal* and the cruiser-squadron commodores.

You may be wondering why you're only getting a carrier, another battlecruiser, and two understrength cruiser squadrons. You may even be thinking that you're being expected to skate on ice rings.

Let me tell you, old and honorable friend, that you are exactly right. That is the way we think of the Victoria Squadron right now. I don't recall a Navy unit performing quite so far beyond what we usually expect in the last fifteen years. (You can show this part of the letter to anyone you think needs a chance to *kvell* over their status as miracle workers.)

We're also thinking that unless the Baba is reinforced back up to her full strength, what you'll have should be enough. If she gets that or more, we can pull some ships away from Alliance-watching elsewhere, and send them to Alliance-watch off Victoria.

I don't know whether the Tuskers have any bright ideas of expanding their involvement in Victoria beyond the trouble they've already made. Rumor is that the fight between Antahli and Syrohdi is going to force a Diet general election, for the first time in nearly ten years. This may keep the Fleet looking over its shoulder at the politicians, or they may feel that they're freer to act than usual. I'm glad I don't have the job of guessing what the Tuskers are going to do next.

Speaking of what happens next, our bet is still up in the air. You said Frieda Hentsch was going out. I thought it would be Coletta or somebody brought in from outside the Eleventh.

It looks like neither of us is going to be proved right for a while. The Pocket Pistol says she's been sending the Hentschmen to Victoria because it needs them and they need experience. She hasn't applied to go herself. I expect she will expect this selflessness to be repaid with a shower of stars, etc., on the Hentschmen, if they earn it. Nobody has ever said Hentsch wasn't ambitious, but like you, she's never been stupid about it.

As for Coletta, he's being transferred out of the Eleventh. Apparently they're putting together a talent task force for a major-caliber housecleaning in the Eighth, and Coletta is going to be one of the official ass-kickers. Success at the job will almost guarantee him that third star, without having to stick a toe into Victoria's sandy waters, so he's already packing.

All this means that unless Victoria blows up again and bigger than before, you and Kornilov can see the thing through. Kornilov knows the ground, knows most of the people, and is pretty much all right at the strategic and operational level. For tactics he's got one first-class brigade C.O., he's about to get another (even if this will make Victoria look like a Gurkha resort) and Borha is a good reserve for brigade and a first-class task-force leader as he is.

Throw in the politics, and I admit that our friend Mikhail doesn't look so good. But a lot of people are thinking out loud about how impossible the situation was, and could they have done better? I don't know how much of this epidemic of humility is genuine, and how much of it is following Schatz's and Berkson's lead. *They* certainly aren't going to go headhunting, unless somebody really *needs* theirs handed to them on a platter.

This epidemic, incidentally, probably owes a lot to our

friends in the Republic and the Dominion of Victoria, who did a nice job of hanging on against the rebels and then knocking them flat on their dusty arses without too much help from us. If you want to call off the bet, I'd suggest we pool what we were going to spend on my ski set and your boy's graduation present and throw one hell of a party for the nice Victorians who've made us all look good.

Let me know what you think.

Yours, *arokh heorkh he-galuth,*
Naomi

"Here's a third reference to 'special weapons,' " Lieutenant Darlington said. He passed the page of the interrogation transcript across the table to Brian Mahoney.

Mahoney looked at it and sighed. It was the same fuzzy near rumor as the other two references. Somebody had heard that somebody else had said that she'd heard a third somebody had a "special weapon" in reserve in case the rebellion looked like it was going down to defeat.

Well, the rebellion had gone down to defeat and no "special weapon" had materialized. A good many people who'd taken the field as rebels were still unaccounted for, either merged with the general population, gone underground, or fled into the bush. The weather and lack of supplies should bring the last category in fairly soon; as for the others, they were the Republic's problem.

"I think it's another case of the morale-boosting rumor about super-weapons or super-allies or some such." Mahoney said, handing the papers back. "They probably had rumors about improved stone axes in the days of Neanderthal man."

"Likely enough," Darlington said. He yawned and stretched. "I'll flag it, and hand it over to the com gang. Anything happening with our Merishi guests?"

"Nothing, except the usual complaints about the food and the quarters. I think right now they're sort of for the record, but they might get serious if we don't ship them south pretty soon."

"It's still two more days as far as I've heard," Darlington said. "You'd think Fort Stafford would have secure quarters ready sooner than this."

"Oh, I think they've been secure against bombs and rockets for quite a while," Mahoney said. "My guess is they want to keep the media out, too, at least until the interrogation is over."

"The media are going to want Kornilov's blood if they think that," Darlington said. "Oh well, it's not on our watch." Another yawn made the last words barely intelligible.

"Why don't you call it a night?" Mahoney said. "I can wind up here."

"Nobody's going to sleep in our tent until Pocher gets snored out," Darlington said.

"Have you tried waking him?"

"The last time I did, he came up with his pistol aimed right at my nose."

So Karl's still wrestling with nightmares? I'm not going to throw stones at him, unless I come out better from something happening to Brigitte, God forbid.

"Tell you what, Greg," Mahoney said. "Why don't we swap beds for the night? You hit mine now, I'll hit yours when I'm done."

"Fair"—another yawn, the biggest of all—"enough."

Mahoney followed Darlington to the door and watched him lope across the field toward the sleeping shelters. Overhead, the sky was clouding up, but the Prince's Moon was three-quarters full and lit up most of what was still clear.

Two more days, and back to *Shenandoah*, to Brigitte, and to warmth. He hoped neither the ship nor the woman would be offended by the fact that warmth was on his mind more often than the other two together.

An attacker rode overhead, too high and slow to make a sound but all its lights on. For a moment it outshone the Prince, then faded into the clouds.

Lucco DiVries turned over in the bed he shared with Sophie Bergeron. She murmured something wordless but comforting and tightened her embrace.

Sleep was approaching DiVries, but it hadn't arrived yet. He played back memories of lovemaking, knowing that this might keep him awake but thinking the pleasure worth the price. Then his thoughts drifted on to the future—his future.

A future with Sophie? Why not? He was interested, and she was too damned sensible not to let his interest be a factor in her decision.

So—a future together. On Victoria, or someplace else? DiVries had been born here, but he'd also lost no time shaking its mite-loaded dust from his boots and taking to space. He'd come home to help his family, then stayed to help a planet that needed him more than it had twenty years before. Now something else had grown out of this icy desert. Something warm, something that wasn't a gift of Ray or Reesa or the Navy.

His embrace tightened. He would have liked a warmer planet. Or maybe something would happen that would let them settle farther south? Anyway, they ought to be able to arrange something. *After* Sophie had that regen, though, and preferably someplace where her fair complexion wasn't just an invitation to skin cancer. . . .

In Thorntonsburg, Prime Minister Fitzpatrick dreamed of soldiers rampaging through the streets of the city. They wore Federation uniforms, or what looked like Federation uniforms, but all their equipment was black, their faces looked like Baernoi, and they glowed from within.

He woke up drenched with sweat, just short of crying out.

Rose Liddell dreamed of the college drama society's *Sister House*, where she and Josie Atwood had been leads, and their final duet. She forced herself awake before the dream carried her onto the fight they'd had when she said she was joining the Navy.

They'd long since made up, but Liddell's conscience still gave off twinges, like a tooth about to need a dentist.

Brokeh su-Irzim dreamed of the settled hemisphere of Victoria, scarred in half a dozen places with the raw glare of sunbomb explosions. Then it turned into a hemisphere of Petzas, the explosions doubled in number and size, and he woke up with the sentries pounding on his door, asking why he'd cried out.

He was able to explain without telling the truth, which would certainly have meant his being put groundside.

Captain Bogdanov did not dream, that he could remember the next morning.

He put this down to a lapse of memory, but noted that if he couldn't remember at least one dream three times in a row, he would see Surgeon Mori.

Twenty

Mikhail Kornilov was in bed and unaware of his surroundings, but not asleep. His senses focused completely on Indira Chatterje, and from the look on her face she seemed to be returning the compliment.

Eventually the two vigorous but undeniably middle-aged bodies reached their limits. Chatterje pulled the blankets over both of them and curled against her companion's massive frame.

They'd passed from satisfied desire to the early stages of going to sleep when the alarm on the secure circuit chimed.

"Son of a bitch!"

Kornilov sat up, throwing off the coverings. He hoped that whoever was calling here, now, on the secure circuit, was reporting the system's primary going nova or at least a landing by Baernoi strike commandos.

If they were disturbing his sleep for anything less, he was going to disturb theirs with at least the threat of a court-martial. SOP was explicit; they would have violated it; that could be construed as insubordination or some other major offense if Kornilov so chose. He probably wouldn't, but it wouldn't do the disturber any harm to sweat for a few days.

He opened the circuit, and at the last moment remembered that both he and Indira wore only light coats of sweat. He one-wayed the screen just as it lit up.

A handsome and improbably well groomed female MP captain looked out of the screen. Indecently well groomed, for this hour of the night—or rather, morning. Kornilov noted the name on her well-rounded tunic.

"Good morning, Captain Morley. I sincerely hope this is urgent."

"The provost marshal and I believe that it is. General Liu is no longer in military custody."

"He escaped?"

"Sir, we're not sure that his departure from custody was

an escape or an accident. We are trying to find out which while we try to recover him."

This was serious enough that Kornilov decided against threatening a court-martial. A good tongue-lashing might meet requirements.

"Why is there any doubt—" Kornilov began, but Captain Morley had vanished. A map of the Thorntonsburg area replaced her.

Captain Morley's voice returned, cool and crisp, as if ignoring the questions of major generals was a minor matter. She was one of the Hentzschmen, Kornilov knew. From the name she might also be one of the Monticello Morleys, old colonial aristocracy if there ever was such a thing, so maybe she was right.

"General Liu was being transported from the penal barracks at Fort Stafford to a cell in the Thorntonsburg City Jail. You may remember, sir, that the dominion government requested the right to arraign him on charges of bribery of their officials and misappropriation of dominion funds, in addition to the military—"

"Captain Morley, I realize that you are a nocturnal lifeform and that I am not. My memory of what authorizations I have given and what I have not is still clear. Please continue with what happened tonight, not two days ago."

Morley remembered enough military courtesy to say, "Yes, sir," before continuing.

"Because the city jail has no airlanding facilities, General Liu and his escort were transferred at the Thorntonsburg Airport to ground vehicles provided by the Dominion National Police."

Kornilov wanted to grind his teeth. He was not only being given bad news, he was being told things he already knew in perfect syntax. He decided not to risk emergency dentistry and went on listening.

"On the way into the city, a ground truck had skidded into General Liu's vehicle. Both vehicles were demolished and several people were hurt. In the inevitable confusion and concern for the injured, nobody noticed for a couple of minutes that General Liu was nowhere in sight."

"Any question of a security leak?"

"Sir, the dominion authorities were fully informed and entirely cooperative, and have remained so. Informing them was done at your orders, to promote good—"

"I don't need to be told why I showed good sense,"

Kornilov snapped. "Perhaps you should be told why you need to show it by telling the story more quickly."

The "yes, sir" was almost perfunctory. Kornilov decided that trying to teach Captain Morley military courtesy tonight would be futile and cause even more delays than her syntax. Besides, the situation just might be as complicated as she seemed to think.

"The local authorities have taken the casualties to the nearest hospital and are searching the area for General Liu. The provost marshal's office is contributing tactical communications and medical teams, who will remain at the search party's CP until further notice. Considering the area, we feel this will give the maximum amount of help and the minimum amount of provocation."

Kornilov had to agree. The area where Liu had vanished was known as Parrville, a crowded, rather tattered part of the capital city. Houses, shops, small and not so small factories, and accommodations for people who spent most of their time in pubs jostled one another up and down the narrow streets. It was a hotbed of impartial hostility to all authority, and the people with local knowledge seemed to be the logical candidates for sticking their noses into such a place.

"The accident seems to have been genuine enough. The street was icy and the truck was heavily loaded. Also, one of the truck drivers herself is in the hospital, with a broken arm and cracked ribs."

Kornilov nodded. Suicidal attempts to destroy an enemy were something every soldier had to face. Suicidal efforts to help an unknown general escape punishment for his crimes were distinctly rarer.

"So what's the theory on Liu? Escape or injury or both?"

Morley smiled, which transformed her whole face. Kornilov mentally undressed her, and decided that if Indira had meant less to him, she might have had a rival in Captain Morley.

"You've summed it up very nicely yourself, sir. He may have tried to make a break for it. He may have been injured and wandered off. Or he may have been shaken enough to forget why he'd been cooperating with us and tried to escape without really meaning to.

"Since he had no outdoor clothing and it's twenty-five below outside, we're concerned about exposure. We're also concerned about some local troublemaker deciding that it would be a good joke to hide him. That would be a major incident for certain, and a bad one."

Captain Morley was clearly as sensible as she was decorative. *Well, the Pocket Pistol hasn't been known for picking vacuum brains.*

"It seems to me that everything I would have ordered done is being done already. Let me know when the situation changes, and in any case at 0600."

"Yes, sir."

The screen blanked. Kornilov sat on the edge of the bed and groped for his slippers. A moment later he felt small deft fingers massaging the back of his neck.

"Shall we get dressed?" Chatterje said.

"I refuse to lose more sleep just because General Liu has—what's the local phrase, 'done a bunk'?"

"Then I'll see what I can do."

What Chatterje did was one of her famous soothing massages, not as varied as her erotic ones but just as effective. Kornilov was sound asleep at 0600 when Captain Morley called to report that a thorough search of Parrville had turned up no trace of General Liu.

The sun was well up in the sky, and Brian Mahoney was beginning to wonder if the returning advisers had fallen into a black hole somewhere between Mount Houton and the Border Base. Reminding himself that there was enough wind to slow anything short of an attacker didn't help.

Rather than stay at the Service CP and give all the militia the spectacle of a Navy officer fidgeting, he closed up his coat and hood, then went outside. The wind promptly started nibbling at every bit of exposed skin and tried to insinuate itself through his clothing.

The lee of a fragment-scarred boulder let him stop shivering and start surveying the base. It looked as if every unassigned pair of hands around had joined the working parties waiting to load the last shipment of supplies. As far as Mahoney was concerned, if it would get him and Brigitte out of here faster, he'd lift and tote himself.

Most of the unassigned hands wore militia multiform. The only Federation uniforms Mahoney could make out were on the two squads guarding the Merishi, on the eastern edge of the base.

The drone of approaching lifters rose above the wind and penetrated Mahoney's hood. Then the aerial convoy began dropping out of the cloud base. Mahoney counted a good fifty lifters, more than the advisers could have needed. Then he remembered that the Bushranger Republic was sending an aerial escort, as well as most of a rifle company. There'd been reports of last-ditch rebel holdouts filtering back into the Blanchard Canyon area after the Federation search-and-clear force pulled out.

Mahoney wished the Bushrangers much joy in turning over ice-cold rocks. He was beginning to count the minutes to seeing Brigitte, and the hours to being warm aboard *Shenandoah*—and maybe warm with Brigitte—

He jumped as a hand gripped his arm. Karl Pocher's voice spoke to the left. "I think they're splitting up. Yeah, there's about ten of them going down toward the east. That's a long way to haul supplies—"

A moment later it became obvious that the rest of the approaching lifters weren't landing on the pad either. One group settled like a necklace around the summit of Cheek Hill. A second landed halfway down the hill. Meanwhile, the eastern group had not only landed but started disgorging fully armed troops.

From inside the CP, Mahoney heard Captain Huong's voice begin describing the situation. It cut off suddenly, as the howl of jamming blasted everyone's ears.

"I think we'd better go down and find out what the hell's going on," Mahoney said. He unsnapped his holster and saw Pocher chamber a round in his scattergun.

As they reached the level, Mahoney saw that not all of the Bushranger lifters had landed. Four were circling overhead, and it didn't surprise him to see that three of them were the K/G-96 gunship conversions. The last one seemed to have a few nonstandard antennae sprouting in odd places, and Mahoney suspected he was looking at the source of the jamming.

By the time he and Karl crossed the pad, they weren't alone. Jammed radios didn't keep the alert from going out by word of mouth; fully armed Federation troops were coming up behind the two Navy officers. A whole platoon of them, a fine sight until one remembered that the platoon was half the Federation's combat strength at the base.

The Aldrich twins, Booth and Galina, seemed to be in charge of the militia deployed at the edge of the field. Galina stepped out, snapped off a geometrically precise salute, and gave Mahoney a somewhat tentative smile.

"Good morning, Brian."

"Good morning, Lieutenant Aldrich," Mahoney said. "It might be even better if you told me what's going on."

"Brian, I have orders not to let anyone from the Federation—"

"The Victoria Brigade, Gally," Booth said.

"Anyway, nobody from the regulars is allowed on base until further notice."

"Oh?" Pocher said. "When do we get that further notice?"

"As soon as Colonel Borrie finishes conferring with Colonel Luvic and comes down here."

"And when—oh, never mind," Pocher said, spitting on the ground in disgust. His spittle crackled as it froze, loud enough to make several militiamen raise their pulsers.

"Easy does it, Karl." Mahoney said. He saw that he was senior Federation officer present and added, "Okay, everybody, let's back off about twenty meters. I'd suggest a one-squad OP, SSWs deployed, and everybody else try to stay out of the wind. If I know Borrie, that conference is going to last half the morning."

That was Mahoney's one error in judgment. Borrie and Luvic came down the hill less than ten minutes later. Borrie walked with a cane; Luvic looked like someone ready to commit either murder or suicide once she could decide which.

"If you say good morning once more," Luvic muttered, "I'm going to vomit all over your boots."

"Then I'll save everybody's time by being as rude as you are," Borrie said blandly. "The situation is this, people. The governments of the Dominion of Victoria and the Bushranger Republic have signed an Act of Union, making them the Associated States of Victoria. This act will be proclaimed over the planetary news channels in"—Borrie looked at his watch—"about eighteen minutes.

"Associated forces have moved into this camp now, because we want to be the Federation representatives for dealing with the Merishi refugees. If we can have custody of them, we have no further business here."

For a moment Mahoney thought Luvic had decided in favor of having a stroke instead, and was about to have it. Then her face and breathing returned almost to normal.

"Colonel Borrie has shown me an authentic document proclaiming the Act of Union," she said. "He's also let me see an advance copy of Prime Minister Fitzpatrick's broadcast. If it's shit, it's authentic shit.

"The lifters with the rest of the advisers are up there—" pointing at the group halfway up Cheek Hill. "I want officers' call there in five minutes. Where's Captain Huong?"

"At the CP, trying to get through the jamming," Pocher said.

"They're going to jam us until broadcast time. Tell him to get his ass up the hill, or I'll come and drag it out whether anything else comes with it or not!"

Pocher left at a run. Mahoney followed Luvic at a more discreet pace, occasionally looking back toward the camp or forward and uphill for Brigitte.

It took until seven minutes before broadcast time to assemble all the officers and unit leaders. Luvic passed around a copy of the Act of Union while she delivered her briefing.

"If this was a 'you can always take one with you' situation, we'd have already started shooting. We have two rifle platoons, thirty technical people, and eighty-some advisers. The—whatevers—have a full rifle company plus all their 150-odd militia here. We could pretty much wreck them, even if they wrecked us.

"Unfortunately, the lawyers got to Fitzpatrick and his friends. The whatevers aren't seceding. They're just pooling their resources with the Bushrangers. The Bushrangers did secede, so that means the Associated States and the Federation are going to have to negotiate their relationship. But Fitzpatrick lays it on pretty thick about 'preserving a proper climate for negotiation.' He keeps saying that we can trust the Associated States' cooperation; can they trust ours?"

"What about the Merishi?" Huong and Darlington asked almost together.

"I'm coming to them. I've agreed to a truce on two conditions.

"One is that we can evacuate the camp immediately, by attacker if necessary. Borrie and I don't want any incidents.

"The other is that we can ask the Merishi if they want to go with the Associated Schemers of Victoria. Any who don't ride out with us. Merishi ethics may be as scaly as their skins, but they did put themselves in our hands."

Everybody was nodding when a lean, bearded figure came striding up the hill. He wore a Republican uniform complete with their sergeant's stripes.

"Sergeant Esteva," Luvic said. "I thought we'd lost you. And you're out of uniform."

"Well, ma'am, I thought it would be easier to slip aboard one of the Bushranger lifters like this. It was. It even got me through the security perimeter to the Merishi quarters."

"Yes?"

"I got there just as the Ass-ossified troops were handing the Merishi guns. Not just sidearms, an SSW and a grenade launcher. Baernoi-made to Merishi specs, it looks like."

Luvic looked up at the gray sky and the circling gunships. Without looking down, she said, "I will not kill the bearer of bad news. I will not kill the bearer of bad news, I will not kill the bearer of bad news." She looked at Esteva. "What I tell you three times is true."

"Thank you, ma'am."

"I thank you, Sergeant. It never helps dignity to go around asking dumb questions."

Mahoney thought that none of them had much dignity to lose, but decided not to throw what little he had away by saying so. He joined the others squatting on the icy rocks as the clock came around to 1045, the jamming died, and the portable screen came to life.

"My fellow Victorians," came Fitzpatrick's voice. "It is my duty and privilege today to bring you momentous news. Yesterday the Bushranger Republic and the Dominion of Victoria signed an Act of Union, making them one government under the name of the Associated States of Victoria.

"You are entitled to know both the reasons and the implications of this act. The principal reason . . ."

Mahoney gave Fitzpatrick as much attention as he could when he was slowly freezing and the prime minister wasn't saying much his audience hadn't already learned or guessed. He had to admit that Fitzpatrick didn't look particularly happy about the situation, which might mean some divided opinions in high places among the Associates.

But unless the Associates' divisions started *another* civil war, the Federation didn't have the strength to exploit them. The Victorians, Mahoney concluded, had already outsmarted the Federation and were now in a position to outfight them as well.

Until the new brigade landed, at least, and if the Victorians had meanwhile knocked out all existing Federation ground units and bases, where the devil would it land? It could combat-assault in, if it was loaded for that, which it proba-

226

bly wasn't. Even if it was, CAs were bloody messes and didn't do a thing about all the pissed-off Victorians who'd turn guerrilla—

No, even if Fitzpatrick said it, the Federation was going to have to negotiate. So the less shooting, the better.

By the time Mahoney's thoughts reached this point, Fitzpatrick was off the air and a nervous announcer was promising a repeat of the announcement every half hour until further notice. From what Mahoney had seen of the Victorian media, they would probably have the largest audience in their history today.

He stood up, slapped one buttock, and felt a small hand patting the other one. He whirled, embracing the empty air centimeters above Brigitte's head as she ducked, then fell over backward as she leaped into his arms. As they crashed to the ground, Mahoney knew that he'd lost more dignity, but in a good cause.

Captain Liddell tested the round counter in the magazine of Admiral Kuwahara's carbine and noted that it was nominal. Then she hand-counted the rounds to be absolutely sure, and handed the magazine to the admiral.

He accepted it with a bow that was almost a parody and a smile that barely deserved the name. Viewed objectively, it was ludicrous for Liddell and Bogdanov to be sitting in flag quarters, arming and equipping the admiral for his dirtside visit like a couple of squires readying their samurai for battle.

However, on Victoria at any rate, today seemed to have been given over to the ludicrous. Not, thank higher powers, to bloodshed yet. Neither on the ground nor in space, and the Victoria Squadron was on Alert One only because Kornilov was keeping his troops at the same level.

Kuwahara stood up and let Bogdanov adjust his battledress in a couple of tight spots. Then he slung on the carbine, tucked the helmet under his arm, and turned to look at himself in the mirror. He almost managed not to laugh.

"The next time Kornilov proposes a meeting like this, I'm going to insist on setting the uniform. Kornilov may think he looks younger in battledress, but I look like exactly what I am, an admiral—"

"Taking a sensible precaution, if you'll pardon me for saying so," Bogdanov put in. He finished checking the fuses on four thunderflash grenades and inserted them into a pouch. "Your grenades, sir."

Kuwahara picked them up as if they'd been red-hot. "Precaution against what? We can't fight our way out of Government House if they're determined to keep us in. Not without a rifle company, and I can just see the Associates letting us bring *that* to the meeting."

"There are always lone assassins," Liddell pointed out. "Remember Colonel Pak."

"I'm not forgetting him. But we'll have all the security the Associates can muster, plus an MP platoon configured to fight a small war."

"That still might not be enough, if the assassin didn't care about getting away," Liddell persisted. She agreed with Kuwahara about the effect on his dignity, but thought an undignified admiral more useful than a dead one.

Kuwahara threw up his hands in a gesture of defeat. "All right. I'll be doing enough arguing with the Associated Victorians, and on an empty stomach, too. But I doubt that I'm going to end my days under a plastext couch, sniping at would-be assassins with a carbine I can barely aim."

"I don't think so either," Liddell said, "but both Pavel and I didn't want to lose you to even a low-order probability."

Kuwahara sat down at his desk and opened a drawer.

"In case we're all wrong, I've left a few things for both of you. One of them is a back-dated emergency local promotion for Rose, to the rank of acting rear admiral. Somehow I've always thought that was a more dignified title than commodore. So, I suspect, does Captain Prange."

He handed her a code card. "This opens the drawer and accesses my personal file. I won't tell you what's in it, because I refuse to be known as that sentimental until after I'm dead. Since I won't be for some time . . ."

Kuwahara stood up, and his weapons harness caught on the arm of his chair. It would have gone over if Bogdanov hadn't untangled it. He'd just finished when the door chime sounded.

"Your lunch, Admiral," Commander Gesell said, stepping inside. She wore full flight gear including body armor, but carried an insulated container slung over one shoulder.

"Captain Liddell, what have you been doing behind my back?" Kuwahara said. "If you've got full commanders as stewards, what else are you likely to be planning?"

"This commander is planning to take you down to

Thorntonsburg in an attacker she's got warmed up and waiting," Gesell said. "Jensen and I thought you might want a bite on the way."

"You and the captain's steward?" Kuwahara said meditatively. He was sniffing at the container, but the sealing was too good. "You and Jensen, without Captain Liddell's knowledge? I'm surprised at you, Commander."

"So am I," Liddell said.

"Really?" Kuwahara said.

"Completely," Liddell said.

"Captain, lying is a court-martial offense," Kuwahara said. "By the time I return, I hope you'll consider your position. Commander Gesell, I'm at your disposal."

As the door closed, Liddell and Bogdanov heard the intercom blare.

"Now hear this. Now hear this. The captain will address all hands in five minutes. The captain will address all hands in five minutes. That is all."

"I'll take it in here, Pavel," she said, sitting down at Kuwahara's desk and slipping the card into a breast pocket. At least the charade of girding the admiral for battle had relaxed her enough so that she'd look better on the screen.

Twenty-one

Candice Shores's bag came sailing out of the attacker's hatch. It nearly hit her, bounced on the hard ground, and rolled under her feet. She retrieved both it and her balance, thrust a finger up at the attacker's cockpit, and sprinted for the edge of the field.

The attacker went supersonic low and close, kicking up snow and making antennae dance. It climbed until it was a molten sliver against the blue sky, then circled until another joined it. The pair slowed and descended, to join the standing patrol over the Armistice Zone.

"Hey, Captain! Over here!"

Shores turned to see a familiar beard jutting out of a doorway. The face above it was more weathered than it had been twelve days ago, but it was still a pleasure to see.

"Esteva! What the hell are you doing here?"

"Me'n the rest of the Scout advisers—we heard the company was coming in here. Somebody also told us there was an attacker heading this way. So we sort of borrowed space on it."

"What did Top Entemann say about that?"

"He was medevacked. Exposure and concussion finally caught up with him. That left me in charge."

"Anybody besides Scouts on the attacker?"

Esteva shrugged. "Not on ours, I know. I suppose the mob jobs found their own way out of the base sooner or later."

"The base's evacuated?"

"Turned over to the rebel—sorry, the Associated Victorian—militia."

Since there wasn't much in Border Base One that hadn't been provided by the militia in the first place, this made sense. It still hurt a bit to think of the militia squatting where Federation soldiers had died to hold the line until the militia got their nerve back.

Shores reminded herself to be fair. Warriors came in a lot of different shapes and sizes, including some you had to allow one mistake, because if they survived it they wouldn't make any more.

Let's see if the Vics make it.

Now she could see that Esteva was alone. "Where's the rest?"

"I couldn't find you—"

"Did you look?"

"Have a heart, Captain. You just got here. So what difference does it make?"

"Did you look?"

"I got word from some Navy type over at HQ that you weren't in yet, but most of the Company was. So I just turned the people loose, to go home."

The way he said that made Shores realize that Scout Company really was home, to Esteva and probably to others as well. Flattering, but that didn't take care of one little detail Esteva had left flapping in the breeze, along with his tongue. . . .

"No debriefing?"

"What?"

"All the advisers were supposed to be debriefed before RTUing. Did anybody debrief you at the base?"

"I don't remember."

"But if you were betting something important, like your stripes, what would you bet?"

"I'd bet no."

"I thought so. Nothing here, either?"

"We haven't been here that long ourselves, Captain, ma'am."

"Esteva, if you salute, I am going to pull your arm out of its socket and beat you to death with it."

"Yes—okay, Captain." He managed to look and sound sheepish. "If we really stepped in it, I'll take it for the other guys."

"You won't have stepped in it if we get you debriefed before Major Nieg hears about it. Otherwise he's going to do obscene things to both of us."

"Hadn't heard he went both ways—"

"I said *obscene*, Sergeant, not interesting. Believe me, they won't be interesting."

"Except maybe the Chinese way?"

"Exactly. Now pull your mob of ex-advisers together and

231

have them ready for a debriefing in one hour. Otherwise I'm going to take up the Baernoi custom of making gloves out of my enemies' skins."

"Can do. We're over in what used to be the Alliance barracks. They pulled out a couple of hours ago. Rumor says they got orders to recognize the Armistice Zone as Federation territory again, which means they're recognizing the Act of Union."

"Bounce the Alliance!"

"Anyone in particular?"

"Just start with whoever turns you on. *After* the debriefing."

Esteva was grinning as he sprinted off for the barracks. Shores headed toward Major Abelsohn's HQ at a more leisurely pace. She wished she could feel more cheerful about the prospect of spearheading any action Victoria Brigade took over the Act of Union.

The problem was, her Scouts might be a spearhead all right. But it would be a spear thrown at a ghost, or even into the shadows on the chance that something might be lurking there.

She and her people were being subjected to a military version of coitus interruptus. She was finding this no more agreeable out of bed than in.

Since her last visit, HQ had acquired several additional layers of armorplast and beaming plus a roof-mounted missile launcher. The guards had acquired red eyes and armored vests, and the hallways had more blast doors.

Abelsohn looked pretty much the same, except for his shoulder boards. Shores saluted, then embraced him, then tapped the silver wreath.

"Who was giving those away?"

"A promotion board, with a dull day and a sadistic streak. They decided it would be entertaining to promote a perfectly happy captain to field grade."

"Remind me to keep my head down when they're around."

Abelsohn hugged her back, then held her at arm's length and looked almost grim. "Candy, you're going to be a major by the time you leave Victoria. Bet?"

"What were you thinking of betting?"

"I'll figure something out, but right now what's happening in the world?"

"Do you want the briefing report or a brief report?"

"You could also strip to your undershorts," came a

sepulchural voice from the wall, "and give us a report in briefs."

The last words let Shores home in on the sound. She spotted the open ventilation grille and the feet sticking out of it, bent over, gripped the feet, and heaved.

Charles Longman flew out of the ducting, churning up a cloud of dust that set them all to sneezing. This didn't keep Shores from pulling him to his feet by one ear and his hair.

"Lieutenant Longman, weren't you sent down from *Shenandoah* for something like that?"

"Yeah, Charlie," Abelsohn said. "Do you want to apologize to the nice captain? Or do I send you back up to Bogdanov with your last remark tattooed where it might cramp your style?"

Longman pretended to clutch frantically at his groin, then grinned. "Sorry, Captain. Chalk it down to oxygen deprivation in that duct. Major, whoever sold us that preciptator ought to be locked up in there for a week or two."

"Noted, Charlie. Well, Captain?"

"No harm done, Lieutenant. But now Major Abelsohn and I have a little talk to get through." She jerked a thumb at the door. "Launch!"

Longman vanished, trailing dust and sneezes. Abelsohn pulled out a bottle and two glasses. "A dust cutter?"

Shores nodded. Abelsohn filled his and raised it. "To toasting peace on Victoria in something better than this."

"Amen." The liquor cut the dust in her throat, while the dust protected delicate tissue from the bite of the alcohol.

"So. We've got your Scouts and the garrison and you. Anybody else coming out? And when they do, what am I supposed to do for them?"

Shores summarized the situation as she'd heard it from General Langston and Colonel Borha. Everybody was being very careful not to shoot or even make the other side think they might. The fact that Victoria's status was up for negotiation all over again meant that nobody wanted to undercut their negotiating position.

"We're staying on Alert One until Kornilov finishes his conference with the Associate—leaders," Shores concluded. "Meanwhile, what Langston's setting up here is a three-company task force. Half the First/Victoria plus the Scouts, with your people doing support and security."

Abelsohn looked indignant. "I thought Langston's head was too pointed to get that far up his ass. We're field-ready, or we can be in a couple of days. But we don't have the people to be support for a skinny battalion."

"He's sending out support as well, a little right now and a lot when 215 hits planet. The thing is, our major job will be to watch the border with Seven Rivers and *stamp* anybody who tries to jump the border, from either direction."

"Either direction?" Abelsohn's bushy eyebrows rose.

"Hotheads or rebel holdouts might think they've got carte blanche to 'liberate' Seven Rivers. The Alliance might decide to interpret 'hot pursuit' a bit liberally."

"So you're going to be the local referee in this match?"

"Not me. I think the X.O. of the Second/215s coming out. One of the Hentschmen and no Major Nice Guy, but he knows his job."

Abelsohn muttered something in Hebrew. "What's that?" Shores asked.

"A blessing for the Hentschmen. Rough translation: 'Bless, oh Lord, those who are ignorant with the desire to learn.'"

Shores held out her glass. "That might not be a bad blessing for the Associated higher-ups."

"Amen."

Admiral Kuwahara wasn't surprised to find that the local security forces around Government House also looked able to fight a war. They still greeted the two flag officers with smart salutes and even polite smiles, and passed them through to the prime minister's office with minimal delay.

The only delay came over the grenades, which the Special Branch inspector wanted to confiscate. Kornilov flatly refused. Kuwahara didn't care much one way or the other, but had to present a united front with the general.

They finally compromised on turning the grenades over to Captain Morley, commanding the MP security platoon. She and her people would be staying in the outer office, along with the Special Branch and Associate militia contingents.

In fact, thought Kuwahara, looking at the room and counting up the various security details, there were enough people to stop an assassin with bare hands if necessary. Or to create a hideously bloody incident if somebody set off a bomb.

Inside the office, Kuwahara saw Governor-General Gist seated at the table between the president and Father Brothertongue. The governor-general didn't look any too happy to be there, but Kuwahara was ready to make his position as easy as possible. Even if Gist had gone over to the Association, he was more likely to help than hurt. The same couldn't be said of quite a few Associate leaders, starting with Senator Karras.

By the end of the first half hour, Kuwahara's circuits were overloaded, just short of burning out. He'd expected the fifteen minutes of polite chitchat with Brothertongue leading. Everybody was nervous about everything, including letting anyone else know it. He'd even more or less expected the Victorians to push for a political settlement that he and Kornilov had no power to negotiate.

What frayed his temper was their persistence. At the end of forty-five minutes he'd concluded that the Associates would almost prefer that the negotiations broke down in a way that could be blamed on the Federation. Then they could settle relations between the two sets of armed forces on Victoria as they pleased, and if any shooting started, it wouldn't be their fault.

The only argument against this was that Brothertongue and Gist seemed to be going along with it. This was so improbable that he decided there had to be some other explanation. Not, very likely, a more pleasant one.

He decided that the best way to smoke it out would be to lose his temper. The urbane and polished admiral doing that would have more impact than the bulky, loud general.

"So the Associated States have to complete negotiations over their status within the Federation before anyone can consider negotiations with the Alliance," the president said. "Surely the military appreciates the security value of being able to negotiate with the Alliance as soon as—"

Kuwahara interrupted with a long, carefully enunciated sentence in Japanese. Gist actually flushed. The others looked blank.

"Your Excellency, would you care to translate?" Kuwahara asked.

The governor-general gave a heavily censored version of what Kuwahara had just said about the Associates' ancestors, anatomy, and sex life. Then he switched to Japanese and suggested that Kuwahara perform sexual acts with a variety of nonsapient life-forms.

Kuwahara in turn provided a censored translation, then smiled. "Thank you," Kuwahara said. "I think that's enough personal insults for now. I think it's also time to stop insulting each other's intelligence."

"How have we been doing that?" Brothertongue asked.

"By pushing for a political settlement," Kuwahara said. "We can certainly discuss something that we can recommend to the Federation authorities. But the first thing we have to settle is the future relations of the various armed forces on Victoria. We haven't even begun—"

"I've told you," Fitzpatrick practically whined. "With the governor-general present, a Federation representative with the necessary legal authority is—"

"Bugger off," Gist said inelegantly. He flexed his shoulders, as if the black tunic and neckcloth were binding his heavy muscles. "I didn't promise to attend this bunfight to let you twits put one over on the Federation. You can either stop looking for me to approve anything but a military convention, or you can start looking for me in the nearest bar when you're through mucking up the situation."

Kuwahara's smile mixed satisfaction and irritation. It was useful to catch the Associates in a blunder. They'd thought that Gist could be persuaded to perform his usual quasi-diplomatic functions.

Unfortunately for them, they'd forgotten that his presence here might not mean approval of the Act of Union, that half his staff had fled to Fort Stafford, and that the armed forces to back any decision he made were split into several factions glowering at each other all over the Associated States.

It also occurred to Kuwahara that in diplomacy as in war, there was a difference between "economy of force" and "sending a boy to do a man's job" (unless the boy was someone like BoJo Johnson). The Federation had left most of the diplomatic work on Victoria to the governor-general's office, helped out by a small staff of experts on the Alliance and occasionally by Victoria Command Military Intelligence. The experts imported to tidy up the Armistice, the border, and so forth had all left Victoria weeks before the current crisis, mostly on their way to other assignments. The head of legation was more interested in rocks ("including the ones in her head," some people said) than in diplomacy.

Kuwahara nodded at Kornilov. "We can't afford a stalemate, I agree," the general said. "But if you'll agree to drop any political settlement, we'll offer you something like carte blanche on the military convention."

"Well, not quite," Kuwahara said. "We have a few points we need to incorporate, for the security of all parties. What

236

about both parties putting their terms on the screen, for comparison?''

He smiled. "I'll bet a case of anything you can find on Victoria that they'll be fairly close. We can't negotiate a political settlement. We can help one along by reaching a military convention quickly enough to avoid any incidents that would create bad feeling."

Kuwahara was gambling that the Associate leaders had been so determined to push for a political settlement that they hadn't given much thought to the terms of a purely military agreement. Gist was a retired colonel in the Southern Cross Army, but he obviously hadn't given them the benefit of his experience.

As for Alys Parkinson, Kuwahara knew that she was hopping all over the Associated States, trying to pull her new command into some sort of order before there was any danger of its actually having to fight. Since the only troops she could actually *order* to so much as flush a toilet were the militia, she had a lot of negotiating to do.

Parkinson knew her business; Kuwahara expected that she would succeed. But while she was negotiating, her civilian superiors were going to have to get along without her advice.

"Your Excellency, if you can warm up the display, here's our terms."

Kuwahara handed a data card across the table. It had taken him and Kornilov an hour to work out, which was one reason Gesell had taken the long way around from *Shenandoah* down to the Government House pad. The other reason was that she'd been making a complete all-modes record of the position of Associate troops around Fort Stafford, in Thorntonsburg, and in the area between them. Kuwahara didn't plan to start shooting, but he knew that Robert Burns had been a better strategist than a good many war-college graduates, when he wrote about what happens to the best-laid plans.

Displayed side by side on a split screen, the two sets of terms overlapped so much that negotiations moved smoothly for the next hour. Both sides were to hold on to what they had, except for transferring Border Base One to the Associated States—a fait accompli if there ever was one.

Neither side was to allow leave or liberty in the other's territory. This effectively ended off-base leave and liberty for Victoria Command, which could mean a serious problem once 215 Brigade landed. However, it would also prevent the kind of incidents that could become a serious problem, starting when the bars opened tomorrow morning!

Various forms of technical assistance (medical, maintenance, mapping, critical spares) could be provided by either side, depending on their own requirements. Personnel providing such technical assistance would be exempt from the movement restrictions, but would not be allowed to carry more than personal weapons.

The only place the two lists clashed head-on was over General Liu.

Victoria Command wanted him found, if necessary with the help of a search of Thorntonsburg, and returned to their custody.

The Associated States considered that they were the legitimate Federation authority to have custody of General Liu. They could carry out the search themselves, with less risk of incidents.

"If you agree to our proposal," Brothertongue said, "we may be able to come to an agreement on the status of the Merishi refugees."

"What kind of agreement?" Kornilov asked impatiently.

"We could authorize you to assume custody of them, pending a final decision on their request for asylum."

"Authorize—" Kornilov snarled, then swallowed the rest of what he'd been going to say and looked at Kuwahara. The admiral shook his head. Kornilov glared for a moment, then Kuwahara's message reached him and his heavy face nearly split apart in a smile.

"We can't recognize your right to custody of General Liu or your right to authorize anything about the Merishi." Kuwahara said. "That implies recognizing your political authority in a way we've already said is impossible. If you push this point, it's going to wipe out our hopes for a military convention.

"General Kornilov and I are going to feel somewhat insulted at being led around by the nose for an hour, right back to where we started from. We're also going to have to inform the nearest responsible Merishi authorities about your illegal attempts to transfer their citizens."

"Illegal?" the prime minister said, frowning.

"The Merishi have clearly expressed a preference for you as representing the Federation on Victoria, instead of Victoria Command. That's all right with us. You're capable of

238

keeping them secure, and their eventual place of residence is open to negotiation.

"But trading them to us for General Liu violates the noncoercion clause of every political-asylum agreement I've ever heard of. The Merishi will hear of it. They may decide to retaliate by withholding recognition of the Associated States as a legitimate Federation authority. What happens if one of the most powerful races in the inhabited galaxy will only deal with Victoria Command or its successors?"

Fitzpatrick's pencil snapped. Brothertongue's face was too dark to show a flush, but he didn't meet Kuwahara's eyes. Gist was trying not to laugh.

Kuwahara decided to rest his case. In this area of space, being on bad terms with the Merishi risked the kind of isolation that Victoria's war-battered economy could hardly face.

Kornilov laughed. "Citizens, Your Excellency, I think you forget that we wear our armor externally, not in our heads. Try to to remember it next time."

Negotiations returned to course within twenty minutes, helped by a round of drinks escorted in by Captain Morley and the Special Branch inspector. When the meeting finally broke up, Kuwahara's stomach was reminding him that lunch was a fading memory. But the Military Convention was ready to submit to Governor-General Gist, Victoria Command, and the full Military Council of the Associated States.

"Who are the Republicans putting on it?" Kuwahara asked as he let the president help him into his cloak.

"We've been asking them for—since we decided the Act of Union was a good idea," she said. "They haven't answered. If they don't answer soon, I'll send Phil Karras north and have him drag back the first six people he finds."

"I'll help him," Gist said. Kuwahara looked at the man, only a hair shorter than Captain Bogdanov and considerably broader, and decided that he wouldn't want to be someone Gist chose to drag anywhere.

Outside in the reception room, the three security units were more or less keeping to themselves, except for Captain Morley and Special Branch Inspector Gevhru. They had their heads together over a portable screen. Kuwahara saw that the screen was covered with hieroglyphics that seemed to move as he watched.

"What's that, Captain?"

Morley stood up and saluted. "Dance steps, sir. I was

trading Inspector Gevhru some of my Caucasian dances for some of his Romanian ones."

"Dances?"

"Yes, sir. Both of us turn out to be historical folk dancers."

Kuwahara looked Morley up and down, an agreeable task. His gaze stopped at her light-infantry badge, a nonregulation one with the parachute flanked by two scimitars.

Memory dawned. "Kemali Academy?"

"Yes, sir."

"Good work."

"It was certainly work, sir. Whether it's good or not—captain's too soon to tell."

"Can you and Inspector Gehvru teach your dances?"

"Yes, sir."

"Good. We're going to have to use everything we have to provide on-base entertainment. You and Inspector Gehvru are now appointed joint chairs of the folk-dance club. You might talk to Captain Bogdanov, too. I think he knows something about Russian folk dances."

"I'm sure he does, sir. But I suspect they're overchoreographed Soviet-era versions. Not authentic at all."

From behind Kuwahara came the sound of Kornilov strangling a laugh.

"As you wish. Meanwhile, Captain, in case you haven't noticed, General Kornilov and I are ready to leave. Let's lift out."

"Yes, sir."

On the twilit planet below, the lights were coming on in Port Harriet. Rose Liddell chased the last fragment of omelet to the edge of the plate and off it with her chopsticks. Jensen's marvelous omelets weren't really designed to be eaten with chopsticks, but Liddell wanted to stay in practice. It was going to be a while before she saw an Asian restaurant.

Unless . . .

"Admiral?"

Kuwahara swiveled his chair away from the screen to face her. She was relieved to see his face no longer drawn with the pain of his migraine, only with fatigue.

"Captain Liddell, I must apologize for being not only unworthy but nearly uncivilized as a host. I haven't had a migraine ambush me like this in ten years, but that's an explanation, not an excuse."

"Sir, I don't think you've had to use your head to butt with this much in ten years."

"Probably not," Kuwahara said. He adjusted his lounger. "What's on your mind?"

"Thanking you for the dinner invitation. Also, following up Captain Morley's example."

"Which example? Her dancing, her attending the Academy, or her treatment of her superior officers?"

"She's apologized to Captain Bogdanov already, Admiral. I was thinking of her work with Inspector Gehvru. We and the Associated States should try pooling our resources for recreational activities.

"It might ease the tension. Not just because it'll be easier to have fun, but we'll be establishing a protocol for cooperation among the various forces. Once we've established the protocol for one area, we can extend it to others."

"Such as the Merishi?"

"Admiral, have you taken up mind reading?"

"If I had, I might have done more to keep us out of this morass to begin with. But I agree. The Merishi are too valuable a source of intelligence to let go indefinitely. At the very least, we have to impress the Associates with the importance of completing the interrogation. Their relations with the Alliance might be at stake."

"How so?"

This was new territory for Liddell, uncharted except for a number of labels on the order of "HERE BE PLOTTERS." But ever since *Shen* rode into Victoria orbit, it had been practically impossible to turn around without tripping over somebody plotting something. The map might be incomplete; it was hardly inaccurate.

"The Merishi almost certainly know more than anyone else about the relations of the Alliance and the Bushranger rebels," Kuwahara said. "Specifically, between Alliance Intelligence and the hardcore fanatics who now think they've been betrayed by their paymasters. That's something the Alliance badly needs to know—or rather, the Baba's squadron and the Bonsai Force."

Liddell realized that she was dangerously tired when she took a whole thirty seconds before saying, "Hollings is working with Intelligence?"

"Carrying on a passionate affair with it, would be more my way of putting it," Kuwahara said. "Kornilov and I have gone over every other possible explanation of what's going on across the border. We don't think any of them cover as many facts."

"It would make sense," Liddell said slowly. "Hollings has been pretty bitter about his retirement. If he thought having Field Intelligence owe him a favor would get him back on active duty—"

"Except that he was retired for good and sufficient reasons: he was totally inept as a general officer. He could be reinstated, let alone promoted, only over the opposition of most of the Alliance Ground Forces. I think Field Intelligence is leading him around by the nose, pandering to his delusion that they can do the impossible if he just helps them enough."

"Or they could have finally achieved enough power in the Pentarchy to override Ground Forces High Command," Liddell said.

Kuwahara put his head in his hands. "Captain, if we speculate very much along *that* line, I'll have a headache all over again."

"Sorry, sir."

Josephine Atwood stared at the words on her screen.

"—the appointment of representatives to a Military Council by the former Bushranger Republic has proceeded remarkably swiftly, after much foot dragging."

"Former." That was the problem, even though this was a background feature, not the straight report she'd already wrapped up.

"Former" implied that the Bushranger Republic had ceased to exist, with the Act of Union that formed the Associated States. But that act hadn't been recognized by anybody yet. Even the Military Convention was going to need a stack of ratifications and approvals that might take several days. When and if the Act of Union would be recognized even as a basis for negotiation, only the Lady knew and she wasn't offering unsolicited advice.

Erase "former." In fact, erase the whole bloody be-damned feature and start over again in the morning, after a good night's sleep following a good evening's drunk.

"Erase and close down," she told the computer. The screen darkened and the shield slid down over the display and board. Atwood stood up, brought her arms behind her back until good tension replaced vague aches, then raised them over her head.

She punched in her photographer's code.

"Hello, Frank? You free tonight, or at least severely discounted? What do you mean, no action tonight? Are you slipping? Anyway, I was thinking of keeping our relationship purely professional. That's right, neither of us pays the other a cent. See you at eight? Okay, nine. Bring a thirst."

She stripped off her robe as she headed for the shower, and wriggled as the needle spray prickled and tickled her body. Frank deserved a night on the town after putting up with not only traveling separately but traveling aboard that damned heavy-lifter *Imre Farkas*. She'd been the next ship outbound for Victoria and she'd got him there, but heavy-lifters were all the same—cubic parsecs of space for their cargo, the odd millimeter or so for their passengers.

Not to mention that *Farkas* was owned by a joint human–Merishi consortium, and the humans on the supply staff had forgotten that some of their fellows liked beer, as well as wine and that lethal stuff the Merishi distilled from *okugh*. For Frank, thirty-seven Standard Days without a beer constituted punishment for more crimes than he could probably commit.

The door to D-4 was locked but the sign outside was blank when Elayne Zheng came home. She inserted her key card and opened the door, both silently.

Fortunately the people inside weren't silent. Their happy noises gave Zheng plenty of warning. Her retreat would have been hard to detect even for people not literally wrapped up in each other.

So Brian and la Tachin have finally faced the obvious, not to mention each other. Hallelujah, I think.

She wondered if they were trying to cram themselves into one of the bunks, or using bedding spread on the floor. Either would be a bit tight, when one of the partners was as long as Brian.

Now if it was Brigitte and somebody my size . . .

Come on, Elayne! With them just getting started, Brigitte probably one-way by preference, and you still on light duty?

Zheng called herself uncomplimentary names in several of her ancestral languages and turned toward the D-Deck Lounge. Her roommates' enthusiasm would eventually give way to sleep, and then she could bunk down.

Or she could always return to sickbay, for a night of fasting and prayer. Sickbay food certainly counted as fasting, and she could undoubtedly think up something to pray for if she could decide whom to pray to.

No, wait. One piece of unfinished business, as a courtesy to friends who forgot to signal "do not disturb." Zheng walked back to the D-4 door and started on the keys of the message board.

Her message marched across the screen in the closest thing the dim-witted door brain could manage to gothic script: *Wie lebt in glashausen, sollte im keller bumsen.*

As an afterthought, she added a translation, for the benefit of those who hadn't had a Schneeheim ski instructor to teach them German, skiing, and several interesting sexual variations: "People who live in glass houses should do their bouncing in the cellar."

Twenty-two

Josephine Atwood finally sent her feature out three days later. It concluded:

> Now that the Military Convention has been ratified by all the necessary parties, both sides are beginning to reckon time from the proclamation of the Act of Union. Everybody seems to hope that this will be the last really planet-shaking event for some time. Those who think otherwise (and there must be some) are keeping their heads down and their mouths shut.
>
> So this is Josephine Atwood, Trans-Rift Media, on U + 3, Victoria reckoning, joining her hopes to everyone else's, that peace is about to break out on this troubled planet.

U + 7:

Sophie Bergeron was crossing the street as Lucco DiVries IDed himself into his apartment building. She broke into a run, dodged a cargo tug, and caught him just as the door slid shut.

When they untangled themselves she said, "Lucco, we're going to have to stop meeting like this."

DiVries's mouth opened. Before he got it closed to say something stupid, his reflexes made him hold Sophie out at arm's length. She was wearing a smile and brand-new black plastic major's tabs.

"Congratulations." They got somewhat tangled again.

"I hope you'll think so after I give you the details." She held his arm as they walked to the elevator.

Two people didn't crowd DiVries's cube if one of them sat on the bed. DiVries propped himself in one corner and watched Sophie stretch out in the chair.

"The lady said something about details, I believe?"

"A reassignment goes with this promotion. They're setting up a training center in Kellysburg. I'm going to help design the tactics course."

"The congratulations stand."

"Even if I can't wangle transport on weekends?"

"I can't leave Mount Houton. Dr. Nosavan's got too much work and too few hands for it. Some of the hands he's got aren't attached to brains."

"Like the visiting medics?"

"Chatterje's medforce has pulled their weight. She screened them pretty thoroughly. Some of the rest—well, Dr. Nosavan's Hippocratic Oath has been a bit strained, putting up with them."

Bergeron bent and started pulling off her boots. "They'll up tails and out if the shooting starts again."

"Isn't that killing the bugs by burning down the house?"

"The fire may start again whether we want it or not." She pulled off one boot and sat holding it in her hand. "I just wish I could be sure we'd heard the last of the terrs and crazies. But for every one we killed off in the rebellion, I bet we made two more."

The thought made DiVries need a drink, and want dinner. He punched codes into his com.

"I feel like I'm living on the floor under a nest of K'thressh," Bergeron went on. "They've dropped a couple of shoes. But with all their feet, they can go on dropping more, every hour on the hour until morning."

"K'thressh don't wear shoes," DiVries said.

"One proof of their superior intelligence," Bergeron said, pulling off the other boot and starting to rub her feet.

"Here, let me do that," DiVries said, kneeling and starting a foot massage.

Bergeron leaned back in her chair and closed her eyes. DiVries was sure he heard her purring.

"When you've finished with the feet—"

"By the time I'm finished with the feet, drinks and dinner will be here. You have big feet, my lady, or hasn't anyone ever noticed?"

Bergeron sat up. "Lucco, you paid last time. It's my turn."

"Not when I know what they're paying the Army, and when I just found a three-K deposit in my account."

Bergeron now not only sat up, she stiffened. "Where did it come from?"

246

"I checked. Brother Ray, either making a friendly gesture or a bribe. I don't care which. It's good either way."

"Is it?"

"Legally, or some other way?"

"I'm sure the deposit's legal. But—where is somebody with a seven-person organics plant and a family farm getting three thousand stellars to throw around?"

"Probably from Reesa, if it's a peace offering. If it's a bribe—"

"Whatever it is, it could also be funds he was holding for the rebels. This isn't the first time somebody suspected of rebel sympathies has showed up with extra cash."

"I know."

Two cases that DiVries knew of personally involved suppliers to the orphanage. Superintendent Eddings was ready to pluck herself bald over them. The children needed the money. But it was coming from people who'd only weeks ago hadn't cared if the children were killed.

"The problem is that there's no way I can find out," he added.

"What about asking Teresa?"

"That'll work only if it was her money, and maybe not even then. Otherwise—if it's rebel money, asking Reesa isn't enough punishment for Ray. If it's family money, it's too much."

A metallic crash in the corridor made Bergeron draw her pistol and DiVries lock the door. A moment later somebody shouted, "Anybody on this floor order dinner? The robot just blew its guidance."

Fortunately the robot had only rammed into a wall without spilling anything. DiVries salvaged dinner, rolled the robot on to the elevator, and pressed the "down" button. From here on, the robot was somebody else's headache.

When he got back, Sophie's clothes had joined her boots on the floor and she was in bed under the blankets.

DiVries set down the covered tray. "You don't mind if dinner gets cold?"

"Better it than me."

"You have a point." He began pulling off his own clothes.

U + 13:

The two ancient red dwarf stars at the heart of this lonely system seemed more active than usual. Brokeh su-Irzim

247

stared at the screen, trying to tell if both were flaring or if one of them had flared so violently that the gas jet had reached its comrade.

It would be easy even for an amateur astronomer like him to tell if one of *Night Warrior*'s telescopes turned to the stars. But they were all busy setting up for the next Passage, except for one that was monitoring the approach of the water tanker.

The system's planets were as worn and weary as its primaries; none of them had any life or economically valuable resources. The system's great virtues were a convenient location and excellent seeing conditions.

A single Passage from half a dozen of the People's planets could bring a ship into the system. Half a day's work with a telescope and computer could set up the next Passage—and that next Passage could reach more than a dozen Smalltooth planets, Victoria among them.

While the Guidance staff peered and pondered, the last supplies were going aboard. The squadron had made its Passage from Petzas with half the supply ships still with it, for reasons that su-Irzim still did not know in spite of his position.

Rumors certainly ran about, ranging all the way from a human attack on Petzas to the fleet commander's whim. Su-Irzim was more inclined toward the latter; whims were not something most commanders liked to discuss with their staffs, particularly not the Inquirers.

A black shape cut across the red stars, growing as it crept toward *Night Warrior*. The water tanker was about to come alongside. Su-Irzim hoped that they were steering a course that would keep them clear of the telescopes. Then they would have to link up and pump their load across so gently that the telescopes would stay trained where Guidance wanted them.

Never mind that our computers are every bit as sound as the humans', and can keep a telescope aimed even if a ship is rotating around its axis. The Guidance tradition is to scream if they are jiggled, and scream they will.

Far off in the blackness below the stars, light flared. Proof that the telescopes had to be pointing the other way; the glare of a beam test could seriously damage the navigational opticals. The tanker could maneuver freely, on this side of *Night Warrior* at least.

The universe suddenly lost interest for su-Irzim. He killed

the screen and squatted on his couch. This wasn't the first day he'd spent with an unoccupied mind.

Data from the Victoria System had grown sparse since the Federation refused to declare war over the Act of Union. There was less military signaling to intercept, and only occasional squirts from agents in place. It was possible that the squadron would arrive on its mission of exploiting a human crisis to find that there was no crisis left to exploit.

On the other tusk, it might find that the crisis had erupted due to humans using the People's sunbombs on one another. In that case what might happen would depend on whether the Smallteeth knew whence came the bombs.

If they remained ignorant, the squadron might still have an opportunity—to retreat, if nothing more. If they knew—that line of thought hardly bore pursuing.

Su-Irzim turned his squat into a sprawl and let his mind ramble down more agreeable paths. The asteroid bases had involved a number of new techniques to make them hard to detect. Would it be possible to apply these techniques to building undetectable sets of navigational beacons in systems like this one so that a squadron could take only half a watch instead of two or three to prepare for its next Passage?

Maybe. Su-Irzim began to work out the details, cheerfully ignoring factors like cost, shipping space, and overlapping departmental spheres of authority. The plan therefore made as much sense as some of those fantastic novels he dipped into as a way of judging public opinion, in which the People finally broke out of human encirclement and swept all before them, to the applause of a grateful cosmos.

However, it also kept him from brooding about the sunbombs—which was as much sense as it needed to make. He was opening his lap computer when he heard the faintest of jars as the water tanker hooked a heated transfer pipe to *Night Warrior*.

The air already seemed fresher, although he knew that had to be his imagination. It would take a quarter-watch to transfer the whole load, and a whole watch before the fresh water was replacing the old in *Night Warrior*'s atmosphere.

Imagination, definitely. But then, without an imagination, what use was an Inquirer?

U + 16:

"We are not alone," Rahbad Sarlin solemnly intoned as he entered F'mita ihr Sular's cabin.

She looked up from the screen. At the look on his face she froze the passing play of *Master of the Thunder*, the recreation of the life of the Great Khudr's artillery commander.

"Is that a philosophical observation or an invitation to a sexual engagement?" she asked.

"I lack the philosophical mind," Sarlin replied. "As for the latter, I would like to know whether you mean to encourage me or complain about my raising the matter."

"What I would like to know is the truth about what you meant. And if you ask 'What is the truth—' "

"The truth is that Fleet Commander su-Ankrai's scouts have completed their Passage. The rest of the squadron will be in-system within four days."

"Good."

"I wish we could be sure of that."

"I wish I could stop listening to riddles."

Without invitation and ignoring the frozen screen, Sarlin sat on the couch by the door. "I promise no more riddles. But I must ask you for something—and no, it has nothing to do with sex!"

"I did not mean to be insulting. Forgive me." She now recognized weariness in too many lines of his body. He also had something that looked remarkably like a burn on one ear.

"Gladly, if we can work together. The asteroid's commander wants to hide our loss of contact with *Fireflower*."

"Does he want to pretend that we still have contact? Or merely hide how long ago we lost it?"

"Does it matter? Either will involve altering message logs and records aboard both the asteroid and *Perfumed Wind*."

Which could mean twenty years of corrective confinement, and never to space again after I get out.

The selfish thought gave way to a different one. *For Rahbad Sarlin the confinement could be for life. Or he might face death, if someone is able to interpret it as treason.*

"I'll be happy to cooperate in shoving him out an airlock—"

Sarlin pointed a finger at his burned ear, then at the walls. "I learned the commander's plans from a friend aboard the asteroid. Two can play at this game."

"Of course." Ihr Sular turned to her terminal, switched it to the log, and coded for "Communications." Data scrolled past, blank of any mention of *Fireflower*.

"Good. If there's someone aboard ready to alter the log, he hasn't done it yet. I'll make some copies of the original log, clean the record of any trace of the copying, and let you wield the gloves from there on."

Sarlin looked ready to weep with joy and relief. Ihr Sular smiled. "Have you lived in the world of secrets so long that you've forgotten how to trust?"

"Perhaps I have. Actually, what I did not expect was that you would be able to deal with the problem so quickly."

"You flatter me. Anyone with the same degree of skill on computers could have done it. I admit that it will take a little more to alter the records so that no one can detect even the alteration. How good a computer expert do we have to fear?"

"Aboard the asteroid, no one as good as you seem to be. Aboard the squadron—no limits, and therefore no guesses."

"I'll give it my best, then." She coded in the orders to copy and activated the printer for a solid backup. "Computers were what really took me to space. I got bored with the problems I had to solve on ground-based ones. Calculating a Passage from a triple-star system, on the other hand—that never grows dull."

The copies filled her terminal; the printer whispered. In a single advance the job was done. She handed Sarlin the solid copy.

"Now, if the crew's inhibitions about betraying the Mistress have just slowed the wits of any spy—"

"I will pray that they have. And I will pray for you to be rewarded. 'Danger always looks greatest when one sees no way out of it.'"

Rahbad Sarlin was one of the few people she'd ever met who could quote the Great Khudr as though he found meaning in the words. Most quoted the sayings in the same tone they must have heard them from teachers, as something heard too often to have a single bone of meaning left in them.

"How great is the danger?"

Sarlin looked at the walls and at her, then tapped his ear again. "As great as our friends' chances of bypassing the disablers on the bombs."

She took the message. *I should not be telling you this, and with others you should pretend ignorance.*

"How great are they?"

"It depends on whose estimate of the humans is accurate. The Fleet doubts they have a way of bypassing the disablers. We Inquirers, I think, do them more justice."

251

"But the humans and the Merishi would have to cooperate, wouldn't they? At least to use *Fireflower* for delivering the bombs?"

"Desperate, vengeance-driven humans and young Merishi who think well of themselves and are bold to strike for a new division of the spoils? They might very well find that they had enough enemies in common to cooperate more than we had expected."

"I think the asteroid commander and others who think like him fear the passing years more than most," Sarlin added, half to himself.

"The commander is five years younger than you are, my friend." Ihr Sular couldn't help a tusk-baring grin.

"Indeed, I underestimated your talent for intelligence work," Sarlin said. "Is that why you set me aside? Thinking that I am—ah, aged past usefulness?"

"If we ever do put the matter to the test, I do not expect to be disappointed. You wear your years well. The commander does not."

"His life has not depended on his speed with weapons or nails. He isn't alone, either. There seem to be quite a few of the older commanders—I give no names—who want to strike a final blow before they pass on the gloves. They find valuable partners in discontented young Merishi."

"At least that's what they probably call them," ihr Sular put in. "They should remember the Great Khudr's words after the Battle of Gudjar: 'I dread alike the zeal of those who have everything to learn and those who have nothing to lose.' "

In *Master of the Thunder,* she'd learned where the Great Khudr made that remark—after a battle that should have been decisive but turned into a bloody stalemate because two commanders advanced without orders. One was young, in his first battle, eager to raise his family's name to new heights. The other was old, his banner already victory-studded, but knowing himself to be dying and determined to take a good escort of enemies with him.

The years, it seemed, were long, memories were short, and there was no lesson so old that it did not have to be learned over again.

Paul Leray didn't know if the split screen had its usual meaning. When Pak's face shared the screen with a Victorian desertscape, it meant that his message was in the free cryptic he and the two senior officers of *Audacious* had worked out.

This time, however, the desert scene could be quite legitimate. Leray decided to assume the worst and have a decrypted interpretation of the conversation ready to compare with Jo's.

"In this area a clandestine arms depot has been discovered," Pak said. "The discovery was made by officers of the Border County Patrol, after a sighting by a training flight of the Third Battalion."

Decrypted: *the 96th won't get the credit for it, and we wouldn't be wise to even ask, because that would make trouble between us and the prefect.*

"The depot seems to have been in existence for some time."

So why didn't the police, who said they had everything in hand, find it sooner?

"It contained few arms, but showed signs of several shipments having passed through."

Let's pray that they haven't been passed out *to potential rebels in Alliance territory.*

"Cooperation with the police is being increased in order to discover any other depots in the area."

Although if we can't persuade the governor to lean on the prefect, we may have to risk trouble with at least the latter. We can afford angry prefects, but not dead soldiers.

"The present deployment of the 96th Regiment seems adequate for this cooperation. However, the more naval support we can expect on short notice, the fewer potentially provocative changes we will have to make."

It's in nobody's interest to make already nervous Federation commanders even more nervous. We have to exercise the right of self-defense, but discreetly.

"If a naval liaison officer is required to facilitate this cooperation, the Navy recommends one with previous experience in that role."

Leray stared at Jo Marder. She'd delivered her remark in a tone so perfectly matching Pak's that for a moment he thought she was joking. Her face sent a different message.

I want to go back down there, badly enough to want to wrestle the chain of command for the job.

"Subject to the other demands for the services of such qualified officers, I concur," Pak said.

You have the job if you want it and it won't make trouble higher up.

Leray forgot how Pak's report ended, other than with a map showing several colored triangles—he couldn't remember how many or what color. They were, as he recalled, the areas where the search for arms depots was concentrating.

The signal was scrambled, but if the potential rebels had reasonably sophisticated electronics, they could record, unscramble, and be warned. Maybe Pak was thinking of *sending* such a warning—covertly, indirectly, whatever . . . ?

Before Leray could put that question in free cryptic, he found himself staring at a blank screen. He only stopped staring when Marder pushed her translation notes onto his knee.

He almost pushed them right off, but stopped himself and picked them up, without looking at them. His eyes were on Jo's face.

"What the devil—"

"Is that a safe question to ask, Paul?"

"Meaning, can Intelligence use it? I don't see how. Intelligence may block your volunteering because of what you did to Lorne. But they can't get any madder than they already are, over our discussing the risks."

"I wasn't thinking professionally, Paul. I was thinking—do you really want an answer to that question?"

Leray wasn't sure about that. His own thoughts weren't entirely professional.

Audacious had been nearly as efficient without Marder as with her. The cruiser's captain hadn't been quite so lucky.

The only problem with mentioning this was that it would step over an important boundary—exploiting their relationship to steer Jo professionally.

Another excellent argument for not falling in love with my executive officer, if the matter hadn't been settled five years ago.

"I suppose I ought to know. I—no, I'll ask once. If my guess is wrong, I'll shut up."

"Launch." Her smile was thinner than usual, like the rest of her. She'd lost weight or at least water down on Victoria.

"Is Pak keeping his bargain?"

"Yes."

Leray jumped up and kissed her. If Pak was keeping his bargain, then she wasn't going down to be freer to drink.

Marder accepted the kiss without returning it, then picked

up the two notepads. Leray tore off the top sheets and popped them into the scanner hole of his portable computer.

"Let's let the Golem do a semantic analysis and comparison while we celebrate."

Her smile wasn't so thin, but she didn't reach out to him. "Is the Golem still secure?"

"Even more. I ran up a new batch of nonsense data while you were dustside."

"Actually, there was more snow and rock than dust, where I was."

"Just as loathsome. Weather is a blot on the face of the Creator's handiwork. Anyway, now any tapper gets five minutes of interesting but irrelevant files, then the machine shuts itself off unless it receives a code that only I know."

"All right. You can give it to me afterward."

They were in his cabin, so it was easy for him to kneel in front of her, pull down her pants, and begin his worship of her body. She sighed as his lips tasted her, but her fingers didn't twine themselves in his hair as usual. They lay quiet, almost flaccid, until they tightened at last along with the arching and flexing of her whole body.

Leray lay on the bed while she knelt beside it and returned the favor. His thoughts were churning so that it seemed hours before pleasure took over.

Should I give Jo the code when I've been putting all my doubts about her in there? Or when Intelligence might bring charges over Lorne, then bribe her to switch sides by offering to drop them?

Intelligence could do that. They might even throw in the offer of an assignment where nobody would monitor her drinking. It would be a trap, designed to get her out of space and into a position where they'd have a clear case against her. Would she realize that, or would he have to tell her? In her new mood, would she *listen* if he told her?

255

Twenty-three

Under Alert One, Communications Primary held nine people, including three watch officers. Brian Mahoney hoped he wouldn't have to experience an Alert One while he was a Communications J.O.O.W. trainee. Even with five people, the place was a sadist's idea of a labyrinth. You could see freedom just beyond the last console, but you had no idea of how to thread your way past the consoles and couches to reach it.

A display's lights slowly changed color, and a chime murmured, as if afraid of being overheard. The petty officer at the display spoke; her throat mike passed the words to the master-signal display.

"We're getting a very diffuse signal, more like an emergence pulse than anything else but not really like that either. Could be natural."

"You're recording?" the watch officer asked.

"Of course, sir."

"There's no 'of course' in a situation like this," the lieutenant said.

Mahoney silently watched the displays, which would have made it clear that the petty officer was on the alert. Lieutenant Rosza, Mahoney decided, was one of the things fate had sent him to compensate for his award and Brigitte.

Maybe even finding what I've been looking for in the Navy—

"Heads up," Rosza said. The communications officer, Lieutenant Commander Rothbard, walked in, perfunctorily returned Rosza's salute, and looked around the compartment.

"The crypto gang's done their number on that Alliance signal you picked up at the beginning of the watch," she said. "From the fragments, they were discussing sighting and interrogating an unidentified ship."

Mahoney felt a prickling start somewhere at the base of his

256

spine and work toward both neck and toes. He also felt sweat under his collar.

"Did they identify the ship?" the petty officer asked.

Rothbard's reply cut across Rosza's glare. "They're working on it. They've also sent a request to the Chennault Observatory for a record of any Alliance signals they may have picked up."

"A bloody lot of good that's going to do, with Kuttelwascher's hand on the valve," somebody out of Mahoney's sight muttered.

"Miracles can happen," Rothbard said. "Even Kuttelwascher shouldn't mind giving us enough to refine our ETA on the Baba's reinforcements. Right now it's twenty-three hours plus or minus four. We'd like to take out some of the 'plus or minus.' "

What Mahoney would really like to do was take Baba Lopatina's reinforcements and place them somewhere about four Jumps from Victoria. The Federation reinforcements were in-system and coming fast, but their ETA was something just short of seven Standard Days.

If something happened to make the Alliance thoroughly pissed at the Federation before then, Baba Lopatina might be able to carry out her notion of turning the Victoria Squadron into an orbital debris problem. Mahoney didn't really expect any such thing to happen, but he'd picked up the infantryman's rule of "When in doubt, keep your head down." Far down, when you faced a superior enemy and weren't sure about your flanks or rear.

Rothbard looked ready to go and Rosza looked ready to let her leave. Mahoney remembered the casual dismissal of "special weapons," and the fact that nothing of the sort had turned up in the rebels' surrendered arsenals. It hadn't even been detected in the sensor scans for fugitive rebel bands.

He also remembered that Rosza didn't like him, regarding trainee J.O.O.W.'s as a burden and heroism on the ground as no excuse for letting them mess around with his equipment. He remembered a number of other things, and they pushed him back and forth until he had to hold on to the arms of his seat to keep it from swaying under him. The final memory was his tactics instructor at OCS:

"You can't prepare against all your opponent's capabilities. But you can—you *must*—be aware of them all, and as soon as possible."

"Ma'am," Mahoney said as Rothbard turned to leave. "We've got another signal the crypto people might want to play with. It smells a little like an emergence pulse. If it is, the observatory might help us get a triangulation—"

"Lieutenant—" Rosza began.

"Excuse us, people," Rothbard said. If she'd looped a microfilament line around Rosza's neck, he couldn't have followed her more dutifully.

Mahoney called up the communications log and started updating it to include the suspicious signal and Rothbard's visit. He'd just finished the updating when Rosza came back alone.

"Next!" shouted the same invisible humorist, mimicking the tones of a luxury hairdresser.

Mahoney unstrapped and ambled out into the passageway. He was too relieved at a chance to stretch his legs out of Rosza's sight to care much what Rothbard might say.

The communications officer was standing with her hands behind her back, "Thanks for the information," she said. "But what made you think it was worth embarrassing Rosza?"

Mahoney's answer came out more fluently than he'd expected. "The unidentified ship, mostly. The mysteries are just piling up too fast."

"Next time, assume that Rosza doesn't like mysteries any more than you do and has a strong sense of duty. If he didn't, you wouldn't be getting the rating you're working on. Assuming you didn't just blow it, of course, but I think I can see to it that justice is done."

"Thank you, ma'am."

"Thank yourself and Rosza, first. Incidentally, how did you get so familiar with com equipment? Rosza was surprised to learn you'd never had communications duty before."

"Testing all those simulators helped, I guess. It's not the same as live equipment, of course. But you do get a head start on knowing what to pull and what to push.

"Also, it isn't quite true that I never had any communications duty. I was sort of odd-jobs man in the Traffic Control Division on Jeremiah Station. In slack times, when there wasn't an officer around, they'd let me fill in while they—ah, put in some time elsewhere."

"I see. No wonder it wasn't in your record. We may need a traffic-control team if all these funny little signals turn into ships around Victoria. Want to volunteer for it if we need it?"

"Will that count toward my com J.O.O.W. qualification?" Mahoney phrased the question more politely than he felt. *Nobody, not God Almighty, is going to jerk me off course again—*

"If you stop butting heads with Rosza, I'll interpret the regulations so that it does. Fair enough?"

This bordered on blackmail, but . . .

Mahoney nodded.

"Good. I know Rosza thinks he's the only person around who knows anything about communications. I even sometimes suspect he knows more than I do. But I don't want to have to ask the Alliance to start a war just to keep you two out of each other's hair. Or mine. Understand?"

"Aye-aye, ma'am."

Rothbard was right. She was also being lenient. The next time it would go up to the Hermit or even the Old Lady, and then Elayne and Brigitte might suddenly find they had D-4 all to themselves.

Sophie Bergeron was visiting the supply dump because both of the corporals she'd tried to have promoted to sergeant were on duty tonight. They probably didn't blame her for not getting promoted, but they would surely be angry.

Tonight would be her last chance to tell them who to be angry at. Her suitcase was sitting by Lucco's bed; the rest of her baggage was already on its way to Kellysburg. Tomorrow morning at 1030, she would be following it—a late flight, but one she'd chosen so that if she didn't get to sleep early—

"Storage Area Twelve. Storage Area Twelve. Passengers for Storage Area Twelve."

The military bus had a human driver, probably someone given the assignment to keep him in uniform and out of the refugee camps. He'd certainly OD'd on self-importance, shouting out each stop on the route as if he had thirty passengers instead of two.

Bergeron pulled up her hood and mask, nodded to her one fellow passenger, a sergeant from Seventh Battalion, and climbed down. The bus was already purring away down the tamped-down gravel road when she realized it had dropped her at the far side of the area's landing pad.

It was a long, windswept walk and mostly in darkness. Even with her superior night vision, Bergeron stumbled twice on icy ruts. By the time she saw the light above the main door, she'd sworn a solemn oath.

If I make colonel, and if a colonel's salary is worth anything by then, and if the Victorian economy can produce a spare groundcar, I will buy my own transportation.

Not to mention that if she owned it herself, nobody could object to her transporting Lucco in it. Lucco, and anyone who might in time come to join the family—

She told herself that the stinging in her eyes was wind-blown dust.

The sentry at the door was also human. A rough female voice called: "Halt! Who is there?"

"Major Bergeron."

"Advance and be recognized."

Bergeron saw the sentry pressing a button, but then heard her curse as the spotlight over the door neither came on nor tracked. What the sentry did after that, Bergeron didn't notice, because her attention leaped elsewhere.

The main building of Area Twelve was a U-shaped monster, a former light-industrial complex, built on the edge of a cliff. The cliff made it secure on three sides, and the U-shape gave the building two loading areas. The one Bergeron had just crossed served both lifters and ground vehicles. The area inside the U faced the cliff and let lifters fly directly in to load practically at the door.

Or it had, until a couple of accidents with hot pilots made Brigade ban lifter landings inside the U. Area Twelve held several tons of ammunition, as well as other miscellaneous supplies for the Brigade. "We want that ammunition exploding on enemy targets, not in our own dumps," was the way the brigade commander put it.

So why was a lifter flying out of the U, slowly, almost silently, and dropping out of sight below the edge of the cliff?

Bergeron could swear by her night vision. What she'd seen was what had been there. But before she started running after explanations, it would be wise to question the two corporals she'd come to see. If they were innocent, they might talk. If they weren't, they'd stay corporals.

The light finally came on. Its beam slapped Bergeron in the face, dazzling her for a moment as she fumbled for her ID.

She wasn't too dazzled to see the door behind the sentry

open, the sentry step aside, and one of the unpromoted corporals step out. He looked grim, on the way to angry.

Not much she could do about it if he was. She'd start by quoting Lucco DiVries's prayer, when she'd complained about the two corporals and he'd complained that Dr. Nosavan was still a captain, because the reign of the clerks was setting in fast.

"From ghoulies and ghasties and bureaucrats that we bump into in the night, and in the day, and in the morning and the evening, good Lord deliver—"

Something punched her hard, twice, in the stomach. The second punch was so hard that she doubled over, then lost her balance. She fell with her face toward the door, so she saw the corporal's expression change from grimness to surprise. He fell forward, throwing out both hands as he sprawled facedown at the sentry's feet.

A tall burly man in civilian bush clothes stood behind the corporal for moment. Then he knelt and put a pulse pistol—Bergeron saw Army markings on it—in the corporal's outflung right hand.

The corporal didn't seem to notice. A moment later Bergeron didn't notice anything either, because the pain struck. She rolled onto her ravaged stomach, not caring if that made the pain worse, only hoping that grinding her face into the frozen ground would stifle her screams.

If they think I'm dead, maybe they won't finish me off. Then maybe I can stay alive until the next bus comes and warn it, give the alarm. . . .

She writhed, remembering too late just how much belly wounds hurt. She felt a scream bubbling up in her throat, then realized that it was blood.

I'm not going to last that long.

Despair made the pain seem worse, if that was possible. She would have screamed then, except that now she was too weak to roll her mouth clear of the ground. . . .

The lieutenant behind the desk looked at Lucco DiVries as if he'd just pissed on the floor. Then he motioned DiVries to a chair and the two policemen to corners of the little room.

"I'm sorry about your connection with Major Bergeron," the lieutenant began. DiVries stared at him. It was 0400 or a little after, but he had managed a couple of hours' sleep before word of Sophie's death came. He shouldn't be hallucinating.

Or maybe he should hope that everything since he went to sleep was a hallucination, and that when it was over he'd wake up, in his own bed, with Sophie beside him? Sophie, alive and warm and loving and above all *not dying of a gut wound facedown in a frozen puddle of her own blood.* . . .

"Are you all right, Mr. DiVries?" the lieutenant asked. Only the words were solicitous. DiVries noted that both visual and sound recorders were on.

"What would you expect?" DiVries snapped. "I don't know why either of us is here, or what it has to do with catching Sophie's killers. Tell me, and then I'll tell you everything I know."

"Fair enough." The lieutenant rested his hands on a notepad. "You know that Corporal Rentschler is suspected as Major Bergeron's killer?"

"No, I didn't."

"The murder weapon was the pulse pistol he was issued for sentry duty. His fingerprints were found on it, and nobody else's. Do you know any reason he might have had to be hostile to Major Bergeron?"

"No. I—wait a minute. He and another corporal—she'd recommended them both for promotion to sergeant. The recommendation didn't go through. But—that wasn't her fault. He wouldn't be angry with *her.*"

"He might not show it. But he could have been hiding it. Also, if he was already a part of the plot—"

"What plot?"

"You don't need to know that."

"You've just mentioned it, you bastard! You can't get away—"

The lieutenant pulled a thump pistol out of his desk drawer and pointed it at DiVries. "Lieutenant, I'll forgive you this time. I'll even tell you about the plot. On one condition."

"What's that?"

"I want a complete history of everything Major Bergeron said to you."

"In bed or out of it?" DiVries kept his mouth moving to give his brain time to catch up. He had the feeling that the situation was already outrunning him by several meters a second.

"If she said anything in bed that might explain why she was visiting Area Twelve tonight, I'd like to know it. I'm sure you've known people who could pretend complete loyalty until it was time for pillow talk, then let their—"

DiVries's brain caught up with the situation, then leaped ahead to grasp what the lieutenant was implying. A heartbeat later DiVries himself was leaping over the desk. He got the pistol away and was actually pounding the lieutenant's head on the carpeted floor when the two policemen pulled him off.

They held him up between them, and the lieutenant wobbled to his feet. Now he looked as if Divries had pissed on *him*—which in a way, DiVries supposed he had. The two policemen tightened their grip, and the lieutenant threw all his weight into a punch at DiVries's solar plexus.

Paralyzing DiVries's breathing didn't paralyze his brain. Its oxygen reserves supported a single thought. *If I ever get loose—*

Then he was loose, as the two policemen dropped him. He fell to the floor, curling up against the kicks to the groin he knew were coming next.

They didn't. Instead he heard a cold voice say, "Lieutenant, enough!"

"But he assaulted—" began one of the policemen.

"I wasn't asking you." Now the voice sounded oddly familiar. "I'm ordering you all out of here."

"But—"

"I can see about adding disobedience of a direct order to brutality and neglect of duty. If I do, they might decide it's worthwhile to court-martial you all. Or reassign you to the Loch Prima labor crew."

The silence above him made DiVries feel better, almost as much as his breath coming again. The Loch Prima labor crew wasn't technically a penal company, but nobody went there unless they'd really stepped on their equipment. Not everybody who went there came back.

DiVries stretched out and lay quietly until he heard three sets of footsteps parade out and the door close behind them. When the chair creaked, he lurched to his feet, and nearly sat down again.

Behind the desk, wearing a lieutenant colonel's insignia on his sweater, was the man Brigitte Tachin had been trying to attract that day at Hennessey's. He'd added a mustache

263

and he wore a rumpled bush suit, but it was unmistakably the same man.

"How's your brother, Lucco?" the man said.

DiVries didn't shake the offered hand. It wasn't that he wanted to be rude. It was just that he had to catch up with the situation again.

"If you're a light colonel, you probably know better than I do. Ray made a few remarks about me and—anyway, he should have kept his mouth shut. I haven't heard from him in quite a while."

"I wasn't trying to pump you, believe it or not."

"No, and I don't think you're trying to play 'soft' interrogator after getting rid of the 'hard' ones. Loch Prima's not a threat you use for playing games."

"No, it isn't. But I'd like your cooperation. If the lieutenant hadn't got his priorities arse-end foremost, he'd have told you about the theft from Area Twelve before he questioned Major Bergeron's loyalty."

"I'd have jumped him no matter when he did that. I'll jump you, too, if you—"

"Will you shut the bloody hell up long enough to listen to something besides your grief?"

DiVries shut up, for two reasons. One was that jumping the colonel was less practical than jumping the lieutenant. The senior officer was bigger, younger, and looked both tougher and faster.

The other reason was that the colonel was right. He couldn't imagine any reason for questioning Sophie's loyalty, but maybe his imagination didn't go far enough. Certainly grief and rage weren't helping.

"All right. You can even question Sophie's loyalty, if you tell me *why*."

"Very simple. As of six hours ago, two columns of armed Associated States citizens crossed the border into Seven Rivers Territory. They've proclaimed its independence from the Alliance at Anvil of the Winds.

"The total strength of the two columns seems to be at least a short battalion of light infantry. They seem to be composed about equally of pardoned rebels, fugitive rebels, and ordinary citizens. Plus a few deserters from the Army."

DiVries didn't quite see the light, but he saw a less impenetrable darkness. "And Sophie was shot in connection with this crazy stunt?"

"She wandered in on a major arms theft. One of her corporals seems to have deserted. Corporal Rentschler—well, we know what happened to him. So the question has to be asked—could Major Bergeron have been seeking their promotion to sergeant to put them in a better position for aiding the rebels?"

Lucco DiVries wanted to run away and hide from a world even madder than before. Instead he shook his head.

"I can't see how. She was loyal, I swear. She never said anything to make me think she wanted another war.

"I think she did want an independent, united Victoria. But she wouldn't have lifted a finger to help a crazy stunt like this. I swear to God, she'd have shot both of those bastards herself if she'd thought they were in on it!"

"Is there any chance she might have mentioned their names where rebel agents could have overheard?"

"Everybody in the brigade knew their names. Are you going to arrest the whole brigade? If you do, who's going to stop the rebels? Or are we going to let Colonel Pak shoot our dog, because we're too busy suspecting each other to trust anybody with a gun . . . ?"

DiVries knew that he was almost incoherent and forced himself to stop. The colonel stood up.

"Mr. DiVries, what you've said is pretty close to what I've heard. I'll need more confirmation, and I'm not going to make any promises. But if you want to bet, bet on both you and Bergeron being clear. Just don't get into a dust-up with any more policemen."

"I'll try. And—what the hell is your name, by the way? I can't go on thinking of you as 'the light colonel Brigitte Tachin tried to make' forever."

"I wasn't any kind of officer then. But my name's still Peter Bissell. How is the elegant Lieutenant Tachin, by the way?"

"Still elegant, and I think paired off with Lieutenant Mahoney."

"The long lanky dark-haired one?"

"You've got a good memory."

"I'm not sure it's a blessing. If all I could remember was which end of a pulser the slug comes out of, they might have given me a combat unit." He rose and held out his hand again. DiVries took it as a knock sounded.

"That'll be your medical treatment. Good luck, Mr. DiVries."

"That's Lieutenant DiVries," a voice said from beyond the door. DiVries started, not only at the rank but at recognizing Dr. Nosavan.

The doctor entered as Colonel Bissell strode out. Nosavan wore an open overcoat over tunic and trousers and carried a medical bag.

Both the overcoat and tunic showed a full colonel's insignia with the Medical Corps caduceus. DiVries stared at them and went on staring until he heard a gurgle and saw the doctor pouring out a stiff glass of brandy.

"That's the first medicine I'm giving you. I'll scope you for internal injuries as soon as the lieutenant gets out of the examining room. I must say, it strained my Hippocratic Oath to treat him after I learned what he'd done."

DiVries emptied the glass in two gulps. "Don't worry, Doctor. If I run into him again, he and his muscle won't need a doctor. They'll need a mortician."

"I didn't hear that, Lieutenant."

"What the hell are you doing calling me 'Lieutenant'?"

"Because you are now a first lieutenant in the Medical Corps of the Associated Victorian States Armed Forces."

"I'm not a doctor!"

"You're a good administrator and troubleshooter. We need—"

"The only trouble I want to shoot is the bastards who got Sophie! Leaving her like that—dying of a belly wound . . ."

This time the image hit him harder than before. He started to shake, then started to cry. Dr. Nosavan put his arms around DiVries and held him until he'd cried himself out, which might have taken minutes or hours, DiVries never knew.

He only knew that when his eyes were finally dry, the brandy bottle was almost empty, but he was still completely sober. Dr. Nosavan divided the last few drops, and DiVries managed to sip them instead of gulping.

"All right. So I'm a lieutenant. Really?"

"As real as me being a colonel. General Parkinson flew in a few hours ago with a stack of promotions. Apparently word about frozen promotions got down to Thorntonsburg, and she thought it was a bad idea.

"Of course, the first thing she heard about was the invasion of Seven Rivers. It would be a considerable understatement to say that she was unhappy. But she decided that the promotions would go through."

Nosavan leaned back in his chair in a way that hinted he'd done his share with the brandy. "She said that if the people do their jobs, they'll deserve the promotions. If they don't, they can always be broken. And if they die, it hardly matters what rank they die in. Sorry, Lucco."

It was the first time Nosavan had used DiVries's first name.

"No problem."

Well, not quite. There is a problem, but the last time anybody was raised from the dead was a long time ago.

Twenty-four

In the last hour, Brian Mahoney had learned that Communications Primary really was a mob scene under Alert One. Even a simulated alert meant a full crew, plus an observer, one of Commander Charbon's lieutenants who seemed to have no purpose aboard *Shenandoah* except to help the first lieutenant make a bigger nuisance of herself.

Actually, they'd lost one officer as a simulated casualty when the alert sounded. The senior O.O.W. was supposed to have been "trapped in a passageway" by "damage-control measures."

This left Rosza and Mahoney. Rothbard was at her Alert One station, in the Combat Center. Mahoney had stopped wishing that Rosza would become a nonsimulated casualty, but they were still short of being each other's favorite people.

Mahoney sipped from his bulb of tea, then set it down and locked it into place inside the left arm of his chair. With all the technical seats filled by people well up to *Shenandoah*'s standards, there wasn't a lot for a trainee J.O.O.W. to do.

Things would be a bit different when he shifted over to do his qualifier in Weapons, with all the heavy equipment continuously in use, but then his background in maintenance and damage control would help. So would Charlie Longman, if he got back from dirtside exile in time and in the right frame of—

The damage-control warning whined, shrieked, and whistled. At least that was the way it always sounded to Mahoney. He was already in shipboard survival gear; now he pulled his hood and mask up, checked airflow, and jacked the mask's electronics into his board.

Around him the rest of the com gang were doing the same. Mahoney was happy to see that he'd been among the first three to rig up. The observer finished her masking, then tapped Rosza on the shoulder.

"You're a casualty. So are the people on Board Two. Lieutenant Mahoney, you are now in charge of Communications Primary."

Rosza assumed lotus position, with a horribly uncontemplative smirk on his face. "What caused the casualties?" Mahoney asked.

"Internal explosion leading to an electrical surge."

"Cut Board Two off the circuit," Mahoney said. "Do we have a clear venting?" Fires aboard spaceships could be incredibly dangerous if you couldn't open the compartment to vacuum, ridiculously minor if you could.

"No."

Mahoney ran through all three remote-control systems for the extinguishing system. The observer smiled grimly, Rosza was positively smirking.

"Dalkey!" Mahoney called. "Get on Board Two with the extinguisher. Freeze Board One. The people on it, clear away the casualties. Board Three, full power. You've got inship communications."

Mahoney's own board was Four. As three people converged on Board Two with fire extinguisher and first-aid gear, he punched a signal through to Combat Center, with a repeat to Damage Control Primary.

"Communications Primary, Mahoney. Three personnel casualties and one board out. Request transfer of all intership communications to Combat Center boards."

Before anyone could acknowledge, he saw someone at Board Three signaling frantically. He mimed using the telephone and heard an almost equally frantic voice in his headset.

"Sir, we've got a priority signal from *Imre Farkas*. Report they're coming in damaged after meteorite collision."

"What the—" Mahoney, Rosza, and the observer said in chorus. When the trio was done, Mahoney went on.

"This isn't simulated?"

"Not that I know of," the observer said. She borrowed the nearest untended headphones and listened. "No, that's not one of ours. Looks like she's really coming back."

"Shall I interrogate her on condition and ETA?" If he'd actually been on his own, Mahoney would have had the interrogatory on the way already. But by common consent, the drill was suspended until they'd settled with reality, and part of reality was two senior officers.

"Yes, and cut Combat Center in on it," the observer said.

269

She pulled down a folding seat and straddled it. "Also, secure from drill until we finish the talktalk or the Old Lady turns the job over to Combat Center."

Rosza sat down at Board Four and started composing the message for *Imre Farkas*. Mahoney made a visual scan of the compartment and noticed that Dalkey had actually pulled the safety lock on the fire extinguisher. If he'd triggered it, the results would have been nonsimulated, messy, and expensive.

Mahoney decided in favor of a gentle reminder in private. Not roasting juniors in front of an audience was even more an armor-clad rule when the audience included Rosza and one of Charbon's professional nuisances.

Colonel Pak's personal screen lit up and the "urgent" chime sounded. Pak and Commander Marder swiveled their chairs away from the display of the ground tactical situation.

"Shield tactical display," he ordered the computer. "Activate personal screen."

Marder frowned. If she'd known just how paranoid everyone on the ground had become, she might have stayed aboard *Audacious*.

Pak's request for her services as naval liaison hadn't been an order. Paul was too busy helping the Baba and Uzel brief the reinforcements on the situation off Victoria to have time for a confrontation with her, even if he'd been short-tempered enough to allow one. And the Bonsai Squadron was, if not safe territory, at least territory whose mine fields and booby traps she knew, not to mention less accessible to Intelligence agents or Investigative Division types acting for Intelligence.

The screen lit up; Paul Leray stared out of it. "Report on an intercepted communication from the Federation squadron. *Imre Farkas* is on her way back, after taking meteorite damage just prior to jumping. She lost all secure long-range communications in the collision and didn't want to open up otherwise, because she'd detected an unidentified ship."

Pak and Marder looked at each other. The unidentified ship the reinforcements had detected on the way was a wild but not particularly threatening variable. After all, a force of three battleships, a carrier with two attacker squadrons, and a half-dozen cruisers should be able to take on any unidentified ship and the Feds as well.

It was, however, data that ought to be fed into Baba Lopatina's next captains' meeting. If the unidentified ship was a hallucination or a ghost, then Feds, Allies, and merchant ships were all seeing it.

"I've communicated the intercept to the flagship. It's been acknowledged. I received no orders against communicating it to our ground forces."

Probably because you had the sense not to raise the question, Marder thought. *I wish you were as intelligent about people as you are about tactics. Or did having to suck up to the Pentarchs cripple that part of your brain?*

"Thank you, Captain," Pak said. "Your evaluation?"

"Except for the unidentified ship, the whole thing seems routine. I'm going to recommend to the admiral that we formally request a pooling of information about this unidentified ship."

"I concur."

"Thank you, Colonel. And good hunting."

The screen blanked. Pak swiveled his chair back and had the tactical display opened before Marder stopped staring at the featureless gray plastic.

"Commander?"

"Sorry. I was trying to think if you needed to change any of your plans because of this development."

Pak's thin smile reminded her that they hadn't discussed any of the 96th's plans yet. *Clumsy, Jo, clumsy.*

Marder had already decided to make her next relationship one with someone outside the Navy. She now considered making it with someone who could be out of her mind completely when she wasn't with them.

The two officers studied the display. One thing stood out, for Marder.

"It looks as if the situation could go either way. Get very serious very fast, or go back to being completely trivial."

"That's been our estimate for at least the last day. The total hostile forces involved are no more than a light-infantry battalion. *Very* light. Almost fluff-weight, one might call it. The 96th could hammer them flat in any kind of straight fight."

"But they're not giving us the opportunity for that," Marder pointed out. "They've seized Anvil of the Winds and the two corridors leading from it to the border. We can't move into the town without risking heavy civilian

271

casualties. We can't operate against the corridors without risking border violations."

"Have you thought of transferring to the Army? That was not entirely a joke, by the way."

"Let's think about this after we're not up to our midriffs in organics," Marder said. She bent over the display.

"What we have to worry about, I would guess, is resupply and civilian support. In fact, I suspect that civilian support is going to be the big factor in their supplies. The Feds may actually be willing to close the border."

"With—oh, you're right; 215 Brigade's only six days out now. If they CA a battalion down on the Bushranger side of the border, that would seal off the invasion from any supplies or sympathizers in—whatever you want to call the other side of the border. Even the task force in the Armistice Zone might begin that job."

It was ironic, that after all the freedom the Alliance had enjoyed thanks to the Feds' inferiority on the ground, two Alliance officers were praying for the prompt arrival and successful deployment of forces that would shift that balance. However, it wasn't the first time that Alliance and Federation leaders had made common cause against generalized chaos and those who deluded themselves about profiting from it.

"Are we doing anything to move the Feds along?"

"If I could, I would. But stepping over the boundary into what Hollings might interpret as negotiating with foreign powers would be risky. The governor might forget that he has no spare C.O. for the 96th."

"The Baba could reverse your relief."

"Then how much cooperation could she get from the governor? Not to mention that *she* could be reversed. What would the 96th do while everyone waited to see if that would happen?"

Marder's mouth felt as sour as it ever had after a binge. She nodded.

"What I want from the Navy is medium-altitude backup for a TacAir ring we're going to draw around Anvil. If we can't get in, the rebels can't get out. Not in force, anyway, and the threat of being detected should keep odd sympathizers from trying to slip in.

"Once the ring is solid, we can lift a battalion into the space between those two corridors. It may have to work too

272

close to the border for much air support, so the Navy can stay west of Anvil. Unless the rebels deploy enough AD to interdict resupplying the battalion, in which case we'll want Navy firepower *and* orbital resupply."

"I don't see problems with any of that, Colonel. Although I'd recommend that you pick a second naval liaison, attacker-qualified and equally senior. Attacker squadrons work better if their spokescreature with the groundpounders wears the thunderbolt."

"That might not leave you with much work."

"I hope you don't think—"

"No, I don't. But I—" Pak appeared to go off into a brown study for a minute. *Except that on Victoria it's more like a gray study. If this was the only planet I'd seen, I might agree with Paul that space is the natural human habitat.*

Pak opened a drawer, studied something in it, then closed the drawer and turned back to Marder. "All clear, for at least five minutes.

"Commander, if you're going to be reasonably free to move but also free of duties, there's something you can do for me. Keep your ears and eyes open about police behavior in the Border Counties."

"What for, in particular?"

"Anything I told you would be a guess. The fact is, both Anvil and several of the communities in the path of the rebel advance went over to the rebels much too fast. In one case, the local citizens came out and guided the rebels in."

"You suspect the police of being heavy-handed?"

"Probably. Either on their own, or because Field Intelligence promised them immunity."

"Intelligence would need Hollings's backing for that promise."

"I think we both agree that he would be quite capable of giving it."

Pak lit an aromatic. "I said, I'm guessing. But Army–police cooperation in the border counties has been nonexistent since a month before the first rebellion. That usually means the police wanting to hide something.

"Maybe our borderers just didn't want to fight people who'd been their fellow citizens, even neighbors, until the Republic. But I'm willing to wager there's more."

"So I see. And I'm one of the things you're willing to wager."

"If it seems like that—"

"No, don't apologize. This—I'm tired of being used. But this isn't using me. Actually, it's something of a challenge. How far can I stick my neck out before Intelligence takes a swing at it?"

To Kornilov, the rebel positions reminded him of the cancer that had killed his mother, just after it metastasized, just before the immune-system boosters went to work and killed her with a heart attack instead of driving out the cancers. There'd been only a four-percent chance of that, the doctors said, even in a woman her age, but statistics didn't revive the dead.

Anvil of the Winds was the main tumor. The reported rebel positions trailing back toward the border along two routes were the secondary tumors. A few offshoots made red blotches to the west of Anvil, and even up north to within five hundred kilometers of Loch Prima.

There were at least one difference between this malignancy and the one that killed Natalya Kornilova. Not all of the red spots were active menaces. The reported invasion force could hardly be occupying all of them even if it put only a single platoon at some of the minor ones. So it wasn't necessary to scattergun the disease and risk massive side effects.

Kornilov hoped Pak saw it that way. Left to himself, the C.O. of the 96th and Brigadier Fegeli probably would. There wasn't much Kornilov could do to influence Hollings and Lopatina, but with the cooperation of the people across the table he might administer a few supportive therapies—no, more like first-aid—to the patient until the doctors took over. . . .

Kornilov straightened up and let the rest of the Associated States Military Council study the display. When he thought they'd all learned as much as a pack of civilians could, he cleared his throat.

"With all respect, Your Excellency—"

Governor-General Gist nodded and cleared his own throat. That was enough to have everyone sit down in one of the chairs circling the display. Kornilov would have liked to remain standing, but he couldn't do that without blocking somebody's view and annoying the governor-general. Presiding over this meeting was a large concession on Gist's part; best to give him no excuse to stamp (or even walk) out to the nearest pub.

"General Kornilov has come to suggest some measures the Associated States may take to disarm this crisis," Gist began. "I trust you've all read the advance reports?"

Everyone nodded. Senator Pappas frowned. "How up-to-date are they?"

"They were printed three hours ago. At the rate the rebels are moving, there probably haven't been any significant changes."

"If they're not moving, where's the threat?" Pappas asked.

Prime Minister Fitzpatrick nodded. "I think that's a legitimate question."

Kornilov managed to keep his voice low if not friendly. At this moment he wished that the family legend that one of his ancestors had been a werewolf was true. He didn't need ears, a tail, or hair, but a display of fangs might help.

"The presence of forces that are technically Federation ones on Alliance territory is an act of war. If you're going to claim that they aren't Federation forces, then what is the status of the Associated States? I hope we don't have to waste any more time arguing over the—legal—nonsense." The tone had fangs, anyway.

"Now just a minute—" Pappas growled, and the prime minister looked ready to jump out of his seat.

"I'm sure General Kornilov won't need more than a minute," Father Brothertongue put in. He looked around. "I was opposed to holding this meeting until General Parkinson returned or sent a report. However, she is too busy in the north.

"General Kornilov may not be unbiased, but he's the best military expert available. Let's assume he knows his arse from a mitegrubber's burrow and listen to him."

Brothertongue's phrasing fixed everyone's attention. The governor-general laughed out loud.

Kornilov used the opening. "It probably won't take more than a minute. The other reason for taking action is that if we don't look as if we're repudiating the invasion, the Alliance will suspect we're behind it. In that case, they may interpret the right of hot pursuit rather freely."

275

"As we did," Brothertongue pointed out.

"I'm not denying it, nor that it seemed a better idea at the time than it does now. But precedents cut both ways, as I'm sure your legal advisers could tell you. Sorry, I won't snipe at the lawyers anymore, as long as they don't come up with any more bright ideas for a few days."

Without waiting for agreement, Kornilov raced on. It was partly true that the first-aid would be simple. It was also true that it might be only marginally effective for the next few days.

"I remind you that if the Alliance does act, they currently have both space and ground superiority."

"Won't it take a few days for the new battlewagons to become effective?" Pappas asked.

Kornilov shook his head. "Effective in ground support, yes. But battleships are primarily space-to-space systems. They don't need local knowledge to keep the Victoria Squadron busy while the Bonsai Squadron and the attackers go low and blast a path across the border. Admiral Kuwahara would not thank us for putting him in that position, I assure you."

And if that doesn't retire the Understatement of the Year Award for the whole planet—

"So what are you proposing?" Fitzpatrick asked.

Kornilov stepped up to the display, feeling a sense of release in being able to stand. He ran a finger along the seven hundred kilometers of border that the invasion had penetrated.

"Here. I want permission to move the task force in the Armistice Zone, plus up to another battalion. I also want you to promise a full battalion of your own forces."

"That's going to strain our supplies," Pappas said.

"Once the battalion's in place, we'll take over the logistical support," Kornilov said. "On that basis . . . ?"

Brothertongue nodded. "I could live with it. But what would it do besides cut off supplies?"

"That's quite enough for people who can't get resupplied locally."

"And if they can?"

Kornilov was angry at being pressured, but once again pleasantly surprised at Brothertongue's knowledge of military matters. "Obviously our rebel friends have some support in the Border Counties. But they're going to be

276

surrounded by a couple of first-class rifle battalions in a day or two. Then they'll be living on stored fat. They'll have to break out or starve."

"Or retreat back across the border?" Pappas hinted.

"Senator Pappas," Kornilov said bluntly. "You're wondering what the Federation Armed Forces will think of a political purge of the invaders and their friends?"

"I think it's rather insulting our intelligence to put it that way," the deputy minister of defense put in. "General Kornilov, I think we deserve an—"

"Oh, bugger the apology," Fitzpatrick snapped. "Just answer, and we can finish this off."

"Very well," Kornilov said. "The Federation Armed Forces haven't taken part in whatever investigation of the first rebellion you're carrying out. Of course, we weren't invited.

"However, I will say one thing, on condition that I can strangle with my bare hands anyone who mentions it outside this room. I need the exercise."

Everyone except Pappas managed a smile.

"It's very simple. If we can avoid a political purge and the Alliance can't, it will hardly matter what happens to the invasion. People in Seven Rivers won't forget that on the other side of the border is a government that didn't run wild against its own citizens."

Kornilov retrieved his briefcase from under his chair and turned toward the door.

"I am returning to Fort Stafford. I'll be there by 1430. At 1700 I'll be taking off for Mount Houton to confer with General Parkinson. I'd like your answer by then, if you don't mind. Your Excellency, distinguished associates, I thank you for your time and courtesy."

Admiral Kuwahara was doing a headstand when his intercom alarm prodded his attention. He was tempted to handwalk over to the screen, then decided to leave such displays to younger folk.

"Kuwahara here."

"Captain Bogdanov, Admiral. Some intelligence I thought you ought to have. That suspected Emergence pulse has been analyzed. We have a seventy-eight-percent probability, plus or minus seven, of a multiship Emergence."

"Any estimates of whose?"

"No. The pulse was too distorted. The analysis suggests that it was well beyond the usual Emergence distance."

"I can believe that." *If it's somebody who didn't want us to know they were there until something they had cooking for us was done . . .*

"Anything else?"

"ETA for *Imre Farkas.* Three hours, twenty minutes."

"Have they requested assistance?"

"No. I'm surprised, too. However, apparently they didn't take any major casualties besides their communications gear. The crew seems to be alive and healthy, if a bit shaken."

"Voice-print analysis?"

"Yes, sir. Stress, fatigue, and maybe some dehydration, but they all pass."

"Good. Have you told Captain Liddell?"

"She was taking a nap, and this didn't seem to be an emergency."

"It probably isn't. Thank you, Captain."

Kuwahara returned to his exercises. Emergency or not, he'd noticed that Rose Liddell had an extra sense or two for things that could affect her ship and crew. He wondered how long it would take for those senses to start operating and interrupt her nap.

As it happened, Kuwahara was in the shower when Liddell called. He wrapped one towel around his waist and started drying himself with the other as the screen lit up.

"Admiral, I've just learned about the Emergence pulse and our friends aboard *Farkas.* Think there's any connection?"

"The unidentified ship couldn't be the pulse maker. The time's all wrong. But she might be the ship you picked up on the way in, or the one the Baba's new boys say they spotted."

"I agree. Shall I organize a boarding party for *Farkas*?"

"Yes. Warn them about it, and don't mention anything except repairing their communications gear. But send trained interrogators and computer experts. If we can get some hard data, maybe we can bargain with the Baba for pooling our knowledge of this mystery ship."

"Unless it really is Alliance."

"If she drags her feet, that in itself will tell us something."

"True. We also have a request from the two attacker squadrons, asking for permission to top off with consumables."

"All of them?"

"Yes."

Kuwahara did mental arithmetic. The dockyard had plenty of everything that twenty-nine attackers would need to make themselves independent for ten days. Ten days, about as long as it would take the invasion of Seven Rivers to either end in farce or start a war.

Ten days, when having all the attackers ready to go into action might make the difference between farce and war. The Associated States had agreed to Kornilov's proposal, but the two battalions and eventually 215 Brigade could do much more with round-the-clock attacker support.

"Permission granted, to resupply up to the maximum capacity of the dockyard. Attackers *not* resupplying are to remain on station. I want at least our four cardinal positions covered by a pair each at all times."

"I'll have the signal up for your authorization in five minutes."

"Good. And another one, too. To Commodore Uehara. I want standard tactical formation for a troop convoy in a hot system, effective immediately."

That would pull the transports into a tight ball, mixed with attackers from *Valhalla*'s squadrons, while the heavy warships formed a globe around the transports. Outside the globe would be more attackers.

"It's going to slow them down, Admiral. Besides—"

"We can afford losing a day or two on their ETA. We can also afford Prange's tantrums over being reduced to a convoy escort. We can't afford losing a ship to a hit-and-run by our mystery friends. And if that multiship Emergence is their friends . . ."

Let's not call them Baernoi.

"Shall I repeat our request to the observatory for a triangulation on that emergence?"

"Let me draft the signal. If you're free in about twenty minutes, come on up to Flag Quarters and have a drink while we edit it."

"Thank you, sir."

Kuwahara stepped back into the shower, needle-sprayed himself with hot, then cold, and started dressing. He also considered declaring a space emergency, which would force Director Kuttelwascher to cooperate with the Navy.

That consideration took only two of the twenty minutes he'd given Captain Liddell. Nothing was happening in space to justify slapping the system's best-known scientific installation in the face. The invasion of Seven Rivers was slightly above the level of comic opera—people were being killed—but it wasn't in space. Vice-admirals and higher had been retired over declaring space emergencies to handle ground situations.

Privacy and free movement in space was essential to civilians, and most of the time no more than a minor inconvenience to the Navies. Kuwahara hoped this wasn't one of the other times.

On a whim, he started looking up rites of propitiation against bad luck. He was studying with horrified fascination a Ptercha's recipe for a potion to give courage in battle when Captain Liddell arrived.

Twenty-five

Aboard *Fei-huang*, Admiral Uzel spared a quick glance for the display at the end of the conference table. The squadron was in a tight globe, as neat as you could get in a computer simulation. If it hadn't been for the possibility of EI, the Baba could have held her captain's conference by scrambled tight beam.

Uzel wished she had. The ragtag invasion force couldn't have any EI gear worth mentioning. The Feds certainly did, but could they really have anything to do with this latest piece of nonsense?

"Probably not," the Baba had said. "But they let themselves be caught by surprise. To me, that means rebel sympathizers in their organization. Anything Kornilov or Kuwahara learned from us would certainly be in rebel hands sooner or later."

"If it's later—"

"It might be. But if it was sooner? How many of Pak's soldiers are you ready to throw away on being optimistic?"

When the Baba took that tone, it signaled the end of argument. At least she seldom used it except when she was almost certainly right.

Uzel turned both his eyes and his mind away from the display and went back to his more immediate duty of greeting the new C.O.'s as they filed into the conference room.

In the hold of *Imre Farkas*, four pairs of eyes stared at a radar repeater. Two were human, one brown and one blue. The others were the silver gray of Merishi eyes adapted to a light level comfortable for humans but almost twilight for Merishi.

"If we go in fast, good fortune will ride our shoulders all the way," one of the Merishi said.

"Provided that radar plot of the squadron's accurate," a human said.

"He who loses faith at the moment of decision loses fortune," the other Merishi quoted. The words were ponderous, but he smiled as he said them. At least it was a smile for a Merishi and those humans who weren't intimidated by the Merishi display of teeth.

"Faith or no faith, they're giving us the best they can," the other human said. "We can't unlimber our own radar until we've dropped. *Farkas* is supposed to have her electronics patched up out of bits and pieces and the odd spare. She can't really probe the squadron without looking suspiciously healthy."

"So be it," the senior Merishi said. "Are the deadman links on the release gear active?"

"I programmed them myself," the other Merishi replied.

"Confidence polishes no scales," the first Merishi said. "But I will assume that you tell the truth." He swiveled his seat and adjusted the harness for his tail.

"Time for a shuttle check," he said. Two claws tapped plates with deceptive delicacy. The four boards that displayed the status of the four shuttles also sharing the heavy-lifter's hold came up.

"Shuttle One, full status data, please."

"New ETA for *Farkas*, Lieutenant," the petty officer at the intership board said. "Thirty-eight minutes."

Brian Mahoney made mental calculations. "That's slow, considering their last reported position."

"I know. Shall I query them about any new problems?"

"Yes."

The light-speed delay between *Shenandoah* and *Farkas* was down to fractions of a second. The reply came quickly.

"They're having drive-field modulation problems. Not critical, but they'd like to find an orbit that keeps them well clear of anybody else. The navigator quoted the old bit about a space collision ruining your whole day."

Mahoney switched to the intercom; the news flew up to the O.D. and a reply crawled back. *Farkas*'s ETA was down to thirty-two minutes when the reply finally reached Communications Primary.

"Tell them they're authorized to choose any orbit that will keep them two hundred kilometers clear of other ships. Offer them assistance in calculating the orbit if they've lost too much computer capacity to do it themselves. We'll shift the boarding party over to one of the shuttles."

The eight people scheduled to board *Farkas* and go over both ship and crew with a micrometer had been standing by in full EVA gear for nearly an hour. With the ship only a few kilometers from *Shen,* they could jet over, or ride one of the freight tenders. With her hundreds or thousands of kilometers away, they needed something more comfortable.

Captain Rosie, Mahoney decided, must be a little on edge over this latest bit of Victorian nonsense. Otherwise she'd never have given a "hurry up and wait" order to the boarding party, or even passed one along from Kuwahara.

He didn't blame her at all. The crisis on Victoria was like a relapsing parasitic infection. Just as you thought you'd routed the last of the little buggers out of your system, here they came again. Not to mention the rumor that the Emergence pulse might be Baernoi, coming to see what they could see and dig their tusks into any likely target.

"Heads up, everybody!" Rosza's voice came from behind him. "Control problems are no joke."

Mahoney jerked his head. Rosza was always tense. Now the situation was making him revert to the standards of his last duty, power-pile watch officer aboard *Horton.*

"You shall watch all displays with absolute attention at all times" made sense when you were introducing matter and antimatter and hoping they'd get along energetically instead of explosively. On communications watches, it was just one more excuse to be disagreeable—not that Rosza really needed many. . . .

Far out from Victoria's sun, F'Mita ihr Sular personally steered *Perfumed Wind* through the screen of flying rocks around the asteroid base. Rahbad Sarlin would have grumbled, if he hadn't had a job that kept him too busy—making sure that *Night Warrior* and her mates were following in *Wind*'s wake. The fleet commander would hold them equally responsible for even a minor collision, and he was not notorious for benignity, warmth, or charity on such occasions.

In the hold of *Imre Farkas*, the sensor display showed clear of major targets. For twenty-five minutes, the ship had been steering such an erratic course that the four people now strapped into couches had begun to wonder. Was the drive field really going unmodulated?

If it was, did this mean sabotage of the mission, so close to its conclusion?

"What's that last target?" the senior Merishi asked, pointing at the main display.

"Communications relay satellite," a human said. "One of the old ones. It's got a short-range collision warning suite and a one-shot evasive-action system. Can't do a thing to us unless we ram it by accident."

"Good."

The shuttle displays showed all four shuttles ready to drop. The altimeter wound down, passing sixty kilometers. Another twenty would be good, another forty would be perfect, but forty would take long enough to make anyone who detected them suspicious—

"Stand by for release," came a voice from the bridge. "Good luck and good hunting."

"Kytano!" the senior Merishi said. He spoke so quietly that one of the humans didn't hear him, and the other was surprised. He'd thought that was always shouted or even screamed.

Then all his thoughts returned to his job, as *Imre Farkas*'s midsection opened and *Fireflower* dropped free.

At long ranges, it needs a big radar to pick up a small target. A big target, like *Imre Farkas* or *Fireflower,* can show up at long range even on small radars, like the ones carried aboard Scout Company's gunships.

Candice Shores was riding in the copilot's seat of one of the gunships, in the first echelon of the task force, when the blip on the radar screen suddenly split in two. At least two, she amended; for a moment it looked as if there were three or four more smaller blips circling the two big ones.

Rules said you called up the task-force C.O. before hitting any buttons, panic or otherwise. Rules also got people killed when they delayed responding to a hostile missile launch—and if this wasn't that—

"Interrogatory on the IFF, those blips," she told the com operator. She succeeded in not raising her voice.

"No way, Captain. Ask the C.O. Her set just might punch through—"

"As you said, no way." Shores took a deep breath. "All-hands circuit."

The operator's mouth gaped for a moment, without slowing her hands. The all-hands circuit came up.

"Task force, emergency call, repeat, emergency call from Huntress. Have detected suspected missile launch, distance

180 kloms, bearing 310 true, altitude forty-five thousand meters. Recommend all units go to nuclear-alert condition. Repeat, recommend nuclear-alert conditions immediately."

Shores didn't wait for acknowledgements, let alone arguments from the C.O. She shifted to Scout Company's circuit and made it an order. By the time she'd finished, the gunship was snugged down, windows polarized, everybody strapped in, helmets locked and faceplates down, and the pilot ready to turn the lifter into the blast wave to reduce the impact.

"I'd like to keep us under power until something actually blows," he said. "That way we'll lose less distance on the rest of the formation. And by the way, ma'am, could my copilot have her seat back?"

Shores realized that she'd been too busy getting everyone else ready to protect herself. She scrambled out of the seat and popped into the spare gunner's seat. Harness down, locked, and hooked. Helmet sealed, radio tested—*Hades and herpes, the helmet set had lost a couple of frequencies!* —sidearms and equipment strapped down, because flying objects were the big killer in an airborne lifter caught in a nuclear blast—

The copilot sat down, the radio operator reported that the C.O. was on the horn, and Candice Shores jacked her helmet into the lifter's set. She'd just acknowledged the C.O.'s call when the sky caught fire.

Fireflower skimmed the mountaintops for fifty kilometers to let the shuttles get on course for their targets or at least clear of her own weapons effects.

Then she pulled up into a vertical climb, straight for the Alliance squadron, and dumped a four-megaton fuser with a delayed-action setting.

Coming at your enemy out of the sun was as old a tactic as flying. Generating your own sun was as old as space warfare.

The fact that both tactics were venerable didn't make them any less effective against the Alliance squadron.

Paul Leray was aboard his own *Audacious* when the alarms started screaming all over the squadron.

The last time he'd talked to the flagship, Admiral Uzel had made it clear that his not being in the conference was no slight. The last report he'd sent over was so complete that it answered questions the Baba hadn't even thought of asking.

"Besides, we need somebody who knows local conditions on watch. He'll pick up on any funny business faster than one of the newlies." Leray managed not to smile at the term "newly" applied to a rear admiral and four captains, one of them with the Medal of Honor.

"I'll try to live up to your hopes, sir."

"You will," Uzel said, and blanked the screen.

Leray had permitted himself a smile and a sigh of relief. Not only was he being trusted with the post of the squadron's sentry, he didn't have to face a mass of Pentarchy-connected rank. Oh, they would be so graciously polite to someone who after all wasn't responsible for his being spaceborn or his long service with the Bonsai Squadron.

But the bastards won't let me forget exactly what they think of both, either.

That was as far as Leray got in remembering the conversation when the alarms went. He dropped his tube of beard cream, snatched up a shirt, and plunged out into the passageway.

For a moment he thought he saw Jo dashing out of her cabin, half-dressed and the half of her that wasn't dressed looking even better than he remembered it. Then he remembered that she was down on Victoria, doing a job that might suddenly become a devil's own lot more dangerous—

"Nudet alert! Nudet!" the intercom screamed. It wasn't just the equipment; the talker was on the ragged edge of control. Leray made a mental note to get the talker's name; if the clown started a panic over a suspected nuclear detonation—

Action stations sounded. Ahead of him Leray saw hatches sliding shut. There were only five of them between him and Battle Command, but that looked like being at least one too many.

He broke into a run, plunging through the third as it started to close, diving for the fourth. Only the hatch's sensors kept it from closing on him. Someone manually overrode the fifth, letting Leray half leap, half fall into Battle Command.

"Somebody started coming up from the planet. Then they popped a megaton fuser. They may still be coming, but the EMP's scrambled all our sensors."

"Let's hope it did the same for theirs."

286

Hope was all they had, and not much of that. The oncoming ship would be hard to detect against the cloud of radioactive particles from the bomb. The Alliance squadron would be silhouetted against the cold background of space.

That wasn't the only unfavorable factor in the squadron's tactical situation. Normally a squadron's globe was large enough that ships could fire and maneuver in all directions. When it was tight, the center was usually packed with attackers, ready to hit anything that might leak through the outward-aimed defenses of the heavy ships.

Now the squadron was almost defenseless to any attack that got inside the globe. Unless they started maneuvering radically, and if they did that they couldn't raise their shields, but if they shielded they couldn't use any mass-generating weapon—

A new alarm jerked Leray's attention from the theory of saving the squadron to the urgent need of saving his own ship. Two missiles were locked on, and the weapons officer's face had "Shield or maneuver?" written all over it.

"Launch all antiship buses, and prepare for evasive maneuvering. Engage with lasers and beams until the launching is completed."

Leray's decision missed being the right one by a matter of seconds. The lasers took out the first missile, so violently that it erupted in a cloud of fragments. Those fragments didn't cripple the second missile, but they did deflect enough of the lasers and beams to save its circuitry.

As for jamming, it didn't occur to anyone aboard *Audacious* that the missile would include a simple-minded visual guidance system that nothing electronic could affect. With the growing image of *Audacious* fed into its tiny brain, the missile rode in and detonated just as the automatic overrides raised the cruiser's shield.

For a fraction of a second, until the shield generators turned into gas, the shield contained the fireball. Then it vanished, and the cloud of plasma, gas, and fragments that had been *Audacious* erupted outward.

Only a handful of the ship's crew lived long enough to feel anything. Most were dead before they knew that they were dying.

Fireflower now had other advantages besides surprise, a self-generated sun, and missiles too stupid to know they were supposed to be jammed.

The destruction of *Audacious* created another EMP and an immense cloud of debris. The Alliance's attackers were racing to intercept, but they had to slow down to avoid damaging debris impacts. Even that didn't keep the EMP from scrambling their sensors.

By the time some of them had reached a position where *Fireflower* was above them, the enemy ship had closed most of the distance to the squadron. The squadron was dispersing as rapidly as it could, using shield and drive alternately to provide both acceleration and protection.

It still hadn't dispersed enough to allow the attackers to shoot freely when *Fireflower* rode right into the middle of the expanding globe. Her missiles leaped in all directions, lasers chopped into her from all directions, and great pieces of half-molten metal peeled from her hull.

Her drive was intact, though, and the last command of her crew was flying through the computer to the drive. *Fireflower* slowed, took more hits, then accelerated on a collision course with *Fei-huang*.

Admiral Lopatina gripped the controls of the display tank as if she could undo what she'd just seen. *Brilliant* was crippled, *Dayan* had taken a near miss that must have done major damage—

A fireball completely swallowed *Frohman*. Behind her Lopatina heard what might have been a sob, must have been from the battleship's captain. Then the collision alarm went berserk, and so did every weapon aboard *Fei-huang*.

The power surge killed the display for a few seconds. That was long enough for *Fireflower* to close most of the remaining distance to the Alliance flagship. Two kilometers from her target, her drive finally died. The ship herself was also a dead thing, without sensors, crew carbonized corpses at their stations, trailing now completely molten debris—

Fei-huang's shield rose, catching *Fireflower* half inside it, half outside. The inevitable result followed: the shield generators overloaded and died. Not explosively, just irreparably.

The dead generators had done their work, however. *Fireflower* became an expanding cone of fragments. Dozens of them slammed into *Fei-huang*, at relative velocities of up to twenty kilometers a second. Hundreds of them missed, enough to have reduced the flagship to another collection of fragments as if they'd all hit.

Admiral Lopatina felt the stomach-twisting demise of the

shield generators. No figure of speech, that; she gripped the display controls and vomited all over the screen. The sound of others doing the same replaced the sobbing of *Frohman*'s captain.

She also felt the first three fragment impacts. The fourth was less than twenty meters away. The shock wave tore through the flag suite, ripped the conference table off its mountings, and sent it scything through the officers in the room.

An immense padded hammer smashed Lopatina across the ribs. She felt herself flying through the air, almost as if the artificial gravity was off. Then she knew it wasn't, because the deck came up and slammed her across the back of the head. Even the carpeting didn't soften the blow enough. She saw the ceiling insulation splitting, cracking off, and falling down on her in pieces that seemed as big as *Fei-huang* herself. Before the pieces could crush her, she lost consciousness.

The attackers maneuvering to engage *Fireflower* were too late to save their squadron or their carrier. They weren't too late to take out one of the shuttles. Going down to low altitude, they escaped the worst of the radioactive particles. The shuttle pilot helped by not being as fond of low-altitude flying as she should have been.

So the attackers caught the shuttle and blew it apart over the Pfingsten Mountains. Then they spread out, looking for the other shuttles, hoping to be homed in on them, and ready to attack somebody—anybody—if they got a sighting with their own sensors.

Twenty-six

The Baernoi asteroid was seventy-four light-minutes from Victoria. They had no ships closer than that, and even if they had, it would have made no difference. No starfaring race had yet developed a safe method of Passage so deep within a planetary system.

So the news of *Fireflower*'s death spread across Victoria and the space around it, ringing both knowledge and nightmares. Aboard the asteroid and the ships now masquerading as more rocks, ignorance remained intact.

One virtue of the Federation armed forces was that officers could get their hands dirty. When a job came up short and an officer was available, he was expected to pitch in.

At this point, Charles Longman would have been helping pack equipment even if it had been a court-martial offense. Sitting around was impossible—had been, ever since the sky blazed with fusion explosions.

Fortunately he'd been in charge of the working party that was packing up some Navy gear. With the Army taking over the Armistice Zone, everything they wouldn't need was scheduled for shipment back up to the dockyard and redistribution among the squadron.

"Hey, I just thought—" began one of the third-class techs.

"So where does it say in your MOS that you're supposed to think?" Chief Dalmas interrupted.

"Easy, Chief," Longman said. "Is it a thought worth sharing?"

"Maybe. What if they want to base attackers out of here?"

"They'll bring their own stuff, if and when," Longman said. That was no more than a semi-educated guess, but it made him sound halfway intelligent.

The storeroom door opened and Major Abelsohn stuck his head in. "How's it going?"

"We're about two-thirds of the way down the list," the

chief said, ignoring Longman. "Another half hour. We can cut it if they're sending transport sooner."

"Lord only knows when they're sending anything," the major said. "But keep at it. If you sit on your thumbs, sure as Merishi climb they'll show up asking for it ten minutes ago. And I'd like a word with Mr. Longman."

"Carry on, people," Longman said. The idea of getting off this dustball and back home to *Shenandoah* was presenting itself, in a way no sex partner ever had, and right now a hell of a lot more enticing.

"Lieutenant, I know you'd like to snatch a lift with the equipment back to your squadron. But frankly I can't spare you or any of the Navy people for a while."

"A while? Until somebody lays a fuser on us and we're all hot molecules like the Alliance ships?"

"Lieutenant, I'll admit it's partly my fault that you and your people are suddenly indispensable. I should have kept a better watch on the task force. They carried off everybody who could walk and everything that wasn't bolted down. I don't blame them, but it doesn't mean that you Navy people are now about half my strength."

"Strength of what? A sitting target?"

"Maybe. But the last I heard, they're still planning to stage a battalion through here, to join the task force. Maybe use it as a major base, too. I can't handle that job with what my dear devious comrades in the Army left me."

"What about arranging for the battalion to leave some people when it comes through?"

"If you're willing to wait that long, I'll do what I can. But I won't have the rank and the battalion C.O. will certainly have the excuse."

Longman's frustration remained, but it no longer threatened to spill over into insubordination or raw rage. It wasn't Abelsohn's fault that radio reception was out over half of Victoria from all the bombs, or that land lines were few and far between on sparsely settled Victoria.

"Okay. I'll go back and tell the people there's a nuclear-conditions freeze, or something like that. For all I know, they might have declared it and we just didn't hear."

"Good man."

Longman slapped the opener on the storeroom door and braced himself for the looks he'd get when he passed on the bad news.

291

Look on the bright side, Charlie. Think of it as practice for your next little family chat with Aunt Diana.

Wobbling and weaving erratically, *Imre Farkas* climbed up from Victoria toward a stable orbit. She reached the point for maneuvering into that orbit, passed it, and seemed to be heading for the dockyard.

Laser signals flashed from *Shenandoah* and the dockyard. Debris attenuated them, but not as much as radioactive particles scrambled radio. Ships and craft, from light cruisers down to drone handlers, began to move in a complex orbital ballet.

"*Weilitsch* has acquired Bus 16," Chief Nakamura said.

On her board in Weapons Primary, Brigitte Tachin read the same thing in her displays and gave a thumbs-up. She also wished that Nakamura would stop treating her like a brain-damage case—except that actually, this was the first time he'd done so in months.

This was also the first time *Shenandoah* had been on a live nuclear-conditions Alert One. The first time for the ship, and the first time for her.

It didn't help that her job was done for the moment. She'd handed Bus 16 over to the light cruiser trailing *Farkas* in case she needed extra firepower to either destroy the ship or defend herself.

Nobody wanted to destroy *Farkas*. It was obvious to everyone aboard *Shen* that the heavy-lifter might be a treasure trove of intelligence. She wouldn't have to reveal much, either—as Commander Zhubova put it, "Any positive quantity is greater than zero."

Which was what they knew right now about the ships that had come out of nowhere to strike down the Alliance squadron. Six ships destroyed or crippled; two thousand crew dead or dying.

Who had done it and why? There might be clues aboard *Farkas*. There would certainly also be booby traps, and right now there was a computer steering her on a collision course for the dockyard, which Captain Steckler had buttoned up and ready for maneuvering—

"*Weilltsch* has a laser burn-through aft on *Farkas*," Zhubova reported. "Drive pulses are erratic—fading—gone. She's a hulk."

Still a potentially lethal hulk. But now that *Farkas* was no

292

longer under power, robot service craft could be locked on to her. A few nudges with their rockets would put her into an orbit safely clear of anything vital to the Federation. Then only the boarding party would be in danger if anything went wrong.

Tachin thanked God that Brian was assigned as a Communications trainee. With his medical rating cleared, if he'd been assigned to Damage Control, the fates would surely have picked him for the boarding party.

Charlie Longman would have probably volunteered outright. It surprised Tachin a bit to realize how much courage she took for granted in *le petit Charles*.

I think an apology for some of what I have said about him is in order, now that he will not mistake it for a proposition.

Farkas launched for shuttles along with *Fireflower*.

Brilliant's attackers killed one. A second steered the wrong course to approach Silvermouth and had to climb over the Pfingstens instead of staying low over the sea. The air defenses of Silvermouth were up to their work; the shuttle went down forty kilometers short of its target, without launching its missile.

The third shuttle did pick a course in over the sea, launched a missile that failed to ignite, then vanished from the radar screen of the one attacker that had picked it up. Nobody ever saw the missile or the shuttle again.

Fort Stafford had never been intended as a major strategic headquarters. After the nonprovocation doctrine went into effect for dual-sovereignty planets, it became actually illegal to turn it into one

So the deepest room in Victoria Command HQ was only thirty meters down. Kornilov knew perfectly well that a four-megaton bomb would turn it into a glazed crater. Since everybody else knew it too, he put the matter out of his mind.

When he'd settled down behind his desk, however, the chief of staff showed up with a few matters he couldn't dismiss so easily. Radio communications with the squadron erratic, thanks to the EMP effect. Orbital debris creating meteoritic impacts; none in populated areas so far but a lot of spectacular trails making people even more nervous than they were already. The Military Council requesting that all available transportation be used for evacuating major population centers—

"*Sookin sin!*"

"Who's a son of a bitch, sir?" Colonel Vesey asked.

"Nobody in particular." Actually it was to the credit of the Military Council that it was sitting, debating, and coming to conclusions, even if some of the conclusions made a soldier's hair stand on end.

"Message for the Military Council. 'Cannot spare military transportation for evacuation of civilians at the present time. Deployment of troops against invasion of Alliance territory *must* be completed if Alliance is not to suspect Federation of hostile intent. Such suspicion greatest single danger to peace on Victoria.

" 'Will inform Council when troop deployments completed. Meanwhile, we will make volunteers available for maintenance on civilian lift and request Council to plan for housing and feeding of evacuees.'

"Get that off Priority One."

"Yes, sir. Do you really think the Council will call your bluff, about the housing and feeding?"

"Colonel Vesey, will you either keep quiet about my bluffing or have an affair with me? I offer this choice because only Colonel Chatterje has the privilege of being that blunt."

"Sir, if you won't be offended—"

"You'd rather keep quiet?"

"Yes, sir."

"Good. As for your original question—the Council has sprung quite a few unpleasant surprises on us. I'd be delighted to see a pleasant one for a change, but I'm not going to hold my breath."

Vesey left to put the message on its travels and Kornilov tried to relax. He couldn't have made any other decision about the evacuation. Langston needed all his battalions' organic transport and most of the TUCE lift; he could barely spare a groundcycle. The tactical formations had to go to nuclear dispersal, the battalion going in against the invasion's supplies had to be lifted, and both had to be done at the same time.

Otherwise either the bomb throwers or the Alliance would have too many vulnerable military targets. Until 215 Brigade arrived, Kornilov had no margin for error in ground troops. Losing a battalion would be a disaster and even a company would hurt.

He also had no illusions that the sudden, brutally acquired Federation superiority in space could compensate for lack of ground strength. Not when the other side's ground strength was the 96th Regiment and their C.O. was Colonel Pak.

Time, time, time! Napoleon said, "Ask me for anything but time," yet now I am not only asking for it, I would beg for it on my knees if I thought that would do any good!

Not all the debris from the Alliance squadron plunged into Victoria's atmosphere, to frighten citizens. Much of it remained in orbit, creating an appallingly dense patch of "junk space." Add the orbiting debris problem to the EMP disruption of communications, and it wasn't surprising that most of the Federation's attackers were out of touch with anyone more than fifty kilometers away.

Most of them were also too high to detect the last shuttle as it crept from valley to valley through the Roskill Range. Even the ones who detected it couldn't get a clear IFF or signature. With neither one, even the bolder attacker pilots balked at taking their ships down through a cloud of flying debris heavy enough to gut larger ships than attackers.

One pilot who was low enough to get a clear signature was Commander Gesell, wave-hopping onto her station just outside Alliance territorial waters and doing a 360-degree scan as she went.

"That's one of the standard Merishi shuttles," Gesell's EWO said. "But what the Hades is it?"

"Taking a fishing party up to the trout streams in the Roskills," Gesell said, and punched "Attack Stations."

Everyone had learned that you didn't wait for the Old Lady to explain herself. You jumped first, and she might explain when you came down. Everyone was locked and buckled and sealed by the time Gesell took over the controls.

The attacker climbed at Mach Two until they reached twenty thousand meters, where Gesell could feed in all the power. The Mach numbers shot up to five and stayed there, while the weapons officer fed targeting data into the missiles so fast that he seemed to have more than two arms.

Gesell prayed to hear her EWO signal Alliance AD launching or even getting radar lock on the shuttle. Meanwhile, she steered a course based on what she would call a theory if she lived to defend it, but right now seemed a pure hunch. The two biggest Alliance targets left were Silvermouth itself and the two-battalion task force in Barnard's Crossing. Either one would finish the job of crippling the Alliance on Victoria.

Except that the last she'd heard, the task force was moving out against the invasion. That meant Silvermouth. Of course, if she steered to meet an attack on Silvermouth and the shuttle's crew attacked Barnard's Crossing, it might look like she'd been the diversion for the attack. . . .

Hell with it. Decisions and death—the only way you can escape either one is not to be born.

Gesell's already dry mouth went drier, as she realized what taking a Federation attacker into Silvermouth's alerted air-defense zone might do. She checked the weapons-status panel, then switched on the intercom.

"We're going to have to head the bad guys off before they launch on Silvermouth. It doesn't look like the Alliance has picked up the shuttle.

"This may mean our heading into the Silvermouth AD zone, *looking friendly*. Use our own IFF, no jamming, no decoys, no maneuvering we don't need to stay on target, and yelling loud and clear.

"We've got a couple of minutes to spare. Anybody doesn't want to ride this thing through, I won't squawk if you want to punch out."

Three helmeted heads swiveled toward her. Stinging eyes joined a dry mouth as she saw the faces. The weapons officer was the only one to speak.

"With all due respect, Commander, ma'am, go shove your head up the antimatter feed."

"Okay. Hope your insurance is all paid up."

Mach Five became Mach Six. The attacker went ballistic, risking climbing into the path of orbital debris to get a look from high ground.

It was a short look and a fuzzy one; at this altitude the EMP effects were stronger. But the shuttle was now out over level terrain, which compensated. Gesell saw it clearly—clearly enough to see the missile launch.

She'd guessed wrong; the missile was going for Barnard's Crossing. She could still stop it with some good long-range shooting, if she came straight in over the base. Its AD zone was smaller than Silvermouth's, but if you were inside it, that didn't matter. Not to mention the Alliance's own attackers—

By the time Gesell finished the thought, the power plant was on max. Aerodynamic and thermal loads on the outer skin hit the red line, then passed it. Gesell was sure that everyone was like her—praying, but silently, and hoping that higher powers wouldn't mistake attention to the displays for lack of reverence.

"Radar lock from Crossing." That was the EWO. Then:

"Laser beam bearing 245.

"Attacker target, bearing 85 and closing.

"Missile launch from attacker."

"No evasive action," Gesell said. Just possibly, that Alliance attacker on their side of Barnard's Crossing would be salvation. If ground AD was afraid of hitting a friendly target—

"Lock on enemy missile." The EWO again.

"Missiles armed and ready." The weapons officer.

"Then fire the bastards!" Gesell snarled.

Gesell watched the missiles' signatures in the displays, and the Alliance attacker turning to engage them. She didn't mind that as long as it didn't hit any of them. They had to survive the attacker, then the AD—*and please Lord, don't let the AD get so distracted by our missiles that they don't spot the enemy's*—

Gesell turned her attacker, as tightly as anything can turn at Mach Six, and slowed down. Evasive action might not be absolutely a bad idea now, and besides, your own lasers and beamers were more accurate if you slowed down.

The Alliance attacker, flustered by not knowing who was trying to do what to whom, shot at Gesell's missiles and missed. It shot at Gesell's attacker, and missed again. Then the AD system of Barnard's Crossing let fly, taking out two missiles and their own attacker.

Gesell screamed curses at fate and orders at her EWO. Target data on the incoming missile now went straight to the radio and out to everyone within receiving range, in plain language. If she couldn't kill that fuser sneaking up on the town herself, Gesell would do her damnedest to help somebody else do it.

The attacker's turn was wide enough to take them through the extreme inland side of the Barnard Crossing AD zone. A pop-up missile proximity-detonated close enough to rip the attacker's hull and wreck the controls for the matter-antimatter feed.

The book said to put the attacker into a climb and punch out before the uncontrolled feed and mixing cooked off the power plant. Gesell mentally erased that page of the book and played with her controls.

Good. We've got a laser, we've got some missiles, and we've got enough control to ram it if we can't do anything else.

The laser killed the enemy missile. Gesell had time to watch the missile nose down, then tumble out of sight. She had time to launch four more missiles at the rapidly retreating shuttle. Then she had time to die, as an Alliance attacker plunging from fifty kilometers drove a laser beam into her cockpit.

It was a quick death. The rest of her crew joined her moments later as the attacker cratered the desert at Mach Three.

Colonel Pak could have claimed an "assist" on the shuttle. By the time Gesell's attacker hit the desert, he knew what was going on. He personally ordered the attacker pilot to leave the missiles alone, but follow them up if they missed.

He also ordered all units under his command to ignore any orders except his own, for hostile action against Federation forces. Then he settled down to wait.

Two minutes, and the shuttle went down, ripped apart by three direct hits.

Five minutes, and the attacker reported the position of Gesell's crash.

Six minutes, and Pak ordered the attacker to orbit the AD zone and go to AEW mode until further orders or until more attackers arrived.

Fourteen minutes, and Pak finally managed to get through to an attacker flight leader, to call up reinforcements for their lone aerial sentinel.

Twenty-five minutes, and he began to suspect that Hollings and Fegeli were going to overlook his order about no hostile action against the Federation. Of course, they hadn't actually ordered him or anybody else to take such action, so maybe it would be—what was the phrase—"least said, soonest mended"?

Except that this nightmare from which they could not awake would take a great deal more than silence to mend it.

He turned to Commander Marder.

"Commander, would you like a drink?"

Marder shook her head. She wanted to say something, but didn't want to break the control she'd fought for and won in the past few minutes.

But if that control lasts too long—

She consigned psychologists and their theories to prolonged and vicious tortures, and shook her head again. Then she swallowed, and nodded.

A glass appeared in her hand as if by magic. She'd emptied it before she noticed the robot rolling away. She thought of calling it back for a refill.

If I take more than one drink, I don't know where I'll stop. There's too much to do. There's always too many people with an image of me I don't want to live down to.

Audacious deserves a better memorial. It was several seconds before she added Paul Leray's name to his ship's.

"Commander, I want you to go over every scrap of data on this engagement. I am as sure of the Federation's friendship as I am sure of my fingernails, but we need proof."

She lowered her voice. "And my other work? Not that this isn't more important—"

"It is. But you're right. It's possible that whatever—errors— were made in picking our political friends—had something to do with this. . . ."

Pak called the robot back, took a drink for himself, and let it circle them until Marder sent it away. As it vanished, she glared at the colonel.

"Sir, don't we have more important things to do than test my self-restraint?"

"Yes, and more important than asking stupid questions, too. I simply wanted to leave the decision up to you."

Leave the decision up to me?

The words had sound but not sense. Maybe they would be different tomorrow, or some day after that. Marder filed them for reference and drank the water left from her first drink.

"Start the investigation immediately. I'll try and let you work on the other project without leaving this HQ. I have a friend, a former captain in Homicide in Silvermouth, who's been reassigned to the Border County Patrol."

"I can ask for him as police liaison to the task force we're putting in against the invasion. That should keep him down here until we're ready to leave. Can you finish your investigation in three days?"

"Maybe. If I can borrow anybody I need—"

"Give me a list as soon as you can."

"Aye-aye, sir." *Although the more work I do myself, the more it will keep the pain away, until I can stand it.*

"I think the captain was reassigned because he asked too many questions. So walk carefully. Intelligence may be watching."

"I will." *Unless they get in the way of my finding out who killed my ship and Paul.*

From the western foothills of the Roskill range, a pair of night scopes were focused on where the shuttle crashed.

"Want to check out the site?"

Thick, stubby fingers danced with unexpected grace across computer controls.

"Too far, not enough cover, and no vehicles."

"Not time to steal one, either?"

"With everybody expecting God knows what to bite them in the *cul* each time they turn around? We would have the police and Field Intelligence out here in a day."

The computer operator held up a large, roughened hand. "No, we needn't be afraid of them if there's a worthwhile goal. But there isn't. Not when the Alliance Navy will investigate better than we could. To draw in the police and the Intelligence—they could ruin such an investigation."

"So let their Navy plant, and we can reap?"

"Exactly."

"I trust Major Nieg has a few good reapers in place?"

"Have you ever known him to fail?"

"There is always a first time."

"You are pessimistic tonight, *mon vieux*."

"It's this planet. Too much rock, not enough growing things."

"Better then to fight over it, and leave the fertile places in peace."

"Better still not to fight at all."

"*Sans doute*, but we are past that point, I fear."

A nod, and two pairs of mountain boots moved silently across the slope and down toward the foot of the Micaela Glacier.

*   *   *

Kuwahara had seen too many fictions in which soldiers of Japanese descent conjured up the image of samurai ancestors to strengthen them in times of crisis.

This was certainly a crisis. As for what he conjured up to strengthen himself—his family had no known samurai ancestors. The ancestors whose memory came to him at times like this were both railroad people.

One was an engineer, who'd stayed at the throttle when his train was attacked from the air. Escaping steam scalded him to death, but he stopped the train and let the passengers escape.

The second was a vice-president of one of Akhito's early railroads. After a tragic bridge collapse, she neither resigned nor committed suicide. She stuck to her post, in the face of criticism almost as scalding as her ancestor's steam, learned what happened, and had the bridges redesigned. Some of them were still standing, thanks to that redesign, and so was their patron's reputation.

The present drove away images of the past. "Captain Steckler's calling," Captain Liddell said.

Even with his voice chewed by static, Steckler's indignation was unmistakable. "Sir, I'm inquiring about your order to check every item of cargo brought in by *Imre Farkas*."

"It stands. Anything else?"

"Sir, with all due respect—"

"No amount of respect will make me change it. But I'm open to suggestions about the best way of doing it."

Dockyard now held about two hundred tons of cargo unloaded from *Farkas*, on the stop she'd made before being hijacked. Kuwahara's guess was that the hijacking had been partly an inside job. That could mean sabotage of the cargo, anything from loosened wires to suitcase fusers.

"Aye-aye, sir. Most of what's already been issued was checked out at the time. It was clean. The rest—I'd suggest we simply stuff it all into one of our spare people pods and tow it out fifty kilometers. A few critical items, I'd like to check out. Otherwise we can just put the load on a shelf where if it does fall off it can't hit anybody."

"What about security?"

"I've got twenty people who can rig the pod with alarms and benign booby traps using one hand and one foot. Let me turn them loose, and we can have the stuff out of here in a couple of hours."

301

Kuwahara was about to give permission when Steckler rushed on. "Sir, under other circumstances we'd have plenty of people to do the inspections on the spot. But it occurred to me that there's both a legal and a moral obligation to give the Alliance squadron all the help we can. I don't want to have to say that we can't give it because half my techs are running tests for poisoned beard cream!"

"I think I'll leave you to get on with your job, Captain. Hearing you being diplomatic is more of a shock than my system can take right now. I want the pod and the rescue parties on their way in two hours."

"Aye-aye, sir."

Fleet Commander Eimo su-Ankrai stared at the screen, Brokeh su-Irzim stared at him and saw the blood drain from the older commander's face as if the screen had sucked it away.

The screen blanked, and silence hung in the cabin. No, several silences, one for each commander in it, and not hanging. Each commander held silence in front of him like a shield, as if it would fend off the message the screen had brought.

"*Fireflower* has appeared," Su-Ankrai said at last.

"Is she returning?"

"She attacked the Alliance squadron off Victoria. Seldom in history has one ship done so much damage to a superior force. All the Alliance's heavy ships were destroyed or damaged beyond fighting."

"They used the sunbombs," su-Irzim said. It was not intended as a question. He had spoken before he realized that it was also monumentally silly.

Fortunately only the fleet commander heard. His brows drew together and his lips curled back from his tusks. For a moment he looked two generations younger.

Su-Irzim hoped that would last. They would need all of su-Ankrai's old strength and cunning to fight their way through this situation.

Even then, they would hardly be fighting their way to victory. To hiding the traces of their involvement, perhaps—and if they did that, *then* they might think of victory.

Rose Liddell rubbed a helmet-battered ear with one hand and rested the other on the console in front of her. The strength that had flowed out of her along with her adrenaline supply in the past hour was creeping back in, as long as she touched some part of her ship. Even the pain in her ear was fading.

The killers had come out of their hiding place. Not the warriors, who knew what they fought for and what price was worth paying for it. But the killers, who did not care how many died if they could win, or counted the deaths themselves as a victory.

They had come out, and their madness had devoured ships and crews. It did not take much imagination to hear *Shenandoah* crying out for the dead, as her captain wanted to do.

ABOUT THE AUTHOR

Roland J. Green is an active SFWA member, and the author of the PEACE COMPANY series, as well as co-author (with Jerry Pournelle) of two military SF novels in the JANISSARIES series. *A Division of the Spoils* is the second book in his STARCRUISER *SHENANDOAH* trilogy. He lives in Chicago.